Three
Screenplays

Books by Richard Price

THE WANDERERS

BLOODBROTHERS

LADIES' MAN

THE BREAKS

CLOCKERS

THREE SCREENPLAYS

The Color of Money
Sea of Love
Night and the City

Richard Price

3

THE COLOR OF MONEY

SEA OF LOVE

NIGHT AND THE CITY

Screenplays

HOUGHTON MIFFLIN COMPANY

Boston / New York 1993

The Color of Money copyright © by Touchstone Pictures.
Sea of Love copyright © 1989 by Universal City Studios, Inc. All rights
reserved. Licensed by MCA Publishing Rights, a division of MCA, Inc.
Night and the City copyright © 1992 by Twentieth Century Fox Film
Corporation. All rights reserved.

Library of Congress Cataloging-in-Publication Data

Price, Richard, date.
  [Screenplays. Selections]
  Three screenplays / by Richard Price.
  p. ; cm.
  Contents: The color of money — Sea of love — Night and the city.
  ISBN 0-395-66924-3   ISBN 0-395-66923-5 (pbk.)
  1. Motion picture plays.   I. Title.
PS3566.R544A6   1993   93-12236
791.43'75 — dc20   CIP

Printed in the United States of America

Book design by Robert Overholtzer

BP 10 9 8 7 6 5 4 3 2 1

A Special Angle of Vision

An Interview with Richard Price
by Neal Gabler

Born in New York in 1949, Richard Price won instant acclaim at the age of twenty-four with his first novel, The Wanderers, *the story of five teenage gang members living in the Bronx housing projects where Price himself was raised. Over the next decade, he solidified his reputation as a fresh and powerful voice of urban America with* Bloodbrothers, Ladies' Man, *and* The Breaks. *Turning to screenwriting, he won an Academy Award nomination in 1986 for* The Color of Money, *his first produced script. His screenplays for* Sea of Love, *Martin Scorsese's "Life Lessons" segment of* New York Stories, Night and the City, *and* Mad Dog and Glory *have earned him recognition as one of the most gifted screenwriters and as the undisputed master of realistic dialogue. He returned to novels in 1992 with* Clockers, *for which he received a National Book Critics' Circle nomination.*

Neal Gabler is a cultural historian and the author of An Empire of Their Own: How the Jews Invented Hollywood.

NG: Years ago, before you had written a screenplay, you said, "The best thing I can do for the movie industry is write novels." What changed your mind?

RP: The first two books that I'd written, *The Wanderers* and

Bloodbrothers, were made into movies, and I'd always been courted by Hollywood because of the way I wrote my novels. I grew up as much on television and film as I did on literature, and it showed in the way I wrote; I always envisioned the story in my head as if on a screen. But instinctively I had always put off screenplays. I wanted to keep writing novels. Then there came a time in my life, in the process of writing *The Breaks,* where I felt it was too much hard work for too little reward. I felt temporarily bankrupt as a novelist. I had to step back and have a different type of life for a while and then come back.

So I called up one or two of these people who had been courting me over the years and said, "I'm ready." They said, "Hey, that's great news. Got an idea?" I came up with this thing called *Wingo,* which was the story of a guy who works in a post office and wins the lottery and how it changes his life. That was sometime in the early eighties. I had no idea how to write a script. It was sort of like, earn while you learn. And the way I learned was by watching movies and pretending I was the writer of what I was seeing. I avoided textbooks and workshops because I knew that the more I learned about the rules, the more jammed up I'd get regarding inspiration. So I just winged it.

NG: We always hear horror stories of successful novelists emasculated by Hollywood, yet you continued to write scripts.

RP: Writing novels is a very lonely process. You can have cobwebs going from your head to the pen. Writing scripts, the phone never stops ringing, and there's always coast-to-coast flights, and every once in a while you've actually got to write something. But I enjoyed that. It's not lonely, and that's very seductive. Hollywood is a form of cultural crack. You've been feeling very bad about yourself in one art form, and all of a sudden you find another art form, and you don't know yet that "wonderful," "marvelous" and "terrific" all mean "This stinks." It was just the flattery and the interaction and the money and, "Well, we're not going to do anything with this fabulous script, but here's even *more* money to write another fabulous script we're probably not going to do either."

It's addictive. I mean, not to be facetious, but part of the reason I was falling apart as a novelist was that I had developed a drug problem, and so I gave up on novels thinking, "Well, if I'm a drug addict, I might as well be a screenwriter. I have to do something that doesn't require so much brains." Ultimately the drugs were very easy for me to give up; the screenplays were harder. The screenplays and the whole world around them became new addictions for me.

NG: Were there things you felt you could express on screen that you couldn't express in the novel form?

RP: Part of the jam that I was in as a novelist was that I kept going back to my autobiography for material. And if today is Wednesday, and I was up to Tuesday with my life in print already, well, what's going to happen today because I've got to have another book out. Life is hard enough without it having to be perpetual material too. I felt like a cannibal eating his own foot. Once I became a hired pen out there, for the first time in my life I was forced to leave my own autobiography to research my characters' lives, and I learned, with great gratification, that talent and autobiography are not joined at the hip, that talent travels. If you have enough imagination and empathy, you can write about anybody.

That was probably the only good thing, *tangible* good thing, that came to my writing through screenwriting: knowing that I could go anywhere and learn and bring it back home and turn it into art.

NG: But it must have required an enormous psychological adjustment to move from a form over which you have total control and are top dog in the creative scheme to one over which you have so little control and are low dog.

RP: You have to understand that a superior attitude out there goes only so far and then it gets tired. You know the rules, and you can pose and play the artist all you want, but if you're going in there you better have your Screenwriter's hat on, not your New York Novelist's hat. You're getting paid by them. It's their project. They've got to sell it in the morning. Now what *I* have to do is write stuff that I can live with and they can live with.

NG: You were once quoted as saying that there were three "arts" to screenwriting: the "pitch," the "first draft," and the "negotiation."

RP: First, you've got to sell them on it, just so you've got a job. Brevity is the soul of salesmanship out there. You're in and out — as fast as a knock-knock joke. Never talk for twenty minutes when you can say it all in ten because the more details you give, the more there's a chance they're going to hear something they might not like. "High concept" basically means low concept. "High concept" means something that is so simple-minded you can tell the whole story in one sentence. That is a particular art.

NG: Now the first draft.

RP: The first draft is basically: No matter what you told them, you do what you want to do because they're not going to remember anyhow — hopefully. And you give it everything you've got because in case they *do* remember, you have to win them over to your secret agenda once the draft is in their hands.

NG: And stage three — the negotiation?

RP: What you've given them with the first draft is basically like yogurt and bulgur wheat — tastes like shit, but very, very good for you. *They're* going to say, "No, no, no. People want Turkish Taffy and Count Chocula." *I* say, "I don't do Count Chocula." And they say, "Listen, you ain't doing bulgur wheat either because it's our money." So I say, "All right, let's talk. I tell you what — how about fruit salad?"

NG: Obviously you don't have to negotiate a novel, but were there ways you had to change your *technique* in moving from novel writing to screenwriting?

RP: What you bring from novels over to screenplays is nothing but trouble. Because the essential elements that make a novel memorable are death in a screenplay: the life of the interior mind, the psychological history, the author's ability to speculate and create commentary, the weave and texture of the narrative, the *words* — none of this is relevant to a screenplay.

NG: What about dialogue? Is there a big difference between writing dialogue in a novel and writing dialogue for the screen?

RP: In a novel you can just start out with small talk, pick up speed and then coast into a coda because seconds aren't precious. In a screenplay I can't have a dialogue that warms up and *then* goes full speed. You're always jumping in in the middle and trying to imply what went before and what's to come. You've got to figure out how to essentialize these five indulgent pages of novel dialogue into a half-page exchange. In a script, momentum and efficiency have the highest priority. It's speed chess.

NG: You called yourself a "hired pen" when you're writing for the screen, which I assume is something you would never say about yourself as a novelist.

RP: The big difference between novels and scripts is the issue of art. A screenwriter is not an artist; a screenwriter is a craftsman. You have a job. Your job is to create the blueprint for a movie. Here is another metaphor. It's just like when you were a kid playing a game of telephone. The first kid whispers a nonsense sentence to the second kid. "Eugene obliterated my pet panther recently." Now this kid's got to whisper that to a third kid and so on, until the tenth kid down the line announces what he heard, and everybody has this big giggle over the difference between what the first kid said and what the tenth kid heard.

Well, the first kid is the screenplay, the tenth kid is the released movie. And all the kids along the line — they are the director, the actors, the studio, the editing room, the marketing system. That's why you're just a craftsman. Because an artist has a vision, and an artist is in control of that vision to the very end. But a screenwriter is just serving somebody else's vision. On the other hand, people should never come out of a movie theater saying, "Boy! Was that a good script!" Because if they're saying that, it means that the rest of the movie didn't come up to snuff, and the screenplay stuck out. So either way you lose as "the artist."

NG: And publishing the screenplays is a form of protection?

RP: The whole point of this book for me is that as a screenwriter you are constantly surrendering your vision. And what I am saying now is that my vision, my role as an independent artist, ended with these drafts. Which is not to say that a lot of the stuff that was done after these drafts was not good and necessary. It's not like I'm the pure poet and everybody else is some kind of venal Babbitt. One thing to remember is that the only screenplays that don't get fiddled with are the screenplays that don't get made. I'm just saying, "This is what my work table looked like the first time I said, 'Done.'"

NG: Of course, the logical step, then, would be for you to direct your own material.

RP: I think the only type of writer who should become a director is the writer who identifies himself solely as a screenwriter, doesn't have fiction or theater to retreat to, and feels like he has to move deeper into filmmaking to protect his work or he'll commit suicide.

But because of novels, I've always thought of myself as a writer and nothing else. I've never thought of myself as a filmmaker. And I know in Hollywood I'm a hired pen. This is what I do to replenish my juices when I feel burned out as a novelist. This is what I do to make money so I don't have to worry about how little or how much I'm getting as a novelist.

NG: Let me play devil's advocate, or Richard Price's advocate, here. Whether you are the master of the finished product or not, I think anyone who reads these screenplays will find continuities of character, theme and vision among them and between them and your novels, the way *auteur* theorists find continuities in the oeuvre of studio filmmakers who were also, most of the time, hired hands.

RP: That's not something I am able to say on my own. I don't want to be disingenuous, but at the same time, if we go into too deep an analysis of these scripts, we might end up giving me more credit, really, than I deserve.

NG: Well, let's take the idea of the outsider. Every major character you have written is an outsider, a loner, trying desperately to get inside, to make some kind of connection, to find some kind of authenticity.

RP: That probably reflects my own feeling of where I fit. I'm always writing about people on the outside because I feel as if *I'm* on the outside. That's why I'm a writer. If I were on the inside, I'd be a lawyer. I'd be a team player. But, yes, my characters are all outsiders. They all have a special angle of vision, occupationally and attitudinally. They all have an angle that romanticizes their isolation.

NG: And yet your characters aren't sulking, laconic loners. They are all extremely verbal men who use talk to avoid intimacy or real engagement.

RP: They're all con artists. They're all liars. They can all paint great pictures without any canvas behind them. It's the art of the flowing lie. Frank Keller in *Sea of Love* is the hunter-loner using bullshit to lay his snares. Frank's whole thing is he's flattering and manipulating and lying and he's spinning stories to trap the bad guys. Then you've got Fast Eddie Felson in *The Color of Money*. He is an adjunct professor in the art of cynicism. The whole movie he is giving these lectures on manipulation to young Vincent until he can't do it anymore because his priorities shift, and then he becomes almost innocent. And Harry Fabian in *Night and the City* is talking to keep his head above water, constantly. His mouth is his major asset. It is also his major liability.

They're word dancers, but then the words become the Red Shoes. Frank the cop gets stung by his own sting. Fast Eddie suddenly realizes he doesn't believe or doesn't *want* to believe anything that he's been proselytizing. Harry Fabian talks himself into a corner he can't get out of.

NG: Which brings us to another issue. The primary hue of these screenplays is dark, the tone rueful, pessimistic, even hopeless.

RP: I don't feel they're hopeless. I think at some point people have to take a beating before they find a new path in life. The reward for the drubbing that they take is this small getting of wisdom, this little moment of grace, this little rest stop or this little niche. What happens at the end is this new acceptance of things, this new accommodation — the great unclenching — if they're lucky.

In *The Color of Money*, Eddie turns to Carmen and he tries to tell her, "I was wrong. I found myself again." He's playing pool again. Whether he's going to make a career out of it again or get his chops back, we don't know, but at least he's doing something to heal his soul. In *Sea of Love*, Frank realizes how much he has to lose, and the only way he can get it back is to say to Helen, "I confess. I don't want to be this way. Can you trust me now?" He goes through hell, but he winds up with somebody, and there is the chance something is going to come of this. Harry in *Night and the City* does the same thing with *his* Helen. It's like this burst of, "I'm a bad man. I did bad things. I want to make it up to you. I have to go out on a note of grace."

NG: All three characters have been screwing over someone for the entire course of the film. Then they beg forgiveness.

RP: You can screw people so deep that you wind up getting screwed yourself. And the only way out is to come clean.

People change not because one fine day they wake up and think, "I feel like changing," but because the pain of maintaining the status quo is finally greater than the pain of transformation. Sometimes people's lives get so untenable that they have no choice but to strip themselves down of all game plans and all scams and say, "The only way out of here is to be naked." This is when the characters are least entertaining, least dazzling verbally, so these are always incredibly awkward moments.

NG: At least in the cases of *Sea of Love* and *Night of the City* your screenplays end less optimistically, more problematically than the movies do.

RP: Big, happy endings for a studio film are more or less mandatory, but happy endings are really tricky for me because it is so hard to earn them in a real way. I always feel that the big happy ending is the most painful part of the compromise for me. You want to be true to the scale of values that you've been writing about all along. You want things to be earned, and things that are earned are precious and small.

NG: There were eight years between *The Breaks* and *Clockers* — eight years when you were doing screenwriting exclusively. We talked about the transition from novels to screenwriting. When you went back to write *Clockers,* was it different because you had been writing screenplays?

RP: Well, the funny thing is that when I went around to all these editors and tried to set up *Clockers* without having done any writing, just telling them the story line, as though I were pitching to Hollywood studios, one of the things I said to them was, "Listen, I've been working out in Hollywood pretty successfully for eight years, and Hollywood's about momentum, and none of my books historically has been tightly plotted, but if there's one thing I learned out there, it's how to plot and make things move." And they all believed me. And then I turned in a 1,400-page first draft with no ending because I was so happy to be back in novels and not to have to write any of the Hollywood bullshit. I denied and discarded eight years of screenwriting.

NG: And were you scared or exhilarated by that?

RP: Oh, it was great. I mean, in Hollywood they look at a page and if it's got too much black, too much ink on it, they say, "Shit, it's freeze-the-camera time." But now, I just said, "God, I'm going to do monologue after monologue. I'm going to make them all dazzling and 'nonsequiturious' and some of them are going to pay off later, and some of them are going to exist just for the joy of their own words."

NG: Are you going to continue now moving between screenplays and novels?

RP: I'm going to go back and forth. In a way you need the screenplays to heal yourself from novels and you need novels certainly to heal yourself from screenplays. But screenwriting is like drugs. You kick it and you're clean for four years and write a novel and say, "Well, I haven't touched the stuff in years. I guess I can do a quickie. I can handle it now," and the next thing you know you're back in the rut. I'm on my second screenplay since *Clockers*.

But this time I'm going to join SA, Screenwriters Anonymous. That's when you get up there and say, "Hi, I'm Richard Price. Well, it's been ninety days since my last screenplay." People all applaud and chain smoke, and there's coffee and Pecan Sandies at the back of the room and every month, half-year, year, you get a different-colored progress tag for your key chain and you have all these haggard but clean writers doing thumbs up as they pass each other on the moving sidewalk at LAX.

THE COLOR OF MONEY

NG: The provenance of each of these screenplays is different. *The Color of Money* was not only adapted from a novel, but it was a sequel to a cherished and beautifully written film, Robert Rossen's *The Hustler*. How did you approach that task?

RP: Well, it was kind of daunting. I remember sitting there with Martin Scorsese and Paul Newman, and Newman saying, "By the way, this should be better than *The Hustler* or at least as good, otherwise what's the point in making it." *The Hustler* was so good it was intimidating. The way I decided to deal with that was to completely disregard *The Hustler*. This movie's got to stand up on its own terms with its own definitions.

NG: Did you feel any obligations to Walter Tevis's novel?

RP: I read the novel, and then I respectfully put it aside. It didn't lend itself easily to movies because it was about a man's inner journey, and it was a very leisurely novel. In fact, most of the characters in the movie didn't exist in the novel.

NG: Had you roughed out the plot and characters with Scorsese before you sat down to write?

RP: I wrote for Scorsese as opposed to writing for Paul Newman. I was always attracted to dark characters, characters who take a precipitous drop in spirituality, and that's how I envisioned Eddie Felson. He's not playing pool anymore, and he's going to be filled with bile, and he's going to be manipulative. He's doing the very thing that George C. Scott did to him in *The Hustler*. It's sort of like the abused child becomes the abusive parent. I made him very manipulative, very blunt, very cold. I mean, the best hustlers out there are not slick, they're dry. Snakes are very dry. Everybody just thinks they're slimy. And I wrote a very unsentimental, very un-studio film. Nobody was lovable. Eddie was basically talking to the kid about hate, schooling him in the usage of hate.

NG: That sounds like a Scorsese film.

RP: Somewhat. But what happened was, we gave it to Newman and he got about halfway through the script and he says, "Fellas, I don't *like* this guy. I can't *play* this guy. I don't feel any sympathy for him." I felt like throwing my hands up then, but Scorsese said, "What we have to do is to start all over again. We have to learn what Paul's about, pick up his sensibilities, and we have to accommodate that."

That's what happened. We'd meet once a week, twice a week, at Newman's house, in Newman's office, and we'd hear his thoughts. It took about a year, of writing ten pages, going in there, discussing ten pages, writing twenty more pages, going back fifteen pages, going ahead thirty-five pages.

NG: When it was all finished, did you feel that it had been compromised beyond recognition?

RP: No, but it was a compromised achievement. It was also a crash course in how you make a script functional and savvy enough to be the skates under a studio film that's going to actually move now. But that's the way it gets done.

NG: There is one article that interprets the film as a parable of your own experience in Hollywood. *You* are the virgin who Eddie corrupts with money or perhaps you are Eddie himself, poised between the literary world and Hollywood, just as Eddie is poised between the purity of pool and the taint of the hustle.

RP: I thought that was a kind of simplistic take. I don't feel I'm enmeshed in this great personal drama for my artistic soul. I'm happy I can do both kinds of writing.

NG: Eddie is certainly aware of the compromises he has made.

RP: Eddie has been away so long that he has forgotten the way back. He's become Rappucini's daughter. He is filled with poison now, and he's going to bite somebody. But in finding himself a nice, young virgin, Vincent, he gets trapped into remembering his own virginity. He didn't plan on that. And when he sees Vincent tossing out all this carefully orchestrated cynicism, he hears the music again that he thought he couldn't hear anymore.

NG: Essentially Vincent and Eddie switch roles.

RP: You teach him how to be a prick and he teaches you how to be a virgin. Eddie is rediscovering what he's about. It's almost as if he's becoming a baby again, but all of a sudden he realizes that it's not so easy. When you take the shell off the first time, it's kind of tender.

NG: You're talking about the scene where Eddie gets hustled himself.

RP: I've got to be very careful how I pick my words here because it is very easy to sound corny. But it's dangerous to have feelings again. It leaves you open to all sorts of wounds. You become unmanned by your own optimism. But Eddie's reaction to it is to plunge in deeper, because even though it was a humiliation, it was a start. *The Color of Money* is ultimately about resurrection, about the gift of a second chance in life — no small thing.

SEA OF LOVE

NG: With *Sea of Love* you were once again working with a major star — Al Pacino. Did you customize the script for him as you did *Color of Money* for Paul Newman?

RP: Well originally, I wrote it for Dustin Hoffman. Hoffman approached me after *Color of Money* saying "I'd like to work with you." And I told him I had this idea for *Sea of Love*, which was basically coming off one of my novels, *Ladies' Man*, about how an urban male deals with sexual longing and loneliness. I figured, "I know how to get *Ladies' Man* made into a movie. I'll give the guy a gun."

Now, I didn't know anything about cops, but the guy had to be a cop. So I decided to hang out with cops and see what I could get off that. In the first draft of *Sea of Love* I indulged myself in my own fascination with what I had discovered — cops' eyes, what cops see on a day-to-day basis as opposed to what civilians see. And that became a much more personal script for me than *Color of Money.*

NG: What happened to Dustin Hoffman?

RP: Hoffman got sidelined on *Rain Man,* and he asked me to come on *Rain Man* for a rewrite. That was an unhappy experience. It was one of those you-can't-fire-me-I-quit situations. So then he pulled out of *Sea of Love.* Everybody loved *Sea of Love* because Dustin Hoffman was attached. Dustin Hoffman pulls out, all of a sudden, nobody loves it anymore. The words didn't change, but we lost our five-hundred-pound gorilla. And so it lay there for a year. The minute Pacino came on board, our *new* five-hundred-pound gorilla, it was everybody's favorite script again.

NG: Pacino said about you: "He starts with the character and then builds everything around the character."

RP: Basically, I've always started out with nothing but a character. I always begin with an interesting character in search of a story. For example, in my first draft of *Sea of Love* there's nothing *but* character. The story doesn't come together until the last twenty pages of the script. It looks like a dumbbell with the weight all at one end. It's almost like the story was beneath contempt: "I'm creating a great character here. Leave me alone." Of course nobody will make a movie of that.

NG: Were you deliberately thumbing your nose at Hollywood conventions?

RP: Not at all. Part of my problem as a screenwriter is that I'm much more engaged by the moment, the *veracity* of any particular moment, than by what happens next. Think of a screenplay as a pyramid; you've got four characters on the bottom, you have two hours, and they all have to converge at the apex of the pyramid. Well, my problem perpetually is that my guys constantly wander and mosey on their way up, because there's something very interesting ten feet from the base, and there's something over here forty feet up from the base, and they might not ever get to the top of the pyramid except that I have to do it. My heart is in the moment.

NG: So then the negotiations began.

RP: My first draft of *Sea of Love* — the draft published here — was totally unshootable as a studio film. So producer Marty Bregman was asked by the studio to make it into a studio film. A major problem was that the female lead of the story doesn't come in until thirty or so pages from the end. The studio is thinking, "What big-star actress do you think we're going to get who'll agree to come on in the last half hour of the movie? What are you, crazy? We have to get this lady who now lives on page ninety living on page two." I said, "I can't *do* page two with her." "All right. Then we want her in on page ten." I say, "How about page thirty-five?" They say, "How about page twenty-five?" *Sea of Love* was unbearable. I worked on that thing for two years, two solid years and what seemed like hundreds of drafts, pounding it into this sort of genre shape. And I fought tooth and nail the whole way. But at some point your resistance goes. The seventh or eighth or ninth time they're telling you, "I think we have a problem here," you can't fight anymore.

NG: Reading this draft of *Sea of Love* I was struck by the similarities between it and *Clockers*. There is a brilliant speech in *Sea of Love* about the "cycle of shit" that cops observe, the generational wheel of poverty, crime, and cruelty. It was excised from the movie *Sea of Love*, but it reappears in *Clockers*.

RP: I ran into a cop one night who told me about the cycle of shit, and I stole it, just literally stole it. The "cycle of shit" is how cops feel. "I know what's out there but I can't really *change* anything, so . . ." But it's also part of the romance of isolation that they have. There are three jobs in this society in which people grant the possessors demigodhood: priests, doctors, and cops. Because when you find out that you're talking to a priest, a doctor, or a cop, you can never for a second forget that you're talking to a priest, a doctor, or a cop. And cops get off on that. It's a power, a glamour that they're granted and that's very seductive to them, and they don't want to give it up. But it's a double-edged sword. A lot of them think that the only person who'll relate to them as a *person* is another cop.

What happens to a guy like Frank Keller is once you start hitting your "twenty," retirement age, once you're at an age where you're on borrowed time, you're like a celebrity athlete who just got cut from the team. What do you do with yourself? You're forty-four years old, and its over for you at an age where any other man would be approaching the professional prime of his life. Suddenly you're a nobody. You lost your godhood. And that's a jarring realization. I never meant *Sea of Love* to be a thriller, though it may have been lucky for me that it was remolded that way. To me, *Sea of Love* is about Frank finding out how to realign his values to keep from going under, to keep from eating his gun.

NIGHT AND THE CITY

NG: In *Night and the City* you were in the strange position of remaking someone else's film.

RP: I wrote it for Scorsese in 1985 before I wrote the other two films. That was my entree. Bertrand Tavernier told Scorsese, "You know, there's this Jules Dassin film, *Night and the City,* that's ripe for a remake." And Scorsese was looking for a writer to do it, and that's how I met him. I did it in about three months. He liked the script, but I think what happened was, it was too Scorsesean in its touches. He felt like he had already "done" in all his other films what I proposed in my script so there was no challenge for him here. I sort of outsmarted myself, and it stayed in limbo all these years at Fox.

Ufland–Roth productions were involved in *Night and the City.* Then at some point Joe Roth became head of Fox, and I called him up and said, "You remember that script that I wrote for you and Harry Ufland way back when? Guess what? You run the studio now. How's about it?" So he sent it out, and a lot of actors were interested, but it never got off the ground until Irwin Winkler, who had produced a number of Scorsese movies, had a reading one day with Robert De Niro. The script had been dead for six years but after a casual two-hour read-through they decided to do it, and it was done, in the can, six months later.

NG: Did you have any trepidations about remaking a film that already had a cult following?

RP: I never thought *Night and the City* was that great a movie to begin with. I mean, the only movies that get remade are B movies. Nobody would dare remake *Citizen Kane.* I watched the movie once, just to absorb it, and then I watched it a second time and just basically took notes on the sequence of events. I never watched it again. The reason you have to do that is that there is a danger in becoming too worshipful of your source material. You become too self-conscious of how *they* did it, how the director did it. And in order to make it yours, all you want from the original is the essence, the spirit of the dilemma. With *Night and the City*, all I wanted out of the earlier film was the smell of it and the mechanics of the plot.

NG: When you watched the original *Night and the City*, were you thinking about the thematic affinities with your work?

RP: No. All I saw was the character. The character of Harry Fabian. It seemed like it would be a tremendous amount of fun to put words in his mouth. I love writing about fast-talkers. I like wheeler-dealers. I love the art of yackety-yak. I love that because what keeps me fresh as a writer is improvisation. I've got to create scenes in which my character has got to improvise because then *I* have to improvise *for* him. And, basically, this guy starts out at ninety miles an hour, then he goes to 120 miles per hour, crashes and burns. I could really kick up with this type of character. The guy is a mouse in a room full of cats, who thinks he's a cat simply because the *real* cats let him live, temporarily.

NG: Though in the movie he's still alive at the end.

RP: I killed him in the original draft because I felt it was the natural end. But no studio is going to let you kill your main character — unless he's a historical figure we all know dies. You can't have JFK alive at the end of *JFK*.

NG: As you know, what critics find most striking about your work is the very thing you found most appealing about Harry Fabian: facility with dialogue. It's almost as if language is a character in your films — certainly in *Night and the City*.

RP: My affection for and fascination with how people speak started out really early. Before I was a writer I was a mimic, somebody who could watch TV and go downstairs with his friends and then "do" *The Twilight Zone* or *The Untouchables* with Walter Winchell's narration. It's in your mouth, the way you metabolize information. Some kids were into athletics. For me it was always the ability to imitate and mimic. And as I got older, I acquired writing skills, and all of a sudden I could do that on paper.

A very early inspiration for me was *The Essential Lenny Bruce*, the transcripts of Lenny Bruce's comedy routines. Without ever having heard Lenny Bruce, I knew exactly what register the voice was in, what his sighs sounded like, his tongue-clucks, his stops and starts. By simply *reading* the transcripts. And it just hit me that you can make the ear work for you on the page. Good dialogue is not somebody's ability to write authentic speech as heard in real life. If that was all there was to it you could just push a button on a tape recorder, go get a sandwich and when the guy's finished speaking, push Off, and then go collect an Oscar or a book award. Good dialogue on the page is the *illusion* of reality. It's the essentialization of how people talk. You've got to know how to edit what people say without losing any of the spirit.

NG: Your characters also appropriate the world through language.

RP: I'm fascinated by the way people construct a sequence of words, the misnomers, the malapropisms, and how that reveals how they process the world. It's not so much what they saw; it's how they *verbalize* what they saw. It's an oral Rorschach test. And that's another frustrating thing for a screenwriter: you're not in charge of the music that's going to come out of people's mouths. I have an obsession with perfect pitch in the delivery of dialogue.

NG: Talk is the street music of New York, and you are the quintessential New York writer. One critic even called *Night and the City* your "feverish love lyric to New York" and "one of the great New York movies."

RP: What is consistent in my work, from book to movie, to movie to book, to poem, to play, to essay is that the fourth character is always New York City. Part of this is for simple security on my part. I know New York so well. I often think of New York and night simultaneously. I think about New York in the night, and I think of it as this great urban, nocturnal ocean, in that all the characters, all the inhabitants of New York, are various forms of prey-fish or lantern-fish, you know, these strange fish that you rarely see except from these superbathyspheres. I'll often indulge myself in secondary and tertiary characters. Look, here comes a Wang-fish! Here comes a goddamn *dragon*-fish. What the hell *is* that! And all my characters are floating in this fluid urban night, and they're looking for things. Somebody might be looking for love, somebody might be looking for power, somebody might be looking for redemption of some kind. But basically I think of my people as floating . . . in an ink black sea, in the New York nocturnal sea.

The Color of Money

This draft was written in 1985 and 1986 and
is the shooting script, the nearest line-by-line
representation of the filmed movie. — R.P.

VOICE-OVER

Nine-ball is rotation pool. The balls are pocketed in numbered order. The only ball that *means* anything, that *wins* it, is the nine. A player can shoot eight trick shots in a row, blow the nine and lose. On the other hand, a player can get the nine on the *break* if the balls spread right. Which is all to say, that *luck* plays a part in nine-ball.

But for some players, luck itself is a skill . . . or an *art*.

OPENING CREDITS

1. WE SEE, almost totally in shadow, a pool player, frozen like a mounted suit of Samurai armor. He's immobile, seated, waiting, surrounded by his sacraments; his cue (held like a staff), a small table by his side supporting a tiny hill of baby powder and a full ashtray. The only motion in the frame is a thin stream of wafting cigarette smoke from the ashtray.

2. Faces, frontal and profile, also immobile, impassive, waiting.

3. OVERHEAD SHOT of a pool table. A diamond-shaped formation of nine balls centered at one end, a player's hands and stick emerging from shadow to shoot the break shot at the other. WE SEE the break in slow motion.

4. OVERHEAD of the shadow-player running all nine balls. Normal speed.

END OPENING CREDITS

1 INT: THE "HI-CUE" BILLIARDS AND
GAME CENTER — DAY

There's a red cigarette-scarred wall-to-wall carpet, a bar/grill, a jukebox. Along one wall a bank of video machines.

The players range in age from kids to senior citizens; in ethnicity from white to black to Latino to Chinese.

The only sanctuary for serious players is a two-table niche near the bar bordered by roll-out aluminum bleachers. The tables are in reasonably good shape, well lit and the vibes are those of concentration and money on the line. There's an invisible shield between this niche and the rest of the room.

THE BAR

TRACKING SHOT along the bar top. WE SEE various drink and cigarette still lifes, hands; hear snatches of conversation, and in the background the sporadic yet ever present clack of pool balls.

During this TRACKING, the man's voice we hear is Eddie Felson.

> EDDIE (OS)
> Check this out. Old MacDonald. More like Young
> MacDonald but it tastes like six year bonded.

WE SEE Eddie Felson, in his fifties, liquor salesman. He's got a clipboard, a bottle standing upright in an open attache case.

He's feeding a shot of liquor to the bartender, Janelle, in her forties. She leans on her crossed forearms towards Eddie.

> EDDIE
> (*carefully feeding her*)
> To your health.

Eddie dries her lips with his thumb and watches for her reaction.

> JANELLE
> (*making a pass at her own lips*)
> That's good stuff.

> EDDIE
> That's *very* good stuff.

A young long-haired lanky kid in a black heavy-metal T-shirt stands slightly behind Eddie and taps his shoulder. The kid is wearing a fingerless black weightlifting glove. He's holding a cue stick. Eddie ignores him.

EDDIE
Tastes like top shelf, right? I get you a case of that for
thirty-five fifty less than your wholesale on Jack Daniels,
forty-five fifty less than your wholesale on Wild Turkey.

JANELLE
A case . . . What am I, a hotel chain? Who are you trying
to sell?

EDDIE
I don't "sell" . . . I'm doing it for you . . . for family.

JANELLE
Come to my house tonight . . . I'll make you an omelette.

EDDIE
I make the omelettes.

JANELLE
OK (*pause*) you make the omelettes.

EDDIE
What? You forgot the omelette I made you?

JANELLE
No — I didn't forget.

EDDIE
Yeah? What was it? What was in it?

KID (JULIAN)
Yo, Eddie . . .

EDDIE
What was in it?

JANELLE
(*hesitatingly*)
Sweet sausage?

EDDIE
(*sounding horrified*)
Sweet sausage! I never made sweet sausage. Who the hell
made you sweet sausage?

> JULIAN
> Eddie . . .

> EDDIE
> (*to Janelle*)
> Excuse me.

> EDDIE
> (*patient*)
> Julian . . . what am I doing here . . . am I working?

> JULIAN
> I'm working too . . . I got this guy . . .
> (*shrugs and semi-whispers*)
> He's up for twenty a rack.

> EDDIE
> (*to Janelle*)
> It was sour cream and caviar.
> (*to Julian*)
> What guy?

Julian nods over to the bank of video games where a twenty-year-old Italian kid, his back to us, his cue leaning between the video machines, is going berserk on a game of Q-Bert. This is Vincent, easygoing, nice kid.

> JULIAN
> We're playing two, two and a half hours for five a game.
> (*beat*)
> He's up thirty.

Eddie raises an eyebrow.

> JULIAN
> Aw c'mon, man, I been playin' him off.

Julian turns to his buddies, other dark lanky guys, lounging around the hustlers' niche, for verification. Even though they're out of earshot they nod to Eddie in agreement.

Eddie shrugs, dips in his pocket, peels off a twenty. Julian snaps it up, strides back to the niche, stroking the length of his cue stick the whole way, props the stick on the rail, hunches over. His gestures are amphetamine-fueled.

>   JULIAN
>   (*shouting across the room to the video bank*)
>   Yo, Vincent!

Vincent is going nuts on Q-Bert, doesn't answer. Julian looks back to the bar at Eddie. Julian and his buddies are laughing.

>   JULIAN
>   (*shouting*)
>   Vincent! We're on!

Vincent just raises his hand OK, his back to the action.

2 INT: HI-CUE — DAY
ANOTHER ANGLE

Eddie turns back to Janelle.

>   EDDIE
>   Sweet sausage!

>   JANELLE
>   I get off at ten.

>   EDDIE
>   I'll come pick you up. No. Better still get the sweet sausage
>   guy to pick you up.

>   JANELLE
>   I'd rather you.

>   EDDIE
>   (*pouring and leaning forward to Janelle*)
>   I'm talking bourbon. You know the secret? These people?
>   They got a hold of aged kegs. You know what aged kegs
>   to a young bourbon is like? That's like getting bootleg
>   thoroughbred sperm and slipping it to a police horse . . .
>   leave the other horses back in the precinct house . . . So
>   what are you tasting? You're tasting a low fusil oil content

. . . you're tasting a low acidic content. Just like the big
guys . . . it's the kegs.

> JANELLE
> (*laughing*)
> Low fusil oil content. Where'd they get the kegs? You
> can't just get aged kegs like that.

Julian taps Eddie's shoulder.

Eddie pulls out another twenty without turning around. Julian
grabs it. Eddie grabs Julian's wrist.

> EDDIE
> (*slightly pissed*)
> What happened?

> JULIAN
> I slipped.

Eddie lets him go.

> EDDIE
> (*to Janelle*)
> He slipped . . . where'd they get the kegs? Look . . .
> (*with a conspiratorial wink*)
> they just do. Do whatever you want. It's gonna leave the
> warehouse one way or the other.

> GIRL'S VOICE (CARMEN; OS)
> On the snap, Vincent!

The sound of Vincent's break . . . a thunderclap.

Eddie instinctively turns his head to the game, studies Vincent for a
brief moment.

> EDDIE
> Kid's got a sledgehammer break, huh?
> (*pours himself a shot*)
> Bottoms up . . . You know who loves this stuff? The
> Chinese.

Eddie jerks back a thumb at the Chinese.

JANELLE
(*smirking*)
It must be the low fusil oil content.

EDDIE
Don't kid yourself . . . It has its effect, it's just one of those
things you never think about but can make your day . . .
like electricity.

Julian is behind Eddie again tapping his shoulder.

JULIAN
(*sheepish*)
Eddie . . . throw me another twenty?

EDDIE
Hey! That's *six*ty!

Julian shrugs, slightly embarrassed.

EDDIE
(*hesitating*)
Julian, who you working, me or him?

JULIAN
He's on the ropes, Eddie, he just lucked out . . . you know
me . . .

Eddie gives Julian another twenty.

As Julian returns to the table, Eddie casually checks out Vincent.
The kid is talking to a girl, Carmen, young, dark, T-shirt and jeans.
Vincent is fooling around with his cue stick, working it like a
samurai sword; slipping it behind his back, holding it over his head,
slipping it into an invisible scabbard at his hip.

Eddie, watching Vincent, absently gives Janelle a twenty-dollar bill.

EDDIE
Pick some nice wine for tonight.

JANELLE
Red or white?

>   EDDIE
>   (*double take; snatches back his money with mock
>   outrage*)
>   Well screw the whole thing if it's gonna get *com*plicated!

Janelle laughs.

>   EDDIE
>   (*winking*)
>   A nice white . . .

>   CARMEN (OS)
>   On the snap, Vincent!

We hear the sound of Vincent's break again. Another thunderclap.

Eddie turns at the sound. Looks at Vincent with real interest for the
first time.

3 INT: HI-CUE — DAY
EDDIE'S POV

WE SEE Vincent work the table with fluid precision. Eddie slowly
rises.

>   JANELLE
>   Eddie, how about some labels . . . can you get me some
>   Wild Turkey labels?

>   EDDIE
>   (*on his feet, moving towards
>   the table; distracted*)
>   I'll see what I can do.

Eddie casually saunters over to the game, takes a seat on the aluminum bleacher next to Carmen and watches. Vincent starts to run
the rack as Julian stands there without ever getting a shot.

>   EDDIE
>   (*to Carmen*)
>   Kid draws a bead, hah?

Vincent drops the nine. Julian looks over to the bar for Eddie. He
doesn't realize Eddie's right there. Julian hands the twenty to Carmen. Eddie beams up at Julian. Julian is flustered.

EDDIE
(*offering Julian another twenty;*
sarcastic)
Play him again . . . I think he's *really* on the ropes now.

VINCENT
(*to Julian*)
We doin' it again, chief?

JULIAN
(*mortified*)
Eddie, I gotta split.

EDDIE
I'm sure you do.

VINCENT
(*to Julian*)
You goin'?

JULIAN
I gotta see somebody.

VINCENT
C'mon, one more game.

JULIAN
I'm bust.

VINCENT
So let's just play play.

JULIAN
(*squinting*)
Play play?

VINCENT
Yeah . . . just play . . . for play. Show me what you got.

CARMEN
(*exasperated*)
Hey, *Vincent* . . .

Julian looks at Eddie, incredulous. No one just "plays" when they can play for money.

> VINCENT
> Hey. I just want your best game, man. I think the money's throwing you off.
> *(beat)*
> I tell you what. *I* win — no money . . . *you* win . . . I'll go for twenty.

Julian splits without a glance, as if Vincent is dangerously whacked.

> CARMEN
> *(to Eddie)*
> You want to play him?

> VINCENT
> *(imitates a boxer who just scored a K.O. — arms raised high in a V for Victory)*
> Carmen! Who's next!

> EDDIE
> *(mock intimidated)*
> Me?
> *(beat)*
> Sure.

> CARMEN
> Twenty a rack?

> EDDIE
> Five hundred a rack.

> CARMEN
> You serious?

> EDDIE
> I never kid about money.

> VINCENT
> *(to the room)*
> Next! Next! . . .

Eddie grins at Carmen. She doesn't know what to do.

VINCENT
Cowards . . . c'mon . . . for the table . . . just for the table
. . . no money.

4 INT: HI-CUE — DAY

Vincent goes back to the video bank. Carmen is blown away by the
size of Eddie's offer. They stare at each other.

EDDIE
You don't know what you're doin', do you?

CARMEN
What do you mean?

EDDIE
You just blew five hundred dollars. That kid had both
arms in traction he could beat anybody in the room.

CARMEN
Yeah . . . he could . . .

EDDIE
So I'll offer you again . . . I'll play him for five hundred
dollars.

Carmen is still paralyzed.

EDDIE
You don't know what to say, huh? Maybe I'm hustling
you . . . maybe not. You don't know . . . but you *should*
know . . . you know when to say yes . . . you know when
to say no . . . you know that . . . everyone goes home in a
limousine.

CARMEN
So what should I say, yes or no?

EDDIE
You should say no . . . you know why? Because I'm an
unknown and it's too much money. See, *he* should be the
unknown . . . that would be beautiful . . . you can control

that . . . play with that . . . you follow me? So I'll offer
you again . . . I'll play him for five hundred dollars.

> CARMEN

No.

> EDDIE
> (*rising*)

Actually you should've said yes . . . but you wouldn't
know that . . . I don't know how you could . . . It's very
complicated. It's like . . . which twin has the Tony . . .
> (*shrugs*)

Maybe they *both* do or maybe they're really *bald* . . . or
maybe Tony's some *guy* . . . How would you know? . . .
See what I'm getting at? *Plus* like everything else, you need
money.

> CARMEN
> (*laughing*)

You're crazy.

> EDDIE
> (*calmly, seriously*)

No I'm not . . . I'm just common sense.

They stare at each other a beat.

> EDDIE

Let me take both you guys to dinner tonight . . .

> CARMEN

You should ask Vincent.

> EDDIE

No, *you* should ask Vincent.

5 INT: SEMI-FANCY SALAD-BAR-TYPE
STEAKHOUSE — NIGHT

The three of them at a table.

> EDDIE
> (*in mid-conversation*)

. . . Yeah, well, there's *lots* of good players.

But let me explain. It really doesn't matter — Vincent, you
beat Julian. You know the last time Julian lost for me?

> VINCENT
> It's a *game,* man . . . balls and a stick.

> CARMEN
> (*laughing with admiration for the understatement*)
> Balls and a stick . . . This is Vincent.

Vincent pinches Carmen's cheek.

> VINCENT
> I'll tell you, man . . . nine-ball's not that tough. You know
> what's tough? Q-Bert.

> EDDIE
> Q-Bert . . .

> CARMEN
> It's this video game, Vincent's the best at.

> VINCENT
> Pool . . . the balls . . . they're just sitting there . . . You
> take your time . . . set up the shot . . . Q-Bert, that little
> bastard's moving so fast, right? . . . and you got those
> other guys after him.
> (*Vincent imitates twirling and punching and pushing
> knobs and dials*)
> You got no time to think . . . to study . . . it's go! go! go!
> Man versus machine.

Eddie grins.

> EDDIE
> Can you make any money doing it?

> VINCENT
> I tell you what I can do off Q-Bert . . . Ten years from now
> I can get into West Point . . . it's all coming down to video
> game reflexes . . . computerized tanks . . . Ten years from
> now a guy who can score heavy on Q-Bert is a shoo-in at
> the Point . . . Just you wait.

EDDIE
(*grins affectionately*)
You're beautiful.

VINCENT
You don't believe me?

CARMEN
What do you mean *money?*

EDDIE
Money-money . . .

CARMEN
Really.

EDDIE
Hey, look . . . you have an area of excellence, you're the *best* at something, *any*thing . . . rich can be arranged, rich can come fairly easy.

CARMEN
Really.

EDDIE
Hey, Vince, other than this Q-Bert, do you have an area of excellence?

VINCENT
Nine-ball!
(*to Carmen with a squeeze*)
Right?

EDDIE
You're *some* piece of work.

VINCENT
I'm some piece of work.

EDDIE
You're a natural character.

VINCENT
(*to Carmen*)
I have natural character.

EDDIE
No . . . no . . . That's not what I said . . . you *are* a
natural character . . . you're an incredible flake . . . I'm
serious . . . It's a gift . . . guys work all their *lives* to
develop a character like that . . . You go into a pool hall
guys nowhere in your league would *fight* each other to
play you . . . you're a *master*piece.

Vincent is silent; he doesn't know if he should be insulted or not.
Carmen is all ears.

EDDIE
You got all that but the fact of the matter is, kid, the way
you go about things . . . you couldn't find big time with a
road map.

Eddie pauses to let that sink in.

EDDIE
Pool excellence is not about excellent *pool*. It's about
be*com*ing something.

VINCENT & CARMEN
What . . .

EDDIE
A student. You study *hu*man *moves*. All the greats are
students of human moves . . . to the man.

VINCENT
Student of human moves, hah?

EDDIE
That's *my* area of excellence.

VINCENT
(*grinning*)
Oh yeah?

EDDIE
Human moves. See that guy at the bar with the girl . . . ?
on the end?

EDDIE'S POV

WE SEE a couple talking at the bar across the room.

> EDDIE
> From *here,* where I sit I say
> (*Eddie squints, speculating*)
> they come in separate, he's busting his ass trying to score
> and he's gonna give it up in
> (*consulting his watch*)
> thirty . . . thirty-*two* seconds. You want to bet me a
> dollar?

Eddie takes off his watch and passes it to Vincent to keep time.

> VINCENT
> Go.

Vincent is nose-down staring at the second hand. Eddie winks at
Carmen. Carmen studies Eddie.

> VINCENT
> Ten seconds.

> CARMEN
> What do you mean "rich can be arranged"?

> EDDIE
> (*shrugs*)
> I'm just talking . . .

> VINCENT
> Thirty seconds . . . thirty-one seconds . . . thirty-*two*
> seconds, cough it up please!

Eddie casually glances at the bar, peels off a dollar.

> EDDIE
> Uh . . . there he goes.
> (*the guy leaves*)
> I'm off a few seconds. You want to up the bet?

> VINCENT
> Sure.

> EDDIE
> The check for this meal says I go up there and I leave with
> her in two minutes.

> VINCENT
> You got it.

6 INT: STEAKHOUSE-BAR
ANGLE — THE BAR — NIGHT

The woman, Diane, in her twenties, short hair, attractive in a
secretary way, sucks her drink through a straw.

She looks at him, nods hello.

> EDDIE
> Look . . . I know this sounds crazy but, ah, come outside.
> Look at my car for a minute.

> DIANE
> (*hesitating*)
> Your *car?*

Eddie rises and gestures for her to come with him. She silently
gathers up her stuff and complies.

ANGLE — THE TABLE

Eddie and the woman walk past Vincent and Carmen. Vincent
looks awed, Carmen amused. Eddie bends down to Vincent.

> EDDIE
> Human moves, kid. You study my wristwatch.
> (*Eddie takes it back*)
> I study you. You get the check.
> (*Eddie drops a five dollar bill*)
> Cab's on me.

7 EXT: PARKING LOT — NIGHT

Eddie and the woman stand outside the restaurant.

>   DIANE
> What's with the car, Eddie?

>   EDDIE
> (*shrugs*)
> Nothing. I'll give you a ride home. You shouldn't be
> sitting in there alone, Diane, it's depressing.

8 INT: DARKENED BEDROOM — JANELLE'S HOUSE —
NIGHT

Eddie on his back in bed next to Janelle. Eddie looks lost in thought.
Janelle examines her nails. Postcoital, Miller time.

>   JANELLE
> (*dryly*)
> Where'd you go?

>   EDDIE
> What?

>   JANELLE
> You sure weren't *here*.

>   EDDIE
> (*wryly*)
> I was here . . . you kidding me? The *earth* moved . . .
> didn't it move for you?

>   JANELLE
> (*fighting a grin*)
> A little bit.
> (*beat*)
> I mean it wasn't like San *Juan*. You want to talk *earth*
> moving you talk to San *Juan*. You remember that
> waterbed we had? Sometimes I think about that week,
> Eddie, you know when I'm at the bar? I say to myself, I'm
> buying a waterbed, don't tell Eddie. Make it a surprise.
> Make us some rum and pineapple juice . . .

Janelle notices Eddie's lost in thought, not listening.

> JANELLE
> (*sadly*)
> You couldn't tell me one thing I just said to you, could you?

> EDDIE
> (*glassy in thought*)
> Huh? No . . . yeah . . . a waterbed would be great.
> (*coming belatedly alert*)
> You remember San Juan?

Eddie retreats into his thoughts again.

9 INT: HI-CUE — NEXT DAY

A liquor delivery is being wheeled through the front door. Various cases topped by two cases of Old MacDonald.

ANGLE — THE HUSTLERS' NICHE

Eddie elbows on knees on the top tier watching Julian play some other guy.

Carmen strolls over. She's without Vincent.

Eddie nods hello.

> CARMEN
> What did you mean last night "rich can be arranged"?

> EDDIE
> (*rises*)
> Come to my office.

10 EXT: PARKING LOT IN FRONT OF HI-CUE — DAY

Eddie digging for his car keys, Carmen walking slightly behind.

They get in the front seat of the car.

11 INT: CAR/EXT: HI-CUE — DAY

> EDDIE
> Rich can be arranged.

> CARMEN
> You want Vincent to quit his job and become a pool
> hustler?

Carmen and Eddie stare at each other for a long beat.

> EDDIE
> Smell . . .
> *(waves his hand palm up)*
> You smell anything?

> CARMEN
> Leather?

> EDDIE
> Six months ago you'd of smelled leather half a block away
> . . . when it gets faint like this it's time to get a new car.

Carmen gets in. Eddie turns radio on. Music.

> EDDIE
> This car looks very good on you.

> CARMEN
> This is liquor money?

> EDDIE
> Some . . . And some is human *moves* money . . . I invest.
> You know what I invest in?

> CARMEN
> Excellence.

Eddie studies her. He's smiling.

> CARMEN
> You think Vincent is that good?

> EDDIE
> He's got the tools . . . He's got the eye . . . He's got the
> flake . . . But can he flake *on* and flake *off?* . . .

control . . . can you teach that? It's not clear. You gotta
learn to be yourself but on *purpose*. Do you understand?

CARMEN
Yeah . . . yeah I do.

EDDIE
You like to travel?

CARMEN
Sure.

EDDIE
You like hotels?

CARMEN
(*fighting down her excitement: you have to be cool
with Eddie*)
They're OK.

EDDIE
You gonna help me with him?

CARMEN
That lady you picked up last night . . . you knew her from
before, right?

EDDIE
(*soberly*)
I think you should consider cultivating a less cynical
attitude towards people.

CARMEN
(*not thrown*)
And that guy . . . you probably had his schedule down
cold . . . What . . . he works the night shift somewhere?
He's your brother-in-law?

EDDIE
(*mock serious*)
You're a hard broad, you know that? What's Vincent see
in you?

CARMEN
Vincent's the best. *That's* what he sees in me.

EDDIE
(*grinning*)
I bet you guys have been together since the beginning of time, right?

CARMEN
We been living together about a year . . . Vincent *made* us get a place together. You know how we met? My old boyfriend last year got busted breaking into Vincent's parent's house . . . we met at the police station, me and Vincent.

EDDIE
You were bailing him out, your boyfriend?

CARMEN
I got busted too . . . I was driving the car. You see this?
(*she shows Eddie a medallion on a chain*)
This is Vincent's mother's.

EDDIE
He gave that to you?

CARMEN
No. It's from the robbery. Vincent says his mother has one just like it . . . Vincent's sweet.

EDDIE
Where does Vincent work?

CARMEN
(*wincing*)
I don't have to go there with you, do I?

12 EXT: TODDLER TOWN — TWO HOURS LATER — DAY

It's a warehouse-sized store on a miracle mile stretch. On the roof is a giant rotating plaster baby.

13 INT: TODDLER TOWN — DAY

It's a cavernous acre of cribs, bibs, toys, playpens, etc.

Working the floor are Vincent and four coworkers; each wearing a black T-shirt with his name ironed on the chest (Frank, Tom, Vince, Lou).

Eddie cruises the room.

EDDIE'S POV

Vincent is pitching to a young couple. He holds a baby harness, straps and clamps trailing to the floor in each hand.

> VINCENT
> (*holding up one harness*)
> The problem with *this* one is . . . it's made in Taiwan . . .
> (*Vincent shrugs*)
> You want something for your kid to bounce in? What country comes to mind. Bounce . . . think bounce . . . what animal bounces?

> YOUNG GUY
> Kangaroo?

> VINCENT
> Who lives where . . .

> YOUNG GIRL
> Australia.

> VINCENT
> Bingo . . . This is the Bounceroo.
> (*holding up the other harness*)
> . . . Australian made . . . I'll be perfectly honest with you, twice as expensive as Taiwan, here . . . but it's three times the goods. Plus, I'll throw you fifteen percent off.

They nod OK. Vincent spies Eddie.

> VINCENT
> Tommy! Write 'em up . . . fifteen percent off. Tommy'll take care of you . . . he's a good man.
> (*to Eddie*)
> Hey! What're *you* doing here, Mr. Felson?

> EDDIE
> Eddie . . .

> VINCENT
> Eddie.

> EDDIE
> Carmen told me where you work.
> (*regarding young couple*)
> That was nice.

> VINCENT
> Thank you. It *is* better stuff. If you believe . . . they believe.

> EDDIE
> Me and you . . . where we can talk private?

14 INT: DOLL DEPARTMENT (OR VENDING MACHINES) — DAY

Vincent and Eddie stand in either a narrow aisle flanked by towering shelves of dolls which stare at them, or a refreshment area. Vincent eats a candy bar. Eddie eats a bag of Planters peanuts.

> EDDIE
> Listen up . . . there's a nine-ball tournament end of April in Atlantic City. There's gonna be a lot of action . . . We should go.

> VINCENT
> (*flipping a doll like it's a baseball*)
> We?

> EDDIE
> Me, you and Carmen.

> VINCENT
> That sounds like fun.

> EDDIE
> Now the best part is that we oughta leave tomorrow.

VINCENT
(*joking*)
Tomorrow?! Hell, why wait? Why don't we go now?

EDDIE
Yea, we could do that. Hey, if you're gonna take the
plunge, give yourself a fair shake. You do this half-assed
then nobody's gonna do any good. Go on the road . . . six
weeks . . . get some seasoning . . . put together some stuff.

VINCENT
(*backing off*)
Why don't you take Julian? He'd be into that, right?

EDDIE
Julian's a face . . . he's known. You're nobody . . . I'll get
better bets down with you . . . if I can be more honest
about this you have to tell me how.

VINCENT
C'mon, Eddie, this is my job.

EDDIE
You think so? Well I don't think so. I think it's your
problem.

VINCENT
What is?

EDDIE
(*deep exhale*)
You love Carmen?

VINCENT
(*cautious*)
Sure.

EDDIE
Crazy about her, right?

VINCENT
(*embarrassed*)
This is a little personal, here.

Eddie just stares at him seriously.

> VINCENT
> (*wary*)
> What . . .

> EDDIE
> You're losing her kid.

> VINCENT
> What do you mean?

> EDDIE
> (*no sarcasm*)
> She don't see the al*lure* of this place.

> TOMMY
> (*leaning into the aisle*)
> Hey, Vincent!

> VINCENT
> (*to Tommy, with irritation*)
> Wait . . .
> (*to Eddie*)
> What?

> EDDIE
> You ever take a good look at her?
> (*shrugs*)
> She's starting to pack.

Vincent stares at him.

> VINCENT
> You don't know her.

> EDDIE
> I didn't know that lady at the bar last night either . . .
> She's *bored*, Vincent. Do you follow me?

> TOMMY
> Vincent!

Vincent ignores Tommy.

VINCENT
So what are you sayin'?

EDDIE
All I'm saying is, me, you and her, six weeks on the road
. . . she'll be a couple of years catching her breath.

TOMMY
Vincent! . . . these people got a babysitter. Time is money,
hah?

VINCENT
Hey. Can't you see I'm talkin' here!

EDDIE
Take some time. You should think about all of this.
Everything I'm saying. You know where I am. Come and
talk to me.

Vincent, frazzled, pulls his eyes away from Eddie and walks down
the canyon of dolls.

EDDIE
And Vincent, listen . . .

Vincent turns.

EDDIE
(*fucking with Vincent's head*)
. . . don't worry about it.

15 INT: HI-CUE — BAR AREA — NIGHT
EDDIE AND JANELLE

Janelle brings a bottle of JSW Brown over to Eddie.

Eddie holds up his hand in a don't pour gesture.

EDDIE
You know there's this island in the Bahamas . . . Green
Turtle Cay . . . They make this drink down there called a
Bahama Breeze.

> JANELLE
> Yeah?

> EDDIE
> I think . . . me and you . . . as beverage service
> professionals, we should investigate that island soon.

> JANELLE
> (*smiling*)
> A fact finding tour?

> EDDIE
> Uh-huh. With a two-hour layover in San Juan.

EDDIE'S POV

WE SEE Vincent enter with Carmen.

Eddie looks at Janelle and nods in the direction of a back office.

16 INT: HI-CUE — SMALL BACK OFFICE — NIGHT

Eddie stands by filing cabinets behind a desk. The office is cluttered
with papers, boxes and liquor cases.

Vincent knocks, tentatively enters.

> VINCENT
> Hi, Eddie? . . . What we were talkin' 'bout yesterday? I
> wanted to ask you some more questions . . .

> EDDIE
> (*cuts Vincent off halfway through above line*)
> Here, I got something to show you. Take a look at this.

Eddie hands a beautiful velvet cue case to Vincent. Vincent opens
it. WE SEE cue stick in two pieces resting in blue velvet.

> VINCENT
> God Damn!

> EDDIE
> A Balabushka.

VINCENT
This makes the others look like a stickball bat. Is this yours?

EDDIE
You want it?

VINCENT
Aw, no way . . . This isn't for me — this is for . . . for . . . I don't know *who* this is for! Babe *Ruth,* if he played pool, would carry this . . . John *Wayne* would carry this.

EDDIE
G'head . . . take it.

VINCENT
You're pushin' pretty hard.

EDDIE
Yes I am. I've been thinking about nothing else all day.

VINCENT
I don't know what to tell you, Eddie.

EDDIE
Whatever . . . doesn't matter . . . try it. You don't like it? Bring it back.

VINCENT
OK.
       (*hesitates*)
You know, Eddie, I was talking to Carmen? Feeling her out? I think you're wrong, man. She's doing good . . . real good.

EDDIE
       (*gracious*)
Good . . . glad I'm wrong . . .

Vincent hesitates.

17 INT: HI-CUE — POOL ROOM — NIGHT

Vincent walks out past Carmen and the young hustlers. Everyone spies the case. No one says anything about it though.

ANGLE

Eddie exits from the office, watches Vincent from across the room. He stands near Carmen.

> CARMEN
> What's happening?

> EDDIE
> (*eyes on Vincent, sighing*)
> That boyfriend of yours . . . I dunno.
> (*looks at Carmen*)
> I need a little help here.

ANGLE

Vincent stands over a pool table. The two parts of the sticks are separated in his hands.

VINCENT'S POV

WE SEE the hustlers' niche. Carmen's not there.

Vincent leaves the stick on the table and walks over to Janelle at the bar. Pulls potato chips off a clip rack, drops a quarter on the counter. Surveys the room. Still no Carmen.

Julian walks over to the bar. Vincent tears open the chips.

> VINCENT
> You see my girlfriend?

> JULIAN
> She went out.

> VINCENT
> Out where?

> JULIAN
> Hey, she's *your* girlfriend, man.

Carmen enters the room tapping a fresh pack of cigarettes against the back of her hand.

> VINCENT
> Everything OK?

CARMEN
(*shrugging*)
Yeah.

VINCENT
Where'd you go?

CARMEN
I went to get cigs.

VINCENT
They sell cigarettes here.

CARMEN
So I got 'em across the street, so what.

VINCENT
What, you mean, you wanted to get some fresh air?

CARMEN
Fresh air? There's ninety thousand cars out there.
(*beat*)
What is your problem?

VINCENT
No problem . . . no problem.

CARMEN
(*looking at him screwy*)
Glad to hear it.

VINCENT
I just didn't know where you went . . . I was looking for
you.

CARMEN
I'm gonna sit down now, OK?

VINCENT
Great.

CARMEN
I might go to the bathroom in about ten, twenty minutes.

       VINCENT
OK.

       CARMEN
I'll come and tell you when, OK?

       VINCENT
Hey . . . I just didn't know where you went . . . Let's not make a federal production out of it, OK?

       CARMEN
OK.

       VINCENT
Good.

Vincent returns to the empty table, screws the stick together and powers a monstrous break. He studies the spread. Can't concentrate. Puts down the stick and strides over to Eddie.

       VINCENT
Let's do it.

CLOSE-UP — CARMEN

casually looking across the room to Eddie.

Eddie catches her glance, nods, looks away.

18 INT: J.C. PENNEY PACKERS — TWO HOURS LATER — NIGHT

Restaurant/bar; fake Tiffany lamps, mock Victorian, hanging-plants-type lounge. Sporty joint; lots of hitters, fifties jazz jukebox.

Eddie and Janelle are dancing. Fox trot.

       JANELLE
So this one island they got down there I never got out of the airport. We land I gotta go to the john, I walk into the men's room by mistake and I see these urinals screwed up on the wall here — eye level. I said, Jesus Christ, what do they breed out here, giants? I mean, I know how much I can handle . . .

They go back to the bar. Chuck the bartender pours them drinks without asking.

> JANELLE
> So I just grabbed the next plane out . . .

> EDDIE
> (to Chuck)
> How's that Old MacDonald working out?

> CHUCK
> You're drinking it now.

> EDDIE
> (startled)
> You serious?
> (shrugs)
> Good stuff.

Julian, who's been having a drink at the other end of the bar with some girl, makes his way to Eddie.

> JULIAN
> (coked up)
> Yo, Eddie, my man.
> (to Janelle)
> Hey . . .

> EDDIE
> (staring hard at him)
> You should look in the mirror before you leave the john, Julian.

> JULIAN
> (as Eddie drinks)
> Better than that shit.

Eddie is disgusted. He hates drugs.

> JULIAN
> Listen, you gonna be around Monday? There's a guy I got set up in Camden.

> EDDIE
> I'm gonna be out of town for a few weeks on business.

Janelle looks alarmed.

> JULIAN
> Bullshit . . . What . . . you gonna take that guy on the road? What's his name?

> EDDIE
> I don't know his name . . . And it's none of your business.

> JULIAN
> (*coke rap*)
> That guy's a *chump*. What he do, beat me one night? I put the nine ball up *both* your asses. Are you serious? Takin' him on the road. When was the last time you did the road? Nineteen sixty? They didn't even have cars then. What, you banging his girlfriend?

Janelle looks away, smiling.

> EDDIE
> (*stares at him for a beat, as if contemplating smacking him down, then smiles*)
> You're the best, Julian.

> JULIAN
> Let me play him again tonight . . . Winner gets in the car with you.

Janelle exits. Eddie doesn't see this.

> EDDIE
> I said you're the best, Julian.

> JULIAN
> Hey, Eddie, you're not the only stakehorse around, you know that?

> EDDIE
> I'll see you in Atlantic City, Julian.

> JULIAN
> Don't look *too* hard for me, OK?

Julian exits. Eddie turns to see Janelle has gone. He exits.

19 INT: J.C. PENNEY PACKERS — CLOAKROOM LOBBY —
NIGHT

Eddie catches Janelle putting on her coat.

> EDDIE
> Hey, we're goin' to the Bahamas. I just didn't say *when.*

> JANELLE
> This "road" trip. I appreciate hearing about it from that
> dope fiend. It really makes me feel high on your intimacy
> list.

Julian abruptly shows up.

> JULIAN
> That guy *sucks,* man . . . and so do *you!*

Julian exits.

> EDDIE
> (*to Janelle*)
> Listen . . .

> JANELLE
> (*rising, cold*)
> You got anything you need at my place I'll leave it in a
> suitcase out front.
> (*she splits*)

> EDDIE
> Wait a minute . . . hey . . . *shit* . . .

20 INT: CARMEN AND VINCENT'S APARTMENT — DAY

Eddie stands against a wall studying the two-room tatty layout
(neat but filled with thrown together pickup furniture; improvised)
as Carmen and Vincent do last-minute packing.

EDDIE

. . . I cover all expenses, rooms, food, everything. I cover the entry fee, everything. For that . . . I get sixty percent of everything you win . . . all bets . . . I lay the bets so I also take the losses if you lose, but I take the sixty when you win.

CARMEN

Sixty percent? What are you, a slum lord?

EDDIE

You find a newcomer's got a better deal — let me know and we'll talk.

VINCENT

Hey, I'm not gonna lose often.

EDDIE

Yeah you will. I'll teach you . . . sometimes if you lose you win.

21 EXT: CARMEN AND VINCENT'S APARTMENT — DAY

They walk down wooden staircase at rear of Vincent's house. They walk towards Eddie's car.

CARMEN

Who's the heaviest guy?

VINCENT

What are you asking *that* for. I'm the heaviest, right?

EDDIE

(*dismissing the question*)

It goes in streaks . . . The balls roll funny for everybody . . . There's a kid, Grady Seasons . . . he's makin' the most money straight up on paper but that doesn't mean anything . . . the real money's in the practice room . . . that's where we'll get you some good games . . . A guy can get wiped out on the first day of the tournament, hang around the practice room for a few days, make more money than the guy who won.

VINCENT
(*gung ho*)
. . . the *practice* room!

21A EXT: CADDY ON HIGHWAY — DAY

22 INT: ROADSIDE RESTAURANT — DAY

A waitress puts down food in front of them. Carmen studies her balefully.

CARMEN
(*correcting the waitress*)
That was *three* on the side, not *four*.

EDDIE
Where did you work?

VINCENT
She was a killer waitress over at the Acropolis. She just quit yesterday.

Eddie looks surprised.

CARMEN
What do you think, Vincent's the *only* one who has to work?

EDDIE
(*embarrassed — he never thought of this*)
No . . . I just . . .

VINCENT
How come you don't play anymore?

EDDIE
I quit . . . actually, somebody retired me. Sometimes you get hooked up with the wrong people, you know? That was a long time ago . . . back East. It's dead and buried . . . I don't even remember . . . what the hell, you look it up, in the history books, I won more 'n my share of medals.

VINCENT
You ever feel like pickin' it up again?

EDDIE
Now? . . . Nah . . . I'm too old . . . my wheels are shot,
it's a grind standing up there hours a guy like me, plus my
eyes are less than they were . . . it's a young man's game.
Besides, there's drugs now . . . kids playing on speed, coke
. . . I dunno, when I was younger . . . it was booze, it was
more human.

VINCENT
Yeah, huh?

EDDIE
I'm serious. Booze goes back to the Bible . . . wine. The
Bible never said nothing about amphetamines.

VINCENT
You religious, Eddie?

EDDIE
Me?

VINCENT
(*without malice*)
Is there a masters' tournament you can play in? An old-
timers' game?

CARMEN
If you're too old to cut the mustard you can still lick the
jar, right?

EDDIE
Oh yeah? Nobody ever asked me for a refund.

23 EXT: HIGHWAY / INT: CAR — DAY

EDDIE
Look . . . we're talking *around* something here. If you
haven't figured this out yet, it ain't about *pool,* it ain't
about *sex,* it ain't about *love.* It's about *money.* The best

is the guy with the most. That's the *whole* show. The best
is the guy with the most . . . in *all* walks of life.

>   CARMEN
> Are you the best liquor salesman?

>   EDDIE
>   (*beat*)
> Yeah . . . you bet your sweet ass I am.

Eddie taps his dashboard as if the Cadillac signifies his success.

24 EXT: DOWNTOWN JERSEY CITY — DAY

The three of them stand around the street from a narrow walk-up
entrance squeezed between two modern storefronts.

>   EDDIE
> This place is an all-time classic.

Eddie notices Vincent has the Balabushka under his arm.

>   EDDIE
> Oh no . . . put that in the trunk.

>   VINCENT
> What am I gonna play with?

>   EDDIE
> You play with a house cue for now . . . you walk in with
> that nobody'd go near you with a nickel.

25 EXT: NARROW ENTRANCE — DAY
ANGLE — THE THREE OF THEM

file into the narrow stairway facing a steep flight of stairs.

>   EDDIE
>   (*puts out his arm for Carmen to touch*)
> Feel . . . goosebumps . . . I love this.

They start trudging up the stairs.

26 INT: ENTRANCEWAY AT THE TOP OF THE STAIRS — DAY

> EDDIE
> We're just gonna sit and watch for a while. I have to find this guy.

Eddie pushes inside.

The three of them stand in shock, staring out at a sea of piled carpets and rugs. It's a carpet clearance outlet.

27 EXT: STREET — DAY

Eddie walking back to the car faster than Carmen and Vincent who trot to keep up. Eddie looks like he just got smacked in the back of the head with a bag of nickels.

> VINCENT
> (*wryly*)
> Sixty percent, hah?

> EDDIE
> Just get in.

Carmen and Vincent pile into the car after Eddie. Eddie peels rubber.

28 INT: CRANDALL'S BAR — ONE HOUR LATER — DAY
CLOSE-UP — TOMMY

An old guy with a voice vibrator stuck in his trachea, sinking the nine on a coin op table. His friends cheer.

Vincent hands over twenty.

> TOMMY
> You had enough, junior?

> VINCENT
> Hold on.

Vincent approaches Eddie and Carmen at the bar.

EDDIE
What the hell you doing, Vincent, for Chris' sakes, beat
him, eat him and get out.

VINCENT
(*wincing*)
I know, I know . . . I can't take this guy's money. This
guy's breaking my heart, man. What's it so far, sixty
bucks? No big deal.

EDDIE
No big deal?

VINCENT
You want me to quit?

EDDIE
Yeah, I want you to quit if you're just gonna keep
*dum*ping.

VINCENT
(*pleading*)
Eddie, man . . .

EDDIE
Unless
(*beat*)
. . . Sh*ow* me . . . you wanna dump? *Fine* . . . go ahead
. . . But I want a real per*for*mance. You show me you
know how to dump like a pro it'll be worth it.

VINCENT
(*turning to the table*)
Let's go, chief. I'll play you for thirty!

CARMEN
That's eighty bucks.

EDDIE
OK.
(*handing her the keys*)
Go out to the car . . . pull it up to the front.

> CARMEN
> You, what are you doin'?

> EDDIE
> Do what I say.

Carmen splits.

> TOMMY
> Let's do it.

Eddie eases off the stool and saunters out of the bar unnoticed.

29 EXT: OUTSIDE FRONT WALL OF CRANDALL'S BAR —
DAY

Eddie leans against the wall smoking a cigarette. Carmen sits in the car, engine humming.

Eddie sneaks a peek inside.

30 INT: CRANDALL'S BAR — DAY
EDDIE'S POV

Vincent flings a hand in exasperated self-disgust at a blown shot.

Tom cackles electronically.

31 EXT: CRANDALL'S BAR — DAY

Eddie ditches his cigarette, he's tensed, waiting, winks at Carmen, turns again to peek inside.

32 INT: CRANDALL'S BAR — DAY
EDDIE'S POV

> TOMMY
> (*menacing*)
> Where's the money, kid?

Vincent searching the bar bewildered.

> VINCENT
> Eddie . . . He must've gone out for a second.

Vincent takes two quick steps away from the table.

> TOMMY
> Where's the *money,* ya little prick!

33 EXT: CRANDALL'S BAR — DAY
CLOSE-UP — EDDIE

We hear the sound of Vincent getting whacked with the cue, a fist landing, an exhalation of breath, scuffling feet.

Carmen charges towards the door. Eddie holds her back.

> EDDIE
> (*angry*)
> I know what I'm doing! Get back in the car!

> TOMMY (OS)
> Get his face!

Eddie waits another beat then barrels inside.

34 INT: CRANDALL'S BAR — DAY

Eddie strides forward, pulling two men off Vincent, then grabs Vincent by the shirt front, yanks him to his feet, and starts screaming at him.

> EDDIE
> You stupid little *bast*ard . . . what'd I *tell* you.

There's a chorus of angry "fuck offs" and "beat its" to Eddie.

> EDDIE
> (*enraged*)
> I'm his *father!*
> (*to Vincent*)
> Did I tell you *not* to play? . . . or to *play?*

Another guy puts his hand on Eddie, Eddie whips around.

> EDDIE
>
> *Hey! Back* off! This is *family!*

Eddie ushers Vincent out of the bar by the scruff of his neck. They walk through a gauntlet of hostile but disoriented men.

> EDDIE
>
> You think *this* was bad in *here?* You know what's gonna be at *home?*

Vincent suddenly hisses in pain and jerks to one side. Someone just took a cheap shot to his ribs. Eddie distractedly pushes Vincent to the door.

Eddie stares at the guy, nose to nose. We don't see what Eddie does, but suddenly, the guy drops to his knees, his presence obscured from our view by Eddie's back.

> EDDIE
>
> He had enough.

35 EXT: FRONT OF THE BAR / INT: CADILLAC — DAY

Vincent's already in the back seat. Eddie slides in next to him.

> EDDIE
> (*to Carmen*)
>
> Get out of here . . . go . . .

Vincent is dazed and shaken. Carmen peels out as men come to the door of the bar.

36 EXT: ROAD / INT: CADILLAC — DAY

> EDDIE
>
> The *nerve* of that bastard . . .

> VINCENT
>
> What happened!

> EDDIE
> (*amused*)
>
> What happened?

Vincent, still dazed, sits in silence.

> CARMEN
> Where to . . .

> EDDIE
> Pick up the Parkway South . . . you know how to get to
> the Parkway?

> CARMEN
> No problem.

> EDDIE
> (*to Vincent*)
> Let me see your face.

He touches Vincent's chin. Vincent snaps his head away.

> EDDIE
> You *never* . . . I mean *never* ease off on a guy like that.
> Not when there's money. *Never.*
> (*beat*)
> The problem with mercy, Vincent, is that it's not
> professional.

Vincent doesn't react.

> EDDIE
> You'll live.

Eddie stares at him, a small smile playing on his lips.

> EDDIE
> You're gonna live, right?

> VINCENT
> Get outa my face.

Long beat.

> VINCENT
> My *father*.

> EDDIE
> (*grinning*)
> Saved *your* ass.

Long beat.

EDDIE
Carmen . . .

CARMEN
What . . .

EDDIE
What are we talking about?

CARMEN
(*beat*)
Nice guys finish last?

VINCENT
Is that original or did you just make that up?

CARMEN
You look sexy with that bloody lip.

VINCENT
(*blushing*)
Yeah, right.

CARMEN
I'm serious.

EDDIE
(*playing Cupid*)
You want me to drive?

CARMEN
I'm good.

EDDIE
(*to Vincent, after a beat*)
You're a good kid.

VINCENT
(*to himself*)
Goddamn slime-ass sonofabitch . . .

EDDIE
(*uptight and defensive*)
Hey . . .

> VINCENT
> Shove that throat pipe out the back of his goddamn head
> . . . come back with a *cannon.*

> EDDIE
> (*relieved*)
> Next time, kid.

> VINCENT
> What you do to that guy?

> EDDIE
> (*mock innocent*)
> What guy?

Carmen looks at Eddie via the rearview mirror.

37 EXT: STREET — DUSK

A one-way street so driver's side of car is near curb. Caddy pulls up
to three guys on a street corner.

> EDDIE
> Where's the Triumph Motel?

> GUY #1
> Left on Aurora right on Seneca.

> EDDIE
> Is Chalkie's still around?

> GUY #2
> Chalkie's?

> EDDIE
> The pool hall.

> GUY #2
> (*feisty*)
> I know what it is. Yeah, it's still around. It's supposed to
> *go* somewheres?

Eddie's face relaxes.

EDDIE
Some things never change, hah?

GUY #3
I wouldn't bet on that.

38 INT: VINCENT AND CARMEN'S ROOM — NEXT DAY

Vincent is sitting on one of the two double beds. He's on the phone. The TV on its swivel base is blasting out the weather. Vincent has changed into his black "Vince" T-shirt. Eddie's Balabushka is enshrined — in its open case — atop the TV.

As Eddie enters, Carmen goes into the bathroom, turns on the shower and starts to strip. Eddie can see her in the full-length mirror on the ajar bathroom door. The mirror is rapidly misting over but it's a jaw-on-the-floor show. Eddie is totally thrown.

VINCENT
I'm getting room service, you want anything?

EDDIE
(*struggling not to stare at the mirror*)
Room service?

Eddie takes the phone out of Vincent's hand and lays it down in the receiver.

Vincent notices Eddie's gaze straying towards the bathroom. Eddie covers for himself.

EDDIE
I hate the weather.

Eddie turns off the TV as if that was the source of his distraction.

EDDIE
Motels don't have room service. C'mon . . . let's check out Chalkie's . . . tell your girlfriend there to speed it up. I'll wait in the lobby.

Just as he leaves, Carmen, nude, stares at him via the mirror before she steps in the shower.

39 INT: MOTEL HALLWAY — AFTERNOON

Eddie leaving Vincent's room. The TV immediately goes back on. Eddie stands there, eyelids fluttering a little stunned by the mirror action.

> EDDIE
> (to the door)
> Vincent?

> VINCENT (OS)
> (yelling)
> Yeah!

> EDDIE
> Don't change that shirt . . . it's a nice touch.

> VINCENT (OS)
> My shirt?

> EDDIE
> And leave the Balabushka.

40 EXT: STREET WITH ENTRANCE TO CHALKIE'S — AFTERNOON

Eddie and the kids check out the street. It's heavy; low-income tough.

> EDDIE
> (awed)
> This used to be a nice average bad neighborhood . . .
> Look at this!

41 INT: CHALKIE'S — AFTERNOON

Spacious, old time. Pressed tin ceiling. Thirty tables. Loud music. Homemade tattoo arms. Goatees. Young male prison-yard types with a sprinkling of old-timers.

Eddie and the kids enter as a man leaves.

>   EDDIE
>   (*to man*)
>   How do we get a table here?

>   MAN
>   Guy over there — with the red shirt.

An old black guy, Orvis, stands nearby.

>   EDDIE
>   Can we get a back table?

>   ORVIS
>   Table fifteen fo' Mister Fast Eddie.

Eddie does a double take.

>   ORVIS
>   Yeah, see, he don't recognize Mr. Orvis from way back
>   when.

>   EDDIE
>   Orvis?
>   (*Eddie extends a hand*)
>   What are you doin' here!

>   ORVIS
>   Now he starting to remember. How long you want it for?

>   EDDIE
>   A couple of hours. Last time I saw you, you were sweeping
>   up at McGurrs . . .

As Orvis talks, they walk to the cage.

>   ORVIS
>   Sweeping up at McGurrs . . . that's right . . . then be
>   sweeping up at Chalkie's . . . then be running Chalkie's
>   when Chalkie's sells cause he's scared of the bad element
>   takin' over . . . now what can I be doing for you . . . you
>   lookin' for some action? Usually I steer for twenty percent
>   but I'll do you for ten . . .

> EDDIE
> Me? Nah . . . I think my friend here is looking for a game.

> VINCENT
> How ya doin'?

Orvis, startled, doesn't answer.

> VINCENT
> (*awkward at the silence*)
> This place is wild.

> ORVIS
> (*ignoring Vincent*)
> What you doin', Eddie? *Stake*horsin'?
> (*to Vincent*)
> You know who you got here *stake*horsin' for you? This
> Fast Eddie Felson. Who the hell are you, the End of the
> World?

> EDDIE
> Give it a rest, Orvis.

Carmen exits.

> ORVIS
> Yeah, OK . . . him I steer for fifteen since he staked by
> Fast Eddie the *Stake*horse.

Vincent follows her.

> EDDIE
> (*embarrassed*)
> Fine . . . fair enough.

42 INT: CHALKIE'S — AFTERNOON
ANGLE

Vincent and Carmen check out the room.

> VINCENT
> Maybe you should go back to the motel.

> CARMEN
> Why?

> VINCENT
> *Why?* What, are you kidding me? There's probably two dozen rape artists here.

> CARMEN
> Maybe *you* should go back to the motel.

> VINCENT
> Me?

> CARMEN
> Pretty boy like you.

> VINCENT
> (*blushing*)
> Cut it out.

> CARMEN
> Cute boy like you.

> VINCENT
> (*laughing, disarmed*)
> I'm serious.

> CARMEN
> Cute boy.

Eddie comes up behind them and steers them to a bench.

> EDDIE
> Awright, killer, here's the scoop . . . you see that guy over there? With the tie pin in his nose?

EDDIE'S POV

A huge Leon Spinks type complete with tiny cowboy hat that makes him look even bigger.

> EDDIE
> That's Moselle . . . him we stay away from.

> VINCENT
> No shit.

EDDIE
Grow up . . . him we stay away from because he's the
main stick around here . . . you beat him you scare away
that gentleman over there.

EDDIE'S POV

WE SEE EARL, fifty, fat, white mutton chops and a conservative
suit. He's also wearing a skipper's cap à la Count Basie.

EDDIE
That's Earl . . . he comes in here, he's got five, six
thousand in his pockets.

VINCENT
Jesus!

EDDIE
Yeah . . . he runs the numbers. Orvis says he doesn't mind
losing his money but he don't *give* it away . . . beat
Moselle and old Earl there loses interest.

VINCENT
So what happens now?

EDDIE
Nothin' for a while . . . he's gonna be watching you play
. . . but you're gonna be playing over here.
(*Eddie raises his hand and makes a wavering gesture
implying half-speed*)
He'll come to you.

VINCENT
Who'm I gonna play?

EDDIE
(*pausing, nervous*)
Me.

VINCENT
You? Wait . . . one thing . . .

EDDIE
What?

> VINCENT
> I want her to go back to the motel.

> CARMEN
> Oh Christ . . .

> VINCENT
> I don't like her here . . . this is goddamn *Bird*land.

> CARMEN
> I been worse places . . . I dated worse guys.

> VINCENT
> (*upset*)
> Who!

> EDDIE
> Carmen . . . Carmen . . . tell Orvis to call you a cab.

> VINCENT
> Who!

> EDDIE
> (*nodding, implying she's working against things now*)
> Carmen . . .

43 INT: CHALKIE'S DUSK
ANGLE — POOL TABLE

The balls are already set up on the table.

Eddie and Vincent rolling cues on the table, testing for warp.

> EDDIE
> No thunderbolt breaks, OK? No runs over four balls. Just play it nice and easy.

> VINCENT
> She never went out with anybody like these guys.

> EDDIE
> Vincent . . . pay attention 'cause that guy Earl's gonna be paying attention . . . you hear what I said?

VINCENT
Yeah, yeah . . . you want to break?

EDDIE
Let me break.

Eddie seems tense. He draws a bead, stands up, hunches down, stands up.

EDDIE
(*grabbing his back*)
What they do, saw down the legs? This is a *dwarfs'* table.

VINCENT
C'mon, c'mon, no excuses . . . I wanna see some heavy legend action here.

EDDIE
(*hunching down to break*)
I swear I see thirty-five balls.

Eddie slams into pack, drops three.

EDDIE
Yeah . . . not bad, hah? Ah . . . this ain't pool. This is for *ban*gers. *Straight* pool's *pool*. This is like *hand*ball . . . it's like *crib*bage, or something.

Eddie starts to work the table.

EDDIE
Straight pool, a guy had to be a *surgeon* to get over. It was all *finesse*. Now everything's nine-ball because it's *fast*. Good for TV. Big loud break shot. What the hell, checkers sells more than chess I guess, hah?

Eddie runs the table. Despite his contempt for the game, he's glowing, excited.

EDDIE
Not bad for a blind man, hah? Rack 'em up.

VINCENT
Yes suh, boss.

Eddie fast-shrugs his shoulders, working out kinks.

> EDDIE
> See what I mean? I haven't played serious pool in twenty-odd years . . . right off the bat I'm laying waste . . . watch this . . . nine on the break.

Eddie breaks, wide spread, but nothing goes on.

Eddie shrugs it off . . . it happens.

> VINCENT
> (*studying the lay*)
> Eddie, that was phenomenal . . .

> EDDIE
> I'd like to play that big dude Moselle. I bet you he ain't that good.

> VINCENT
> (*not listening now, sinking the nine*)
> You know, Eddie, maybe you're right . . . maybe this is just for bangers.

44 ANGLE — SECOND GAME
CLOSE-UP — EDDIE

hardened face.

Vincent sinking the nine.

> VINCENT (OS)
> But the thing is . . . even if it's just for bangers . . . everybody's doin' it.

45 ANGLE — THIRD GAME

Vincent sinking the nine, looking up at Eddie.

CLOSE-UP — EDDIE

tight and angry.

> VINCENT
> If everybody's doing it, that's *a lot of guys* doing it.

46 ANGLE — TABLE

Vincent lining up a combo on the nine.

CLOSE-UP

> EDDIE
> (*hissing low*)
> Dog it, hot shot.

> VINCENT
> A lot of guys doin' it . . .
> (*sinks the nine*)
> Only *one* can be the best.

Eddie walks away from the table, looking like he could kill. He replaces the cue stick in the wall rack and marches out.

> VINCENT
> Where you goin'?

47 EXT: FRONT OF CHALKIE'S — NIGHT

Eddie's in the car. Vincent trots out.

> VINCENT
> What . . . those were easy plays, man . . .
> (*shifting gears*)
> Eddie . . . I'm sorry . . . I was being a smart ass . . . I was showing off . . . I'm sorry.

> EDDIE
> You know what this is turning out to be?

> VINCENT
> What.

> EDDIE
> A waste of my *time* . . . and a waste of my *money*.

Vincent reaches for the door handle. Eddie drives off.

48 INT: EDDIE'S MOTEL ROOM — NIGHT

Eddie lying on his bed staring at the ceiling, lost in thought.

Rises, looks out the window at the trucks going by on highway —
a stream of headlights.

>   EDDIE
>   (*hissing*)
>   *Child*-care.

49   INT: MOTEL HALLWAY — NIGHT

Eddie knocking on the other door.

>   EDDIE
>   Vincent?

The door swings open. Carmen is standing in her underwear. Behind her the TV is on and the bed is rumpled.

Carmen returns to lying on the bed watching a movie.

Eddie stands there in the middle of the room, embarrassed again.

>   EDDIE
>   Vincent back?

>   CARMEN
>   (*not moving*)
>   Yeah, but he's out.

>   EDDIE
>   What do you mean "out"?

>   CARMEN
>   *Out* . . . like, *not* in the *room* . . .

>   EDDIE
>   You mind getting dressed?

>   CARMEN
>   Are we going somewheres?

>   EDDIE
>   A guys walks into a room . . . what if I was somebody
>   else?

CARMEN
Like who?

EDDIE
That's not the point.

CARMEN
I'm not *naked* or anything.

EDDIE
(*uptight, covering it with officiousness*)
And another thing . . . work *with* me, not *against* me . . .
don't go saying to Vincent stuff like you said in Chalkie's
. . . you get him all upset . . . if you're gonna use that
thing, use it right.

CARMEN
(*fake innocent, breaking his balls*)
Use *what* thing?

Eddie doesn't answer, he looks lost in thought. Abruptly locks the
door then steps forward, grabs Carmen's wrist.

CARMEN
(*shocked*)
What are you doin'!

EDDIE
(*brusque*)
C'mon . . . me and you . . .

CARMEN
What!

EDDIE
(*scary*)
I like doin' it in the shower . . . a fast one before Vincent
gets back . . . let's go.

Carmen pulls her hand away. She's freaked and scared.

Eddie sits on the edge of the bed. The sexual threat evaporates.
Suddenly he's all business. The come-on was a put-on.

EDDIE

Hey . . . I ain't your daddy, I ain't your boyfriend so don't you be playing *games* with me, kid . . . I'm your *part*ner . . . You don't come *on* to me, you don't *flirt* with me . . . You take a shower . . . You close the damn door.

CARMEN
(humiliated, holding up a shred of pride)
Don't flatter yourself.

EDDIE
(cutting through her pose)
Don't waste my time with bullshit, Carmen.

There's an awkward beat, Eddie realizes Carmen's totally shamed.

EDDIE
(gently)
Look . . . me and you . . . we got a *race*horse here . . . a thoroughbred. You make it feel good and I teach it to run . . . do you understand me? We're *bus*iness people.

CARMEN
(still shaken)
Gotcha.

EDDIE
(trying to make light)
Besides I'm old enough to be your relative.

Eddie smiles at her, lets his eyes stray around the room.

EDDIE
(alarmed)
Where's the Balabushka?

CARMEN
Vincent took it.

EDDIE
You said he was *out*.

CARMEN
Yeah! He was in, then he went out.

> EDDIE
And he took the *cue* stick?

> CARMEN
Uh-huh . . .

> EDDIE
And you *let* him?

> CARMEN
So what.
> (*dawning realization*)
Shit.

> EDDIE
> (*leaving quickly*)
Goddamn *child*-care.

50 INT: CHALKIE'S — NIGHT
CLOSE-UP — MOSELLE

stretched across the table for a shot.

PULL BACK TO REVEAL Vincent watching the same sitting on a high chair . . . the cue case under his arm.

Moselle makes a difficult shot, a two-cushion job.

The guy he's playing curses and passes him a twenty.

> VINCENT
Nice shot.

> MOSELLE
> (*nodding towards the case*)
What you got in there?

> VINCENT
> (*grinning*)
Doom.

51 EXT: HIGHWAY — NIGHT
Eddie's Caddy flying down the road.

52 INT: CHALKIE'S — NIGHT

Moselle is playing Vincent. James Brown is playing over the PA.

There's a major mob watching the game.

Vincent is dancing to the music around the table, dipping to the felt to make shots, dancing to the next set-up, making that. It's a massacre.

53 INT: ENTRANCE TO CHALKIE'S — NIGHT
ANGLE

Eddie strides towards the cage. Orvis looks at him sadly, shrugs and nods to a mob around a table.

CLOSE-UP — EDDIE

pissed.

EDDIE'S POV

WE SEE Earl watching the game, impassive. The crowd reacts as Vincent makes a shot. Earl snorts, shaking his head.

> ORVIS
> (*casually, elbows on the cage counter*)
> Fast Eddie the *Stake*horse.

> EDDIE
> Up your ass, Orvis.

> EARL
> (*walking past them*)
> That boy is *hot!*

Eddie makes eye contact with Vincent. Vincent waves, raises the Balabushka and kisses it, turns to the game and sinks the nine ball.

> EDDIE
> Shit.

ORVIS
Eddie . . .

EDDIE
What.

ORVIS
When you finish fuckin' up with that boy . . . you come
on back here, by yourself.

EDDIE
Fat chance.

Eddie leaves.

ANGLE — MOSELLE

handing a wrinkled twenty to Vincent.

The crowd has no hard feelings. Vincent has put on a spectacular
show.

MOSELLE
(*murmuring*)
That's some nasty stick . . . So when you leavin' town,
right now?

54 EXT: CHALKIE'S STREET — NIGHT

Eddie is standing up against the Caddy. Vincent exits, still dancing.

VINCENT
(*eyes glistening, almost shouting*)
Did you see me tonight, or *what!*

Eddie grabs the cue case from under Vincent's elbow and, grunting,
flings it down the street.

Vincent, shocked, laughs. Eddie just glares at him.

VINCENT
What! I made money!

> EDDIE
> You *lost* money! This town is *dead* for you now . . . what
> is the matter with you? Am I not speaking your native
> tongue? What is it?

> VINCENT
> (*incredulous and angry*)
> You give me that stick and you want me to lay *low?* That
> goddamn thing. You put it down, it *jumps* at you, man!
> Are you *kidd*ing me?

> EDDIE
> You don't de*serve* that stick!

> VINCENT
> (*retrieving the case; calmly*)
> No . . . *you* don't deserve that stick. I'm a fucking *pool*
> player . . .

Vincent starts briskly walking backwards on the road, thumb out
for a ride.

> VINCENT
> (*shouting*)
> I'm a fucking *an*imal!

He beats on his chest with one hand like an ape while holding the
cue case high.

Still holding the cue case overhead, he turns his back to Eddie
and marches down the road, thumb out. Exploding with righteous
energy, he's a walking celebration of himself.

CLOSE-UP — EDDIE

staring at him through the windshield. Eddie looks tired.

ANGLE — EDDIE

driving the car at a crawl alongside Vincent.

> EDDIE
> Vincent, get in the car.

VINCENT
No.

EDDIE
C'mon, Vincent, this is embarrassing. You're acting like some girl got felt up in a drive-in. This looks terrible. Get in.

VINCENT
Tough shit.

EDDIE
(*patiently*)
Vincent . . . What you take off that Moselle, I heard a hundred.

VINCENT
One fifty!

EDDIE
A hundred fifty!

VINCENT
Yeah! A hundred and fifty!

EDDIE
You go in a shoe store with a hundred fifty dollars, you come out with one shoe! A hundred *fifty!* We were working on five thousand! C'mon, get in the car . . . it's cold.

Vincent pauses. Then gets in.

EDDIE
(*sober, almost awkward*)
Do you know how *hard* it is for me to tell you to lay down? When you're on
(*shakes his head*)
I watch you . . . Hey . . . But . . . the reality of it is, I got to hold you down . . . See . . . when I was you, your speed, nobody ever told me that, about control, restraint . . . *class* — I had to have my head. You don't *know* what I

blew . . . what could have *been* for me . . . You *got* to start
listening to me, Vincent. I'm gonna *make* something of
you . . . *if you* listen.
> (*Eddie gestures with helplessness; hand out*)
Gimme.

> VINCENT

What?

> EDDIE
> (*smiling, but serious*)
Ninety bucks. Sixty percent of one hundred fifty is ninety
— so, ninety dollars —

Vincent hands him the money.

> EDDIE

I could cry . . .

55 INT: EDDIE'S HOTEL ROOM — NIGHT

Eddie on the bed, hands on his chest, looking at the ceiling. The
phone is cradled between ear and jaw line. He's calling Janelle.
Eddie looks beat, troubled.

> EDDIE

Hey. I wake you? . . . Want me to hang up? You're not
still pissed at me, are you . . . If you are, I would
understand, but you're not, right? . . . Great . . . Good . . .
Thank you . . . Hey . . . What kind of rent do you pay?
. . . That's criminal . . . Well listen . . . After the
Bahamas? I think you should move in with me . . . y'know
a practice run . . . yeah.
> (*beat*)
What do you mean? *No!* Everything's fine. What're you, a
shrink? I miss you and I say nice things to you . . . yeah!
Everything's fine . . . I mean, a couple of curve balls here
and there . . .
> (*tired*)
nothin' much but y'know, there and here . . .

56 INT: DINER ON THE ROAD — BREAKFAST HOUR — DAY

Eddie and company share a booth. The place is packed with truckers and locals.

> VINCENT
> (*wolfing food*)
> I love this, man . . .
> (*gestures to the parking lot and the highway*)
> . . . on the *road!*

Carmen rolls her eyes.

> VINCENT
> Hey . . . you shoulda seen Eddie play last night.

> EDDIE
> (*changing subject*)
> You think we could make some money today or am I still talking to Our Lady of the Cueballs, here?

> VINCENT
> (*finishing up*)
> Make some money! *Definitely!*

> EDDIE
> You ever hear of a hustle called Two Brothers and a Stranger?

> VINCENT
> The guy in the Bible with the many-colored coat, right?
> (*laughing*)
> I'm kidding, I'm kidding, relax . . .

> EDDIE
> (*mildly, peering speculatively*)
> Did I get through to you last night? Because if I didn't, I can run it down to you another way . . . If you kicked ass in any other place but Chalkie's, Atlantic City would be dead for us . . . those guys last night don't leave the street, otherwise it would be all around . . .

> VINCENT
> Eddie . . . last night? People don't talk to you like that.
> You really *talk*ed to me. I really appreciate that.

Vincent gives Eddie a hug.

> EDDIE
> (*embarrassed*)
> Hey . . . don't worry about it. You're a good kid . . .
> you're a good kid . . . OK . . . Two Brothers and a
> Stranger . . .

57 EXT: STREET — DAY

Eddie's car comes to park. Vincent exits, cradling the Balabushka
in the crook of his elbow.

> VINCENT
> Give me two hours. They'll be building me a trophy wall
> in there.

> EDDIE
> (*as Vincent walks into pool hall*)
> Look at that kid — gets to have all the fun.

58 INT: POOL HALL — DAY
CLOSE-UP — TWENTY BUCKS

dropped on felt, scooped up by Vincent.

PULL BACK TO REVEAL the hall — half busy. Vincent's table is
surrounded by a half dozen guys. Vincent folding the twenty over
a small roll. The Balabushka leans against the crook of his armpit.

> VINCENT
> Who's next?

> PLAYER
> Forget it.

> VINCENT
> Hey . . . I'll spot you the break.

> PLAYER
> (*hesitating*)
> I want the eight ball too.

> VINCENT
> (*shrugging*)
> You got it.

Guys crowd around the table for the coming game.

59 EXT: STREET IN FRONT OF POOL HALL — DAY

Eddie stands with Carmen. Puts his arm around her shoulders.

> EDDIE
> Lock and load.

60 INT: POOL HALL — DAY

Vincent shooting.

VINCENT'S POV

He sees Eddie with his arm around Carmen, go to the bar and sit.

> VINCENT
> Six off the three.

Vincent misses.

Eddie laughs. Vincent looks up. Everyone turns to him.

Eddie, oblivious to the attention, puts his nose in Carmen's neck, says something. Carmen pushes him away, blushing.

Vincent gets angry — half putting it on.

Player #2 shoots his shot, misses too. Eddie laughs again.

> GUY IN CROWD
> Whyn't you keep it shut, hah?

> EDDIE
> What I say?

Eddie nuzzles Carmen again.

> VINCENT
> Seven off the three.

He makes the shot.

> EDDIE
> Shit . . .

> CARMEN
> Eddie . . . shut up.

> VINCENT
> Hey, *mouth* . . .

> EDDIE
> (*offended*)
> Excuse me?

> VINCENT
> It's a money game here, you mind? Six off the three.

Vincent hits balls. Makes it.

> EDDIE
> (*to Carmen*)
> Big money match.

> VINCENT
> Yeah. That's right, a big money match. So, why don't you
> take your hand off your daughter and watch a pro play.

> EDDIE
> What do you care where my hand is, mind your own
> business.

> VINCENT
> Hey, gramps, put your teeth back in, get your hand
> off that girl and pay attention, you might learn some-
> thing.

> EDDIE
> (*rising*)
> Hey, sonny, are you trying . . .

PLAYER #2
(*interrupting, to Eddie*)
Hey . . . we got a game here . . .

EDDIE
(*to Player #2*)
What you playing for?

PLAYER #2
Fifty . . .

EDDIE
(*to Player #2*)
Fifty? You wanna win? I'll bet five hundred on this man here.
(*to Vincent*)
You look like a choker to me. Five hundred says you choke right now.

VINCENT
Go take a walk, will ya?

EDDIE
(*to the crowd*)
Anybody wanna bet five hundred, sonny here chokes?

CARMEN
(*acting upset*)
Eddie, cut it out.

EDDIE
Any takers?

CARMEN
Eddie! I'm gonna leave.

EDDIE
Any takers!

VINCENT
Jerk . . .

BARTENDER
You wanna go for a thousand?

Eddie slowly turns to the bartender; Eddie's face is beatific.

61 EXT: SIDE STREET — POST POOL

> VINCENT
> (*to Carmen*)
> What was that?

> CARMEN
> What?

Vincent grabs her breast, Carmen pushes him away. Eddie whips an arm around the kid, and walks him away.

> EDDIE
> Hey! Hey!

> VINCENT
> You get off on that, Eddie?

Vincent pushes him off, starts marching back to Carmen, who this time starts backing up. Eddie grabs him again.

> EDDIE
> Hey!

Vincent walks away from both of them.

> EDDIE
> I'm a little disappointed in you, frankly.

> VINCENT
> (*walking in circles*)
> Frankly, your *ass*. I've *seen* you, man. So don't *give* me that. I've *seen* you!

> EDDIE
> Seen *what?*

> VINCENT
> Hey! Screw this. I don't need this. I'm gone. C'mon, I'm goin' home.

> CARMEN
> The hell you are.

VINCENT
The hell I *am*.

CARMEN
Then you're going home alone.

VINCENT
Alone, huh? Oh, I'm going home alone. Is that right?

EDDIE
Hey, hey, listen. You played your part . . . *nice* . . . when I put my hand on her? That's *my* part. It's *act*ing, don't you get that?

CARMEN
What do you think, every time you see people kissing in the movies they go home together? They're pro*fess*ionals.

EDDIE
That's what *we're* trying to be . . . professionals. Does it sink in? Huh?

CLOSE ON VINCENT

confused, trying to shrug it off.

VINCENT
(*giving in, mumbling*)
Yeah, well, it's a little rough on me, that's all. I'm not used to that . . . I dunno . . . I dunno . . .

EDDIE
(*affectionately*)
Vincent . . . Vincent the Kid . . . You are gonna be one of the *greats* . . . I have a very good feeling about this.

62 MONTAGE OF POOL ENCOUNTERS

Vincent wearing glasses, shoots the cue off the table in an old vast pool hall. Everyone around the table laughs, including Eddie. His opponent is a burly middle-aged man.

The opponent forking over a fistful of cash to Vincent.

63 Eddie driving at night. Vincent and Carmen sleeping.

64 Vincent, seemingly drunk, playing a tall skinny guy in granny glasses and a ponytail. He dogs a shot. The skinny guys offers him a joint. Vincent nods no, holding up his drink.

The skinny guy giving Vincent money. Vincent takes his joint, takes a drag, gives it back.

65 Vincent driving at night. Eddie and Carmen sleeping.

66 Eddie playing alone.

67 Carmen sitting at a bar, and watching Vincent play a young Latino trucker in the bar mirror behind her.

Vincent hands over money to the trucker.

The trucker hands over money to Vincent.

The trucker hands over more money to Vincent.

The trucker hands over even more money to Vincent.

The trucker takes a swing at Vincent. Vincent kicks him in the balls and runs.

68 Motel room, bathed in blue TV light. Vincent and Carmen, fully dressed, crashed on top of the bed. Eddie sitting in a chair in his T-shirt and socks — glass of bourbon — watching TV.

69 EXT: MAVERICK CLUB — NIGHT

It's a long cinderblock painted bar on a highway, the name hand-painted along the side. It looks like a bucket of blood.

70 INT: MAVERICK CLUB — NIGHT

Eddie, Vincent and Carmen enter. It's smoky, honky-tonk. A narrow long line of pool tables stretching the entire length bordered by those aluminum foldout bleachers.

>   EDDIE
>   (sniffing)
>   Huh . . . you smell what I smell?

> VINCENT
> Smoke?

> CARMEN
> Money . . .

> EDDIE
> Let's take a stroll around, see what's what.

ANGLE

They cruise the tables. Money changes hands. The players are good; concentrators, no bangers. Eddie does a double take at the last table. He holds up the procession and makes them sit on the bleacher.

> VINCENT
> What's shakin'?

> EDDIE
> (*intense, mind going ninety m.p.h.*)
> Check this guy out.

Eddie tilts his chin towards one of the players, skinny, early twenties, quick, speedy, chain-smoking. He wears continental slacks, Italian loafers, and a dark polyester shirt, buttoned at the neck and wrist — his hair is longish and blow-dried — a wispy moustache. He shoots like a machine — never a false or wasted move. He doesn't miss.

> VINCENT
> (*mildly*)
> *That* guy?

Eddie pulls Vincent and Carmen aside.

> EDDIE
> This is what's called a *Gold*en Opport*un*ity . . . you know who that is? That's Grady Seasons, the best money player in the world . . .

> VINCENT
> (*leaning past Eddie to stare at Seasons*)
> *That's* Grady Seasons?
> (*shrugs*)
> You want me to play him?

> EDDIE
> (*fervent*)
> You *bet*. But you're gonna *dump*. You're gonna lose
> something fierce. You're gonna ask for a *spot,* you're
> gonna ask for the *break* . . . *ev*erything. It's gonna be
> *hu*miliating. This is beautiful.

> VINCENT
> (*shocked*)
> What do you mean *dump!*

> EDDIE
> (*to Carmen*)
> What do I mean, *dump* . . .

> CARMEN
> (*half speaking to Eddie*)
> Because if you lose bad *now,* to this guy, you'll be a *super-*
> nobody in Atlantic City and the odds on you'll drop to
> nothing, right?

> EDDIE
> (*ushering them to the bleachers; to Vincent*)
> See? *She* learns.

They take a seat on the bleachers closest to the game.

> VINCENT
> Let me ask you something. I see these guys — they hustle
> and they *win* . . . How come I always gotta play the jerk?
> Why can't we get a hustle where *I* win?

> EDDIE
> (*for his ears only*)
> Because this is better than that . . . there's something at
> the end of this . . . I wouldn't tell you to do this unless the
> payoff would be phen*om*enal.
> (*long beat*)
> Hey . . . you *do* what you wanna do . . . Do it your way
> . . . whatever you want.

> VINCENT
> (*a resigned beat*)
> I'll do it for you.

> EDDIE
> (*to Grady*)
> Hey, Seasons!

71 INT: MAVERICK CLUB — NIGHT
ANGLE

Grady playing Vincent.

Grady running balls.

> GRADY
> (*to Vincent*)
> It's like a nightmare, isn't it?

ANGLE

The roll-out bleachers. Eddie sits, elbows on knees, on the top row. Carmen on the bottom row, closest to the action.

ANGLE

Grady continues his run.

> GRADY
> It just keeps getting worse and worse.

Vincent is black-faced at this arrogant patter. He looks up to Eddie. Eddie nods sympathetically, gestures with his hand to cool it.

Grady misses finally, leaving Vincent a bitch of a shot.

> GRADY
> Oh! The impossible dream!

Vincent studies the table, quick-glances at Eddie, resigns himself to a muffed shot.

> GRADY
> Don't clutch now . . . it's not that hard a shot.

> VINCENT
> (*slow burn*)
> Don't *clutch?*

Vincent makes the shot, then sinks the rest of the table.

Amused, Grady starts racking up as Vincent, ignoring Eddie and Carmen, grinds chalk into his tip.

> VINCENT
> (*hunching down to break*)
> Hey, *Brady* . . .
> (*Vincent smashes the pack*)
> Up your ass with the spot . . . OK with you?

ANGLE

Eddie and Carmen watching from their separate positions on the bleachers.

ANGLE — THE TABLE

Vincent shooting a ball, patrolling the table, sinking another.

ANGLE — THE TABLE

Both kids playing bust-out pool.

ANGLE

A crowd is starting to shape up.

ANGLE — CLOSE-UP — EDDIE

He looks sphinx-like, riveted to the action.

ANGLE

Carmen looks irritated by the crowd, by Vincent blowing the game plan.

ANGLE — THE GAME
FAST MONTAGE OF SHOTS

Grady and Vincent cut with CLOSE UPS of Eddie's impassive but attentive face and CLOSE UPS of Carmen's growing fury.

ANGLE

Carmen rises, heads for the table.

> CARMEN
> (*leaning against the cushion*)
> Hey, baby?

VINCENT
I'm playing.

CARMEN
C'mere for a minute.

Carmen puts her arms around Vincent's neck in a hug.

CARMEN
(*deadly earnest*)
You win one more game, you're gonna be humping your
fist for a long time.

Carmen kisses him on the mouth.

CARMEN
Yeah? OK?

Carmen gives him another hard kiss, then returns to the bleachers.

ANGLE — CLOSE-UP — EDDIE

He's frowning, alert.

CARMEN
(*twisting her head to speak to Eddie above her. Softly
so no one can hear outside of Eddie — acidly*)
What are you doing up there, *med*itating?

Eddie, rapt, transported by the action, doesn't hear her.

ANGLE

Vincent, thrown, bends to shoot, stares at the ball.

CLOSE-UP — THE BALL

missing the pocket.

72 INT: VINCENT AND CARMEN'S MOTEL ROOM — THE
NEXT DAY

There is a knock at the door. Vincent goes to it.

> VINCENT
> Yeah?

> EDDIE
> It's me.

Vincent opens the door.

> EDDIE
> (*coming in*)
> Can you give me the Balabushka?

Vincent gets Balabushka.

> VINCENT
> You gonna play, Eddie?

> EDDIE
> Yeah . . . maybe.

> VINCENT
> You . . . you want me to come?

> EDDIE
> Nah — it's OK.

> VINCENT
> You mad at me?

> EDDIE
> No . . . no . . . you did good, kid.

Eddie exits.

> CARMEN
> Where's he goin'?

73 INT: BAR AND GRILL POOL HALL — HALF HOUR LATER
— DAY

Eddie cruises in, cue under his arm. There's three tables. It's a small place. Half a dozen guys at the bar. No one playing. Eddie walks casually over to a pool table, puts down his cue case, reaches into his pocket, peels off a hundred dollar bill and places it on the rail. Ignoring the six guys at the bar he starts to rack up.

> ONE OF THE GUYS
> (*to the bartender*)

Call Dud.

74 INT: BAR AND GRILL POOL HALL — DAY
ANGLE — TWO HOURS LATER

The bar — twice as many guys drinking. Eddie is playing a huge man, Dud, bearded. He wears a T-shirt that has "EAT ME" stenciled on the chest.

Eddie is shooting. He sinks the nine. Dud digs in for a hundred.

> DUD
> Frank? 'Nother Drambuie and Potato Salad. An' another JSW Brown for Eddie here.
> (*to Eddie*)
> One more time?

> EDDIE
> (*in a great mood*)
> Absolutely.

75 INT: BAR AND GRILL POOL HALL — DUSK
ANGLE — TWO HOURS LATER

The bar is wall to wall.

Eddie and Dud are still going at it. One table is still deserted, the other has a young fat guy playing solo. Eddie looks red-faced, blinky but happy still.

> DUD
> That's all she wrote.

> EDDIE
> Good book, though.

> DUD
> (*nodding to the bar*)
> Buy you one?

> EDDIE
> I'm gonna play a little.
> *(to the fat kid, Amos, at the next table)*
> Feel like a game?

Amos shrugs OK.

76 INT: BAR AND GRILL POOL HALL — NIGHT
ANGLE — HALF HOUR LATER

Vincent and Carmen entering the bar, looking for Eddie.

Carmen spots him playing Amos.

ANGLE

> AMOS
> *(working the table)*
> Then after, I got a job working at the university? Strictly
> for the experience.
> *(calls a shot)*
> Guess what I was . . .
> *(misses)*

> EDDIE
> What.

> AMOS
> What?

> EDDIE
> What were you?
> *(calls a shot, hits)*

> AMOS
> I was a subject.

> EDDIE
> A *what?*

> AMOS
> *(as Eddie runs table)*
> A *sub*ject . . . in the psych department. I was a subject for
> experiments . . . reflexes, memory things. But I didn't do

anything where I get shocked . . . well, I did once but just
for the experience.

> EDDIE
> (*sinks the nine*)
> Game.

> AMOS
> OK. That's eighty.
> (*tosses a twenty on the felt*)
> Screw it . . . I earn the money the old-fashioned way . . .
> I in*her*it it.
> (*laughs*)

> EDDIE
> (*proud of himself*)
> One more, kid?

> AMOS
> Yeah, sure.

> EDDIE
> Double or nothing?

> AMOS
> Double or nothing?

> EDDIE
> Is there an echo here?

> AMOS
> (*laughs*)
> Let's do it.

Vincent and Carmen saunter over.

> VINCENT
> Hey, Eddie . . . how you doin'?

> EDDIE
> (*grinning*)
> Holdin' my own . . . a little of his . . .

> VINCENT
> (*mildly*)
> Good man.

> EDDIE
> (*semi-joking*)
> Hey . . . now we got *two* guns. Cover the street at *both* ends.
> (*to Carmen and Vincent*)
> Have a drink.

ANGLE

Carmen and Vincent watch Eddie play from the bar.

77 INT: BAR AND GRILL POOL HALL — NIGHT
ANGLE

Amos shooting a combination. The nine rolls towards pocket.

> AMOS
> Go! Go! Go!

The nine goes in. Amos jumps in the air. Eddie shrugs it off.

> AMOS
> That it?

> EDDIE
> Do it again.

> AMOS
> Double or nothing?

ANGLE

Carmen and Vincent at the bar.

78 INT: BAR AND GRILL POOL HALL — NIGHT
ANGLE

Amos on the snap — the nine goes in on the break.

> AMOS
> Hey! *That* is *bull*shit . . . I never did that . . . *that* is *luck* . . . I am *really* sorry.

>   EDDIE
>   (*dropping two hundred on the felt*)
> You a hustler, Amos?

>   AMOS
>   (*hurt*)
> Hey, Eddie . . .

>   EDDIE
> You a hustler?

>   AMOS
>   (*hands up in submission*)
> Hey . . . you don't want to pay me? I don't want bad
> feelings. A guy loses . . . I lost, I paid, but . . .

>   EDDIE
> You a hustler, Amos?

>   AMOS
>   (*slight hardness beneath the jollity*)
> You want to quit?

>   EDDIE
> Fuck you, kid . . . double it again.

79 INT: BAR AND GRILL POOL HALL — NIGHT
ANGLE

Four hundreds drop on the felt, Amos scooping them up.

>   AMOS
>   (*breaking down his cue and staring
>   at Eddie with a devil grin*)
> Hey . . . I want to ask you something and I want you to be
> honest with me.

Eddie stares at him. He's trying to control his rage, his shame.

>   AMOS
> You think I need to lose some weight?

Amos grins, head cocked, mouth open, waiting for Eddie's reaction. Eddie makes the slightest tilt with his body towards Amos, using all his willpower not to fly at his throat. Amos knows it.

Amos splits, laughing.

Eddie stares at the felt, casually picking lint at random. He picks up a ball, grips it like a baseball, then still staring at the felt, lightly drops the ball into a pocket. He suddenly laughs to himself, a scary false laugh.

ANGLE

Carmen and Vincent at a table. Eddie strides over, takes Carmen's drink, and still standing, takes a gulp.

> EDDIE
> It isn't *easy* . . . You *really* have to work *hard* . . . I mean you *really* have to put in the *time* and the *effort* to show your ass like that. The *si*gnals that have to be ig*no*red . . . I mean *really hard hard work* here.

Eddie floats down into a chair, stunned.

> VINCENT
> (*lightly, slightly nervous*)
> Hey . . . you'll nail him next time.

Eddie doesn't hear, he's lost in his own turmoil. Suddenly he erupts in anger and anguish.

> EDDIE
> *Je*-sus!

Eddie rises and marches out the door.

80 INT: STAIRCASE OF POOL HALL — NIGHT

Carmen and Vincent cautiously emerge from inside to check on Eddie. Eddie stands on staircase.

VINCENT
Eddie? You OK?

EDDIE
(*resolved, self-absorbed*)
How much you need to go it on your own from here to
Atlantic City?

VINCENT
Why?

CARMEN
(*wary*)
What do you mean?

EDDIE
(*furious at himself*)
I should've wiped the floor with that bastard.

CARMEN
Yeah, so?

EDDIE
(*all business*)
So how much would you need to go from here to Atlantic
City?
(*reaches for his wallet*)
A thousand?

VINCENT
Hey, Eddie, you had a little too much to drink — forget
about it.

EDDIE
(*brusque*)
I got nothing else to teach you . . . that was the last lesson
back there . . . take some money and front yourself . . .
you'll do fine.

VINCENT
(*stunned*)
You're walking *off*?

CARMEN
(*angry, amazed, flat*)
You're dumping us.

EDDIE
(*shouting*)
*Dump*ing you! I'm giving you a thousand dollars as a
stake! I showed you all I *got*. I showed you my *ass* in there.
What else you *want?* That's *it* . . . That's *all.*

VINCENT
What are we supposed to do! Where we supposed to go!

EDDIE
(*blazing*)
Hey . . .
(*spreads his arms — right hand*)
. . . here's *you* . . .
(*left hand*)
. . . here's Atlantic *City* . . .
(*distance in between his hands*)
. . . here's three *weeks,* twenty-seven goddamn pool halls,
and a thousand *dollars.* What the hell else you want, an
Indian guide? Use your brains!

VINCENT
Somebody comes around, plays you for a chump, so
you're out of here? So you get him next time!

Eddie goes down the stairs. Vincent runs down and stops him.

VINCENT
It ain't right. You can't do it!

EDDIE
What the hell you want from me? You always do what
you want anyhow. I say do this, you do *that.*

VINCENT
(*overlapping*)
Don't you tell me that!

EDDIE
(*continuing*)
I'm tired!

VINCENT
(*overlapping*)
I try to do everything you say. Don't tell me that! I do everything!

EDDIE
You don't need me. I got nothing else to give you. Take the money.

VINCENT
What . . . You wanna buy me off? You wanna give me money?

Close to violence.

VINCENT
C'mon, man, give me money, give me money . . .

EDDIE
(*reaching for his wallet*)
You're very *young*, Vincent, you don't understand.

VINCENT
Give me money.

EDDIE
(*with distracted, delayed anger*)
Hey! You don't *know* what I'm about, so don't . . .

VINCENT
(*cutting him off*)
Shut up! Give me *money* . . .

Eddie sighs. There's no words for this. He's got to get out. He extracts some bills.

CARMEN
(*cold, angry*)
Make it fifteen hundred.

> EDDIE
> (*pauses*)

You got it.

> VINCENT

Make it sixteen hundred! Make it two *thou*sand.

Vincent suddenly flings the cue in Eddie's direction.

> VINCENT

Y'know something? *Keep* your fucking money!

Eddie stands there in shock at the rage in Vincent. Vincent leaves.

Eddie turns to Carmen. He vaguely gestures for her to take the money. Carmen hesitates, then snatches it. Last glance at Eddie, then walks after Vincent.

81 INT: CHALKIE'S — DAY

Eddie stands in the doorway for a long beat.

Orvis in the cage.

Eddie saunters in, the pool cue under his arm.

Orvis stares at him for a long beat, nodding.

> ORVIS
> (*unsurprised*)

What table you want, Fast Eddie?

> EDDIE

Nine-ball's shit pool . . .

> ORVIS

It's *money* pool . . . it's the arena, my man.

> EDDIE

My eyes are shot.

> ORVIS

Yeah, well . . . we take care a that.

ANGLE

Eddie staring at an empty table. Pours the balls on the felt. Rolls them with his hands. Sits down, holding the cue stick like a staff. The pool hall is almost deserted.

82 ANGLE — ONE HOUR LATER

Eddie studying the spread of balls — making shots — more tables occupied.

83 INT: CHALKIE'S — NIGHT
ANGLE — FULL HOUSE

Eddie stands in front of the cage, rolling his neck, feeling the strain.

> ORVIS
> Feel good, don't it?

> EDDIE
> I'm blind . . .

> ORVIS
> You don't want a game? I can get you three games tonight . . . you lookin' not too bad.

> EDDIE
> I don't think so . . . What time you open up tomorrow morning?

84 INT: MOTEL SWIMMING POOL — NIGHT

Eddie dives in, swims a slow strong lap, scoops himself out on the opposite end of the pool, mouth gaping, greedily sucking in air.

85 EXT: CHALKIE'S FRONT — NEXT MORNING

Orvis pulls up in a butter-yellow Cadillac. Sleep in his face, he fumbles with his keys to open up.

Eddie emerges out of *his* Cadillac across the street. He's been wait-ing for Orvis to show up. He saunters toward Chalkie's, pool cue under his arm.

86 MONTAGE

EDDIE'S POV

A black eye doctor testing Eddie's vision.

> DOCTOR
> (*adjusting instrument*)
> Better? Same? Worse?
> (*adjusting again*)
> Better? Same? Worse?

87 INT: CHALKIE'S — DAY

Eddie wearing glasses, alone at Chalkie's at 10:00 A.M. He's sitting on the rail of a table reading a newspaper spread out on the immac-ulate green felt.

88 INT: CHALKIE'S — DAY

Eddie shooting alone, at noon — a few players.

89 INT: CHALKIE'S — DAY

Eddie shooting alone at three — place three-quarters full.

90 INT: CHALKIE'S — DUSK

Eddie sitting, beer in hand, cue across his lap, scanning Chalkie's from his table — 6:00 P.M.

91 INT: CHALKIE'S — NIGHT

Eddie squinting down, adjusting his glasses — getting used to them as he plays — 8:00 P.M.

92 INT: CHALKIE'S — NIGHT

Eddie standing at his table, rolling his neck — 9:00 P.M.

93 INT: CHALKIE'S — NIGHT
ANGLE

Orvis and Moselle come up behind him.

> ORVIS
> I like the glasses.

> EDDIE
> (*embarrassed*)
> Yeah?

> ORVIS
> Fast Eddie, this here is Moselle.

> EDDIE
> What's up?

> MOSELLE
> That's a pretty stick.

> EDDIE
> I want the break.

Orvis nods OK.

> EDDIE
> What's the book?

> ORVIS
> Fifty on Fast Eddie wins a hundred. Fifty on Moselle wins
> twenty-five.

> EDDIE
> Thanks a lot.

> ORVIS
> Facts of life, my man.

> EDDIE
> (*to Moselle*)
> How about a hundred on the side?

MOSELLE
Read my mind.

ANGLE — CLOSE-UP

Many nonwhite hands passing cash, Orvis's hands grabbing the money and scrawling names and amounts in a dirty notebook.

94 MONTAGE

Surrounded by noisy bettors:

Eddie shoots, Moselle shoots, Eddie shoots, Moselle shoots.

95 Eddie paying Moselle a hundred dollars.

96 Eddie's Cadillac barreling down the road.

97 CLOSE-UP of a rack of nine balls. An anonymous player smashes a break.

98 CLOSE-UP of Eddie shooting.

99 CLOSE-UP of young, wiry guy, hillbilly-looking, shooting.

Eddie paying hillbilly.

100 CLOSE-UP of Eddie shooting.

101 CLOSE-UP of tough-looking woman shooting.

Eddie paying woman.

102 CLOSE-UP of Eddie shooting.

103 CLOSE-UP of basketball tall black man shooting.

Eddie paying black man.

104 Eddie shooting.

Black man paying Eddie.

105 Eddie shooting.

Woman paying Eddie.

106 Eddie shooting.

Eddie paying hillbilly.

Hillbilly paying Eddie.

Hillbilly paying Eddie again.

And again.

107 INT: CHALKIE'S — NIGHT

Crowded. Eddie and Moselle playing surrounded by the crowd.

Eddie shoots. Moselle shoots. Eddie shoots. Moselle shoots.

108 INT: CHALKIE'S — NIGHT

Moselle paying Eddie in front of Orvis.

> EDDIE
> You guys going to Atlantic City?

109 EXT: HIGHWAY — DAY
CLOSE-UP — EDDIE

driving — squinting anxiously at the distant hotels spaced out like gap teeth, the sea mist reducing them to silhouettes.

110 EXT: CASINO — ONE HOUR LATER

Eddie walking through a sea of slot machines and players towards the lobby. He carries his cue under one arm, a small leather suitcase in one hand.

111 OMIT

112 INT: EDDIE'S ROOM

Walls and ceiling a light chlorine-blue. Eddie lies flat on his bed staring at an oversized TV screen.

On the screen is an in-house station teaching you how to play Blackjack.

Eddie bolts up in bed, rubs his eyes with the heel of his palms.

113 INT: SIGN-IN DESK FOR THE TOURNAMENT

Eddie stands on line with other players before a collapsible card table where a young black woman in a casino jumpsuit is doing the registration. He looks like he's hiding or signing up for unemployment.

ANGLE

A registration card and five hundred-dollar bills dropped on the table. Card reads "Eddie Felson."

SEATED CLERK'S POV

WE SEE Eddie.

> CLERK
> Knock 'em dead.

114 INT: TOURNAMENT HALL — DAY

Eddie walks into the room — a huge arena under soft lights — it's big enough for a prizefight crowd. Eddie takes on the sea of impeccable tables, the miles of shining empty aluminum bleachers. The place looks twice as large because Eddie's the only one in the room.

115 INT: REGISTRATION DESK — DAY

> EDDIE
> (to the clerk)
> Where's the practice room?

> CASINO CLERK
> The Green Room . . . two rights and a left.

> JULIAN (OS)
> Hey, Eddie!

Eddie looks up. Julian and Elmo, another young player from the "Q," are there with their cue cases.

JULIAN
(*grinning*)
Eddie! Where's your man?
(*Julian notices Eddie is carrying his cue; drawling in
amused disbelief*)
No-o *shit* . . .
(*laughing*)
Eddie, you playing?

EDDIE
You got a problem with that?

JULIAN
(*laughing*)
Not me.
(*to Elmo*)
You got a problem with that?

ELMO
(*jerks back his chin*)
No problem at all.

116 INT: THE "GREEN ROOM" — DAY

The practice room. Walls and drapes lime-green like a hangover.
Eight tables. Plastic chairs for fans. Security guard in a uniform; old
guy with glasses.

Six tables are occupied by younger players. Girlfriends watch. They
talk and move like they own the place. Their dress ranges from
Heavy Metal to Casino Flash.

ANGLE

Eddie rolling out a tray of balls, getting to work. Eddie tries to
concentrate on his game, but he's in the midst of what he dreads:
the heartless immorality of youth.

Eddie bends down to shoot.

We hear the murmur and shouts of a large crowd.

117 INT: TOURNAMENT ROOM — DAY

PAN OF CROWD

It's the tournament room, the bleachers are filled.

There are players at every table warming up. There's a dais of judges and scorekeepers on an elevated platform and overhead along one entire wall is an opaque projection of who's playing at what table with score boxes. It's similar to the scorekeeping projection at a bowling tournament. A giant shadow hand is writing in names.

At each table is an attendant in white shirt, bow tie, black pants, short red apron and white gloves who racks the balls and grooms the felt. The attendant wears a miniature speaker-headset to communicate with the judges.

CLOSE-UP — DUKE DUKAS BREAKING

Duke is middle-aged, heavy, nervous, glasses and a moustache. Sharkskin pants and a Guyabera shirt which hugs his gut.

Duke breaks — nothing goes in.

> DUKE
> (*to himself*)
> I didn't deserve that.

WE SEE Eddie — polo shirt, gold slacks. Everything loose for comfort. Eddie smiles at him — guys who say shit like that beat themselves. Eddie puts baby powder on his hands, rubs powder on the length of his stick, and approaches the table.

> EDDIE
> This your first tournament, Duke?

Duke doesn't answer.

118 INT: TOURNAMENT ROOM — DAY

ANGLE — TWENTY MINUTES LATER

The projected screen showing scores. The giant shadow hand is marking up another game for Felson. The score is Felson — nine marks, Dukas — one mark.

119 INT: TOURNAMENT HALL — DAY
ANGLE — EDDIE SHOOTING

In the room we hear sporadic shouts and applause for shots made at various tables.

Eddie sinks the nine. Some applause for Eddie. He's won the race to ten.

The attendant, speaking into the headset, murmurs something to the judges, then shakes hands with Eddie.

Eddie shakes hands with Duke.

>   DUKE
> I didn't deserve that.

>   EDDIE
>   (*casual, yet emphatic*)
> Sure you did.

120 INT: BAR IN THE CASINO — NIGHT

There's a young attractive group on a small stage singing "Aquarius" or "Up Up and Away" to half-empty tables. The tables separate the stage from a long dimly lit bar.

Young pool players make up half the bar crowd, talking loudly, laughing among themselves.

Eddie sits alone nursing a bourbon. He seems less tense than he's been since deciding to play in the tournament.

>   VINCENT (OS)
> Wait a minute . . . wait a minute . . . I have to win only eight games to your *ten?*

>   PLAYER
> That's right.

>   VINCENT
> And all I have to put up is eight hundred to your twelve hundred?

PLAYER
You got it.

VINCENT
Carmen . . . that's a good deal.

CARMEN
This guy won the Akron Open, Vincent, don't be a jerk.

VINCENT
(*angry*)
I can win eight games! Don't blow this.

PLAYER
Sure.

CARMEN
(*to player*)
I don't like it . . . I tell you what. I tell you what . . . What if you make your end fifteen hundred.

VINCENT
Hey, Carmen . . .

PLAYER
No problem. OK. 12:30.

Eddie smiles to his drink as he overhears this conversation.

Carmen and Vincent watch the guy from Akron head off.

VINCENT
(*calmly*)
Fifteen hundred?

CARMEN
Not bad.

VINCENT
(*low key acid*)
Not bad, hah?

CARMEN
(*defensive*)
He wouldn't *go* for more.

VINCENT
Yeah . . . *You* wouldn't go for more. That guy had two
thousand dollars written all over his *face,* Carmen. He just
made five hundred dollars off us . . . *Thank* you.

Vincent turns away in disgust, sees Eddie, who's heard all this.
Vincent's face hardens, relaxes.

Vincent is dressed to kill in a hustler sort of way. Italian slacks,
rust V-neck sweater, chains and tasseled loafers. He strolls over to
Eddie's table.

VINCENT
(*reserved but in control*)
Hey . . . glasses . . . they look good.

EDDIE
(*cautious*)
Hey, Vincent the Kid . . . Carmen . . .

CARMEN
(*a little cool*)
You looked good today.

VINCENT
So how's it going?

EDDIE
Can't complain . . . how about you guys?

Vincent half-pulls a thick wad of money out of his front pocket.

VINCENT
(*casual, low-key pride*)
We made like four thousand on the road in two weeks . . .
could've been better, could've been worse.

EDDIE
Great . . . I'm happy for you.

VINCENT
(*long beat*)
About twelve, twelve-thirty in the Green Room, I'm

taking out that lame from Akron. Did you see what we did to him? You want to get in on it?

> EDDIE
> (*grateful for the gesture, relieved*)
> I'm gonna pass, kid. I got a game at ten in the morning . . . I'm gonna pack it in early.

> VINCENT
> It's on you, chief.
> (*long beat*)
> Anyways, good luck tomorrow.

> EDDIE
> Same to you.

Vincent splits. Carmen stays at the bar.

> EDDIE
> You guys doin' good, huh?

> CARMEN
> We did OK . . . you were right, you know . . . we really *didn't* need you anymore.

> EDDIE
> (*with a twinge*)
> See? Didn't I say so?

> CARMEN
> You wouldn't believe Vincent now . . . you wouldn't even recognize him.

> EDDIE
> A new man, hah?

> CARMEN
> Why didn't you take him up on tonight?

> EDDIE
> I told you, I'm playing tomorrow early.

Carmen stares at him, hesitates (as if to say something), walks away.

121 OMIT

122 OMIT

123 INT: TOURNAMENT ROOM — DAY
ANGLE

Vincent breaks.

Julian breaks.

Grady breaks.

Eddie breaks.

ANGLE — VINCENT

sinking the nine off a tough combination.

> VINCENT
> (*to Grady*)
> It's like a nightmare, isn't it?

ANGLE — EDDIE

breaking. The nine is on the rim of the pocket, the one ball right on line.

Julian, looking disgusted with himself, sweeping the nine in with the side of his cue to concede the shot and the game.

> EDDIE
> Wipe your nose, Julian.

> JULIAN
> You're going down.

ANGLE — GRADY

blowing a shot, arching back in melodramatic exasperation.

> VINCENT
> It's like a nightmare, isn't it?

ANGLE

Vincent wading through the crowd accepting congratulations.

124 OMIT

125 INT: EDDIE'S HOTEL ROOM — DUSK

Eddie enters, flings his cue on the couch.

Stands there, snapping and clapping, wired with joy.

He starts pacing, humming to himself, eyes darting around the room for some kind of outlet. He moves towards the TV, thinks better of it.

Grabs the phone, dials.

> EDDIE
> Janelle . . . hey . . . how *are* you? Good . . . good . . .
> when was the last time you were in Atlantic City?
> A*maz*ing, right? You remember the diving horse? The salt
> water taffy? Gone . . . everything . . . I haven't been here
> in maybe *ten* years? *Fif*teen years I don't even know . . .
> just a*maz*ing . . .
> > (*beat*)
> You know I'm *play*ing, yeah, and ah —
> > (*from the heart*)
> I'm doin' so goddamn *great*, Janelle . . . just *great*.

126 INT: LOBBY OUTSIDE THE TOURNAMENT HALL — DAY

A room bordered by collapsible tables covered with pool related articles for sale, T-shirts, buttons, cue sticks, warm-up jackets. There's a hot and cold buffet along one wall. Mounted on a huge stand-up easel is a diagram of tournament games, who beat who, and who's playing who next.

Eddie traces his progress; his defeat of Duke Dukas, his defeat of Julian. The field is down from 64 to 16.

WE SEE his next draw is Vincent.

CLOSE ON EDDIE

nodding to himself, destiny calls.

127 INT: GREEN ROOM ENTRANCE — ONE HOUR LATER —
DAY

Eddie standing on the threshold watching Vincent play ring-pool
(rotating multi-player pool) with some hustlers.

Vincent's at ease — they all are — laughing and heckling each other's shots.

Eddie moves towards the folding chairs, watches Vincent in his
element. Eddie feels a mixture of envy, fondness and anxiety.

At one point Vincent spots Eddie, laughs, waves and aims his cue
like a rifle at him.

Vincent makes a gun sound.

Carmen enters, sits next to Eddie. Eddie doesn't acknowledge her.
He looks like he's in a trance, staring at his hands — as if something
momentous is being worked out in his head.

> EDDIE
> (*brightly, suddenly coming to life*)
> I'm gonna beat him. I'm definitely gonna beat him.

> CARMEN
> Huh . . . Is that a fact.

> EDDIE
> *Bank* on it.

Carmen stares at Eddie for a beat. They both turn to watch Vincent
play.

128 INT: EDDIE'S BEDROOM — NIGHT

Eddie opening the door to see Janelle in his bed watching TV. She
clicks off the set on the remote control. Smiles at Eddie. Eddie looks
surprised and happy.

129 INT: TOURNAMENT — DAY

Eddie and Vincent crouched down lagging simultaneously. Vincent wins.

130 MONTAGE — TOURNAMENT — DAY

of Vincent and Eddie shooting, interspersed with scratch marks drawn on the overhead scorecard, interspersed with CLOSE UPS of Grady, Julian, Carmen, Janelle in the crowd.

Eddie watching as Vincent makes shot after shot. Vincent misses an easy shot, Eddie draws a breath.

Eddie sinks the nine.

Vincent sinks the nine.

Eddie calls a safe forfeiting his own shot, to leave Vincent a difficult situation (by burying the cue). Vincent busts out, sinks the nine.

Eddie breaks — sinks the nine. Shakes his fist tensely in triumph — pure luck.

On the overhead, scratch marks register neck and neck games to nine even.

131 INT: TOURNAMENT — DAY
THE LAST RACK AT NINE AND NINE

Vincent breaks, drops two balls on the break, moves like a machine up to the six, misses a bank.

Vincent sinks to his knees, holding his cue, forehead between his fingers, shaking his head.

Eddie sinks the six, the seven, the eight, the nine, wins.

Eddie draws a huge breath. He's trying to control his terrible excitement as he shakily dismantles his Balabushka. He's almost heaving.

CLOSE-UP — CARMEN

deadpan in the crowd. Huge applause at this upset.

Vincent leans against the table, his back to Eddie dismantling his cue.

> EDDIE
> (*joyous*)
> You shot *great*, kid. The balls roll funny, I told you that, remember? But you shot *great*.

> VINCENT
> Yup.

Eddie walking through the crowd in a daze.

132 INT: EDDIE'S ROOM

Vincent banging on the door. Eddie, in a bathrobe, after too long a beat.

> VINCENT (OS)
> (*knocking*)
> Eddie?

> EDDIE
> Yeah, yeah. Just a minute. Christ!

Vincent and Carmen enter. There is champagne, bucket, glasses, etc., on table.

> EDDIE
> Hey . . . Come in! . . . I got Kennedy in the quarterfinals tomorrow . . . you know anything about him?

Vincent and Carmen don't answer.

> EDDIE
> What . . .

Vincent pulls out an envelope, drops it on the coffee table.

> EDDIE
> What.

> CARMEN
> That's for you.

Janelle enters in a bathrobe.

> VINCENT
> Hey! How you doin'?

Janelle nods hello, sits next to Eddie.

Eddie opens the envelope, it's heavy with cash.

> EDDIE
> What's this?

> VINCENT
> That's your cut . . . I told you I owe you one.

> EDDIE
> Cut of *what.*

> VINCENT
> For the game.

> EDDIE
> (*starting to tense*)
> What game?

> VINCENT
> (*hard, proud tone*)
> *Our* game, man. I *dump*ed. We got a front to lay all four
> thousand on you and I dumped. It wasn't that hard, all's I
> had to do was dog about four shots. You are *definitely* not
> bad. I feel shitty a little getting booted, but what the hell,
> there's other tournaments.

> EDDIE
> (*shocked*)
> You *dump*ed?

> VINCENT
> Yeah . . . Carmen didn't want to go for it, but I told her
> you'd appreciate it . . . of all people.

> CARMEN
> (*tentative*)
> Two Brothers and a Stranger . . . just like you laid it out
> . . . It was beautiful.

VINCENT
(*rising*)
When I kicked the six? When I dropped to my knees like
that? That's the *art* of the *dump!* Right? There's eight
thousand in there . . . I'm telling you, the odds were a
joke. We gotta split, I got Green Room games for like the
next three nights . . . you sure you don't want in?

Eddie just stares at him, devastated.

VINCENT
(*giving Eddie a look — they* might *have
dumped just to headfuck Eddie*)
Hey, good luck with Kennedy.

Eddie looks helplessly at Janelle.

JANELLE
(*awed*)
That little prick.

133 OMIT

134 INT: TOURNAMENT HALL — DAY

Only four games left, so the sea of tables looks vast and deserted.
Eddie's game is at a corner table.

In the bleachers nearest Eddie are all the players that were knocked
out in previous rounds. They sit at various levels — Julian, Grady,
Vincent.

Janelle sits apart.

Vincent sits at the lowest level, elbows on knees, Carmen at his side.
They're barely ten feet from Eddie.

Eddie's break. He looks freaked.

Vincent and Carmen stare at him with a slight irony.

Eddie pauses, looks at them. Those fuckers *did* dump just to mess
with his head.

Eddie breaks.

The crowd whistles, applauds. Carmen and Vincent don't react.

Janelle watches.

Eddie looks aggrieved.

Eddie hunches down to shoot. He begins to play — halfhearted.

Eddie drops two balls. Then:

Eddie straightens up . . . signs . . .

> EDDIE
> (*softly*)
> Forfeit.

> KENNEDY
> (*casual, disbelieving*)
> What are you talking about?

> EDDIE
> You win, I forfeit.

The crowd starts to get murmury, as they catch on.

CLOSE ON JANELLE

She quietly leaves the stands, exits the hall.

> SCATTERED VOICES
> Yo, Eddie, what's up! Play ball!

Eddie, ignoring everybody, casually, purposefully saunters over to Vincent and Carmen in the front row. Hovering over them, but not looking at them, he leisurely dismantles the Balabushka. It looks to the room like he just strolled over to the sidelines at random to pack up.

VINCENT'S POV

Eddie dismantling his cue. Eddie finally looks at Vincent, briefly, eyebrow cocked, reaches into his back pocket, pulls out the envelope with eight thousand bucks, drops it in Vincent's lap.

> EDDIE
> (*quiet*)
> Here. We're even . . .

CLOSE ON VINCENT AND CARMEN

Vincent furtively peering into the barely opened envelope. He looks smug for the most part.

Eddie exits.

135 INT: LOBBY OF THE TOURNAMENT ROOM — DAY

EDDIE'S POV — Janelle standing by the buffet table waiting for him.

> JANELLE
> (*kissing him on the mouth*)
> Let's get the hell out of here . . . the Bahamas sounds real good about right now.

> EDDIE
> (*distracted, tense and not very convincing*)
> Yeah, it does, don't it?

> JANELLE
> (*studies Eddie*)
> Well,
> (*shrugs*)
> in any event, we got to move me in with you first.

Eddie is surprised, not unpleased, but still caught up in his own shakiness.

> JANELLE
> I admire *character*. I don't know if you knew that about me.

> EDDIE
> (*incredulous, half laughing, half crying*)
> *Chara*cter?

Eddie sees Carmen over Janelle's shoulder.

> EDDIE
> (*tenderly, to Janelle*)
> Stay with me, here.

> CARMEN
> (*offering back envelope*)
> Vincent says it's yours. You don't want it, you should give it to charity.

> EDDIE
> (*no effort to take it*)
> You guys . . .

> CARMEN
> (*blowing her top*)
> Hey! Listen to *this* . . . what the hell you ex*pect*. You *jerk*ed him around, you *burn*ed him, you *dump*ed him. How do you *want* him to be?

Beat.

> EDDIE
> (*hoarse*)
> I'm sorry . . .

> CARMEN
> (*thrown, almost in tears*)
> *Sorry*? What's *that* mean? What's *sorry*? I hate it here. I hate everything and *everybody.*
> (*teary*)
> It was supposed to be *real* different. I don't get it. It's so bad. It's so bad . . .
> (*beat*)
> He's *sorry.*
> (*words fail her*)

> EDDIE
> You want him back?

> CARMEN
> Oh, *what* . . . I'm supposed to *trust* you on something now?

> EDDIE
> (*calmly*)
> You can trust me on this . . . you know why? Because it's for *me.*

CARMEN
What's for you?

EDDIE
His best game, it's for me.

CARMEN
Everything's for *you* . . . everything we did, everything
. . . it's always all for you.

EDDIE
(*cutting off her rant*)
Hey! . . . Do . . . you . . . want . . . him
. . . back!

Carmen is startled into silence.

EDDIE
Get him in the Green Room.

Carmen takes a reflective beat.

CARMEN
(*angry, tired*)
He won't play you now.

EDDIE
Sure he will . . . he's got to . . . he knows that.

Eddie takes Janelle's hand and starts backing out of the room.

EDDIE
I'll be in the Green Room.

136 INT: GREEN ROOM — DAY

Eddie, grim-faced. Janelle sitting, waiting with him. He's preparing a tight rack of nine-ball by tapping each ball in the diamond
with the cue ball. (Makes them hug each other for maximum disper-
sion on the break.) It's like a priest preparing for Mass. The room
is still.

Vincent comes exploding into the room — mid-rant. He's got Carmen by the arm.

> VINCENT
> (*as they walk in*)
> Sonofabitch still doin' it, right? Still doin' it. He don't care! How can you start with me again! What do you want, a beating?

> EDDIE
> I want your game.

> VINCENT
> My *game!* You couldn't *deal* with my game, Jack . . . You're out-*man*ned.

> EDDIE
> Give me your game.

> VINCENT
> (*amazed, but unmoved, otherwise*)
> You got *brass,* man, I'll give you that.

Vincent starts backing out, disgusted.

> VINCENT
> Nothing's changed. You're still runnin' numbers, you're still using Carmen . . . hey, Eddie, drop dead, and have a good life.

Vincent turns his back and walks more briskly.

> EDDIE
> (*startlingly sharp*)
> Hey! Don't you leave! Vincent . . . OK . . .
> (*with great effort*)
> I'm asking you . . . I got *no* leg to stand on with you . . . but I'm asking you . . . right now . . . give me your game . . . I got no time for jumps or hustles anymore.

> VINCENT
> Why should I believe you?

> EDDIE
> Because if you *don't,* the way *you*'re goin', you're gonna

wind up making *me* look like a saint. I *know*, I *taught*
you.

Vincent is caught up short. There's an expectant beat. It's in his
court.

> VINCENT
> (*starting to relent*)
> Listen to this.

Long beat. Vincent looks back to Carmen who's blank with her
own expectation.

> VINCENT
> (*exhaling*)
> So what're we playing for?

> EDDIE
> (*relieved*)
> Hey . . . whatever you want . . . *you're* the gorilla.

Vincent bends down to Carmen to take his cue case from her. He
looks at her. Carmen acknowledges.

> VINCENT
> (*looking at Carmen, talking to Eddie*)
> How about we play for the envelope?

Eddie and Vincent lagging for break. Carmen sits. Janelle gets up
and leans against wall.

> VINCENT
> Eddie, what are you gonna do if I beat your ass?

> EDDIE
> Then I tell you to carry that envelope around for me.

> VINCENT
> Oh yeah? Carry it around until when?

> EDDIE
> Next month in Houston, maybe then —

Eddie wins the lag.

EDDIE
Month after that, maybe Tahoe . . . maybe then . . .

CARMEN
You mean Reno. Nothing coming up in Tahoe.

EDDIE
(*smiling at her*)
Tahoe, Reno, I get them confused. In any event . . .
(*hunches down for the break*)
. . . you ain't kicking *my* ass *any*where . . .

VINCENT
What makes you so sure?

EDDIE
(*concentrating on the cue*)
Hey . . . I'm *back*.

Eddie smashes the break.

FADE OUT.

THE END

Sea of Love

This draft was written in 1987 and represents
the first pass at getting down the story. It reflects
no input other than my own and is considerably
different than my final draft, which was the
shooting script for the 1989 film. — R.P.

EXT: BURNSIDE CATERERS — GRAND CONCOURSE — THE BRONX — DAY

A shabby catering hall on a shabby, formerly resplendent commercial avenue.

Two men, wearing dark blue warm-up jackets, the New York Yankees logo prominent on the chest, stand with clipboards in front of the street entrance. Behind them is a large sign leaning on an easel: "EIGHTH ANNUAL MEET THE YANKEES BRUNCH" — INVITATION ONLY. A few guys stand in a loose line waiting for admission.

CLOSE ON — DOORWAY

A young invitee waits as one of the clipboard guys checks the guest list against his invitation.

> CLIPBOARD GUY
> Mazza . . . Mazza . . . Louis Mazza . . . you got some I.D., Louie? A driver's license?

Mazza digs into his wallet, hands over his license.

> CLIPBOARD GUY
> This says Frank Garro.

> MAZZA
> Wait a sec . . .

He takes it back, passes the guy another license with the right name.

The two clipboard guys stare at each other for a brief second, amused.

> MAZZA
> There you go . . . Louis Mazza . . . the game after . . . we
> gettin' box seats, right?

INT: CATERING HALL

A big Yankee banner is strung across a stage. Rows of long folding
tables covered with Yankee pinstripe tablecloths, name cards, and
place settings.

Ray Charles sings his soulful version of "America" over a PA.

The room is half full of guests; twenty-five men, mainly young;
white, black, Hispanic. A dozen guys in Yankee warm-up jackets
usher and escort guests to their assigned seats.

CLOSE ON — FRANK KELLER

forty-three, short, quick, wiry, wearing a Yankee jacket. He moves
from guest to guest, pouring them orange juice, a quart pitcher in
each hand.

He pours for the Maldonado twins. The Maldonados are in their
late twenties, goatees, nattily dressed.

> FRANK
> How you guys doin'?

> OMAR MALDONADO
> Where the Yankees at?

> FRANK
> They're comin'.

> EFRAM MALDONADO
> You a Yankee?

> FRANK
> You don't recognize me?

> OMAR
> What . . . you a *short*-stop?

The twins laugh and high-five each other.

> FRANK
> (*straight-faced*)
> Used to be.

> EFRAM
> What . . .

> FRANK
> (*doing a perfect imitation of Phil Rizzuto's
> patented exclamation*)
> Ho-lee Cow!

> OMAR
> (*jaw on the floor*)
> You the Scooter! Efram, this dude's Phil Rizzuto. Do that
> again!

> FRANK
> (*winking at some fellow workers*)
> Ho-lee Cow!

The twins stand and shake Frank's hand.

> EFRAM
> Yo, Phil . . . how come you pourin' us juice?

EXT: DOORWAY

A dozen more guys waiting to be admitted.

> CLIPBOARD GUYS
> Invites and I.D.s, fellas. Invites and I.D.s.

> INVITEE
> How we gettin' to the game after? I ain't got no car.

> CLIPBOARD GUY
> We got you covered.

CLOSE ON — A SLOW PAN OF FRENCH TOAST, PANCAKES
AND PLACE NAME CARDS

(Reems, Ortiz, Torrio, Jackson, etc.) as the guests scarf down their
brunch.

Frank heads to the stage. The guests applaud. Shouts of "Scooter!" and "Holee Cow!" Laughter. Frank holds up his hands for silence.

Suddenly twenty guys with Yankee jackets file in around the walls of the room, surrounding the guests.

> FRANK
> Fellas . . . fellas . . . I got some good news, I got some bad news . . . which you want first?

Chorus of "bad news" overrides "good news."

> FRANK
> Bad news wins . . . here we go . . . the Yanks can't make it here, guys.

Groans.

> FRANK
> And you can't make it over to the stadium later.

Silence except for one loud "uh-oh."

> FRANK
> We got thirty-five outstanding warrants here eating our pancakes and, ah . . . on behalf of the New York Yankees and the New York City Career Criminals' Investigations Unit . . . you're all under arrest.

Utter silence as Frank and all the Yankee jackets pull out their detectives' gold shields.

The rear wall rolls back on casters, REVEALING a whole booking setup — photographer, fingerprint station clerks . . . even an arraignments judge. It's a major sting operation.

> FRANK
> (good-natured)
> Sorry, guys . . . we got'cha.

The guests slouch and groan in resignation.

> VOICE
> (defeated)
> Fuck you, Scooter.

Laughter from both the cops and the prisoners.

> VOICE
> What's the good news?

> FRANK
> Good news is comin' around . . . l'chaim.

Four cops, holding half gallons of vodka, make their way from guest to guest, converting all the orange juices to screwdrivers — one for the road.

EXT: ENTRANCE TO THE CATERING HALL

Frankie is lounging with two other detectives on the street. They're smoking — day is done.

> DETECTIVE
> Fuck you, Scooter.

They all laugh.

A black guy, Ernest Lee, and his ten-year-old son come running towards Frankie and his pals.

> ERNEST
> (winded)
> Am I too late?

The kid pulls up, also winded, holding a baseball glove. Ernest hands his invite to Frankie.

> FRANK
> (thrown by the presence of the kid)
> Who's this?

> ERNEST
> That's my son.

> FRANK
> Invitation's for you only . . . you Ernest Lee?

> ERNEST
> Hey, man, how'm I gonna meet Dave Winfield without takin' my boy?

Frank whispers to one of the detectives who vanishes inside.

> FRANK
> You got some I.D., Ernest?

As Ernest digs out his wallet the detective comes back out.

> DETECTIVE
> (*in Frankie's ear*)
> Grand theft auto . . .

Frankie sighs, thinks for a beat, ignoring Ernest's I.D.

> FRANK
> We're booked up in there, Ernest.

> ERNEST
> Hey. I got an *in*vite here.

Frankie casually pulls back his jacket so that his gold shield shows.

> FRANK
> (*looking away*)
> I said we're booked up.

Ernest's face turns gray. He involuntarily backs up.

> FRANK
> We'll catch you later.

Ernest nods a barely perceptible "thanks" and briskly walks away with his uncomprehending son.

> CUT TO:

INT: MOVIE THEATER — MANHATTAN — NIGHT
CLOSE ON — THE SCREEN

A wounded bank robber, on his back, stares up into the .44 Magnum of Dirty Harry. The robber's fingers inch towards his own shotgun on the ground at his side.

> DIRTY HARRY
> (*his gun in our face*)
> Uh uh . . . I know what you're thinking, "Did he fire six shots or only five?" . . . Well, to tell you the truth, in all this excitement I kind of lost track myself.

Over this dialogue from the screen we hear a half a dozen drunken male voices from the movie audience.

> CHORUS
> *Shoot* the hump!
> Blow his friggin' head off!

ANGLE — THE SCREAMERS

Six detectives sitting in the dark, blasted on rum and Cokes, which they concoct sloppily in their seats. One of them is Frank.

> DIRTY HARRY (OS)
> But being this is a .44 Magnum . . .

Frank screams in approval. They all laugh at Frank. People in the audience yell for them to shut up.

> DIRTY HARRY (OS)
> . . . the most powerful hand gun in the *world* and would
> blow your head clean off, you got to ask yourself one
> question . . . do I feel lucky?

> FRANK
> Do it, Harry!

One of the detectives unlatches his .38 from a Velcro ankle holster and aims it at the screen.

> DETECTIVE
> *I'll* fuckin' do it . . .

Laughing, they disarm the guy.

ANGLE — THE SCREEN

> DIRTY HARRY
> (*calmly, deadly*)
> Well, do you, punk?

> DETECTIVES (OS)
> (*start chanting*)
> Yeah! Yeah! Yeah!

ANGLE — THE THEATER

Two ushers hover over the six detectives.

> USHER
> Yo, fellas . . . you want us to call the cops?

CLOSE ON — THEIR FACES

looking up at the usher: drunk, armed, smiling, angelic — ready to explode in laughter.

EXT: STREET OUTSIDE MOVIE THEATER — MIDNIGHT

WE SEE the six detectives weaving slightly. Behind them we can read the marquee "Dirty Harry Festival" MAGNUM FORCE THE ENFORCER DIRTY HARRY."

They stand on the street corner beaming at each other.

> FRANK
> Anybody up for the Island of Lost Souls?

> STARK
> (moustache, tall)
> Ah, Christ, I awready got the clap.

> MALONEY
> (stocky, glasses, tattooed)
> I'm gonna go home, throw up, and go to sleep. I promised to take the kids to Great Adventure tomorrow.

The other three, Rizzo, Dargan, Wolfe — white, Catholic, beefy, mid-thirties to early forties, chorus their excuses.

> FRANK
> (walking away, waving them off)
> . . . Mutts.

FRANK'S POV

As the guys pile into Dargan's pickup (New Jersey plates), Stark sticks his head out of the window.

> STARK
> Hey, Scooter! Fuck you!

They all laugh.

INT: WHITE WORKING CLASS BAR — WASHINGTON
HEIGHTS — AN HOUR LATER — 1:00 A.M.

Seedy cop bar. Jukebox. Drink discounts advertised over the mirror.

Some hard-looking women, not whores, but cop groupies, scotch
cigarettes and tight faces, talking to older guys, some of whom are
plainclothes cops half in the bag.

ANGLE

Frank enters.

A ripple of hellos, recognition. Frank shakes hands with a seventy-
year-old red nose, then the bartender, who puts a rum and Coke in
front of him.

An Irish woman in her thirties, Dawn, sidles up to Frank.

>   DAWN
> I hate this scene.

>   FRANK
>   (*withdrawn*)
> Oh yeah?

>   DAWN
> I'm going to California, live with my sister.

>   FRANK
> Oh yeah?

>   DAWN
> I had a dream about you last night.

>   FRANK
> Oh yeah? Why don't we go out back, get some air.

>   DAWN
>   (*pausing, insulted*)
> You know, sometimes a girl likes a guy to buy her a drink
> or something.

> FRANK
> (*ungiving*)
> Oh yeah?

> DAWN
> (*disgusted*)
> Fuck you, Frankie.

She walks away.

> FRANK
> (*to himself*)
> Fuck you, *Scooter*.

INT: ALL-NIGHT KOREAN VEGETABLE STAND/MINI-MARKET
— 2:00 A.M.

Under the fluorescents Frank stands in line with a quart of juice and some ice cream, waiting to check out.

WE SEE from his POV, three women, shopping alone, not ugly, not pretty — all self-contained, absorbed in their actions, ignoring the fact that, like Frank, they're doing their grocery shopping at 2:00 A.M.

CLOSE ON — FRANK

observing them but impassive.

INT: FRANK'S BEDROOM — 3:00 A.M.

The room is in shadows except for

CLOSE ON — FRANK

in his underwear, hunched over, elbows on knees, phone to ear, sitting on the edge of his bed.

He absently plays with a gold chain with a linked miniature handcuff clasp around his neck. A table clock reads 3:00.

> FRANK
> Gruber . . . Frank Keller . . .

(*beat*)
screw three o'clock . . . I want to talk to my wife . . . my
ex-wife . . . just put her on . . . just put her on . . . just put
her on . . .
(*beat*)
Denice . . . did I wake you? I'm sorry . . . I think I got
appendicitis.

ANGLE — FRANK'S BEDROOM — 4:00 A.M.

TV is on to some moronic cable talk show. Room is spare — bed,
wall-mounted TV, some workout equipment — no decoration, no
frills.

Frank is doing sit-ups on a slant board at the foot of his bed.

WE SEE him do a furious set, then stop, fingers clasped behind his
neck, his head three feet below his ankles.

His face suffused with blood. WE SEE Frank's eyes close . . .
finally.

CUT TO:

INT: DETECTIVES' SQUAD ROOM — 20TH PRECINCT —
UPPER WEST SIDE — 4:00 P.M.

It's a long, messy room with rows of facing desks. The desks are
yard-sale specials, Formica, wood, steel, whatever, all scratched or
dented. Telephones and overhead fluorescent lighting. A bulletin
board festooned with sketches of killers and notices of upcoming
softball games. A cubbyhole system brimming with notices and
envelopes for individual detectives.

Two small rooms connect to this central one; the lieutenant's office
and an interrogation room with a broad one-way mirror. Two
detectives on duty are on the phone.

Frank enters from outside. The two detectives wave, phone under
their jaws. Frank heads for the cubbyhole "Frank Keller," pulls out
a fistful of communiqúes topped by a lifelike dildo. The dildo has a
face inked onto the tip. Frank blinks at it, then calmly slips it into
another detective's cubbyhole.

He drops the papers on his desk and heads to a large back room with lockers, a TV, a dining table, a hot plate and refrigerator — the detectives' "rec" room — another shit hole.

INT: REC ROOM

He opens his locker to hang up his sport jacket. On the inside of the door is a photo of a woman, ringed in red, with a diagonal slash across the face à la *Ghostbusters*. This is Denice.

Detective Gruber, much bigger than Frank, but soft and sad-looking, comes up on him.

>   GRUBER
> Frank . . .

>   FRANK
> Yo.

>   GRUBER
> I don't want you calling us three in the morning anymore
> . . . You want to talk to Denice, you call her decent
> hours.
>   (*beat*)
> Next time you call like that, it's you and me.

>   FRANK
>   (*unintimidated*)
> You and me?

>   GRUBER
> Try me
>   (*beat*)
> and I want you to take down that picture of her
>   (*pointing to the cross-slashed portrait*)
> I find it offensive.

>   FRANK
>   (*holding in his rage*)
> You find it offensive?

Frank slams his locker and walks away, leaving Gruber standing alone, infuriated.

ANGLE — FRONT ROOM

Frank heads for his desk with a mug of coffee, "FRANK" on the mug.

Detective Stark (at least a foot taller than Frank), emerges from the interrogation room and hooks Frank's arm.

> STARK
> Lookit.

He steers Frank to the one-way mirror and WE SEE in the interrogation room, a squat, bull-like black teenager wearing surfer Jams. A detective is calmly talking to him.

> FRANK
> What's he do?

> STARK
> We got him for loitering, but we're pretty sure he did three women last night
> (*beat*)
> including your sister.

> FRANK
> Uh uh . . . that's bad luck.

> STARK
> Your aunt?

> FRANK
> My grandmother.

> STARK
> Say when.

Frank takes off his gun, stands five feet in front of the door primed as if for a kickoff, lets Stark enter, waits a beat, then explodes forward into the interrogation room — WE SEE through the one-way mirror almost a horizontal dive at the rapist's throat.

Stark and the other detective tackle him before he can touch the kid.

The kid is back up against the wall, terrified.

> FRANK
> (*struggling to break loose*)
> Hey! Hey!
> (*to the kid*)
> Don't fucking confess to them . . . don't confess . . . My brothers, we want you out on the *street* . . . We're *wait*in' for you.

> STARK
> (*dragging Frank to the door*)
> Who the hell let him in!

Frank breaks into heated, terrifying Italian.

> FRANK
> (*in Italian*)
> Bouna notte! Volare! Mi piace vino bianco! Cavilleria rusticana! Dove la restaurante? Sambucca romana!

ANGLE — THE SQUAD ROOM

WE SEE Frank flung backwards out of the interrogation room. We can hear the rapist babbling in terror, the detectives telling him cool out. The door slams shut.

Frank looks impassive, heads for his desk.

One of the phone detectives, Serafino, Puerto Rican, stocky, squat, heavily tattooed with cartoon characters on his massive forearms, looms over his desk.

> SERAFINO
> Take a ride?

> FRANK
> What you catch?

> SERAFINO
> Burglary on Central Park West.

> FRANK
> (*begging out*)
> I got ten pounds a paper on my desk.

> SERAFINO
> (*shrugging*)
> You see who's here?

Serafino tilts his chin to the fingerprinting corner where a tall Jerry Vale look-alike in a three-piece suit is fingerprinting himself. This is Tom Rizzo, 43, a retired detective, Frank's ex-partner.

Frank rises and charges over.

> FRANK
> (*joyous*)
> Hey-y! It's the gumshoe!

> TOM
> Hey, crime stopper!

They can't shake hands or slap backs; Tom's up to his elbows in ink.

> FRANK
> (*looking at Tom's prints on a print card*)
> Gumshoe, how's the private sector? What the hell you doing? These prints look like you got gloves on.

> TOM
> (*embarrassed*)
> I gotta get a set of prints for Jersey . . . we're expanding . . . How many guys I print up, Frankie . . . look at this . . . I can't do it.

> FRANK
> Gimme that . . . wipe your hands . . . you got enough ink here for the *New York Times*.

Frank rerolls the ink on the print pad, takes Tom's hands finger by finger and makes his card as they talk.

> FRANK
> (*neutral*)
> You're expanding, huh?

TOM
Frankie, I swear, I got clients upstate, Connecticut, out on
the Island, and now two guys waiting on me out in
Flemington, I get this Jersey license . . . *furriers,* Frankie,
furriers . . . nice clean air-conditioned furriers, straight
security consultations.

FRANK
Oh yeah?

TOM
Frankie, last year? I cleared sixty large without the pension
. . . with*out* . . . I put in a swimming pool.

FRANK
All you need is to take swimming lessons.

TOM
I'm not bullshitting . . . we got slots, Frank . . . take your
pension, meet my partners. Fuck the job.

A uniformed clerk pops his head into the squad room.

CLERK
Who's catching?

FRANK
I got it.

Frank picks up a phone on an empty desk, holds it under his jaw
and continues to print Tom.

FRANK
Two-O Keller . . . yeah, Sarge.

Frank jots "D.O.A." on a pad, an address, continues to print Tom
as he talks.

FRANK
How old . . . any drugs . . . anything laying around . . .
what do you think . . . Yeah? OK . . . I'll be down in a bit.
    (*Frank hangs up*)
White male . . . thirty, thirty-five, face down on his bed,

nude . . . entry wound over the ear, no exit wound, no
drugs, no weapons.

> TOM
> Fag?

> FRANK
> (*shrugs*)
> Sounds like a taxpayer.

Tom grunts.

> FRANK
> (*smirking with triumph*)
> Look at him . . . the private security consultant, your
> tongue's hanging out.

> TOM
> Me? No way . . . probably a fag . . . Were the hands tied
> behind the back?

> FRANK
> Did I say they were? . . . Here you go.

Frank holds up the prints on the card.

> Not bad for twenty-two years practice, huh?

> TOM
> Think what I'm talkin', Chief . . .

INT: BATHROOM

Frank washing the ink off his hands at a row of wash basins.

Gruber emerges from a stall, starts to wash. They're very tense with
each other.

> FRANK
> You see Serafino?

> GRUBER
> He went out on a witness interview.

>   FRANK
>   (*beat*)
> You want to go out?

>   GRUBER
> What you catch?

>   FRANK
> Suspicious D.O.A.

>   GRUBER
> Sure.

>   FRANK
> Hey, Gruber . . . I'm sorry about last night.

>   GRUBER
> It's OK.

>   FRANK
> You took her out of my house, you know what I mean?

>   GRUBER
> *Hey!* I didn't *take* nobody nowhere . . . She's a good
> woman. You didn't treat her right, she *walked* . . .
> You want to kick somebody's ass about it, kick your
> own . . . you want to break balls? Break your own . . .
> and take that goddamn picture down or we're really
> gonna dance.

Gruber walks out.

>   FRANK
>   (*voice cracking with controlled fury*)
> Gruber? I'll wait for Serafino to come back. OK with you?

EXT: WEST END AVENUE — HALF HOUR LATER

Row of canopied apartment houses. Two cop cars double-parked
in front of 365 West End Avenue canopy. A cop is taking down
license numbers of all cars near the building.

Frank and Serafino pull up in an unmarked car and exit.

> SERAFINO
> (*to the cop*)
> Get the cars across the street too, OK?

> PATROLMAN
> (*pissy*)
> I know the job.

INT: 365 WEST END AVENUE LOBBY

There's a uniformed fifty-year-old doorman, a long foyer. Serafino and Frank enter.

> FRANK
> (*flashing his badge*)
> Where's it at, Chief?

> DOORMAN
> (*straightening up*)
> 10K.

> FRANK
> Anybody talk to you yet?

> DOORMAN
> (*man to man confidential*)
> No one of weight.

> FRANK
> (*smiling*)
> You ever on the job?

> DOORMAN
> (*flattered*)
> Me? Nah. I'm just a square badge. I was in Korea though.

> FRANK
> (*flattering*)
> Yeah? I could have sworn you did the job.

The doorman almost turns ramrod straight, fights down a grin.

> FRANK
> (*turns for the elevator*)
> I'll come down talk to you later.

>   (*beat; winking*)
>   I'm "of weight."

The doorman almost salutes. He's in some kind of military hog
heaven.

INT: ELEVATOR — SERAFINO AND FRANK

>   SERAFINO
>   (*mocking*)
>   "You ever on the job" . . . shit . . .

>   FRANK
>   It's called making people feel good so they'll cooperate
>   with you . . . You should try it sometime, you fat bastard.
>   And while I'm on the subject, why don't you get rid of
>   those stupid tattoos — they're ridiculous.

>   SERAFINO
>   Hey . . . my kids think they're great . . . saves me money
>   on comic books, VCRs . . . Set my kids down, go like
>   this . . .

Serafino puts his forearms together, fists in front of his face, so that
all the tattoos face Frankie. He starts hopping from one side of the
car to the other, making the tattoos appear animated — a cartoon
show. The elevator shakes.

>   SERAFINO
>   Hey . . . what I do for my kids.

INT: HALLWAY LEADING TO 10K

There's a lone policeman standing guard.

>   FRANK
>   How ya doin' . . . Detective Keller, this is Detective
>   Morales. Crime Scenes here yet?

>   COP
>   Nah . . .

SERAFINO
Where's it at?

COP
In the bedroom, straight through.

Two cops leave the apartment, talking. We hear other voices inside.

FRANK
We got a cherry scene in there?

It sounds like a cocktail party.

COP
Hey . . . I'm out here.

INT: APARTMENT

Serafino and Frank gingerly step inside, hands in pockets so as not to touch anything. They walk down a short foyer into a combination dining room—living room, where two cops and a Hispanic civilian are chatting about baseball.

There are two wine glasses, a quarter full, and a bottle of wine, half full on a coffee table. An ashtray has half a dozen cigarette butts.

A pile of 45 RPM records are stacked sloppily next to a record player on the floor.

YOUNG COP
It's in the bedroom.

The young cop, finishing up a cigarette, ditches it into the ashtray.

Frank hesitates, walks over to the ashtray. All the other butts have lipstick on them.

FRANK
Anybody up here wear lipstick?

The cops don't answer.

FRANK
Anybody up here see who smoked these butts with the lipstick?

They don't answer.

Frank gingerly removes the cop's butt to preserve the purity of the evidence.

> FRANK
> (*patiently*)
> Gimme a break, guys, OK? My catch, my ass. Crime
> Scenes gets that butt, finds out it's one of yours . . . you
> know what I mean?

The cops stare at him. He politely returns the butt to the offending officer.

INT: BEDROOM

Frank and Serafino enter.

Queen-sized bed, bookcases. Wall-mounted TV. Bathrobe in a heap on the rug.

The corpse is a well-muscled man, belly down, nude, on top of his made bed. His face lies on its side, his eyes staring calmly at the wall.

There's no mess, no blood, save for a dried clot over his ear.

Serafino and Frank circle the body. Frank squints at the dried blood. They both go to great pains not to touch the corpse.

> FRANK
> Hey, Serafino, remember to tell Crime Scenes to get I.D.
> prints on those assholes out there. They probably touched
> everything in sight.

> SERAFINO
> Looks like a shooter?

> FRANK
> Probably . . . can't see any exit wound with him laying
> like this . . . can you get those guys in here?

Serafino steps back into the archway. A beat later the two cops and the civilian enter.

FRANK
What's the story?

COP
(*from his notes*)
Eleven hundred hours Mrs. . . . excuse me *Ms.* Jennifer
Allen next door complained to the super that this record
was playing over and over from this apartment driving her
nuts. No one answered the door so the super, Mr. Rivera
here, used his pass key found the victim here and the
record player going out in the living room.

FRANK
(*to Rivera*)
You the super? Who's this guy?

SUPER
John Mackey . . . Mister Mackey . . . he lives here.

FRANK
How you know that's John Mackey . . . he's just about
face down.

SUPER
That's him . . . he's got no thumb on the right hand.

CLOSE ON — THE CORPSE

No thumb, OK.

FRANK
Where's this neighbor?

COP
Next door.

FRANK
(*to the younger cop*)
Tell her I'm coming by in a bit, OK? Mister Rivera . . .
this guy Mackey, what's his story, you know anything
about him? He live here alone?

RIVERA
Yeah . . .

FRANK
Was he gay, straight?

RIVERA
Lots a women, lots a women.

FRANK
Yeah? Any drugs? Any complaints about him?

RIVERA
Not that I know of.

FRANK
Pay his rent on time?

RIVERA
Yeah . . . fars I know.

FRANK
What kind of work he do?

RIVERA
A lawyer? Accountant?
(*shrugs*)

FRANK
Parties?

RIVERA
Nah . . . just a lot of ladies . . . one by one.

FRANK
A real swordsman, hah? Anybody in particular? Anybody
catch your eye? He looked like he had a little party out
there last night. You see anybody come in with him?

RIVERA
Hey man, I'm in the basement not at the door . . .

FRANK
Yeah? Then how do you know about the ladies?

RIVERA
Mrs. Allen next door . . . she tell me every night —
(*he makes a pumping gesture for sex*)
The walls are like paper here.

> FRANK
> (*to a cop*)
> Excuse me, did I ask you to go over next door before?
> Could you please do that? I really need to talk to her.

The cop stares at him before moving out. Frank looks at Serafino, rolls his eyes.

> FRANK
> Anybody hear any loud noises last night, this morning?
> Like a gunshot?

The super shrugs.

> RIVERA
> He was shot?

> FRANK
> Could be.

> OLDER COP
> (*sarcastically*)
> Could be.

> FRANK
> (*irritated*)
> Excuse me?

> COP
> The guy got capped, what's this *could* be . . .

> FRANK
> You see any exit wound? You see any bullets? Could be a
> minor injury. He could've died of a heart attack. He
> could've got hit with something.

The cop, slightly drunk, grabs the corpse by the hair, slightly lifting the head, revealing an exit wound feathered with blasted pillow stuffing. The cop lets the head drop.

> COP
> (*sarcastic*)
> Don't tell the M.E. on me, OK?

CLOSE ON — FRANK AND SERAFINO

exchanging resigned shrugs.

Three technicians bearing cameras and attaché cases enter the crime
scene unit.

> TECHNICIAN
> Everybody out, please . . .

INT: LIVING ROOM

as they're herded out.

Frank corners the super.

> FRANK
> (*almost whispering*)
> This Ms. Allen next door . . . was he bangin' her?

> RIVERA
> (*laughs*)
> I don't think so, man, she's like seventy-five years old.

> FRANK
> You said some record was playing over and over?

> RIVERA
> Yeah. I turned it off.

Frank heads over to the record player, moves around the sprawled
45's. WE SEE titles — all 1950's vintage.

> FRANK
> This the one?

CLOSE ON — A 45, "SEA OF LOVE,"

a golden oldie, still on the turntable.

> RIVERA
> Over and over.

Frank turns on the automatic record changer, pushing the switch
with his pen.

As "Sea of Love" starts to play, a haunting stroll-paced love tune,
odd and dreamy, Frank opens a linen closet, pulls out a pillowcase

and starts to gingerly remove personal effects from desk drawers; address books, memo pads, checkbooks, photos of family, stuffing them into the pillowcase like Santa Claus in reverse.

With "Sea of Love" still playing, he stands in the doorway to the bedroom, pillowcase over one shoulder.

John Mackey's corpse is floodlit for the crime scene photographer — the star of an obscene and heartless movie. The technicians scurry about the bedroom dusting, measuring and collecting. The whole tableau is a clinical rape of a dead man's personal collage to the tune "Sea of Love" — more sad than lurid.

CLOSE ON — FRANK

watching all this — his face is impassive.

INT: HALLWAY

Serafino and Frank waiting for the elevator. Frank idly pushes open the stairwell door.

WE SEE three cartons worth of groceries sprawled in a tumble down the whole length of the stairs to the landing below.

Frank hunkers down and reads the delivery label on one of the cartons still on the landing.

CLOSE ON — "MACKEY — 10K"

INT: SUPERMARKET — THIRTY MINUTES LATER

Frank stands by the checkout trying to catch the eye of the manager — an Oriental who's on two phones at once. His office is a ten-foot-high guardhouse overlooking the whole store. The manager ignores Frank.

FRANK'S POV

WE SEE the cashiers, stock help, delivery boys — all black, Oriental, Hispanic kids in their late teens, early twenties.

Frank climbs the four stairs to be on eyelevel with the manager, puts his badge in the guy's face.

EXT: LOADING ZONE ALLEY

Frank leaning against the rear wall of the supermarket facing three delivery boys and the manager.

> FRANK
> So nobody delivered to Mackey? Yesterday? Today?

They shrug.

> MANAGER
> Where's Quawi at?

> FRANK
> Who's Quawi?

> DELIVERY BOY
> I ain't seen him since this morning.

> MANAGER
> Where'd he go?

> FRANK
> Who's Quawi?

> MANAGER
> Sonofabitch is fired. You see him, you tell him.

> FRANK
> (*exasperated*)
> Hey! Police! You're all under arrest! Who's Quawi, goddamnit!

> MANAGER
> Quawi's a no-good sonofabitch. You try to help people, the guy don't even show up half the time. I tell him five times, Quawi, you gonna deliver for me, those hoe-downs got to go.

> FRANK
> Those *what?*

> MANAGER
> (*running fingers through his hair*)
> Hoe-downs.

BLACK DELIVERY BOY
(*laughing*)
He mean corn rows.

MANAGER
Yeah . . . Scare all these old ladies coming to their door
with his hair in them corn holes.

FRANK
What's his last name?

INT: LIEUTENANT'S OFFICE — ONE HOUR LATER
Frank is having a sit-down with the Loo, running down the case.

FRANK
I wanna go out to Queens, see if I can grab this
(*checks his notes*)
Quawi Benjamin kid. BCI says they got a jacket on him,
something like a few B and E's, a few muggings — great
delivery boy material this kid — I think he puts the
groceries out in the stairwell — Mackey answers the door
waiting for his stuff — the kid's got a gun in his face —
kid marches him back into the bedroom — strips him
down — shoots him in the head — panics — runs out
without taking anything — kicks over the groceries
beating feet down the stairs. The doorman says the kid
came in around nine this morning, left twenty minutes
later — that's a long delivery, twenty minutes. The M.E.
guesses the guy's been dead since about seven, eight, nine
this morning — bingo.

LIEUTENANT
There you go . . . pick 'im up.

FRANK
(*rising*)
On the other hand you got the strange trim. This guy's a
swordsman extraordinaire, right? But he's also a stone
slob. They found pubic and head hair from something like
seven people in his bed. I mean he didn't even bother to

change the sheets — could be some lady last night gets
pissed because he fell asleep waiting for her to turn into a
pizza at midnight now that he's fucked her. She whips out
her .38, shoots him in his sex swamp of a bed, beats feet.
Hell hath no fury and all that.

> LIEUTENANT
> How do you know the trim is strange? Maybe it's a
> girlfriend?

> FRANK
> Nah, it's strange. You know how I know? The 45's. No
> one whips out their old 45's on anything but a first date
> when you're doing your "the wonder of me" thing. You
> know,
> > (singing)
> "Getting to know you." You bring them out to show the
> broad that you kept them after all these years — meaning
> you're a wonderful, sentimental individual. Who does that
> with someone they know? Who gives a shit once you get
> to know each other?
> > (beat; he got all hot and bothered)
> Anyways . . . my money's on the kid.

EXT: MALCOLM X HOUSING PROJECTS — 9:00 P.M.

Frank and Serafino park in front of the projects. The streets are
filled with teenagers and kids. the project is a hell hole of garbage,
noise and promised violence.

Frank and Serafino walk from their car towards a building entrance.
A half dozen hoody sullen young men stand in their path.

> FRANK
> (casually)
> You got the grenades?

> SERAFINO
> I'll *shout* these motherfuckers to death.

Frank walks right up to these dudes as if he's going to plow through
them. His gait is so swift that they involuntarily step back.

> FRANK
> How ya doing, fellas, how's school?

Frank keeps moving for the building.

> KID
> (*recovering*)
> School . . . what's that, something to eat?

> FRANK
> (*laughs*)
> Take care, fellas.
> (*almost as an afterthought*)
> Hey . . . where's Quawi live . . . ten what . . .

Kids turn numbly. Frank shrugs. It's to be expected.

INT: LOBBY

Graffiti, trash, burned-out mailboxes.

There's two six-year-old kids running through the halls even though it's late.

> FRANK
> (*to the kids*)
> Hey . . . Hey!

They halt.

> FRANK
> (*dramatically*)
> Who's Mister Big?

> KID
> (*grabbing his crotch*)
> *This* Mister Big.

Serafino laughs.

INT: HALLWAY ON THE TENTH FLOOR

Long gloomy, a cacophony of noise from behind twenty apartment doors — kitchen sizzle sounds, shouts, music.

Frank and Serafino stand in front of a door. Frank hitches up his pants, takes out his badge and bangs on the apartment door jarringly hard.

The door swings open to reveal a skinny, pop-eyed young woman, two kids coiled around her legs. Frank puts his badge in her face.

>   FRANK
>   (*friendly but with a rapid, slightly*
>   *intimidating delivery*)
> How ya doing. Detective Keller. Quawi Benjamin live
> here? You Quawi's wife?

>   WOMAN
>   (*slow, drawling*)
> I don't know no Quawi Benjamin. I ain't even married.

>   FRANK
>   (*rapid*)
> You're not married? You want to marry me? Get my wife
> outa paying me alimony?

She laughs nervously.

>   FRANK
>   (*rapid*)
> You don't wanna marry me? Quawi don't live here? So
> where's he live?
>   (*Frank puts his hand on the apartment door opposite*)
> Quawi lives here? This his apartment?

>   WOMAN
> I don't know no Quawi.

>   FRANK
> OK. Good night.

Frank knocks with his fist on the next apartment again jarringly loud.

The door swings open with violent speed. A huge, shirtless black man fills the doorway, but before he can say anything, Frank's got his badge in his face. The guy steps back. Frank leans forward.

> FRANK
> (*rapid*)
> Detective Keller . . . you always open your door that fast?

> BIG GUY
> Yeah, well I don't like people *bang*ing on it.

> FRANK
> You should get some *chimes* then. You Quawi Benjamin?

> BIG GUY
> *Who?*

> FRANK
> Quawi Benjamin . . . he your cousin?

> BIG GUY
> I don't know no Quawi.

> FRANK
> So where's he live . . . over here?

Frank puts his hand on another apartment door.

> BIG GUY
> I don't know no Quawi.

> SERAFINO
> How 'bout Little Man . . . he goes by the name Little Man
> sometimes.

> BIG GUY
> (*brightening*)
> Oh *Lit*tle Man! The dude with the corn rows?
> (*beat*)
> Nah I don't know him.

ANGLE — FRANK AND SERAFINO

at the tenth floor elevator. The elevator doors open. A young black
guy with corn rows starts to exit. Quawi Benjamin.

> FRANK
> Hey! You Theotis Clark?

> QUAWI
> Who?

> FRANK
> You're Theotis, right? We been looking for you.

> QUAWI
> I ain't no Theotis Clark.

> FRANK
> Yeah? What's your name?

> QUAWI
> Quawi Benjamin, man, what's *your* problem.

> SERAFINO
> Problem's all yours.

> QUAWI
> Aw shit, *what* . . . the supermarket sent you.
> (*speedy, angry*)
> I got to pay for them damn groceries? Hey any shit that dint spill? like in cans? I ain't paying for *them,* man. That cheap Chinese dude he put that right back on the shelves, make me pay for 'em, then bang out the dents, sell 'em anyhow. Anyways fuck it, I *quit*. You tell that Charlie Chan motherfucker take it out my pay.

Frank and Serafino look at each other.

> QUAWI
> Hey people call up the store send the nigger over with the groceries, you drag that shit three blocks cross a lobby, banging on the damn apartment door for ten minutes, no one home. Hell you throw the damn food down the stairs *too,* man.
> (*beat*)
> Aw hey *wait,* man. I get it now . . . Charlie Chan told you I *stole* the groceries, right? Shit, you wanna come in my house? Check my refrigerator?

Frank and Serafino look at each other.

> FRANK
> (*deadpan*)
> Bullshit.

CLOSE ON — QUAWI

He looks utterly confused.

INT: QUAWI'S APARTMENT — LIVING ROOM — DINING ROOM

Two young girls play on the carpet. An old lady lays under blankets on the couch watching color TV. The decor is bright red velour sheathed in plastic. Lots of framed photos.

Quawi comes bursting in through the door from the hallway. Serafino and Frank stroll in behind. The three women ignore the action.

Quawi, in angry tears, gestures towards the dinette table which is covered with textbooks, notebooks written in laborious script, all having to do with computer maintenance.

> QUAWI
> (*teary rage*)
> Check it out, motherfuckers! Check it *out*. I got three goddamn months for my goddamn degree — *don't* you be laying no bullshit *mur*der rap on me! I'm working too *hard* now.

> FRANK
> (*after a thoughtful beat*)
> What if I say we got an eyewitness says he saw you come out the apartment?

> QUAWI
> (*furious, despairing*)
> Uh-uh . . . uh-uh . . .

INT: CAR — QUEENS — 11:00 P.M.

Serafino is driving through a residential neighborhood of modest homes. Frank and Quawi in the back seat.

SERAFINO
Where's it again?

FRANK
Third from the end . . .

Serafino pulls up to a brick two family house.

ANGLE — FRANK AT THE DOOR

Frank knocks. Knocks again.

An old man, tough looking, maybe a little bombed, opens up. He stares at Frank, spies Serafino and Quawi on the sidewalk.

FRANK
I want you to look at somebody . . . tell me if we got the actor.

The old man continues to stare at Frank, nods and turns to go inside.

INT: APARTMENT

Spotless, spare, like Frank's.

Serafino and Frank sit in two easy chairs. The old man stands in the middle of the room, drink in hand. Quawi stands facing him, confused, nervous, nose to nose a foot apart. The old guy stares at Quawi, sips his drink, stares some more. Finally turns to a little stand up bar to freshen up his drink.

OLD MAN
(*back to the room*)
He ain't the one.

FRANK
You sure?

The old man turns suddenly choleric, red-faced.

OLD MAN
Whata you, goddamn *deaf*?

Frank nods for Serafino to take Quawi out.

> QUAWI
> (*to old man*)
> Hey yo . . . *thank* you.

Frank's alone with the old man.

> OLD MAN
> Jesus Christ . . . I say he's not the one . . .
> (*aping Frank ugly*)
> "You sure?"

Frank sighs, rises, goes nose to nose with the guy.

> FRANK
> (*beat*)
> You sure?

The old man turns redder, stops, regains some sense of himself.

> OLD MAN
> You know, Frankie, in my day guys like that, we didn't
> wind up asking questions until they come out of the
> hospital, and guys like you . . . you worked for the post
> office.

Frank nods, smiling, and starts to leave.

> OLD MAN
> Frankie . . . thanks.

> FRANK
> (*at the door*)
> Take care, Pop.

> OLD MAN
> (*draining his drink*)
> Will do.

INT: REC ROOM — MIDNIGHT

The detectives are calling it a night — Gruber, Serafino, Stark, Frank.

Lockers are being opened, slammed — midnight shift filtering in.

FRANK
(*talking to the three of them*)
So we're back to the broad . . . Actually I tell you the truth one thing about this lady, whoever she is, I admire her directness, you know? The guy fucks around? Falls asleep on her, whatever . . . bingo.
(*shoots his finger*)
Pop him in the head, it's all over. Other women, you do that, they like to put it here,
(*points to his side*)
or here,
(*points to his belly*)
let you walk around and bleed, you know? This one . . . bingo . . . it's the Evelyn Wood School of Speed Revenge, no muss, no fuss, no walking wounded, right, Gruber?

Gruber, enraged, flies at Frank, bulls him into his locker.

Before anyone can break it up, Frank has turned the balance and is beating the shit out of the larger man.

The guys pull him off. Gruber rises to his feet, dignified, bloody, and rips his wife's picture from Frank's locker door, then storms out.

CLOSE ON — FRANK

He looks like Gruber just ripped out his heart.

INT: FRANK'S APARTMENT — 1:00 A.M.

Minimal furniture — tasteful but barren.

We hear shuffling feet — dropped keys. The door finally opens, Frank half in the bag, enters.

Walks into his bedroom, sits on the bed, doesn't remove his jacket. Sighs through his nose. Rises.

INT: TOWER RECORDS — 2:00 A.M.

It's a massive fluorescently lit store awash in rock music and multiple videos.

Under the ice blue light Frank is the only person in the store over twenty-five.

Frank is browsing through tapes in the oldies section.

ANGLE

Frank in check-out line with an oldies tape.

The cashier is an alien-looking girl, 19, spiky but cute.

> FRANK
> (*self-conscious*)
> I feel like I should be looking for my teenager in here or something.

> GIRL
> (*mild, just being polite*)
> You got a teenage kid?

> FRANK
> (*embarrassed, laughing*)
> Me?

INT: LOBBY OF 365 WEST END AVENUE — THE CRIME SCENE BUILDING — 3:00 A.M.

WE SEE Frank enter, talk to the doorman, show his badge and a key. Frank is carrying a portable tape player and a bright yellow Tower Records bag.

INT: HALLWAY LEADING TO CRIME SCENE APARTMENT

There's yellow tape across the door to 10K. Frank gingerly removes it, unlocks the door, enters.

INT: CRIME SCENE APARTMENT

Frank turns on the lights. The place looks a bit like his. The wine glasses, the record player, the records have been removed. Frank moves into the bedroom.

INT: BEDROOM

The sheets have been stripped, a body outline has been marked over the bare mattress. Frank stares at it for a beat.

Frank returns to the living/dining room.

INT: LIVING/DINING ROOM

Frank removes his coat, sets down his tape player, puts in the tape.

As he tries to find a song we hear snatches of oldies, "Earth Angel," "In the Still of the Night," "Angel Baby," etc. Finally we hear "Sea of Love."

As the moody stroll music fills the apartment, Frank starts looking through closets, drawers again.

> "COME WITH ME, MY-HY LOVE
>   TO THE SEA, THE SEA UH-HUV LOVE,
>   I-I WANT TO TELL YOU HOW-OW MUCH,
>   I LOVE YOU . . ."

He sits cross-legged in the middle of the living room with an address book he found in the coffee table drawer, then lays back flat on the rug, falls asleep.

> "DO YOU REMEMBER WHEN WE MET
>   THAT'S THE DAY I KNEW YOU WERE MY PET,
>   I-I WANT TO TELL YOU HOW-OW MUCH
>   I LOVE YOU . . .
>   CO-OME WI-ITH ME-E, TO-O THE SEA . . ."

INT: LOBBY — 9:00 A.M.

Frank coming out of the elevator walking towards the doorman that he befriended the day before.

        FRANK
Hey, chief.

        DOORMAN
How's the job?

FRANK
We're looking for this lady who would've come out of his
place maybe about this time yesterday. You remember
anybody?

DOORMAN
(*wincing*)
Ah Christ . . . I dunno . . . you know if I'm lookin' to see
somebody I'll see 'em, if I'm not . . . Jesus . . . she might've
come when I'm in the package room, walk out behind me,
I'm hailing a cab or something . . .

FRANK
(*nods*)
Who was on duty the night before, maybe the guy saw her
come in.

DOORMAN
We didn't have nobody on the night before . . . the guy
got in a traffic accident — he was in the hospital — they
let the night go without coverage. Hey . . . this guy . . .
guys like Mackey, he probably has a *black book,* you
know what I mean?

The doorman pantomimes thumbing pages of a little book.

DOORMAN
I bet she's in the book.

Frank winks and wags the book he found.

EXT: BUILDING ENTRANCE

Frank exits under the canopy, looks around. Stops a guy smoking a
joint and walking two thin greyhounds.

FRANK
'Scuse me . . . you walk these guys around here this time
yesterday? . . . What are they, greyhounds?

Frank bends down to pet them. They shy away.

> GUY
> Please don't pet them.

Frank rises and shows his badge. The guy freaks, puts the joint behind his back. Frank ignores the joint.

> FRANK
> You must walk 'em like clockwork, right? You were here yesterday, this time? You notice a woman, young, youngish, wearing dinner type clothes coming out the building?

> GUY
> (*paranoid*)
> Uh-uh.

> FRANK
> Some lady looking a little freaked out, maybe rumpled dress up clothes?

> GUY
> Uh-uh.

> FRANK
> Nothin'? No one?

> GUY
> Uh-uh.

The guy jumps and hisses in pain. He's burned his fingers on the joint behind his back.

ANGLE

Frank leaning against a parked car in front of the canopy humming "Sea of Love."

An older woman is leaning out a second-story window, her forearms on a pillow like it's her usual post.

> FRANK
> Morning!

The woman looks down at him, doesn't like what she sees.

FRANK

You notice anybody you never seen before coming out the
building yesterday morning about this time?

WOMAN
(*insulted at his assumption*)
I mind my own damn business.

FRANK
(*raising his badge*)
I'm a detective, lady.

WOMAN
I don't give a shit who you are, you rude bastard.

She slams down the window.

FRANK
(*to himself*)
Book her, Dano.

ANGLE

Frank standing across the street from the building, still humming
"Sea of Love," still scanning the street for people who are habitually
in front of the building at this time every day.

The only other person on the corner is a swarthy, middle-aged man
in a suit leaning against the side of a private school. He looks
nervous. He's staring at Frank. When Frank turns to meet his gaze
he looks off. The guy's nervous alertness, his focus on Frank is very
weird.

Frank walks past the guy.

FRANK'S POV

WE SEE through the guy's open jacket that he's carrying a gun.
Frank keeps walking, goes to a pay phone.

FRANK
(*on phone*)
This is Detective Keller. You got any plainclothes,
anti-crime people I don't know about on West End and
Seventy-Seven? Something going down here I should

know about? No? Yeah, well there's a guy in front of Collegiate School who's heeled. There was a murder here yesterday morning, you want to get me some back up? . . . Thank you . . .

Frank hangs up and casually strolls past the guy again.

The guy seems tenser. He stares at Frank without turning away.

GUY'S POV

WE SEE Frank's gun over his left hip attached to his belt.

Frank looks wired. They're both staring at each other now without pretense — the guy straightens up off the school wall.

Frank's breathing is rapid. The other guy looks like he might have a heart attack.

They simultaneously draw their weapons on each other and start screaming.

> FRANK
> Don't fuckin' move, motherfucker!

> GUY
> *You* drop it! *You* drop it! *You* drop it!

Suddenly three squad cars come flying in on them, cops leap out, guns drawn, join in on the screaming.

There's eight drawn guns on the swarthy guy. Everybody yelling with adrenaline.

Suddenly there's the shriek of a school bell and under this canopy of death charges an army of elementary school kids spilling out on the sidewalk.

Seeing the kids, the guy quickly, suddenly puts his gun on the sidewalk, raises his arms.

Frank charges him, ramming him up against the wall as the kids freeze in awe.

Frank has his gun to the guy's head. The guy starts shouting in broken English.

GUY
I am a bodyguard! Body-guard! I am not know who *you*
are! I am doing a *job* here!

FRANK
(*shaking still*)
Shut up!

CLOSE ON — AN IRANIAN KID

in a blazer. Eight years old. Comes up to the spread-eagled guy.

KID
(*in Iranian; casual, regal*)
What happened?

GUARD
(*in Farsi*)
Explain to them who I am.

KID
(*to Frank*)
He is Iman my bodyguard against bad people. I have been
kidnapped twice. Please call my father at the United
Nations. We are Iranian refugees.

FRANK
(*angry*)
Oh yeah?

Frank whips through the guy's wallet.

CLOSE ON — GUN PERMIT

and other documentation to back up the kid's claim.

CLOSE ON — FRANK

still trying to catch his breath, gain his composure.

FRANK'S POV

Cops and kids stare at him expectantly.

Frank walks away.

INT: SQUAD ROOM — 5:00 P.M.
CLOSE ON — FRANK'S DESK

He's going over a handwritten list of women's names, checking them against the address book he found in the coffee table.

Some of the names on the list have been already crossed out.

> SQUAD ROOM CLERK
> Frank?

Frank looks up. The clerk is with a young woman in a skirt suit.

> WOMAN
> I'm Carmen Cohen, you called me about John Mackey?

> FRANK
> (*standing up after crossing out Carmen Cohen
> on his list*)
> Yeah. Thanks for coming in.

They both sit.

> CARMEN
> (*laughing, nervous*)
> What, did he do something? Break the law?

> FRANK
> (*after an awkward beat*)
> He's dead . . . he was killed . . . shot.

> CARMEN
> (*laughing*)
> What!

She continues laughing.

> CARMEN
> Oh Christ I'm sorry.
> (*still laughing*)

> FRANK
> (*he's seen this before. Mildly*)
> What's so funny?

CARMEN
Nothing! It's *awful*! I can't help it. What do people do
when you hear stuff like that?

She starts laughing again.

CARMEN
I'm so embarrassed!

Frank shrugs.

ANGLE — 5:30 P.M.

Frank fingerprinting another young listee, Deena MacKenzie.

FRANK
(*rolling her fingers gently against the ink pad*)
This stuff is hard to get off, I'm warning you.

DEENA
This is kind of thrilling, being fingerprinted.

FRANK
Yeah? I never thought so.

DEENA
I'm a real murder suspect huh?
(*winks, great smile*)
That's kind of sexy.

FRANK
Oh yeah?

DEENA
(*unabashed*)
Yeah.

Frank looks away, laughing.

CLOSE ON — FRANK'S LIST

Most names are crossed off.

SERAFINO
(*two desks down*)
What's up?

> FRANK

Nothin' from nothin' . . . The prints on that wine glass are
museum quality too . . . Not a lot of tears for this guy,
I'll tell you that . . .

The squad clerk escorts another woman over to Frank's desk.

FRANK'S POV

The woman is attractive, thirty-five, staring straight at Frank all
business. It's Denice.

> FRANK
> (*rises, thrown*)

You looking for Gruber?

> DENICE

For you.

> FRANK

For me? You want to go get some coffee or something?
Cappuccino? Espresso? Double Espresso?

> DENICE

Frank, you have to leave me alone from now on . . .

> FRANK

Hey, Denice.

> DENICE
> (*sitting down*)

You beat up my husband . . .

> FRANK

Beat up . . . hey . . . he started . . .

> DENICE
> (*shaking her head sadly*)

"He started." That's what a *kid* says.

> FRANK

Well he did.

> DENICE

You know what else a kid does?

She produces the ringed picture of herself that Gruber ripped out of Frank's locker. Frank looks at it, embarrassed.

> DENICE
> (*in a childish sing song*)
> Nyah nyah nyah nyah . . . real clever, Frank.

> FRANK
> (*mortified*)
> I dunno, I was hurt . . . it was stupid . . .
> (*beat*)
> You know, Denice . . . I waited until I was thirty-nine years old before I got married. Why'd I do that? You know why?
> (*Frank tries to look cagey, wise, but he can't answer his own question*)

> DENICE
> (*laughing*)
> Frank . . . We get married, all you do is hang out with the guys, drink, screw those . . . cop *pig*lets up at the bars . . . lot of fun for me . . . lots of center . . . I cut you loose, nothing stopping you. All of a sudden you're lonely, you want me . . . woof . . . too much . . . too much.

> FRANK
> Hey . . . I'm in the trenches here every night . . .

> DENICE
> C'mon . . . don't give me that "trench" bullshit . . . you're not in a squad car . . . it's *you*, Frank . . . you're one of the boys . . . good for you, enjoy it . . . you don't have to make excuses. You hate to go home, that's that.

> FRANK
> (*tense, confused, heated*)
> I *can't* go home!
> (*awkward beat*)
> Something's up with me now.
> (*whispering*)
> The nights are real *bad*.

> DENICE
> (*studying him*)
> Yeah well, I know about bad nights.
> (*beat*)
> Look . . . I just need another kind of man than you, you
> know what I mean?

> FRANK
> (*dryly*)
> Donald Gruber . . . a man among men.

> DENICE
> (*defensive, heated*)
> You *bet* . . . he's *there* . . . he's steady like a mountain . . .
> he don't screw around, he don't drink and he sleeps like
> a *rock*.

> FRANK
> Denice . . . do you have any *ink*ling of how *bor*ing a
> *sum*mary of a human being that was?

Denice shrugs, stares at him, grins sheepishly. It looks like Frank
just scored. Frank grins. He puts his hand over Denice's, leans forward.

> FRANK
> (*whispering, confidential*)
> Straight up . . . how's making love with him compared to
> making love with us. You tell me it's as good, I'll call you
> a liar to your face.

Denice stares at him deadpan for a long beat then breaks out in a
radiant grin. Frank beams in triumph.

> DENICE
> (*leaning forward*)
> I'm pregnant.

> FRANK
> (*stunned, whipped*)
> How do you know it's yours?

INT: DETECTIVES' PROMOTION PARTY — CHURCH
BASEMENT — SOMEWHERE IN N.Y.C. — 9:00 P.M.

Two hundred detectives milling around, drinking and eating at a
party put on by ten borough detectives who just received grade
promotions.

CLOSE ON — A DETECTIVE

short, fat, sweating, in a jogging suit, his gun over his hip, moving
through the crowd holding aloft two six-foot-long heroes on plat-
ters, one in each hand.

CLOSE ON — THE MAKESHIFT BAR

Two armed detectives working frantically as bartenders (free
booze).

The cops come in all sizes and ages, all styles of dress from happy
to shoe salesman to chairman-of-the-board natty.

The mood is boozer-friendly. Clusters of men laughing hard —
shaking hands a lot.

CLOSE ON — FRANK

drunk, sweating, squaring off with a young Chinese undercover
detective who looks like a youth gang member save for his .38 in its
belt holster. They're going through a pantomime of a kickbox/Kung
Fu sparring match. Frank is sloppy but fast, despite his drinking.

They're surrounded by laughing detectives.

Frank and the Chinese guy shake hands.

> STARK
> I keep forgetting you know that stuff.

> FRANK
> (*slightly drunk brag*)
> Hey . . . I don't like getting hurt. I get in a beef I hit the
> guy *fast* and a *lot* . . . I don't like getting hurt . . . know
> what I mean?

STARK

Hey listen up . . . I was talking to some guys here from the
one oh nine in Queens? . . . There's a guy there caught a
case like yours.

FRANK

What do you mean?

STARK

Nah I was tellin' them what was cooking with us, you
know, that one of our guys caught a real good murder . . .
They got a guy caught one just like it . . . you know, face
down taxpayer, back of the head in his own bed . . .
(*imitates and pantomimes a gun being fired*)

ANGLE — SHERMAN TOUHEY

Forty-five, fat, beaming, mischievous-faced, easy laugher — a warm,
good-time Charley in a three-piece suit — making the same gun
finger gesture and noise as Stark just did.

SHERMAN

The bullet we can't do nothing with.
(*laughs*)
The asshole had a steel headboard.
(*makes a splat noise*)
Who the hell has a steel headboard?
(*laughs again*)
The bullet's like this . . .
(*holds his fingertips a fraction apart*)

FRANK

We got a *great* bullet . . . Got any prints?

SHERMAN

(*shrugs*)
Yeah . . . nothing showed up on the files though.

FRANK

Let's compare tomorrow.

SHERMAN

You know something? I think my guy got done by a
female.

FRANK
How's that . . .

SHERMAN
We're talking a four star ladies' man here, OK?

FRANK
Yeah? My guy too.

SHERMAN
Hey . . . you play, you pay, right? My wedding night?
I wake up, my wife's got the tattoo needle, the eyeshades.
I look down . . . She's got "Property of . . ." on my balls.
(*laughing*)
I'm only kidding, but you catch my drift? This guy, I had
to interview a dozen broads he's been knobbin' that
month, that we *know* of, right? On top of that we found
the guy's got a stack of thirty letters from this singles
magazine he placed an ad in? He didn't even get around
to opening the envelopes yet.

FRANK
You find any records there?

SHERMAN
What do you mean, files?

FRANK
Records . . . My guy had all these forty-fives . . . old
records . . . there was even one playing on the turntable
when the super broke in . . . "Sea of Love" . . . remember
that one?

SHERMAN
"Sea of Love" . . . yeah, how's it go?

FRANK
(*singing in a self-conscious low murmur*)
Come with me-e, my-hy love
Come with me to the Sea-e-e of Love.

Suddenly Sherman chimes in with a high sweet tenor.

>   SHERMAN
>   (*moving, snapping like a pro*)
>   Ah wanna tell you . . . how'ow much, I love you . . .
>   Do you remember when we met . . .

He gestures for Frank to keep singing. Sherman's voice is so powerful and beautiful that conversation stops in the area around them and a half dozen of the 35- to 45-year-old detectives haltingly join in.

>   SHERMAN (WITH A GROWING CHORUS)
>   That's the day I knew you were my pet . . .

CLOSE ON — SHERMAN

. . . red beatific cherubic face.

>   SHERMAN
>   Ah wanna tell you how-ow much, I love you . . .

SHERMAN laughs uproariously.

INT: TOWER RECORDS — 2:00 A.M.

Frank, somewhat plastered, heads for the oldies section, while keeping his eyes on that cute punky cashier. He's humming "Sea of Love." He grabs a tape without looking and heads for the register ready to put the moves on this girl.

She smiles at him with recognition. Just as he's about to say something, a tall, handsome, chalk white punky guy with charcoal hair slides between her and her high stool, grabs her around the waist and buries his nose in her neck.

Laughing she rings up his tape.

>   FRANK
>   (*thwarted, thrown*)
>   Hey guess what.

>   GIRL
>   (*to Frank*)
>   What.
>   (*to boyfriend*)

Will you stop?
(*laughing*)

FRANK
I just found out like an hour ago? I'm gonna be a daddy.

EXT: STREET IN QUEENS IN FRONT OF FRANK'S FATHER'S
HOUSE — 4:30 A.M.

Frank pulling up to the curb. There's a light on inside. The rest of
the world is dead asleep.

ANGLE — FRANK AT THE DOOR

His father opens up, hasn't been to bed yet either, drink in hand,
turns towards the interior of the house. Frank follows him in.

INT: SCREENED IN PORCH

Frank and his father sit, drinks in hand. Full moon above, making
the yard gleam like bones.

FRANK
(*drinking*)
Hey . . . I like kids . . . I'm not . . . I de*liv*ered one . . . you
remember that? That lady in the projects? . . . just like in
the newspapers . . . cop delivers baby . . . You delivered a
kid too, right? I remember when I was little you come
home . . .

FATHER
(*far off*)
I don't remember . . . probably.

FRANK
And I don't know how many kids I *saved* from one thing
or another over the years . . . choking on things . . . fires
. . . the *par*ents . . . all I'm saying is . . . is that to *hav*e a
kid, like Denice is . . . I . . . you know what I'm afraid of?
. . . I'm forty-two, Pop . . . I have a kid . . . all you think
about is getting old . . . when the kid's graduating high
school I'll be sixty-nine, the kid graduates college I'll be

seventy-three . . . you know what I mean? You start *dy*ing the minute the kid starts *liv*ing . . .

> FATHER
> (*suddenly coming back from glassy-land*)
> Denice is having a kid?

Frank rolls his eyes in exasperation.

> FATHER
> I thought you broke up with her?

Frank shakes his head in sadness and frustration — drains his drink.

INT: LOBBY OF 365 WEST END AVENUE — 8:00 P.M.

Frank drags his ass in past the doorman who's pacing, hands clasped behind his back. Throws Frank a salute.

INT: MURDER VICTIM'S BEDROOM — 4:00 P.M.

Frank dead asleep sprawled out making an "X" with the marked body outline.

Suddenly the doorbell rings. Frank shoots straight up, dazed, disoriented, frantically trying to figure out where the hell he is.

INT: APARTMENT DOOR

Frank, disheveled, dopey with sleep, opens the door on an attractive, slightly chubby woman dressed sportily as if for a foray to a singles bar. She's got half a dozen silver mylar balloons tied to her arms and bobbing over her head.

> WOMAN
> (*giggling*)
> Silver moons
> A lifetime of Junes
> Old rock tunes . . .

The woman stops reciting, waiting expectantly for Frank's reaction.

FRANK
. . . and a bowl of stewed prunes . . . who the hell are you?
What is this, Serafino sent you over? Well I got no money,
honey, plus I'm not in the mood so goodbye.

Frank closes the door in her face, then quickly swings it open.

FRANK
Who am I? What's my name?

WOMAN
(*angry*)
Hey . . . I don't like being treated . . .

FRANK
(*sharply*)
I said what's my *name!*

WOMAN
(*scared*)
John Mackey?

INT: LIVING ROOM

Frank and the balloon lady, Gina Gallagher, sit on opposite sides of
the room.

She's softly weeping as Frank reviews his notes.

FRANK
(*still disheveled*)
So you read his ad in *City Singles* magazine.

GINA
(*still wearing her balloons tied on her arms*)
I don't know why I'm crying, I never even got to *meet* him
. . . it's just so *sad* somebody dying.

FRANK
You wrote him a letter or you called him . . .

GINA
I wrote him, then he called me. Fate sucks, I swear.

> FRANK
> (*kindly*)
> Gina . . . maybe you'd feel better if you took those
> balloons off.

> GINA
> (*morosely*)
> They're the only things keeping me up.

Frank poorly controls an explosion of sniggers. People are just too
much, sometimes.

INT: SQUAD ROOM — 7:30 P.M.

Frank walks in, sees Sherman Touhey, the fat singing detective, sitting at Frank's desk going over some files. Sherman looks up, grins.

> SHERMAN
> (*slightly uptight*)
> The Loo said I could go through the jacket on your case
> . . . I was waiting for you like two hours you know, so I
> finally got down . . .

> FRANK
> (*not liking anyone going through his stuff*)
> Oh yeah?

> SHERMAN
> Hey! Guess what! The prints match! My guy, your guy
> . . . the same do-er . . . ain't that grand?

> FRANK
> (*excited*)
> Are you *kid*ding me? Yeah well I got one for *you*, my man.
> Your guy put an ad in a singles magazine, right? You told
> me that, right?

> SHERMAN
> *City Singles.*

> FRANK
> Well bingo to that . . . my man's in there too.
> (*reciting*)

Silver balloons endless Junes old rock tunes I'll put it in
your moon Wire Palladin . . . something like that.

SHERMAN
You want to hear *my* guy?
Sugar and spice
Fire and ice
We all lost a love
But lightning *can* strike twice.

FRANK
This lady, man,
(*winks*)
she's in the crosshairs.

SHERMAN
The poetry lover.

FRANK
More like she hates it, you know what I mean?
(*Frank mimes a gun with his fingers*)

SHERMAN
Hey I talked to my Loo. Me and you a two man task force
on this, what do you think?

FRANK
(*wary*)
Queens or here?

SHERMAN
Hey . . . I live and work in Queens all my life . . .

Frank waits warily for Sherman's answer.

SHERMAN
(*laughing*)
Just gimme a goddamn desk, man. Jesus I'll take a *toi*let
seat . . . just get me outa there!

FRANK
(*relieved*)
Hey . . . let me introduce you around.

> SHERMAN
> Nah, hey I'll catch 'em tomorrow. I gotta bolt. My wife's
> gonna kill me. I gotta tuxedo fitting now.

> FRANK
> Tuxedo . . . what you have a lounge act?

> SHERMAN
> I wish . . . nah . . . my daughter's getting married Sunday
> out on the Island . . .
> > (*beat*)
> Hey . . . you like weddings?

INT: REC ROOM — 10:00 P.M.

Frank's getting something out of his locker. He's humming "Sea of
Love."

FRANK'S POV

WE SEE Gruber making himself tea. Gruber's face shows signs of
the fight.

Gruber straightens up sipping his tea. They're the only two guys in
the room.

> GRUBER
> I caught a hold up down on Columbus, you want to take
> a ride?

> FRANK
> > (*awkward*)
> Yeah, uh . . . I can't, I got taken off the rotation for this
> Mackey case.

> GRUBER
> > (*shrugging*)
> Yeah? No sweat . . . Good luck on that . . .

Gruber walks out with his tea.

> FRANK
> > (*moves to the doorway*)
> Gruber . . .

Gruber slowly turns so as not to spill the tea.

FRANK
Congratulations . . . I heard ah . . .

Gruber grins, turns to his desk.

INT: CATERING HALL — LONG ISLAND
CLOSE ON — A BAG PIPER

playing a dignified tune. The bag piper is wearing his kilt and
tam over a police uniform — an Emerald Society marching band
musician.

WE SEE he's playing at the entrance to the catering hall chapel.
Couples, all ages, dressed to the nines, are filing in past him. The
men are putting on yarmulkas, ditching cigarettes, draining drinks.
Beauty parlor hairdos and lipstick stained cigarettes for the women.

INT: CHAPEL

Sherman Touhey in a pearl-gray tux with dark gray piping and a
ruffled shirt is slowly escorting his twenty-year-old daughter down
the aisle to the rabbi. A cantor sounding like Richard Tucker is
wailing away in an operatic sobby voice.

The daughter is frozen with the moment but Sherman is tossing off
wisecracks, cracking jokes, and shmoozing with the people in the
pews closest to the aisle as he passes.

WE SEE Frank in a three-piece suit at the end of his bench as Sherman passes by.

SHERMAN
(stage whisper)
Hey Frank!
(he lifts his yarmulka)
I ain't even Jewish . . . it's her mother's side.

SHERMAN'S DAUGHTER
(hissing)
Daddy . . . shut up . . .

Sherman winks at Frank and proceeds down the aisle to give away the bride.

INT: THE PARTY ROOM
CLOSE ON — A ROCK BAND

with a young female lead singer.

She's doing a semi-lame cover of Queen's white soul hit "Another One Bites the Dust" as dozens of cops in suits dance with their wives — a middle-aged armed American Bandstand.

Frank sits at his assigned place-carded seat at the edge of the dance floor watching these outer-borough cops kick up. He's also watching the young singer.

Frank wears the embarrassed smile of someone who is the only stranger in a sea of intimate celebrants.

Three couples at Frank's table are yakking it up as Sherman, making the glad-hand rounds, comes by.

> SHERMAN
> Hey! Hey! Hey!

> WOMAN
> (breathy, dramatically earnest)
> She looks *gorgeous*, Sherm . . .

> SHERMAN
> You'd never know she's knocked up three months, would you?

Everybody laughs and waves him off. Sherman turns to Frank, leans down.

> SHERMAN
> (grinning, under his breath)
> It's fucking true.

Frank doesn't know what to say so he keeps smiling.

> SHERMAN
> What the hell, so was her mother. You don't love 'em less, I tell you that.

ANGLE — FRANK

watches as Sherman, on the bandstand, mike in hand, tears streaming down his cheeks, sings "Sunrise Sunset" (*Fiddler on the Roof*) to his daughter and his guests. Not a dry eye in the room except Frank, who is checking out the girl singer taking five in the archway between the room and the lobby.

ANGLE — FRANK

standing next to her in the archway. We still hear Sherman singing.

>   SINGER
> *You* look bored . . .

>   FRANK
> I just don't know anybody.

>   SINGER
> They say half the people here are cops.

>   FRANK
> Oh yeah?

>   SINGER
> Are you a cop?

>   FRANK
> Yup.

>   SINGER
> So if I offered you a hit off a joint you'd bust me, right?

ANGLE — DRESSING ROOM

Frank takes a toke as the band watches him expressionlessly.

>   BAND MEMBER #1
> They say cops get the best stuff.

>   FRANK
>   (*exhaling*)
> Oh yeah?

>   BAND MEMBER #2
> You carrying a gun?

>   FRANK
> Maybe.

>   BAND MEMBER #3
> You ever shoot anybody?

>   FRANK
>   (*suddenly stoned, relaxed, candid*)
> I don't like these questions . . . you make me feel like a
> frigging extraterrestrial. I'm a person, OK?

He starts to leave, turns.

>   FRANK
> Look . . . I'm sorry . . . thanks for the dope. I appreciate
> it.

He takes his gun from the rear of his belt, shows it.

>   FRANK
> Here . . . .38 police special standard issue. Yes, I've shot
> people . . . one time a guy in the leg who tried to mug
> me and another time a guy who was shooting at *me*. Him
> I shot in the neck. Nobody died. I'm really stoned.
> Thanks again.

ANGLE — FRANK

stoned in his seat.

Watching couples dance slow as the band plays "Feelings."

Frank intensely watches each couple, looks down as if deep in
thought then studies them again.

Sherman slides into the seat next to him, his bow tie hanging and
his collar unbuttoned.

>   SHERMAN
> You want to dance with my twin sister?

>   FRANK
>   (*abruptly*)
> OK . . . You want to know how we catch her? We put our
> own ad in.

SHERMAN
Say what?

FRANK
City Singles magazine. We put our own ad in. A hundred
guys place ads in there a month. They get thirty to fifty
responses each. That's five thousand women minus
multiple responses say four thousand women. What are
we gonna do, track down four thousand women? Hell no
. . . we know she's into the rhyming ads, right? So we put
in a rhyming ad moon June spoon sand dune. Set up dates
with the thirty, forty, fifty ladies who write us, take 'em
out, get their prints on some wine glasses at some
restaurant. Bingo, she's dropped.

SHERMAN
(*laughing*)
I love it . . . it's horseshit but I love it.

FRANK
There was only *three* ads from men that rhymed in that
magazine last month. We know she went out with two of
them — incidentally we should visit the third guy, see if
he's dead but I'm telling you . . . this is a lock.

SHERMAN
(*laughing*)
You're bats.

FRANK
You know something? It's a good thing that it's guys
getting popped. A hundred women put ads in that rag a
month. You know how many guys answer a hundred
women? I checked with the editor.
(*beat*)
Twenty *thou*sand . . .

INT: CAR — BRONX — TWO DAYS LATER

Frank and Sherman are driving to the home of Raymond Brown,
the third "poet" in that issue of *City Singles*.

> FRANK
> (*reciting from the magazine*)
> Loneliness and silence
> envelop a heart that pounds like thunder
> all the love I have inside
> is ripping me asunder
> this city is a raging sea
> But my love is like a rock . . .

> SHERMAN
> (*giggling*)
> So come answer this ad and help me clean my clock.

> FRANK
> Hey c'mon . . . give the guy a break . . . he sounds like a
> major lonelyhearts.

Silence for a beat then they both break into uncontrollable sniggers.

EXT: FRONT DOOR OF A BRICK TWO-FAMILY HOUSE

Frank knocks, idly plays with his shield in its leather case. A woman answers the door, fortyish, housedress.

> FRANK
> Good afternoon. I'm Detective Frank Keller, this is
> Detective Sherman Touhey. Does ah, Raymond Brown
> live here?

The woman is suddenly enveloped around the legs by three little kids. The biggest (eight) bellows back into the house.

> KID
> *Daa-Deee!*

The woman stares at the detectives.

> ALL THE KIDS
> (*in chorus*)
> *Daa-Deee!*

A burly, hair-on-the-back hulk comes lumbering to the door. Raymond Brown.

OLDEST KID
Dad! They're *cops!*

RAYMOND BROWN
What's up, gents . . .

WIFE
(*finally speaking; taut*)
What he do . . .

BROWN
(*irritated*)
I dint do nothin' . . . would you take that face off please?
. . . Jesus Christ . . .

WIFE
(*angry*)
Yeah . . . you never do *no*thing . . . not you.

KID
Dad, what you do?

OTHER KID
Daddy's got a gun! But we can't play with it.

Raymond in the midst of this irritating cacophony spies the copy of
City Singles in Sherman's hand and his face goes white.

ANGLE — RAYMOND BROWN'S BACKYARD

The three men sit on beat up chaise longues surrounded by toys.

RAYMOND
(*whispering*)
I want to tell you guys something . . . I love my family.

SHERMAN
(*reassuringly*)
Hey Raymond, no kidding, we don't give a shit . . . all's
we want is the names of the women you went out with . . .
and all the letters you got back from the other ladies.

> RAYMOND
> (*whispers*)
> Guys . . . I swear . . . I didn't go out with *any* of them . . .
> I threw the letters away . . . I didn't have the *heart*.

Raymond winces and tilts his head for them to look up and behind them.

FRANK'S POV

WE SEE Raymond's wife hovering behind a curtained window.

> FRANK
> (*whispering*)
> Raymond . . . you go to the trouble to make up that
> beautiful poem about loneliness and silence . . . you spring
> three hundred dollars to put an ad in the paper, you spring
> another five yards a month for some love nest in the
> Village, fifty bucks for a post office box and you didn't
> even go *out* with any of them? Please, please . . .

> SHERMAN
> (*whispering*)
> You know what's the worst part of being a cop? Eight
> hours a day all you hear from people is lies . . . I didn't do
> it . . . I wasn't there, it was the other guy . . . blah this,
> blah that.

> RAYMOND
> (*almost in tears*)
> I swear on my child's eyes.

EXT: UPPER WEST SIDE

Sherman and Frank walk around the upper West Side.

> SHERMAN
> I feel for the guy . . . fidelity is an *art,* marriage is an art
> *form.* You cultivate a happy home like you cultivate an
> *oy*ster.

> FRANK
> You sound like a fortune cookie.

SHERMAN
. . . Hey I been married twenty-four years, that's more
than half my life . . . I fucked around once . . . thirteen
years ago and I only did it one night . . . well two nights
but . . . what I'm *saying* is . . . there's a reason why
you should be faithful, it doesn't work if you're not . . .
I know.

FRANK
When I was married? I got *laid* with other women but I
never made *love* to them.

SHERMAN
You sound like a song lyric.

FRANK
Me? Hey, you're the guy that cultivates oysters.

SHERMAN
(*shrugging*)
I like oysters.
(*beat*)
So what do we do?

FRANK
I *told* you what we do.

INT: LIEUTENANT'S OFFICE

Frank and Sherman are pitching the plan to the Loo.

LIEUTENANT
What's the matter, Frankie, you're not getting enough?

FRANK
Hey, Loo, trust me . . . thirty sit downs, thirty sets of
prints. Miss Wrong . . . We got her . . . upstairs gives us
three hundred to put the ad in the magazine, we spring
for a few vinos, a chef salad or two . . . we bag the
wineglasses, the cigarette butts, some silverware . . .
it's all over.

LIEUTENANT
You think I'm gonna ask the zone commander for three hundred bucks so one of my guys can go out on *dates?* Plus *bar* tabs? *Restaurant* tabs?

FRANK
Say it's for a drug buy . . .

LIEUTENANT
No . . .

FRANK
C'mon . . . we're gonna nail Miss Big . . .

LIEUTENANT
No.

INT: TOWER RECORDS — 2:00 A.M.

Frank is prowling the aisles, one eye on the punky cashier.

It's a quiet night.

A long-haired bruiser obviously messed up on something walks through the security arch setting off the alarm with his stolen goods.

CASHIER
Security!

Nothing happens.

CASHIER
Hey! Security!

As the guy continues for the exit no one comes to stop him and the cashier whips around the register and gamely tries to block his path herself. The guy throws her into a counter and continues on his lurching way.

Like a bullet Frank dives at the back of his knees, flopping him on his back, flips him over and has him hand-cuffed at an arm breaking angle.

As an utterly stoned security guard staggers in, red-eyed, brandishing a nightstick, Frank shows his badge.

>   FRANK
> Call for back up, shithead.

Frank on his ass stares across the belly down handcuffed bad guy to the punky cashier who's also on her ass.

INT: FRANK'S BEDROOM — NEXT MORNING

Frank lays in bed watching the cashier get dressed.

>   CASHIER
> You like compliments?

>   FRANK
> Sure.

>   CASHIER
> You are like the oldest guy I ever was in bed with but I
> swear you have a better body than like half the guys
> I slept with half your age.

Frank stares at her. She looks pleased with herself.

INT: STUDIO — GREENWICH VILLAGE — MORNING
CLOSE ON — RAYMOND BROWN'S FACE

He's laying on his cheek in bed staring calmly at nothing. A trickle of blood slides down his jawline from behind his ear.

In the background we hear the door close. His killer has just left.

INT: FRANK'S BEDROOM

Frank, alone, nude in bed, stares at the ceiling. His phone begins to ring.

INT: THE LIEUTENANT'S OFFICE — A FEW HOURS LATER

Frank and Sherman stare at the Lieutenant. He stares back at them, one hand reflectively covering his mouth.

> LIEUTENANT
>
> You are not to take them out of the restaurant. You are not to lay a hand on them. You are not to have *int*ercourse with them. You chit chat, get prints and *split*. You wear a *wire*. We're gonna have a sound van outside and a two-man backup at another table. Keep the restaurant receipts.

> FRANK
>
> What's with the backup . . . What to I need a wire for, what do you think she's gonna do, confess? Shoot me? We're in a restaurant.

> LIEUTENANT
>
> Make me happy, OK? Who's writing the ad . . . who's the poet?

Frank and Sherman look at each other.

INT: FRANK'S APARTMENT — 11:00 P.M.

Frank comes exploding through the front door, his arms filled with shopping bags which he flings on the dining room table.

He vanishes into the kitchen, re-emerges in a full-length apron with a vacuum, some cleaning rags, a few big bowls (the room is a joint dining/living room), races back into the kitchen, comes back in with an armload of liquor bottles.

At breakneck speed, he dusts and vacuums, fluffs couches, then furiously tears open the grocery bags, filling the bowls with bridge mix, Triscuits, Fritos, lining up the liquor bottles, stacking plastic cups, etc.

Suddenly his father, drink in hand, staggers from the bedroom.

> FRANK'S DAD
>
> What are you having, a mahjongg party?

Startled, still in his full-length apron, Frank yells, pretzels go flying and he has his gun half way out of his rear holster before he realizes who the interloper is.

FRANK'S DAD
(*unmoved*)
You shoot me, Frankie, I'll spill my drink.

ANGLE — 1:00 A.M.

The room is filled with cigarette and cigar smoke.

Frank, Sherman, Struk, Dargan and Serafino are fairly ripped as they sit around Frank's dining room table shouting out possible poems to each other.

Bathroom traffic is heavy. There're pretzels on the floor. Frank's dad sits alone calmly drinking in the shadows.

STARK
OK, OK, here we go.
Roses are red
Violets are blue
I got a thing yea long
And it's all for you.

They shout him down, laughing and coughing.

SERAFINO
Hey! Hey! Check it out.
Windswept hallways in my heart
Echo the blackness of eternity . . .

He gets shouted down.

FRANK
C'mon, c'mon, get happy, happy. You guys sound like jumpers and flashers. I'm gonna be sitting across from Morticia Adams with that stuff.

DARGAN
Hey she's a shooter, right?

STARK
(*ominous doom — melodramatic*)
The bells! The bells!

FRANK
C'mon, we're lookin' for love here . . . a little hopefulness . . . How about we just throw her "Sea of Love"?

A phone rings. Serafino picks up.

> SERAFINO
> Dargan!

> DARGAN
> (*groans to his feet; on the phone*)
> Yeah . . . hey . . . I'm workin' . . . when I'm done workin'
> . . . whenever that is . . . hey, read my lips . . .

They crack up and repeat "read my lips."

> DARGAN
> (*one word at a time*)
> I am on official police business . . . I will see you when I
> get home . . . goodbye.

> SHERMAN
> (*mocking a rolling-pin housewife*)
> C'mere, you worm!

Suddenly we hear Frank's dad in the shadows start to recite as they
shoosh each other.

> FRANK'S DAD
> I live alone within myself
>   like a hut within the woods
> I keep my heart high upon a shelf
>   barren of other goods
> I need another's arms to reach for it
>   and place it where it belongs
> I need another's touch and smile
>   to fill my hut with songs.

There's a respectful silence, half amused, half touched, all bombed.

> FRANK
> (*gently*)
> That's pretty corny, Dad.

> SHERMAN
> I think it's beautiful.

SERAFINO
You just make that up, Mister K?

FRANK'S DAD
Frank's mother wrote that in high school . . . 1934 . . .
she was a goddamn beautiful person.
(*beat*)
G'head, use it . . . she would like that . . . she would like
that very much . . .

ANGLE — 4:00 A.M.

Guys staggering to the door in a drunken shuffle. Somebody's dead
asleep in an easy chair. Frank's father is asleep on the couch.

ANGLE — FIFTEEN MINUTES LATER

Frank carrying his father in his arms into the bedroom.

FRANK'S FATHER
(*half asleep — bombed*)
Alls I'm saying by coming here tonight is I'm worried
about you. You shouldn't be like me years on down from
now — it's not right — I didn't mean to come here other
than to say that . . . where you takin' me . . . am I
walking? I'm walking, right?

They disappear into the black mouth of the bedroom.

ANGLE — MID-MORNING

The smokey living room is blasted with light and party debris.
Frank is sprawled belly down on his own sofa. The guy in the easy
chair is still dead asleep from 4:00 A.M.

ANGLE — FRANK'S BEDROOM

Frank's father is on his back, mouth agape, eyes shut, like a corpse
on Frank's bed.

Frank saunters into the room wearing a towel, regards his father,
does a mild double take, gently feels for a pulse in his neck.

Frank's father, eyes still closed, gently pats the hand that is feeling
to see if he's still alive.

INT: SQUAD ROOM — A FEW DAYS LATER
CLOSE ON — THE BULLETIN BOARD

A page of *City Singles* magazine — forty boxed pleas for companionship — is pinned to the bulletin board. Frank's mother's poem is outlined in red magic marker for the perusal of all. It's dead center on the page.

As the CAMERA HOLDS ON the tear sheet, we hear shouts and curses as some unseen act of violence takes place in the squad room — an uncontrollable suspect, someone whacked on drugs, who knows — an anonymous soundtrack of mayhem and desperation.

EXT: STREET ON THE UPPER WEST SIDE — DAY

An unmarked car, Sherman at the wheel.

Frank emerges from a post box rental center. He holds up fistfuls of envelopes for Sherman to see. Many of these are in a variety of pastel shades, purples, pinks, greens, etc.

INT: THE CAR

Frank slides in and passes the envelopes under Sherman's nose.

> FRANK
> You smell a shooter in there?

INT: SINGLES TYPE WEST SIDE RESTAURANT — DAY

It's called Stanley and Livingston's — ferny, woody, indirect lighting, TGIF-type place. Lots of blender drinks, deserted right now save for the help.

Frank and Sherman are sitting in the late afternoon stillness at the bar with the manager — a stylishly slick young guy.

> MANAGER
> So wait a minute . . . you're gonna tie up a deuce all night for like four five *nights?*

> SHERMAN
> Two . . . we need a table for some backup also.

> MANAGER
> Uh-huh . . . be baggin' my glasses, my silverware . . .
> fellas, hey . . . two tables, that's like maybe fifteen
> hundred dollars worth of tabs a night.

> SHERMAN
> Don't worry about it, we'll be ordering stuff.

> MANAGER
> Hey, look. I'm a good citizen and all, but ah . . . whata
> you doin' to me guys . . .

Frank spies an Oriental busboy in kitchen whites coming out of the kitchen.

> FRANK
> What's that kid's name?

> MANAGER
> Kim something.

> FRANK
> Hey, Kim!

The kid comes over. Frank gently but firmly holds his wrist.

> FRANK
> Kim . . . you got a green card? You understand green
> card? You got one, right? Everybody in the kitchen . . .
> everybody got green cards, right?

CLOSE ON — KIM

frightened, looking to the manager for help.

INT: STATION HOUSE SQUAD ROOM — EARLY EVENING

Sherman and Frank sit at desks working off stacks of letters, calling the women, setting up dates.

CLOSE ON — FRANK

> FRANK
> (*on the phone*)
> I dunno, Gloria, I just got this . . . *hope*ful feeling when I read your letter . . . I can't explain it.

Frank's gaze wanders, he pinches the exhaustion in his eyes.

> Capricorn . . .

CLOSE ON — SHERMAN

> SHERMAN
> (*on the phone*)
> Hey! My *mother*'s name was Amanda!
> (*shrugging*)
> Miranda . . . sorry . . .
> (*laughing uproariously*)
> Are you kidding me? I couldn't *stand* the old bag!
> (*more laughter*)
> Yeah? Well, you got a pretty great laugh yourself. We should have a few laughs together . . . I'll bring my mother.

CLOSE ON — FRANK

> FRANK
> You're a what? That's what . . . you like guys *and* girls . . . *or* girls.
> (*beat*)
> That's cool, that's cool . . . me? Yeah . . . well, sometimes, but, ah, mainly girls . . . *women,* you know.
> (*he's blushing*)
> I mean, hey, whatever . . . this is face to face stuff we're talking now . . . no . . . no, I ap*pre*ciate upfrontness like that. I *value* it. In fact, I have a very special feeling about you, Lana, how's eight sound?

CLOSE ON — A HUGE CROSS-GRID CHART

of days, restaurants and hours on Frank's desk. There are twenty women's names inked into the boxes.

WE SEE Frank's pen resting on an open eight o'clock box.

WE SEE the pen slide down past three booked boxes to rest at the open midnight slot.

> FRANK (VO)
> Well, that's cool, let's get crazy then . . . you a night owl?

Frank writes in her name in the midnight box.

> FRANK
> Solid . . .

INT: REAR OF A SURVEILLANCE VAN

Seated, patient, stripped to the waist, Frank is being wired by the surveillance team — there's something both medical and religious about the tableau. Sherman calmly watches the preparation — he's dressed as a waiter.

EXT: STREET — THIRTY MINUTES LATER

Frank wearing a sport jacket, leaves the van and blends into the sidewalk stream.

INT: STANLEY AND LIVINGSTON'S — 6:00 P.M.

Frank, in jacket and tie, sipping a white wine at a table for two. He's alone.

> FRANK
> (speaking as if to himself —
> a murmur)
> Can I get a hi de hi?

FRANK'S POV

WE SEE two detectives, male and female Wall Street types, at their table by the door. They both raise their hands, elbows on the table and casually wiggle their fingers. They seem to be wearing hearing aids.

INT: THE SURVEILLANCE VAN

We hear Frank's voice coming through a PA speaker. He's tunelessly humming "Sea of Love" via his wire.

INT: STANLEY AND LIVINGSTON'S — THIRTY MINUTES
LATER
CLOSE ON — A BEAUTIFUL SIXTY-YEAR-OLD WOMAN

Gray-haired, fine-boned, classy but tense, embarrassed.

We hear Frank as WE HOLD ON her.

> FRANK (OS)
> Look, I think you're being very foolish . . . do you hear
> me complaining or anything? . . . *I* should look *half* as
> good as you when I'm that age . . . *your* age . . . you're
> great . . . you're great.

> WOMAN
> You're very sweet . . . it's just . . . I should have said
> on the phone I'm . . . the age I am.

CLOSE ON — FRANK

> FRANK
> Hey, hey, I wanna tell you . . . you look better *now*
> than three-quarters of the women I know that are *half*
> your age.
> (*beat*)
> Did that come out right?

They both laugh.

Frank flags down Sherman, dressed as a waiter.

> FRANK
> Bourbon and water, right?

Sherman removes her glass, holding it from underneath like a
brandy snifter.

WE TRACK Sherman into the kitchen, where a fingerprint expert
goes to work dusting and labeling it for the lab.

ANGLE — THE TABLE

> OLDER WOMAN
> When Jack died . . . well, it wasn't a great . . .
> (*hesitates*)

You know, sometimes, in a marriage, you confuse loyalty
with love.
    (*awkward beat*)
After a certain number of years . . . it wasn't . . .
    (*beat*)
. . . we didn't have *passion*.

CLOSE ON — FRANK

. . . attentive.

ANGLE — THE SURVEILLANCE VAN

Everyone going about their business.

    OLDER WOMAN
    (*coming in over Frank's wire on the PA, teary*)
But we were such good *friends*.

CLOSE ON — THE FACES OF THE PROS AT WORK

are impassive.

ANGLE — KITCHEN

The labeled glass is slid into a paper bag for safety. The bag is
stenciled "LAB."

ANGLE — RESTAURANT

    WOMAN
    (*laughing nervously*)
Well . . . ah . . . What do we do . . .

    FRANK
Well, I've got this thing with my son in half an hour . . .
the timing is terrible.

    WOMAN
Will I . . . should we have dinner sometime?

    FRANK
Oh . . . hey . . . we'll call you.

    WOMAN
    (*amused, confused*)
We?

FRANK
(*blushing*)
We . . . like I'm still on the job . . . all day on the phone I
say *we* meaning my company . . . *I* . . . *I* will call you.

WOMAN
(*kindly*)
No you won't.

She leans forward across the table, gives him a kiss and leaves.

Frank sits there exhaling with unhappiness.

FRANK'S POV

WE SEE the undercover Wall Street couple looking at him and
returning to their salads.

ANGLE — FIVE MINUTES LATER — FRANK

at bar watching his table being reset.

ANGLE — TWENTY MINUTES LATER — FRANK

at the table with another date.

YOUNG ATTRACTIVE WOMAN
Look . . . I don't believe in wasting time on this kind of
stuff, you know what you know and you *go* with it.

FRANK
Go with what?

WOMAN
You're just not my type.

FRANK
(*wounded*)
You just sat down . . . how do you know?

WOMAN
I believe in love at first sight.
I believe in animal attraction . . .
I believe in this.
(*she snaps her fingers*)
I don't feel it with you.

> FRANK
> I happen to be hell on wheels once you get to
> know me.

She stares at him blankly as if waiting for him to *become* hell on
wheels.
> (*sighing*)
> Would you at least have a drink with me? . . .

> WOMAN
> (*rising, apologetic*)
> . . . nothing personal . . .

> FRANK
> (*coldly*)
> Do me a favor . . . pick up your wine glass.

She tentatively picks up her empty glass.

> FRANK
> Now put it down.

She does.

> FRANK
> (*cold*)
> See you around.

She leaves, shooting him a weird look.

ANGLE — SURVEILLANCE VAN

Frank's voice complains to the crew over the PA.

> FRANK
> Bitch.

ANGLE — RESTAURANT
CLOSE ON — TABLE

being cleaned.

ANGLE — FIFTEEN MINUTES LATER — TABLE
CLOSE ON — WOMAN

> WOMAN
> (*softly*)
> You have a lot of hurt in your eyes. You know that?

She reaches out to touch his face.

ANGLE — KITCHEN
CLOSE ON — FOUR GLASSES

in "LAB" bags lined up on a shelf.

ANGLE — RESTAURANT
CLOSE ON — FRANK'S PALM

being held by sixth date as she traces his lifeline.

CLOSE ON — THE WOMAN

She starts to cry.

CLOSE ON — FRANK

looking down at his palm, alarmed.

ANGLE
EXT: BACK ALLEY — NIGHT

Frank in his sport jacket, Sherman in his waiter whites. They both sit on garbage can lids. Sherman smokes a cigarette. Frank takes a swig from a half pint of something, then looks at his watch. Sherman drops his butt. They return to work.

ANGLE — SURVEILLANCE VAN

We hear a woman's tense voice.

> WOMAN (OS)
> I don't know . . . I get this very weird feeling off you . . . I get this . . . you're not who you *say* you are . . . there's something . . . not *right* about this.

> FRANK (OS)
> Why would I lie to you? You think I'm what . . . what are you thinking?

> **WOMAN**
> You got cop's eyes.

ANGLE — RESTAURANT

The Wall Street couple straighten up in their seats.

ANGLE — VAN

The surveillance crew perks up with interest for the first time all night.

ANGLE — RESTAURANT — STANLEY AND LIVINGSTON'S
CLOSE ON — FRANK

> **FRANK**
> (*awkward*)
> Cop's eyes?

> **WOMAN**
> You look at me I feel like I *did* something.

> **FRANK**
> (*looking away*)
> What do you mean *did* something? Like what?

> **WOMAN**
> (*staring at him, deadeye*)
> Yeah . . . yeah . . . My ex-husband's a cop. What you say?
> You're a *jew*eler? If you're a jeweler I got a dick.

She walks out leaving Frank staring at her glass.

> **FRANK**
> (*to his wire*)
> How many more tonight?

FRANK'S POV

WE SEE one of the Wall Street detectives casually raise two fingers, while looking away from Frank.

Frank, beat, blasted, rubs his eyes absently, scans the bar and freezes.

FRANK'S POV

WE SEE his first date of the evening, the older woman, sitting at the
bar totally blitzed, staring at him with a mixture of anger, confusion, and pride. Her appearance has totally degenerated with her
drinking.

He has no idea of how long she's been watching him.

Frank looks like he wants to die.

She rises unsteadily, moves towards his table as he waits motionless.
She keeps moving straight on out the door, head high.

> FRANK
> (to himself)
> That lady coming out now? Somebody see she gets home
> OK . . .

CLOSE ON — TABLE

being cleaned — restaurant almost deserted. Frank and Sherman
are gone as are the Wall Street–looking undercovers.

INT: VAN

Frank, nude to the waist, is being stripped of his wire. He's numb,
bushed, fucked up.

Sherman is smoking a cigarette. He's still dressed as a waiter.

> SHERMAN
> (in falsetto)
> You have such *hurt* in your eyes.

He reaches out to touch Frank's face in imitation of the date.

Frank swipes Sherman's hand away — harshly.

Frank takes a swig of something, gives Sherman a dirty look.

EXT: STREET — 3:00 A.M.

Frank, tired, heading into the all night Korean grocery stand for his
usual insomniac shopping.

INT: KOREAN GROCERY STAND

Frank, plastic basket on his arm, picking produce from multicolored fruit pyramids under the grim 3:00 A.M. fluorescent lighting.

> WOMAN (OS)
> Hell on wheels, huh?

Frank looks up. It's the woman who wouldn't even stay for a drink with him earlier in the night. Frank stares at her trying to place the face. She's not bad-looking — more character than beauty, though.

> WOMAN (HELEN)
> (*noting his confusion*)
> How quickly we forget.

> FRANK
> (*making the connection*)
> Oh yeah . . . Love at first sight, you live around here?

> HELEN
> You didn't write that poem . . . I read it in the magazine and figured this is either a very sensitive guy or he ripped off some woman's poem or some *girl*'s poem . . . you didn't write it, right?

> FRANK
> (*disinterested*)
> Nope.

> HELEN
> Some *lady* did, right?

> FRANK
> My mother . . . she wrote it in high school fifty-odd years ago . . . that's why my father fell in love with her . . . or something like that.

> HELEN
> (*moved*)
> Really.

> FRANK
> (*shrugs*)
> So he says.

> HELEN
> (*musing, a little internal*)
> Wow . . . that's . . . huh . . . I like that . . . that you did
> that.

> FRANK
> (*tired*)
> Yeah, well . . .

Helen studies him as he picks fruit, then moves to him until she's a
foot away and staring him in the eye.

> HELEN
> Look at me.

Frank looks up, still distracted, then slightly coming to life because
of her intense eyes and her proximity.

> FRANK
> (*suddenly shy, caught off guard*)
> What's up.

> HELEN
> Take me home.

> FRANK
> (*laughing, flustered*)
> Home . . . what . . . *my* home? . . . hey, what happened to
> ah . . . love at first sight there . . . you know . . . ah . . .
> you wouldn't even *drink* with me back there.

> HELEN
> Take me home.

She just stares at him, her intensity, her spontaneous decision and
willfulness an utter turn-on.

Frank, still making laughy, nervous half words, suddenly pours his
fruit back into the display pyramids — a gesture of surrender.

INT: SHERMAN'S BEDROOM IN QUEENS — 3:30 A.M.

Sherman lying like a beached whale on his bed, sleep mask pushed
up to his forehead, wife dead asleep next to him, is talking to Frank
on the phone.

SHERMAN
What are you, fucking *nuts?* What if she's the do-er? We
won't get the print matches until tomorrow. She clears, go
out with her to*mo*rrow night . . . you're crazy, man.
(*beat*)
Yeah, bullshit. What are you gonna do, nail her in bed?
. . . that'll be some great testimony, Frank. "See, your
honor, first *I* whipped it out, then *she* whipped it out."
You catch my drift?
(*beat*)
She's a *sus*pect, Frank . . . just walk away . . . just walk
away.

EXT: SIDEWALK IN FRONT OF KOREAN GROCERY —
3:30 A.M.

Frank is on the pay phone about fifty feet from Helen, who stands
in front of the store.

FRANK
(*to Sherman*)
You're right . . . you're right . . . I swear . . . I'm walkin'
. . . I'm walkin' . . . no sweat . . . nothin' to it, chief . . .
see you tomorrow.

Frank walks over to Helen, sucks air through his teeth.

FRANK
Ah . . . listen . . . something came up.
(*laughs*)
What's your name again?

HELEN
Helen.

FRANK
(*nodding*)
Helen . . .

INT: FRANK'S APARTMENT
CLOSE ON — FRANK AND HELEN

grinding and kissing against a wall. Helen tearing away, walking in
a little circle, then attacking Frank against the wall again.

She pulls away.

> HELEN
> Where's the bathroom . . .

Frank tilts his head.

> HELEN
> Get in bed.

Helen disappears behind the bathroom door.

Frank quickly removes his gun and holster, slips it under a couch
pillow. He's freaking. Pacing. What the *hell* is he doing? He spies
her handbag on his dining room table. He opens it, looks inside.
His face drains of color and he flings his hands up in despair.

> FRANK
> (*hissing*)
> *Je*-sus!

He paces away from the purse, gesticulating, then returns to the
purse.

> FRANK
> (*hissing*)
> *Je*-sus!

He pulls out a pistol from her purse, turns, retrieves his own gun
and lurches for the bedroom.

ANGLE — HELEN

nude to the waist, wearing a towel like a Gauguin primitive, entering the bedroom where Frank lays fully dressed on his bed. His eyes
don't leave her face. He sees nothing but her face.

He holds up her gun.

HELEN
Hey! Where the hell do you come off . . .

FRANK
(*voice cracking*)
You got a license for this?

HELEN
W*hat?* Where do you come off going into my purse?

FRANK
What if I was a cop? You don't have a license. I'd have to
run you in.

HELEN
(*laughing*)
What are you *talking* about!

Frank just glares at her. He's screwed.

Helen sits on the edge of the bed . . . composed, patient.

HELEN
What are you doing going through my stuff?

FRANK
(*in his panic, his despair, turning officious*)
You have a license for this?

HELEN
What are you, the motor vehicle bureau? What's with the
license, it's a starter's pistol . . .
(*beat*)
What are you going through my purse for . . . that's
creepy, Frank . . . are you a creepy guy?

FRANK
(*stunned*)
Starter's pistol . . .
(*looking at it*)
This a *starter's* pistol!
(*joyous*)
What are you doing with a starter's pistol!

> HELEN
> Hey, I work in an expensive store. I carry a lot of money
> to the bank. I used to pack Mace, but I sprayed myself in
> the face once . . . this way nobody gets hurt . . . everybody
> backs off.
> (*beat*)
> Is this helping you, what I'm saying?

Frank starts laughing with relief, his hands to his face.

> HELEN
> (*watching him*)
> You're a very intense guy.

> FRANK
> (*laughing, chatty in his relief*)
> Yeah . . . hey . . . don't mind me . . . it's the full moon.
> I'm one of those full moon guys.

> HELEN
> Full moon guys.

> FRANK
> See the full moon is for real, and it's got enough magnetic
> power to affect the tides of the Atlantic and Pacific
> Oceans, two of the biggest we have, right? Meanwhile
> the human *brain* is eighty percent fluid. Full moon
> comes out, we're *screwed*, you follow me?

> HELEN
> (*laughing*)
> What . . . so guys like you the full moon comes out you
> walk around all night, your brains are like . . . sloshing?
> Low tide high tide low tide? . . .

> FRANK
> You have beautiful breasts, you know that?

> HELEN
> Breasts . . . I like that word . . . Can I have my gun back,
> please? . . . let me put it away. I don't like it out. It makes
> me nervous.

She puts out her hand. Frank hesitates for a tense beat, looks at it one last quick time, then gives it to her.

INT: BEDROOM — MORNING

Frank is asleep. Helen is sitting in bed next to him eating dry cereal and watching Mister Rogers on Frank's bedroom TV.

Frank awakens squinting at the set as Mister Rogers prattles on about somebody named Doctor Platypus.

> FRANK
> Who the hell is that?

> HELEN
> That's my man, Mister Rogers . . . I turned him on once by accident about a month ago. He was saying to the kids, "Did you ever wish someone would come back from their vacation 'cause you miss them so very much and when they finally do you can't imagine why you missed them at *all?*"

Frank just stares at her.

> HELEN
> That's a pretty middle of the night comment for a kiddie show guy, don't you think?

Frank just lays back as Helen continues to eat and watch TV.

> FRANK
> (*stares at her with curiosity*)
> You're something else.

> HELEN
> No . . . *you're* something else.

She lays on top of him and kisses him as Mister Rogers goes into a high squeaky puppet voice.

> HELEN
> You're tight as a drum . . . you're like the most wired guy I ever been with . . . but I bet you're a good man when the

shit hits the fan . . . why am I saying that . . . who knows
. . . it's true, though, I bet.

>   FRANK
>   (*blushing*)
> You never know.

>   HELEN
> I always know.

They stare at each other, nose to nose. Helen laying flat on Frank.

>   FRANK
>   (*getting suddenly tense*)
> I got to make a phone call.

The phone rings as soon as he says that.

>   HELEN
> Wired to the nines.

Frank takes the receiver. They're still nose to nose during the phone
conversation.

>   FRANK
>   (*with Helen on top, as he talks to the police lab*)
> Keller . . . yeah . . . and . . . everybody clears . . . no
> matches . . . nothing . . .
>   (*exhales in relief*)
> you sure . . . thanks . . . thank you.

He hangs up. The tension leaves him.

>   HELEN
> Who's that?

>   FRANK
> Work . . . the print shop.

>   HELEN
> You're a printer?

>   FRANK
>   (*hesitating*)
> Yeah.

> HELEN
> Huh . . . interesting . . . if I had to guess, though . . . I'd
> swear you were some kind of hunter.

Helen goes back to watching Mister Rogers.

EXT: STREET — SAME DAY

Frank is walking down 57th Street looking for an address.

INT: "NICOLE DU BOFF"

Hush, plush, Euro-elegant shoe store. Trendy, wealthy clientele.

A stylishly dressed salesman is down on one knee before a blonde middle-aged matron. He's chatting her up and fitting her for boots.

Helen is at the counter reading the *New York Times*.

Frank saunters in, immediately uncomfortable in the plush vibes. It makes him whisper like he's in church.

> FRANK
> (to Helen)
> I need sneakers, you sell sneakers?

Helen looks up, excited at seeing Frank.

> HELEN
> What are you doing here!

> FRANK
> (under his breath)
> I was in the neighborhood.

> HELEN
> Why are you whispering?

> FRANK
> (embarrassed)
> I'm not whispering.

Two women walk in — blatantly wealthy.

> FRANK
> (*whispering*)
> It's the Carringtons.

> HELEN
> What?

> FRANK
> Who's Nicole Du Boff?

> HELEN
> She's the boss.

> FRANK
> I know a guy named *Vin*ny Du Boff . . .
> (*beat*)
> I'd kiss you but . . .

He makes a gesture taking in the store — a twirling of his hand close to his chest.

Helen blows him a furtive kiss.

> FRANK
> Can I take you for some coffee?

> HELEN
> I can't leave.

> FRANK
> C'mon, ask Nicole.

Two young guys, hip, lean, shades and exquisitely casually dressed, waltz in — they could be Euro-trash or rock stars except there's something of the street animal in the way they walk and talk — something that doesn't jibe with the threads — maybe they're dope dealers or rising Mafiosi.

> GUY #1 (TOMMY)
> (*holding up boots*)
> Willie, check it out.

Willie makes a noise of disdain.

They saunter into the back room as an older, effete man comes waltzing out to the front room.

He's wearing black suede ankle boots with the skeletal structure of the foot trompe-l'oeiled in white on the suede.

He looks expectantly at Frank and Helen for their opinion.

> HELEN
> (*to the man*)
> Crazy, right?

> FRANK
> (*ignoring the guy*)
> Who were those two guys?

Helen shrugs.

> FRANK
> (*muttering*)
> They're not right.

Frank walks to the threshold of the rear room.

FRANK'S POV

He watches them handle the merchandise.

> FRANK
> (*to Helen*)
> They're not right.

> HELEN
> (*shrugs*)
> What size shoe you wear?

> FRANK
> Me? Ten?

Helen disappears.

Frank scans the room — Money Money Money — dungarees under full length minks, diamond pendants — blonde, tightly pulled back buns over winter tans.

> HELEN
> (*returns with a shoebox*)
> Here you go. Don't open it till you get home.

> FRANK
> What is this, a present? What are you, crazy? . . . What do shoes go for here?

> HELEN
> (*shrugs*)
> Can I make you dinner tonight?

> FRANK
> (*wincing*)
> I got to work.

> HELEN
> What do you have, a twenty-four-hour printing service?

> FRANK
> (*momentarily confused*)
> A what? . . . Sometimes.

The two young guys come back through the front room. Frank gives them a hard stare.

> TOMMY
> (*to Helen*)
> Excuse me . . . I come in here like six months ago, you had this beautiful boot . . . the Ti*v*oli? The Vi*v*oli?

Tommy notices Frank staring him down.

> HELEN
> The Vivaldi . . . we're out of stock.

> TOMMY
> (*to Frank, pugnacious*)
> Can I help you with something?

Frank just keeps staring.

> TOMMY
> What's *your* problem.

>   WILLIE
> Tommy, let's blow.

>   HELEN
>   (to Tommy, anxious)
> Can I help you?

Frank just keeps staring.

Tommy, livid, frustrated, does something that shows his roots despite his fine clothing — he spits on the carpet in the general direction of Frank's feet.

Frank doesn't react except to keep staring at Tommy, knowing it's driving him crazy.

>   WILLIE
> Tommy, let's jet . . . guy's a cop.

>   TOMMY
> You're a cop? So like, if I kick your fuckin' ass, I'm
> assaulting an officer, right?

Frank takes one step away from the counter, rolls his shoulders and beckons Tommy forward with little wiggles of his palms-up hands.

Tommy hesitates. Willie yanks on his arm to split. The moment has passed.

>   TOMMY
>   (doing the up and down)
> Piece of shit.

They stalk out.

>   FRANK
> Those guys are not right.

Helen is glaring at him.

>   FRANK
> What.

>   HELEN
>   (irritated)
> You're a cop?

> FRANK
> Yeah . . . so . . .
> (angry)
> so what.

Frank looks around at the store.

> FRANK
> Hey, you let in scum like that and you say that to *me?*

> HELEN
> (confused)
> What?

> FRANK
> (leaning forward and furtively flashing
> his gold shield)
> Let me tell you something about this.
> (the shield)
> All these people here with the hair, the rocks, the furs . . .
> they get robbed, they get raped, they get mugged . . . I'm
> all of a sudden everybody's daddy . . . Come the wet ass
> hour I'm *every*body's daddy.

He marches for the door, turns, holds up the shield.

> FRANK
> The great equalizer.

EXT: STREET OUTSIDE THE STORE

Frank storming down the block.

Helen running from behind, pulls on his arm, turns him around.

> HELEN
> Hey, what's your problem.

> FRANK
> (imitating Helen)
> You're a *cop?*

> HELEN
> Hey, so what if you're a cop. I have no problems with
> that. I got a problem with a guy who sleeps with me, tells

me he's a printer or something, winds up he's lying. *That's* a problem for me. Makes me think maybe he's lying about other things, like he's got a wife or something.

Frank pauses, comes to his senses. He read the situation all wrong and really showed his ass.

> FRANK
> (*grimacing with embarrassment*)
> Oh Jesus. What a jerk.

> HELEN
> (*patient, shrugs*)
> Why couldn't you tell me last night?

> FRANK
> (*thinking fast*)
> Ah . . . Sometimes I can't tell if ah, you know, some people get uptight when they find out.

> HELEN
> (*shrugs*)
> I don't care . . .

> FRANK
> (*smirking*)
> The great equalizer . . . what a schmuck.

> HELEN
> No . . . that was good . . . I liked that.

They're both smiling, embarrassed.

> HELEN
> You're very intense.

> FRANK
> I'm a fucking lunatic.
> (*beat*)
> But I'm not married.

> HELEN
> (*handing him the shoebox*)
> You forgot this.

> FRANK
> (*still smarting from his little display*)
> I can't take this. I'll pay for it, how about that?

> HELEN
> Yeah? These are four-hundred-and-fifty-dollar shoes.

> FRANK
> (*gawks*)
> What . . . is that what . . . *retail*?

> HELEN
> (*kisses him on the mouth, hands on his face*)
> What can I tell you, I work in a shoe store. I'm in love, the guy gets shoes. Call me, I'm freezing.

Helen trots back to the store. Frank gawks after her, a trace of happiness on his face.

He turns and walks down 57th Street circling the shoebox around his waist, hand to hand, like a basketball.

INT: SQUAD ROOM LOCKER AREA

Frank sits on the bench in front of his locker, the shoebox in his lap. He's partially obscured from us by his open locker door.

ANGLE — SERAFINO AND GRUBER

trail into the room to make coffee.

> FRANK (OS)
> God-*damn*!

They turn to Frank. He's obscured by his locker. Emerges to put one foot up on the bench to display a leopard-print shoe.

> FRANK
> These things, they're so soft . . . they feel like *feet*.

> SERAFINO
> And they're subtle, too . . .

Serafino walks out.

FRANK
(*almost shyly, to Gruber*)
Wild, right? My girl . . . this girl gave 'em to me. You got
to wear 'em, right? What can you do?

Gruber catches the message — Frank's got a girlfriend — Frank
wants Gruber and by extension Denice to know that.

GRUBER
(*benignly*)
Pretty jazzy.

FRANK
(*smiling*)
Well, this girl . . . she's . . .
(*laughs*)
I mean, look at these things . . . She's OK, though . . . You
should meet her, you know, sometime . . .

INT: VAN — NIGHT

It's Sherman's turn to be the date, Frank the waiter.

Frank watches Sherman, nude to the waist, a blubbery emperor, as
the technicians wire him up.

SHERMAN
(*singing "I Only Have Eyes For You"*)
Are the Stars
Out to-night
I don't know
If it's cloudy or bright

Frank is wearing his leopard-print kicks, admiring them, his feet up
on a chair inside the van.

INT: THE RESTAURANT
FRANK'S POV

Heading to Sherman's table, Sherman's date with her back to
Frank. Sherman and the girl are laughing uproariously. Sherman is
having a ball, as usual.

SHERMAN
"Sea of Love," you ever hear that one?

GIRL
Uh-uh.

SHERMAN
(*singing*)
Come with me, my-yy love,

FRANK
How you doing, folks, something from the bar?

Frank looks at the girl, sighs. It's Gina Gallagher, the girl with the mylar balloons who showed up for a date with John Mackey.

GINA
(*to Frank*)
I know you . . . you're that *cop.*

FRANK
Easy, babe.

SHERMAN
(*mock-angry*)
You're a *flat*foot?

GINA
(*with compassion*)
Did you get *fired?*

She looks quickly from Sherman to Frank, gets wise.

GINA
(*almost in tears*)
What do you *want* from me!

She starts to rise; hurt, scared.

ANGLE — THE WALL STREETERS

across the room, starting to rise.

Frank puts a gentle hand on her arm.

FRANK
We don't want anything, honey. Have a drink.
(*to Sherman*)
This is Gina. She's good people.

Frank nods to Sherman, implying she's not the one but show her a nice time for the half hour she's scheduled.

INT: PHONE VESTIBULE IN THE RESTAURANT

Frank, in his waiter outfit, is on the phone to Helen. He's holding a glass in a "LAB" bag.

FRANK
I'm wearin' them as we speak . . . on the job . . . right on the job . . . you still like me?
(*grins*)
Yeah? . . . You? . . . You're OK. Can I see you later? . . . I'm cutting out at ten tonight, I thought maybe . . . yeah? Great . . . Great. So . . . you still like me?

INT: RESTAURANT

Frank is taking a drink order from a young woman seated with Sherman.

FRANK
Golden Cadillac?

WOMAN (SONYA)
*Scream*ing Golden Cadillac.

FRANK
*Scream*ing Golden Cadillac . . . what makes it scream?

SHERMAN
(*giggling*)
Getting attacked by a bunch of White Russians.

SONYA
(*giving Sherman a smoky look*)
That's very clever.

> SHERMAN
> Waiter? Make that two.

> FRANK
> You want yours screaming too?

> SONYA
> (to Sherman, sexy, touching his neck)
> You have very tight skin, you know that?

> SHERMAN
> (turned on)
> That's 'cause I'm fat, it pushes the skin out. Whomp! Like balloon rubber.

ANGLE — THE WALL STREETERS

howling with laughter at their table.

ANGLE — SHERMAN'S TABLE

> SHERMAN
> (to Frank, agitated, horny)
> Did you not get the order, or what?

Frank nods. He's about to cry with laughter.

INT: TELEPHONE VESTIBULE — RESTAURANT

> FRANK
> (on the phone to his father)
> Pop . . . Frankie . . . nothin' . . . I was just calling ah . . .
> how you doing? . . . I'm great . . . really great . . . I
> dunno, I was just calling to say ah . . . that ah . . . I love
> you and ah . . . that . . . I'm doing great and ah . . . I don't
> want you to worry about me or anything because . . . ah
> . . . Dad . . . you like shoes? How you doing on shoes . . .

INT: RESTAURANT

Frank standing over Sherman's table.

> SHERMAN
> (*to new date, casual*)
> Let me just ask you something. You ever go out with a guy, make love, the guy's laying there after . . . you pull out a .38, shoot him in the head? . . . back of the head?

The date just stares at Sherman, emotionless, deadpan.

Frank waits patiently.

> SHERMAN
> (*to the date*)
> You ever do that to a guy?

> DATE
> (*drily*)
> I'm trying to remember.

> SHERMAN
> What are you drinking?

INT: BATHROOM OF THE RESTAURANT

Sherman and Frank taking five.

> FRANK
> Serafino's coming on for me in a few minutes . . . I'm cuttin' out.

> SHERMAN
> (*a little bombed*)
> They gonna let Serafino be a waiter here? He looks like the neighborhood butcher.

> FRANK
> Here you go.
> (*Frank tosses his apartment keys to Sherman*)
> Why don't you crash in my place after . . . you're hitting it pretty heavy tonight . . . How was that Golden Cadillac?

> SHERMAN
> Jesus . . . Good thing my dick wasn't wired . . . I woulda blown out the friggin' speakers in the truck . . . short-circuited the whole *block*.

> FRANK
>
> I'll see you tomorrow.

> SHERMAN
> (*suddenly uptight*)
> Frankie, maybe I should go home . . . my wife's gonna
> freak, she wakes up I'm not there.

> FRANK
> Do me a favor . . . crash by me . . . call your wife in the
> morning.

> SHERMAN
> Wer'e gonna sleep together?

> FRANK
> Right . . . I'm ah, I'm gonna stay with this *Hel*en . . . stay
> over at her place . . . check it out.

> SHERMAN
> (*doing Jack Jones, singing*)
> This *guy*'s in love with you, da da da da.

> FRANK
> (*laughing*)
> Kiss my ass, balloon skin . . . I'm nervous, she makes me
> nervous.
> (*taking a swig of something*)
> Sometimes I swear I feel like I don't know how to talk to
> people anymore . . . civilians.
> (*takes another swig*)
> You get out of practice.

> SHERMAN
> You're OK.

EXT: COLUMBUS AVENUE — 11:00 P.M.

Frank and Helen are strolling arm in arm.

> FRANK
> As far as I'm concerned it's like this. The world is divided
> into good guys and bad guys and I'm a good guy. I'm an
> officer of the *law*. People yell police, yell help, I come

running . . . I'm a protector and I get off on that. My
partner . . . my ex-partner, he says Frankie, come in with
me. He's got this security consultants firm. He says come
in with me, your first year you'll bag sixty large nice clean
work — fur coat outlets, polygraphs, we don't go
nowhere that's not air-conditioned. I say to him hey
Tom . . .

Frank stops and points out a parkside bench to Helen.

> FRANK
> You see that bench? Three people died on that bench over
> the last two years . . . one guy OD'd last summer, last
> winter another guy got drunk, passed out and froze and
> something like six weeks ago some old guy had a heart
> attack — this is the devil's bench.

> HELEN
> I never think of that stuff around this neighborhood. I feel
> like I could walk down the street naked, the only thing
> would happen is somebody'd run out and give me a Ralph
> Lauren towel.

> FRANK
> Oh yeah? Nice around here, right? This one block
> (*pointing to a side street*)
> we had three homicides the last year, you see that garage?
> One in there, one across the street, second floor, two
> months later same building one on the third floor.

> HELEN
> OK, I won't go naked down there.

> FRANK
> Just down there? See this nice condo here? Two, three
> years ago when it was a welfare hotel? Three murders,
> two suicides, two people froze and somebody fell through
> a busted bannister. Lots a ghosts in there.

> HELEN
> (*thoughtful*)
> Jesus . . . this whole town must be like a city of the dead
> for you.

      FRANK
      (*defensive, uptight*)
Nah. Why do you say that . . . I love life.
      (*beat*)
Why do you say that? I was just saying . . . pointing out
stuff . . .

INT: RESTAURANT

Nice joint, not too opulent.

A waiter is serving Frank a drink. Frank passes him back an empty
glass from his previous drink.

      HELEN
So why is that . . . I mean you never see a cop get pissed,
freak out, nothing. I remember this guy got hit by a bus
. . . the cop showed up . . . he stepped in the guy's blood
by accident, he asked me if I had a napkin so he could
wipe his shoe . . . he doesn't have to be that way . . .
that cold.

      FRANK
      (*draining his drink*)
Was the vic dead? The guy that got hit by the bus?

      HELEN
Oh yeah.

      FRANK
So what difference does it make? The guy's *dead*.
What's the cop gonna *do*. You want blood on *your*
shoes?

Frank raises his leopard prints to the table.

      HELEN
      (*mildly*)
That's bullshit, you know what I mean.

FRANK
(*flags down the waiter for another*)
Look, a lot of guys on the job . . . we see a lot of shit.
A lot of suffering. Every day . . .
(*beat*)
It's like in the beginning . . . one time when I was in
uniform? I get this call . . . we break in to this apartment
. . . a four year old kid is chained to the radiator . . . the
mother's somewheres scoring dope, who knows, we take
the kid to a hospital, wait for the mother to come home
. . . I start chasing this bitch around the block . . . we bust
her for child abuse, abandonment . . . I'm freakin' six
ways to Sunday, but my partner, older guy, he says, "Hey
Frank, let me tell you something. That lady? She's a piece
of shit. But ten years ago? I busted her *father* for child
abuse. He *was* a piece of shit. This *kid* we saved tonight?
If he *lives* long enough, he's *gonna* be a piece of shit . . .
It's the cycle of shit and there's nothing to do for it so
relax."

Frank's third drink comes.

FRANK
You see what I'm getting at?

HELEN
(*deadpan*)
Uh-oh . . .

Frank, drunk, sighs.

Troy, a guy in his early forties, executive-looking, comes by the
table.

TROY
Helen! Hi!

HELEN
(*brightening*)
Hey! Troy! You having dinner here?

TROY
Uh-huh! And yourself?

He laughs at his own dumb question.

> TROY
> Be well.

> HELEN
> You too.

Troy sits at a table behind Frank. Turned around, Frank watches him for a second.

> FRANK
> (*draining his drink*)
> You went out with him?

> HELEN
> Yeah . . . a while ago . . . he's a nice guy.

Frank turns and studies Troy for a beat.

> FRANK
> (*bombed*)
> I'm not getting through to you on this cycle of shit thing, huh?
> (*laughing*)
> Talk to civilians, I dunno, I dunno . . . OK, look . . . it's like this. I got to function out there, you know? Every day you see heartache, brutality, un*fair*ness . . . you chalk it up to the cycle of shit and you move on — hey, a doctor working the emergency room does the same damn thing.

Frank turns and glares at Troy, flags down a waiter for another.

> HELEN
> Why don't you slow down a bit, Frank.

> FRANK
> If the fucking food would come I wouldn't be drinking, OK?

Frank sits in a drunken sullen stew, turns to look at Troy.

> FRANK
> (*abruptly*)
> Hey, you may think I'm a creep, a bastard, a what*ever* . . .

but you don't understand what's *out* there . . . I gotta
swim through the sewer.
> (*beat*)

Me and a doctor, we got the same head out there and you
know something *else?* We both save lives . . .
> (*beat*)

except I go one better than him . . . I *risk my* life . . . *I'm* a
creep? *I'm* bullshit? You want to see a creepshow, take my
goddamn tour one week, I'll show you *creep*show.

> HELEN
> (*nervous, embarrassed*)

Easy, easy . . .

> FRANK
> (*muttering*)

City of the dead. I *save* lives . . . you know someone tried
to give me a ten dollar *tip* once I saved them from a guy
with a steak knife. Guy comes at him off the street with
a steak knife. I'm in there like a shot, break it up. Pure
luck I was there. The vic throws me a ten, thank you,
thank you. Who does that cheapen, me or him? It
cheapens *him.*

Helen looks like she's about to cry.

> FRANK
> (*wheels and glares at Troy*)

This guy. You meet him through that singles magazine?

> HELEN

Yeah . . . yeah.

> FRANK

How could you *do* that shit . . . go out with guys like that.
I see these women, it's a real victim-time thing . . . you
seem classier than that.

> HELEN

Hey! *You* did it . . . forget how we met?

> FRANK

That's bullshit. I was on the job . . . that was the *job* . . . I
was wearin' a *wire.* I would *never* do that . . . I got my

pride. I don't care *how* much I eat it every day and every
night, I'd *never* do that.

> HELEN
> (*mounting quiet fury*)
> Run that by me again? The wire part . . .

EXT: STREET — MIDNIGHT

> FRANK
> (*drunk on the pay phone*)
> Gruber . . . Frank Keller . . . look, I'm really sorry to call
> now but ah, I really need to talk to Denice . . . I fucked
> something up. I gotta talk to her . . . I really screwed up,
> she knows me, I'm really sorry to call, Gruber . . . this
> is different, I swear . . . she's got to talk to me . . .
> sure . . . sure . . . no problem . . . tomorrow morning . . .
> I'm sorry . . . have a good night . . . I understand . . .
> I understand . . . good night, good night.

Frank steps back from the booth and rips the receiver off the phone.
Walks away.

INT: HALLWAY OUTSIDE FRANK'S APARTMENT

Frank slips his key in the lock. The door only opens two inches. The
chain is on.

> FRANK
> (*banging on the door*)
> Hey, Sherman! It's Frank!

Sherman slips open the chain, stands blocking Frank from his own
door. Sherman's dressed in a towel.

> SHERMAN
> (*queasy, nervous*)
> What are you doing here?

> FRANK
> Ah . . . I screwed up something fierce.

Frank pushes past Sherman.

> FRANK
> Go rack out . . . I'll sleep on the couch.

Suddenly emerging from the bathroom is Gina Gallagher, the balloon girl.

Frank stands between Sherman and Gina at opposite ends of his hallway.

> GINA
> (*freaked*)
> Sherman said it was OK.

> SHERMAN
> (*dying*)
> Frank, we're leaving right now . . . Let me just get dressed.

> FRANK
> No, no, no . . . I'll go down to the precinct, bunk out . . . everything's cool . . .

> GINA
> Sherman said it was OK.

> FRANK
> And so it is.

> SHERMAN
> No, Frank, aw Christ.

Gina goes into the bedroom, closes the door.

> SHERMAN
> (*gutsick*)
> You said she was clear, man.

> FRANK
> No problem, Sherm . . . glad to see you're human.

> SHERMAN
> (*moaning*)
> Don't say that . . . don't rub it in.

> FRANK
> Hey, relax, relax.

Gina comes flying out of the bedroom fully dressed.

> GINA
> I got to go.

She leaves the apartment, the two cops.

> FRANK
> (*shrugging*)
> Screwed it up for you, huh? I'm sorry.

> SHERMAN
> I should go too.
> (*suddenly angry*)
> . . . I told you I should've gone home from the *git*-go!

> FRANK
> (*grabbing his arm*)
> Stay . . . stay here . . . get dressed, we'll get a drink . . . I got to talk to somebody about tonight . . . I'm like, not fucking human anymore, man . . . somebody *talk* to me about how to be a *per*son! . . . This girl was a terrific girl. A *great* girl, Sherm.

> SHERMAN
> (*writhing*)
> I gotta go home . . . my wife . . .

> FRANK
> (*violently grabbing his arm*)
> *Talk* to me!

> SHERMAN
> (*looking miserable*)
> OK . . . OK . . .

> FRANK
> (*sinking, suddenly sober*)
> Go home, chief . . . it's OK . . . it's OK . . .

ANGLE — THIRTY MINUTES LATER

Frank on his couch hunched over the phone. He's calling Helen. We hear the ringing — no one home.

INT: THE RESTAURANT WHERE THEY HAD DINNER —
1:00 A.M.

Frank ducks in the door — scans the room down to three diners and two people at the bar. No Helen.

INT: STANLEY AND LIVINGSTON'S — THE DECOY PLACE —
TEN MINUTES LATER

Frank ducks in, scans the room, also somewhat barren, no Helen.

Frank starts to leave, hesitates, gives in, drops into a bar stool.

>   FRANK
> Rum and tonic.

Frank regards his leopard-print shoes, laughs, curses himself out, laughs again. Scans the bar. There's four people: a couple, the bar manager going over the night's credit card receipts, and the woman who was juicing up Sherman — the one who ordered a Screaming Golden Cadillac — Sonya.

Frank makes eye contact with her, tilts his glass in a toast. She's either drunk or very sleepy. She barely acknowledges.

Frank concentrates on his drink, staring at the ice cubes, lost in his own thoughts.

Sonya starts crooning "Sea of Love" half to herself, like a lullaby.

Frank, not taking his eyes off his drink, slow-smiles; nods his head as if in self-affirmation when he hears the tune.

He half turns his head to her, smiles almost shyly and croons along at the same half murmury pitch.

ANGLE — FRANK AND SONYA

are slow dancing by the bar to their own hummed version of "Sea of Love."

Sonya seems in a narcoleptic trance, eyes closed, barely standing.

Frank holds her in a gentle bear hug, pressing her to him and rocking her back and forth in a slow circular shuffle.

> FRANK
> (*in her ear*)
> You got something for me, baby?

Sonja just dreamy-hums the song.

INT: ELEVATOR IN FRANK'S BUILDING — 2:30 A.M.

As the elevator makes its creaky ascent, Frank is still holding Sonya in that dance-hug. Sonya might be sleeping to the point of dreaming now.

> FRANK
> You got something for me?

INT: FRANK'S BEDROOM

Dimly lit. Frank has her leaning against a wall murmuring to her, slow, sensuously frisking-fondling her, his hands traveling the length of her body from her feet to her ribs.

> SONYA
> (*eyes closed*)
> Come wi-ii-th me-e
> to-o the sea

Frank gently lays her down on his bed. She stretches sensuously, eyes closed.

Frank lying on his side, rubbing her stomach. Her purse is spread out over the bed.

> FRANK
> Where's it at, mommy . . . where you hiding it?

Sonya falls asleep.

> FRANK
> You the one, mommy . . . you the do-er.

He kisses her cheek.

ANGLE — 3:00 A.M.

Frank standing in the doorway of the bedroom, Sonya's purse dangling from his fist.

He watches her sleep, turns for his living room.

ANGLE — 3:30 A.M.

Frank sprawled on his couch, a drink balanced on his chest, his hands clasped across his belly. Sonya's purse on the coffee table in front of him, alongside his gun.

HOLD FOR a long beat which is abruptly shattered by the shrill buzz of his front doorbell.

Frank carefully reaches for his gun, so as not to spill his perched drink.

ANGLE — DOORWAY

Frank, back to us, gun casually held behind his back, opens the door to Helen.

> FRANK
> (*stunned, happy, casual*)
> Hi!

> HELEN
> I guess it couldn't be helped tonight . . . you know, with the wire and all that, right? I mean the circumstances were the circumstances, right?

> FRANK
> (*pause*)
> Right . . .

> HELEN
> But I can't hang in with anybody who drinks like you, that's another story altogether.

> FRANK
> (*shrugging*)
> That can be dealt with . . . I was thinking about that myself.

> HELEN
> (*long pause*)
> I got an eight year old son.

> FRANK
> (*small smile*)
> Yeah?

> HELEN
> Can I sleep with you tonight?

> FRANK
> (*embarrassed, laughing*)
> Ah . . .
> (*he shows her his gun*)
> . . . No . . . I got this murderer in the house right now . . .
> (*laughs*)
> I'm serious . . . tomorrow night, *defi*nitely, though . . . or
> tomorrow *day*, how's that?

ANGLE — DAWN

Frank sprawled on his couch, sleeping as light streaks the room.

ANGLE — 8:30 A.M.

Sunlight strong now. Frank is watching Mister Rogers on a portable
TV on the coffee table. He's on the phone waiting for someone to
pick up.

> FRANK
> (*turning off the TV*)
> Yeah . . . this is Frank . . . you run last night's prints
> through? You got a match, right?
> (*he smiles*)
> No, let me guess . . .
> (*he lifts Sonya's wallet from her purse*)
> Sonya Peeples?
> (*he flips the wallet back in the purse*)
> I'm Bulldog fucking Drummond, that's how . . .

Sonya staggers out of the bedroom, looking bedraggled rumpled,
confused.

> FRANK
> Morning!

> SONYA
> Where the hell am I?

> FRANK
> There's coffee in the kitchen . . . it's instant.
> (*to the phone*)
> I'm way ahead of you.
> (*looks at his wristwatch*)
> Call Sherman, tell him I got her at my place. He should
> give me a whistle, I'll send her down . . . nah . . . nah . . .
> everything's everything.

Frank hangs up, rises and walks to the doorway of his tiny kitchen.

He watches Sonya fumble with the coffee and the water. Her hands
are shaking.

> FRANK
> (*kindly*)
> You want a drink?

ANGLE — FORTY-FIVE MINUTES LATER

Frank having coffee in his kitchen. We hear the shower, then a
persistent car honking.

Frank goes over to the window. Sherman, looking terrible, is waiting downstairs.

Frank signals "ten minutes."

Sherman nods. In addition to terrible, he looks confused, amazed.

ANGLE — FRANK AND SONYA

at the door.

Frank is in his T-shirt, Sonya ready to split.

> SONYA
> (*disoriented, queasy but a good sport*)
> Did we have a good time last night?

Frank kisses her on the cheek. She smiles bravely, totally at a loss for the evening, then splits.

ANGLE — FRANK

at his window.

Looking down on Sonya, emerging from the building, accosted by Sherman, who shows his shield and talks to her. We can't hear anything.

Sonya starts backing away, obviously upset, protesting. It's been a bad day for her so far.

The two uniformed patrolmen corral her. Sherman conducts a quick frisk and hustles her into the rear of the police car.

As he gets in beside her, he looks up at Frank in his window.

Frank wiggles his fingers in a casual gesture of farewell.

Sherman pantomimes a gun with his fingers.

ANGLE — 9:00 A.M.

Bedroom.

Frank in his underwear, sitting on his bed, setting his alarm.

He sprawls belly down on his bed and closes his eyes.

Long beat terminated by the shrillness of his door buzzer.

ANGLE — DOORWAY

Frank, in his underwear, swings open the door in an irritated fashion.

A tall, thin, intense gentleman, dressed as a UPS delivery man (chocolate-brown pants and jacket) stands in his door — unblinking eyes and a .38 in Frank's face.

SHOOTER'S POV

Frank, nude except for his shorts and his handcuff neck chain, automatically puts up his hands and slowly starts backing into his apartment.

> FRANK
> What apartment you want?
> (*beat*)
> You OK?

The shooter takes two steps into Frank's place, lowers the gun to Frank's crotch and shakes the barrel, meaning take off the shorts. Frank complies.

> FRANK
> (*tremulous, terrified*)
> You OK? What's up? What's . . . How can I help?

> SHOOTER
> You have a good time with her?

> FRANK
> No . . . no way. Who . . . you want a drink?

ANGLE — FRANK'S BEDROOM

Frank being marched into the bedroom by the shooter.

> SHOOTER
> Lay down.

Frank starts to turn. The shooter blocks his turning around with the barrel of his gun against his turning cheek.

> SHOOTER
> Lay down . . . like in sex.

Frank, nude, lays face down on his bed.

CLOSE ON — FRANK'S BUG-EYED FACE

cheek to pillow.

> SHOOTER (OS)
> Can I have a drink?

> FRANK
> (*frantic, forced, sprightly*)
> Help yourself. In the kitchen.

HOLD ON FRANK'S FACE, cheek pressed into the pillow.

There's a long agonizing beat of silence — no movement from the shooter. He ain't going anywhere.

> SHOOTER
> (*laughing*)
> You stupid fuck.

> FRANK
> What's your name?

> SHOOTER
> Did she come?

> FRANK
> Come here? Who?

> SHOOTER
> (*knowing*)
> She didn't come.

> FRANK
> Nobody came, I was alone. All alone. Who you talking about?

> SHOOTER
> She always came with me. All you guys try every trick in the book. You're so handsome, so in with the in-crowd, but she never comes with you. Can I have a drink?

> FRANK
> You want me to make it for you?

> SHOOTER
> Sure.

CLOSE ON — FRANK

Slowly raises his head from the bed.

The barrel of the gun touched to the back of the neck, forcing his head down on the pillow again.

> FRANK
> (*trying to control his fear*)
> I'm a New York City detective.

SHOOTER
(*unperturbed*)
Show me how you did it last night.

FRANK
Did *what.*

SHOOTER
Pretend she's under you . . . show me . . . c'mon.
(*imitating sexual grunts*)
Uh-uh-uh . . . show me and I'll let you go.

Long agonizing beat.

FRANK
There was nobody here.

SHOOTER
I saw you dance and I saw you just about carry her into
the building. Show me and I'll let you go.

Long beat.

FRANK
She slept all night. She was drunk. I didn't touch her.

SHOOTER
(*gun to Frank's head*)
Shut up and show me.

Insane, Frank starts humping his bed, gun to his head.

Long beat of Frank making love to his mattress.

SHOOTER
(*with choked anger and sadness*)
All you assholes . . . she likes to be *kissed* . . .

The doorbell does its shrill buzz, goosing both Frank and the
shooter. Alarmed, the shooter turns towards the door. Intuitively
sensing the turn, Frank twists and leaps for the shooter's back.
Nude, straddling his back, he brings him down to the floor, wres-
tling away the gun and jamming it into the back of his neck.

> FRANK
> (*hysterical, piercing shriek, almost crying*)
> Police! Don't fucking move!
> (*beat*)
> Don't *ever* move!

> SHOOTER
> (*calm, matter of fact, face in the carpet*)
> She doesn't love you, you know . . .

The doorbell rings again.

ANGLE — THE HALLWAY
CLOSE ON — THE DOOR

We can't see who's been pushing the buzzer.

> FRANK (OS)
> (*shouting*)
> Come on in!

A woman's hand opens the door. WE SEE from her POV.

Frank, standing behind the shooter, his arm across the shooter's throat, and his gun pointing down the length of his apartment at the woman who just opened the door — Helen, stunned at the scene.

> FRANK
> (*calmly, casually, whacking the shooter lightly in the side of his head with his own gun*)
> This isn't the lady you been talking about, is it?
> (*whacks him again*)
> Is it?

INT: SQUAD ROOM — DAY

Detectives crowd around the one way mirror checking out the scene in the interrogation room.

INT: INTERROGATION ROOM

Bare save for chairs, table and a video camera.

Frank, Sherman, the Lieutenant, the video operator, and Grady
Peeples, the shooter (Sonya's ex-husband).

> FRANK
> So Grady, you'd sit out there all night in your car across
> from the building your wife went into.

> GRADY
> Yeah.

> SHERMAN
> How'd you stay awake?

> GRADY
> I can dream with my eyes open sometimes.

> FRANK
> You do drugs, Grady?

> GRADY
> No. Do you?

> SHERMAN
> So your wife would leave the guy in the morning, say
> eight, eight-thirty. You'd wait fifteen minutes and head
> on up. How'd you know what apartment?

> GRADY
> I'd see the lights go on when they went up at night . . .
> one time
> (*laughs*)
> I went up to the right floor but I couldn't figure out what
> door?
> (*taps the side of his nose*)
> I smelled it out.

> FRANK
> Sonya never knew you were tracking her, never knew
> what was happening?

> GRADY
> (*shrugs*)
> Nah . . . hey, don't blame her, it's not her fault. She can't
> help what she does. She's out of control.

ANGLE — REAR LOCKER ROOM

Video camera being set up.

> GRADY
> (*stands, facing the cops*)
> I could show you better with something in my hand for
> the gun . . . can I have a pen or something?

ANGLE — LOCKER ROOM

Grady, holding a teaspoon like a gun, slowly marches down a gauntlet of detectives lining the locker rows. He's making an invisible victim back up down an imaginary hallway to an imaginary bedroom. This is being videotaped.

It's a slow, intense, purposeful march. Not a sound, not a breath from the spellbound detectives.

Suddenly Grady swings to face the detectives, aiming his spoon and shouting "BANG!" making everybody jump like children hearing "BOO!"

> GRADY
> (*laughing, flipping the spoon over his shoulder*)
> Shit . . .

An anonymous fist raps him square in the mouth.

INT: FRANK'S BEDROOM — SIX MONTHS LATER — DAWN
CLOSE ON — FRANK'S FACE

cheek pressed into the pillow, eye wide in terror. A gun is pressed to the back of his head.

He jerks up and swings against the gun. There is no gun.

Helen jerks up out of sleep and wraps her arms around him, calming him down, easing him down, soothing him out of the nightmare.

Her head on his chest, her hand against the side of his face, they descend again into sleep.

THE END

. . . .

Night and the City

This draft was written in 1985 and represents
the second pass at the story, which I revised after
I received comments from Martin Scorsese.
The shooting script, directed by Irwin Winkler,
was finalized in the fall of 1991, days before the
start of production. — R.P.

FADE IN:

1 INT: CITIBANK CASH MACHINE ROOM — 8:00 P.M.

A fluorescently lit, littered, deserted, after-bank-hours, glass-fronted cubicle with two cash machines.

Someone enters and heads for a machine. WE SEE from the back a trim, natty, quick-moving guy dressed in a dark tight-fitting suit and white Capezio jazz shoes. This is Harry Fabian, mid-thirties.

CLOSE-UP of Harry's slender hands and the cash machine computer screen.

Harry slips his cash card in the slot.

> HARRY
> (*softly singing to Chris Montez' "Let's Dance"*)
> Hey baby, won't cha *take* a chance,
> Da da *dat* . . .
> Ah lef' mah rubbers in mah *other* pants . . .

The screen reads:

> "Hello, Mr. Fabian! How are you?"

> HARRY
> Fair, and yourself?

The screen reads:
> "What can I do for you?"
> DEPOSIT TO SAVINGS
> CASH WITHDRAWAL
> (etc.)

Abruptly two male voices slide up on either side of Harry — young, menacing.

> VOICE #1 (OS)
> Pull four hundred, bro. That's the daily max, right?

> VOICE #2 (OS)
> Citi lets you pull five.

> VOICE #1
> Take out five.

The CAMERA HOLDS on Harry's hands, his card, the screen asking:

> "What can I do for you?"

> HARRY
> (*fingers paradiddling on counter*)
> Jesus Christ.
> (*disgusted*)
> Here,
> (*drops the card on the counter*)
> do it yourself, my secret number is 382741. Be my guest.

> VOICE #2 (OS)
> Just do it.

> HARRY
> (*softly singing*)
> Hey baby, won't cha take a chance . . .

Harry pushes "balance information." All three wait, Harry humming.

Screen lights up:
> BALANCE $00.00.
> YOU OWE CHECKING PLUS $343.37.

> HARRY
> Know what I mean, chief?

Voices #1 and #2 sigh and hiss . . .

Harry's hands lay still on the counter as we hear the muggers exit.

Hands lay still for a beat longer. Silence. Then Harry starts humming "Let's Dance" again. He digs into his pockets with one hand and reaches for a deposit envelope with the other.

He stuffs a thousand in hundred dollar bills into the envelope.

WE SEE Harry's face as he turns to the street, sticks out his tongue and licks the envelope shut. It's a gleeful, animated gesture of childish triumph.

2 EXT: SIXTH AVENUE AND EIGHTH STREET — 8:30 P.M.

Night time crackle — crowds, traffic, neon glitter. Big lit Crazy Eddie sign setting the pace. Pedestrian traffic flows two ways across wide Sixth Avenue. Coming towards us walking slightly faster than the others is Harry Fabian — he bristles with a little finger popping hip hop lilt in his gait. His face is animated; grinning, alert. He hits the curb like first base, sticks his arm straight out signaling a left turn and heads left.

3 EXT: FRONT OF AN ALL-NIGHT KOREAN GROCERY

Open-front store. Sidewalk an explosive still life of greens, fruits and exotic flowers. Interior of store is fluorescently lit.

Harry stands doing a quick scan of the flowers, plucks a long rose from a coffee can bouquet, raises the flower in one hand, a dollar in the other and pantomimes putting the dollar in the can for the benefit of the Korean at the cash register who nods OK. Harry walks off with the rose and pockets his dollar.

Preoccupied with slipping the rose into his lapel he almost steps in a pile of dog shit but does a Baryshnikov leap at the last second, turns and walks backwards glaring at the pile.

> HARRY
> (*yelling at the shit*)
> Curb your fucking wolf!

He spins around and keeps walking.

4 EXT: GREENWICH VILLAGE STREET

Harry walks down a dark Greenwich Village street.

WE SEE him from the back. He seems to be semi-dancing side to side, periodically stopping to dust imaginary lint from his pants or to raise his leg making a figure four and finger-wiping away a smudge on his white Capezios.

5 INT: WOLFE TONE BAR-RESTAURANT — GREENWICH VILLAGE — 8:45 P.M.

Shadowy masculine joint, woody. Bar divides room into drinking and dining areas.

The bar is almost full up with hulky Stonehenge types, reporters, lawyers, ex-college jocks, a few professional women in skirt suits and briefcases. It's an older crowd — divorced, 35 to 50. Serious drinkers and talkers. No singles bar, no cruisers. All regulars. The jukebox plays fifties jazz and seventies rock, "Round Midnight" or Lou Reed.

The room is below street level and WE CAN ONLY SEE the bottom half of the street entrance door, which swings open REVEALING Harry from his knees to his white shoes. He does a Bill Robinson routine down the four stairs to the floor. Everyone turns. Low-key amused reaction. Harry high-fives his way down to the far end where the owner Phil Nasseros, a small brutal-looking Napoleon type holds court; sipping coffee and bullshitting with a cluster of regulars. Harry is making his way slowly; a politician.

The phone rings alongside Phil's head.

> PHIL
> Yeah . . . He just walked in.

Phil extends the receiver over the bar. Harry steps forward but before he can grab the phone, some guy charging like a bull grabs Harry around the chest and plows him backwards towards the steps. The guy is huge, red-faced, cursing. Everybody is caught off guard. Harry looks terror-stricken.

6 EXT: STREET

Harry being carried backwards up the steps in that crazed bear hug. Three guys from the bar are on the attacker's back, beating on his head. At the top step Harry breaks free and staggers white-faced into the middle of the street.

> ATTACKER
> (to Harry)
> I'll cut ya fuckin' heart out, ya Jew bastard!

Harry, seeing the guy can't get loose, gets brave.

> HARRY
> You want me! You want me?

He fakes a charge forward, grabs some guy's arm and wraps it around his own neck, holding it there with two hands.

> HARRY
> (feigning struggle)
> Lemme go! Lemme go! I'll rip 'is fucking lungs out!

Two cops come running and hustle off the attacker.

> HARRY
> (quick grin then mock-fury; dancing forward
> to the cop car)
> It's yer own fault, asshole! Asshole!

The guy almost breaks free and Harry bolts backwards until the guy's in the cop car.

> HARRY
> (shouting at the back of the cop car)
> And I'm not Jewish!

People pile back into the bar. Harry cackles curses at a smudge on his shoe, straightens his tie, shrugs and heads down into the bar again.

7 INT: BAR

POV of Phil Nasseros and the guys.

Harry walks slowly towards them. He shudders as if it's cold, makes a face, half confusion, half innocence. They're silent.

> HARRY
> (*shooting his cuffs*)
> What the fuck was *that!*
> (*he laughs*)

They don't react.

> HARRY
> (*innocently*)
> Fucking guy . . . You know him, Phil? Who you lettin' in here? What am I, a victim? Fuckin' maniac! Out of the blue . . .

They stare at him.

> HARRY
> *What* . . . it's *my* fault?

No reaction.

> HARRY
> OK . . . OK . . . here's the lick . . . OK? We're in court this morning . . . the case is a fucking lock, I swear. We're in there for the Dobermans . . . three red Dobermans . . . beautiful animals. And *his,* by all that's right, right? I mean the wife is some bull dyke lush, her new boyfriend is some yom fag . . . Calvin Muhammed . . . Calvin makes designer burnooses, I swear on my mother's eyes, designer burnooses . . . a piece of *cake* . . . in the palm of my *hand* . . . The dogs are now living with a lesbian mom and her black fag boyfriend . . . it's like, here Harry, here's a win on a silver platter, just show up, dress nice and say "your Honor" a lot . . . anyways . . . we draw Thurgood Marshall . . . Worthington . . . black judge . . . no big deal . . . good guy . . . the dogs want to live with their daddy . . . very clear . . . anyways this . . . *ass*hole
>   (*pointing to the street*)
> looks up, sees Worthington, sees Calvin Muhammed, turns to me in like this stage whisper that could break glass, he goes "Hey forget it, Harry."
>   (*Harry gestures quickly to an imaginary judge on high and then to an imaginary Calvin Muhammed*)
> "Nigger, nigger . . . we're dead."

Harry makes an open palm gesture of helplessness.

> HARRY
> This is *my* fault he lost the dogs, right? Everything's *my*
> fault. I even had photos,
> (*waves his hand in disgust*)
> the contents of which I don't even wanna *talk* about . . .
> you know, to show how it was a bad home environment
> for the doggies. Jesus Christ were those dogs gorgeous . . .
> I was even thinking of going into business with the guy,
> you know, a kennel . . . stud farm for Dobermans?
> (*shrugs and shifts gears, grabbing the* Post *and
> flipping to the sports section, scanning results*)
> Beautiful . . . Aw fuckin' hoowah Lakers!

The bartender puts a screwdriver in front of Harry.

> PHIL
> I told you take the Mavs last night.

> HARRY
> (*nose down in papers*)
> Mavs.
> (*spying an article*)
> Hey . . . hey . . . you read this?

Harry raises paper with one hand, downs his drink at the same
time, eyes closed. He drinks too fast and coughs.

WE SEE an article bottom of back page — "CUDA SANCHEZ IN
DISCO MELEE."

Harry can't stop coughing — the drink went down the wrong
pipe.

Helen Nasseros, Phil's wife, hard-looking, mid-thirties, appears,
rising from the storage basement below bar. She levitates into our
view standing next to Phil. She's taller than him.

> HELEN
> You shouldn't bolt your drink, Harry.

Harry can't talk yet; waves her away.

> HARRY
> (*gasping*)
> Whata you, my mother? You see this?
> (*raising the* Post)

> GUY AT BAR
> Yeah,
> (*shrugs*)
> Sanchez whacked some drunk Irishman or something,
> some kid.

> HARRY
> (*perking*)
> Irish . . . How do you know Irish . . .

> GUY
> His name's in there. Grogan, O'Grogan from Whitestone.

Harry dives into the paper reading with a finger.

> HARRY
> Gorgan . . . Emmet Gorgan . . . Ozone Park. Phil . . .
> gimme the phone.

> PHIL
> (*tired*)
> Harry, whata you doing?

> HARRY
> Let me use the horn, Phil.
> (*he wiggles his fingers impatiently*)

Everybody exchanges glances.

> PHIL
> (*quiet menace*)
> Use the fuckin' pay phone like everybody else.

> HARRY
> (*pleading*)
> just gimme the phone . . . This is business. Please, Phil,
> just this once.

Harry dials.

HARRY
Yes, yeah . . . Ozone Park . . . a *Gor*gon, Em-met *Gor*gon
. . . no, *Gor*gon not Grogan . . . *Gor*gan like Medusa and
the Gorgons . . . Yes, yeah . . .
    (*Harry scribbles*)
I love you.
    (*Harry dials*)
One ring . . . two . . . yeah, Emmet Gorgon, please . . .
Harry Fabian, Attorney at Law . . .
    (*while he waits he paradiddles the bar top*)
Yeah! Emmet! Harry Fabian, Attorney at Law . . . I'm just
calling, I read the paper . . . let me ask you, how's the
headaches . . . Whadya mean *what* headaches. Blurry
vision . . . depression . . . insomnia . . . bruises . . . What
am I talking about? I tell you what I'm talking about.
You know what you got hit with last night? Registered
weapons . . . bim bam! You're a tough kid with balls I can
tell over the phone, but nonetheless the law states a
professional boxer's hands are registered weapons . . .
which you got hit with . . . OK, big deal, *shoved* . . . so
you got *shoved* with professional weapons . . . We're
gonna sue his ass . . . You got a girl? Yeah? You gonna get
married? Whata you make a year . . . hey look! I'm your
attorney, this is in legal confidence . . . it's like telling your
priest . . . You make *what!* How the hell you gonna get
married on fourteen five? Where you gonna live, in a
migrant labor camp? . . . conservatively? Two . . . three
. . . *hun*dred? Try hundred *thou*sand . . . mental anguish
alone will get that . . .
    (*grins*)
Yeah, I thought so . . . Got a pencil?
    (*Harry covers the receiver, catches everybody's
    eye, winks*)
OK . . . tomorrow you're gonna see this doctor, he's the
best . . . he can do open heart surgery with mittens on . . .
you ready? Pedro Soldano . . . 233 East 111 Street . . .
that's up in East Harlem, take a cab. I'll call him, tell him
you're gonna make an appointment . . . no . . . no . . .
don't see your family doctor . . . this is a specialist in

*le*gal medicine . . . he's a Man*hat*tan doctor . . . Queens
doctor . . .
(*Harry winces*)
. . . listen to your lawyer . . . OK? *Then* I want you to
come see me right after, just jump back in the cab . . . yeah
. . . Harry Fabian, of Fabian Fabian and Fabian . . .
(*makes a whirling motion with his hand at
his own bullshit*)
Yeah . . . Suite 1001 . . . Suite, that's like an office . . .
Suite 1001 . . . yeah, 370 Broadway . . . you're very
welcome . . . you're very welcome.

Harry hands the phone back to Phil.

HARRY
This kid ever had an intelligent thought it would die
of loneliness.

PHIL
(*shaking his head*)
What a fucking shyster.

HARRY
(*outraged*)
*Shy*ster! The kid's a fuckin' victim! We're gonna clean
up. *He's* gonna clean up. I hate what they do to victims.
I fuck victimizers where they breathe.

Phil lifts the hinged part of the bar, slides behind and starts making
Harry a cocktail — soda and cleaning fluid.

PHIL
Drink this . . . get it over with.

HARRY
What?

PHIL
Get it over with . . . nice and easy . . . Sanchez is in
Boom Boom's stable, you putz . . . you wanna sue?
Drink this . . . it's quicker . . . g'head.

HARRY
Boom Boom! Fuck him! He's the *king* of the victimizers.
Is he here? I'll tell him to his face.

> PHIL

Yeah?

> HARRY

Yeah.

Phil comes out from behind the bar, puts a hand on the back of Harry's neck, with implied violence.

> PHIL

C'mon . . . he's in back . . . I'll walk you back.

> HARRY
> (*faltering, resisting the hand on his*
> *neck — wincing and laughing*)

Yeah?

Harry awkwardly moves out from under Phil's grip and shoots his cuffs. Everybody laughs.

> PHIL

G'head, bad ass.

Harry walks to the horseshoe bend that divides the barroom from the dining room. From his POV, WE SEE Boom Boom Grossman, 60, huge ex-pug Jack Dempsey look-alike with meat-hook hands and meat-pie face. He wears an Armani suit which looks ludicrous on his frame. Boom Boom is filled with power vibes. He's eating dinner with a sleek pony of a blonde.

He looks up at Harry. Harry grins and saunters back to the bar, shivering with theatrical fear.

> HARRY
> (*wiggling five spread fingers*)
> Guy goes like this . . . five people die in Oklahoma . . .
> (*tilting his chin in the direction*
> *of the OS jeering*)
> the fuck *you* laughing at?

8 EXT: HARRY'S OFFICE FRONT — BROADWAY NEAR CANAL STREET — NEXT DAY

It's a street-level door in a loft/factory area. A steel door, primer gray, plaque on side of building "HARRY FABIAN — ATTORNEY

AT LAW — ABOGADO — BY APPT. ONLY — (Phone #)." The streets are filled with Puerto Rican factory workers on lunch break, middle-aged garment- and wholesale-type businessmen unloading samples from the backs of station wagons, a few young white loft-owner-types. Storefronts — blouse outlets — luncheonettes — beat-up entrances to artists lofts, exporters, envelope manufacturers, etc.

9 INT: HARRY'S OFFICE

Small, cheap wood paneling, government-issue metal desk, bookshelves with legal codes, diploma from New York Law, signed photos of various minor sports stars, framed gun permit.

Harry, wearing a dark shirt with a gun in an armpit holster, is listening to a client, a sullen black teenager getting chewed out by his obese mother.

> KID
> Devil made me do it, ah *tol* you!

The mother hauls off and whaps the kid upside the head as if to straighten out his corn rows.

The kid makes a grab for Harry's gun. Harry leaps backwards. The mother pulls the kid back by his hair, tears in her eyes. The kid cools out.

> WOMAN
> Oh, I'm *sorry*, Mister Fabian, sorry and *shamed*.

> HARRY
> (*standing flat against the wall*)
> Yeah, listen, let's talk tomorrow, OK? We'll thinka something other than the Devil defense, OK? Nine o'clock, OK? I got a two-thirty coming in now, OK?

The woman shoves her kid towards the door.

> WOMAN
> (*to her son*)
> Miss another day a work cause a *you!*

Slams the door. Harry flops into his seat, checks his gun, squirts a stream of water. Knock at the door.

> HARRY
> Yo!

Door swings open. Emmet Gorgon stands with his arm in a cast. He's huge.

> HARRY
> (*fighting down laughter at the doctor's imagination*)
> Gorgon?

Gorgon stands frozen in the doorway. Harry's got the gun in his hands.

> HARRY
> (*fighting down laughter*)
> You see the doctor?

Gorgon looks bewildered.

> HARRY
> Have a seat.

Harry lets loose with a semi-choked chortle and coughs.

10 INT: WOLFE TONE BAR — 6:30 THAT NIGHT

Harry is at the end of the bar talking to Phil and Helen.

> HELEN
> Marty Fatass been looking for you; he was in and out like ten times in the last hour.

> HARRY
> Yeah? So where is he?

> PHIL
> Hey, Harry, guess what, me an' Helen are takin' off for two weeks.

> HARRY
> (*eyeing Helen as he sips his drink*)
> Where you goin'?

PHIL
London . . . you ever go to London?

HARRY
I never been out of New York, practically . . . one time I
was gonna move to L.A. I wanted to be a talent scout but,
ah . . . London, huh?

PHIL
(*arm around Helen's neck; he's shorter than
her, and he's half pulling her down*)
Helen never been out of New York either. Me, I was only
in Europe once . . . World War II . . . I fucking loved it.

Phil laughs, gives Helen a wet one, almost a bite. Helen throws her
eyes. Harry smiles furtively at Helen.

HARRY
(*singing softly*)
Eng-ga-land swings like a pen-du-lum do . . . Bob-bies on
Bi-cy-culs two by two . . .

HELEN
Shut up.

Marty Kaufman, sweaty, overweight, galumphs down the stairs,
spies Harry, and rubs his hands gleefully. He waddles over and
crowds him into the bar.

MARTY
Harry white shoes.

HARRY
Marty Fatass.

Marty laughs high and hard. Helen and Phil watch.

MARTY
White shoes, you got something for me?

HARRY
You got something for *me*?

MARTY
(*confidential, murmury*)
Look . . . I only got fifteen hundred.

HARRY
No problem.

CLOSE ON HARRY

He extracts a taxi driver's license from a manila folder. It has Marty Kaufman's name and photo.

HARRY
I said two large? You show up with fifteen hundred . . . what's that, three-quarters, right? OK.

Harry starts to tear the license at the three-quarter part as if to keep a quarter.

Marty grabs his hands before Harry can do serious ripping.

MARTY
OK! OK! You goddamn thief.

Marty slips Harry a wad of bills, grabs the license.

HARRY
Me a thief! You want a hack license with three counts of grand auto behind you, *I'm* a thief? A guy like you, I should charge double, you fat fucking ingrate! *Thief,* he calls me . . .

CLOSE ON HELEN

She's staring impassively at the license in Marty's paw.

MARTY
(*grinning*)
Harry . . . thank you, brother.

Marty exits.

HARRY
(*to Helen*)
Could you imagine getting in a cab driven by that ton of bad brains?

Tommy Tessler, a middle-aged sportswriter, squat, balding, a lightbulb with a few hairs, bellies up and Phil moves to him.

TOMMY
Gentlemen! . . . Harry!

HARRY
Yesterday's paper, right?

Harry unfolds a paper to show Tommy's published weekend game predictions: "TOMMY'S TIPS."

HARRY
Tommy's column?
(*reading*)
"Bet these teams *only* if you want to retire to Acupulco — Lakers Celts Knicks Nets." right? Co*llec*tively they lost by thirty-two points . . . you're a sports writer? Who you like tonight?
(*to Phil*)
Fucking Tommy, Phil . . . he took the *Titanic* over the iceberg plus points.

PHIL
(*nodding to the door*)
There he is . . . get em, Harry!

Down the steps descends Boom Boom Grossman. On either side of him are two black fighters, heavyweights, in sports jackets. Boom Boom has an arm on each of their elbows as if he's blind.

BOOM BOOM
Mister Phil, Mister Thomas, Mister Harry, Madame Helen.

A chorus of "Hey, Boom Boom," strained grins.

BOOM BOOM
Everybody, this is Wallace "The Hurt" Fuwad, and this is Alphonse "Downtown" Brown . . . Phil, I'll be in back . . . Tessler, whyn't you join us in like a half hour. I'll give you an item there . . .
(*tilts his chin to the paper*)

Boom Boom ushers his charges around the bend.

Tommy flicks his fingers out from under his chin.

> TOMMY
> Cocksucker. "I'll give you an item there."

> PHIL
> (*referring to Tommy*)
> Another war hero.

> TOMMY
> Yeah? I spit on his grave.

> HARRY
> Who you kiddin', you'll be kissin' his ass in
> (*curls his wrist to check the time*)
> twenty-nine minutes.

> TOMMY
> Twenty-eight.

> HARRY
> That is, unless, you know, you got something, you know
> . . . somebody tips you about something . . .

> TOMMY
> Like what.

> JERRY
> Like the kid that got whacked by Sanchez in that disco is
> suing Sanchez's ass and the lawyer isn't talking out of
> court settlement so it'll be a trial, you can bet your ass
> on that.

> TOMMY
> (*gaping*)
> Are you fuckin' *kiddin'* me, Harry? *You're* takin' Sanchez
> to court? Boom Boom'll eat your eyes *plus* you'll *lose*,
> jerk-off. That kid dint get hurt.

> HARRY
> They said it couldn't be done.

Harry eyes Tommy's note pad greedily. Tommy starts scribbling.

> HARRY
> This is from an undisclosed source, right? Because I can't, myself . . .

> TOMMY
> Totally. I don't even know who the fuck you are.

> HARRY
> Just say I'm "well-placed."

11 EXT: SHERIDAN SQUARE — 4:00 A.M.

The streets are relatively deserted. Harry stands shivering on the traffic island/newsstand subway entrance, a cup of take-out coffee in his hand, watching the newsstand guy open shop. WE SEE 4:00 on the Smiler's all-night deli clock across the street.

A newspaper truck rolls up and drops a bundle of *New York Post*s on the sidewalk. The news dealer trundles out to clip the cord, Harry at his heels. Harry buys a paper and frantically rifles the sports section.

> HARRY
> Yeah!

CLOSE-UP of Tommy Tessler's column. Headline — "Disco brawler to sue Cuda Sanchez."

> HARRY
> Oh yeah! Yes!

Harry walks off.

12 INT: HARRY'S DARK BEDROOM — 5:00 A.M.

Harry sprawled, asleep — sleep mask and tiny red briefs — room in heavy shadow — cookie box under one leg.

The phone rings. Harry is up like a vampire at sundown — totally awake.

> HARRY
> Yo!

13 INT: WOLFE TONE BAR — 5:00 A.M.

Phil Nasseros's office — converted closet — old wood desk file cabinets, stand-up photo of Phil and Helen. Boom Boom Grossman is
sitting on Phil's desk, phone in hand. Phil is standing to the side.

> BOOM BOOM
> (*on the horn*)
> Hey, *cock*sucker . . . I wake you up?

14 INT: HARRY'S BEDROOM

Harry, scratching, sitting on the side of his bed, unperturbed.

> HARRY
> Who's this? I know this voice.

> GROSSMAN
> It's Grossman.

> HARRY
> (*lighting cigarette*)
> Boom Boom?

> GROSSMAN
> What the fuck are you doing to Sanchez, scumbag?

> HARRY
> Whata you mean?

> GROSSMAN
> What's with this case . . . this kid.

> HARRY
> Boom Boom, you wanna talk law? I'm eighty-five an hour.

> GROSSMAN
> Hey, fucko . . . You know what I'm gonna do to you, you
> don't drop this bullshit?

> HARRY
> Boom Boom, wait a sec. I gotta turn on the tape recorder.
> (*makes no move*)

... wait ... wait ... there. OK, what are you gonna do
to me I don't drop this bullshit ...

Sound of hang-up.

15 INT: PHIL'S OFFICE

Grossman stares at Phil.

> PHIL
> Whata you want from *me!*

16 INT: HARRY'S OFFICE — NEXT MORNING

Harry's talking to a female client, Latino, hot pants — looks like
Ronnie Spector.

> HARRY
> No, darling, you don't understand. Entrapment is when
> they come on to *you.* You go up to a cop, offer to clean
> his pipes for fifty dollars, you're not a plumber ...
> they *got* you.

> CARMEN
> I don't do that.

> HARRY
> OK OK ... look ... let's try this, awright?

Harry comes from behind his desk and strides towards the far end
of his office. Carmen sits, watching.

> HARRY
> OK ... I'm you ... you're a john.

> CARMEN
> You're me?

> HARRY
> Just ... shut up and watch, OK?

Harry pretending he's a hooker, starts to saunter as if he's wearing
high heels towards Carmen. Carmen laughs into her hand.

> HARRY
> (*seductively*)
> You know where's a party tonight?

> CARMEN
> (*grabbing his nuts*)
> What you got in there, sweet stuff?

Harry jumps back.

> HARRY
> (*fighting back a laugh*)
> Carmen, I'm serious! I'm tired of bailing you out!

There's a knock at the door. Harry frowns, checks his wristwatch curled on the desk.

> HARRY
> What!

The door opens and two men dressed in business suits — one lawyer-like, the other big, five-o'clock shadow — waltz in.

The lawyer type sits down facing Harry, the big mook lifts Carmen by an armpit.

> BIG GUY
> Let's go, Mother Theresa.

> HARRY
> (*rising*)
> Hey!

The lawyer flips an afternoon edition of the *Post* on Harry's desk. In larger print there's an item about Sanchez again.

> HARRY
> (*smiling*)
> Carmen, give me a call.

The hooker splits.

> LAWYER
> (*wearily*)
> What's this, Fabian?

> HARRY
> You are . . . ?

> LAWYER
> (*throwing his eyes*)
> John Bonney, Sanchez's attorney. Whata you pulling?

> HARRY
> Hey . . . my client got whacked by a world-ranked
> professional fighter.

> LAWYER
> Bullshit.

> HARRY
> Hey! I've got his medical right here, Jack.
> (*taps a manila folder*)

> LAWYER
> Who'd you send him to, Doctor Pedro in East Harlem?

> HARRY
> What if I did . . . the guy's got as much right to practice
> medicine as you got to practice law.

> LAWYER
> No . . . more like . . . as *you* got to practice law.

> HARRY
> (*shrugs off the insult*)
> Hey . . . everybody's over 21 in here, right? So . . .
> you wanna settle or you wanna go to court?

The lawyer studies Harry. He's enraged by Harry's lack of bullshit
as to what he's up to.

> LAWYER
> (*shakes his head in awe*)
> You fucking insect . . . yeah . . . yeah . . .

> HARRY
> (*immune and impatient*)
> Yeah *what*.

LAWYER
Yeah, let's have a hearing . . . OK with you, Counselor?
Practice a little law?

HARRY
(*astonished*)
Are you *ser*ious?

The lawyer glares at him. Harry flashes teeth. He's stepped in shit.

17 EXT: 8TH AVENUE & 40TH STREET — TWILIGHT

Right below Port Authority — a scumbag's Fantasy Island, etc. At
the corner, on the second floor of a two-story building is the wrap-
around all-glass facade of Times Square Gym. The glass is frosted
by heating vent condensation and backlit by the interior fluorescent
lighting, so that from the street WE SEE silhouettes of working-out
fighters as if through a film of bluish ice.

There are faint outline portraits of Ali, Frazier, etc., on the glass
overlooking the street.

Harry, grim-faced, stands on the street looking up to the gym. He
shakes a Tic Tac dispenser into his mouth.

18 INT: NARROW CRAPPY STEEP STAIRWAY LEADING
TO GYM ENTRANCE

Harry, trotting up the stairs. Sounds of radio station disco, shouts
and laughter in Spanish and Carib accents.

19 INT: ENTRANCE TO GYM

Harry stands one hand on a turnstile, staring at a barnlike room in
which two dozen black and Spanish kids skip rope, shadow box,
work with trainers. It's a chaotic third-world aerobics class. Stat-
icky strains of disco come from a PA. Everyone stares at themselves
working out in a ten-foot-high wall-length mirror which doubles
the dimensions and number of people in the room. Over the mirror
hang a dozen full-size national flags. Between the flags and the top
of the mirror are hand-scripted names of the respective boxing

heroes of the country. It's a dreamlike brutal dance hall. Harry stands at the turnstile, mouth open, entranced with the strange violent ritual surrounding him. Abruptly, a sweaty guy in a business suit almost pushes him through the turnstile from behind.

>   GUY
>   (*bellowing*)
>   I need a light heavy for a four-rounder!

The guy charges into the room repeating the request, vanishes around a corner.

On the other side of the turnstile is a ratty desk with a phone. The desk is unoccupied. The phone rings. Like a sleepwalker Harry pushes through the turnstile and picks up.

>   HARRY
>   (*eyes scanning the room*)
>   Gym . . . I'll check . . .
>   (*bawling*)
>   Lester!

Everyone turns at Harry's voice.

>   VOICE (OS)
>   He's in the hospital.

>   HARRY
>   He's in the hospital.
>   (*bawling*)
>   What hospital!

>   VOICE (OS)
>   Roosevelt!

>   HARRY
>   Roosevelt . . . What? Nah, nothing serious.
>   (*Harry shrugs — he doesn't even know
>   who Lester is*)
>   Yeah . . . No, this is Harry . . .

Harry hangs up and wanders, hands in pockets, still open-mouthed, through the gym. He seems quietly thrilled. He's absorbing the power around him. He doesn't look that different than a lot of boxers in the room — quick, ferret-like, alert, hungry. He's home.

At the end of the long room is a ring in which two Latino fighters spar. Standing along the wall are congregations of old-timers hanging out — managers, handlers, and ex-fighters. Harry wanders along the wall through the old guys, his eyes on the kids in the ring. He stands in front of the ring watching the fighters for a minute, steps backwards, and nudges an old manager (glasses, wispy hair, walleye, bad teeth, sport jacket over brown shirt, T-shirt showing at the neck).

> HARRY
> This is wild . . . I was never in a boxing gym before . . . one a these kids Cuda Sanchez?

The manager has a habit of rearing back, baring his broken-dish teeth and glaring for a long beat through his thick glasses before he speaks.

> MANAGER
> (*indignant*)
> Sanchez?

Harry flinches. Manager sprays when he talks.

> MANAGER
> These kids tear a new asshole for Sanchez.
> (*looks away, then rears back, looking at Harry*)
> Sanchez! — These are *my* boys! Sanchez won't get in the ring with them.

> HARRY
> (*shrugs and studies the fighters*)
> Sanchez is pretty good, no?

Manager rears back again.

> MANAGER
> (*spraying and poking Harry in the chest; infuriated*)
> Don't you listen or *what* . . . *Fuck* Sanchez, you watch these kids. *I* could beat Sanchez, *me!* *You* could beat Sanchez!

> HARRY
> (*flattered*)
> I used to do a little boxing. I boxed at Oxford . . . quit
> when I killed somebody.

> MANAGER
> (*cracking a yellow, glassy smile*)
> Yeah? I went to *Cocks*-ford.

> HARRY
> So when does Sanchez come in?

> MANAGER
> There he goes with *San*chez again.
> (*grabbing Harry's arm and pointing at the old guys*)
> Look. You see everybody here except that guy in the blue?
> Everybody here . . . when *they* was fighting? In their
> primes? Sanchez couldna even *spar*red with them.

He waves in disgust, then pantomimes crumpling Sanchez into a
paper ball.

> HARRY
> Yeah?

> MANAGER
> An they fought when the days were the *days*. They'd fight
> ten, twenty fights a year.

> HARRY
> No kiddin'.

> MANAGER
> See that guy with the ears? He beat Tami Mauriello.

> HARRY
> (*faking awe*)
> Hey . . . Tami Mauriello.

> MANAGER
> (*staring for a beat*)
> Tami used to come in here, everybody came in here. Joey
> Giamba . . . Now . . .
> (*waves in disgust*)
> Back then you had ten arenas, no TV, no Felt Forum. Ten

arenas you fight ten, twenty times a year. You go around
the corner, see a fight. Coliseum, St. Nick's, Dykeman
Oval, Fort Hamilton, Star Casino, Hippodrome,
Queensborough, go up to White Plains . . . there's nothin'
now. You watch TV, cable TV, from Las Vegas.

HARRY
How come there's no fights anymore . . . you got a lot of
fighters, right?

MANAGER
What the fuck am I?

Harry shrugs. Something's cooking. The manager walks away enraged, then comes back. He's on a roll.

MANAGER
It's a different class a people. The fighters, they don't give
a shit. The managers, see that guy there? He don't give a
shit. The trainers, they don't *know* shit. Where you gonna
fight? What neighborhood you gonna go into at night?
You watch TV. Promoters? They're scumbags.

HARRY
Boom Boom Grossman.

MANAGER
(*finger poking*)
Now you're talking.
(*grabs Harry's arm*)
You know who used to come in here? *Al* Grossman.

HARRY
Who?

MANAGER
(*rears backward and glares for a beat*)
The *good* one! The good brother!

HARRY
Boom Boom's brother came in here?

MANAGER
Up until, a, about six months ago. He moved to some Jew
retirement village in West Park. He used to hang around

here all a time. Yeah, Al Grossman. He fought Tami
Mauriello . . . No, not Tami Mauriello . . . Maxie Berger,
he lives in Miami, Miami Beach, I think . . .

> HARRY
> Who does?

> MANAGER
> (*infuriated*)
> Who we talkin' about, ya bastid!

20 INT: GYM

Harry's thinking, thinking. Harry walks, hits the turnstile and
splits.

21 INT: STATE ATHLETIC COMMISSION OFFICE —
NEXT MORNING

Room looks like the administration office for a public school.
Chest-high room divider separating secretaries from the public.

Harry is hunched over a pile of papers rapping to a secretary —
Spanish, horn-rims, cigarette.

> HARRY
> OK . . . I fill this out . . . throw it back to you, throw you
> a check for four-fifty . . . form a corporation . . . that's it?
> I'm a promoter?

> SECRETARY
> We run a check on you, you clear that, that's it.

> HARRY
> (*playing*)
> You're gonna run a check on me?

> SECRETARY
> Uh-huh.

> HARRY
> Go into my past?

SECRETARY
Yup.

HARRY
Cause I was involved . . . there are things . . . you know,
OSS . . . CIA . . . I dunno if they'll let you have access . . .
national security and all . . . Burma . . . Macao . . . there
are things . . . what should I call my corporation?

SECRETARY
Bullshit Productions.

HARRY
Bullshit Productions? You want to see scars?
(*starts unbuttoning his shirt, stops*)
Nah . . . I don't like to show my scars . . . tiger cages . . .
sweats in the night . . . Bullshit Productions, hah? I'll
think about it . . . are you married? I'm gonna run a check
on you . . . Bullshit Productions . . . I like it . . . I do.

22 EXT: STREET ON THE UPPER EAST SIDE IN FRONT OF
ELAINE'S — DAY

Harry is standing talking to a runty Irish teenager.

HARRY
Awright . . . so just keep your nose clean until the court
date, Mikey. You wanna take a walk in Central Park leave
the baseball bat at home, OK?

MIKE
Hey Harry . . . I dint do anything.

HARRY
I know, I know . . . just . . .

Harry holds his hand up and nods his head.

HARRY
(*squinting at Elaine's canopy*)
Hey Mike . . . this is Elaine's?

MIKE
I dunno.

> HARRY
> You ever go in here? This is very heavy, this place.

Mike makes a face.

> HARRY
> I always wanted to go in here.

> MIKE
> So go in.

> HARRY
> (*grinning*)
> This is a heavyweight place.

> MIKE
> So fucking *what* . . . you're a goddamn lawyer, right?
> An attorney?

23 INT: BAR AT ELAINE'S

Harry enters, squints around, takes a seat at the bar.

> BARTENDER
> Yes!

> HARRY
> Yes! Vodka tonic.

Harry looks around until the drink comes. He notices someone like Alan King with a woman at the other end of the bar.

> HARRY
> And one for yourself.

> BARTENDER
> (*nodding no*)
> I don't drink, thank you.

> HARRY
> So this is Elaine's, huh?

> BARTENDER
> It better be.

Harry laughs to excess. He's excited.

> HARRY
> (*nodding in the direction of Alan King*)
> Is that, ah . . . ?

Bartender nods.

> HARRY
> Give them whatever they want . . . another round.

The bartender sets them up. Alan King nods thanks.

Harry rises and joins them.

> HARRY
> (*shaking hands*)
> You used to kill me on Sullivan.

> ALAN KING
> Thank you.

> HARRY
> *Thank* you he says . . . it's a *gift* what you give people . . .
> I'm in entertainment too in a way . . . I'm a boxing
> promoter . . . Harry Fabian, Bullshit Productions.

Harry's shocked he let that slip from his banter with the secretary.

> HARRY
> (*blushing*)
> I mean *Knock*out Productions . . . that's an in-joke I have
> with my secretary that Bullshit Productions . . . so ah,
> what happened to you? You doing Vegas mainly? Look,
> look . . . I'm interfering . . . be well, Mr. King . . .

Harry waves and turns, his face a mask of mortification.

> HARRY
> (*muttering and blushing*)
> Chr-rist!

24 INT: WOLFE TONE — 11:00 P.M.

The place is at its peak — six deep at the bar — line for tables for
late dinner. Frantic, loud, slightly saggy seedy drunk.

Harry and Tommy Tessler are squeezed up to the bar, pressed in by the crowd almost nose to nose. Instead of shouting, they're talking *under* the roar.

> HARRY
> (*fingers to chest*)
> Tommy, am I crazy or what? Neighborhood boxing. Bring back the old days.

Tommy looks distracted, antsy.

> TOMMY
> Yeah, well . . .

A guy comes up to Tommy, Tommy's age, tired-looking. Tommy perks up.

> TOMMY
> David! Where you been!

David and Tommy shake hands. David palming off a fold of cocaine in the process.

> DAVID
> (*deadpan, nasal*)
> I got delayed . . . the subway hit a bus.

> HARRY
> (*smirking*)
> I should think you could handle a cab now and then.

> DAVID
> Hey! The theater just broke!

> TOMMY
> (*rising*)
> Harry, I gotta take a leak . . . wait a sec. I think you got a good idea, I'll be right back.

> HARRY
> (*grabs his hand*)
> Hey . . . don't, don't . . . You go in there,
> (*pointing to john*)

come back here all optimistic . . . don't do me no favors,
OK? I need your *head,* not your *mood,* Tommy.

Tommy, sulking, plops back down.

> HARRY
> *Thank* you . . . anyway, look . . . I get a promoter's
> license, four hundred-fifty . . . rent some neighborhood
> hall, a VFW, a catering hall, rent a ring, chairs, security,
> a publicist, some advertising, ticket takers, a press
> conference. We're talking, I dunno, ten thousand bucks,
> maybe fifteen. Then I throw down a bond with the
> commission for seven thousand for the purse, the judges,
> the ref, the ambulance, god forbid, time keeper, doctor,
> whatever . . . So what am I saying? Four-fifty, fifteen
> large, seven large . . . twenty-two . . . maybe twenty-five
> large I can bring back the good old days, local talent, local
> arena, bingo-bango, it's the rage. Hello, 1938, and it'll
> fuckin' catch on . . . What do you think, Tommy? What
> do you think?

Harry's staring into Tommy's eyes, realizes Tommy's dying to do
some coke, raps him on the chest with his knuckles.

> HARRY
> (*disgustedly*)
> G'head.
> (*waves toward the john*)

> TOMMY
> (*coming to life*)
> I'll be right back . . . I got some ideas. I was just thinking
> about what you were saying . . . I was listening.

> HARRY
> Right, right . . . give my regards in there . . .

Tommy splits. Harry turns to the bar.

> HARRY
> (*forearms crossed, fingers paradiddling on
> bar top; in an announcer's voice*)
> Mister Alan King!

He looks up, sees Helen working. Helen smiles down at her work, shaking her head.

> HELEN
> Where you gonna get twenty-five thousand, Harry?

> HARRY
> Where? I'll win it on a game show . . . I dunno. Where'd
> Edison get the light bulb? He went to Con Ed and got the
> money . . . What are you kidding me? I'll beat backers off
> with a club . . . I have some people interested already . . .
> I'll give you one name . . . Alan King the comic . . .
> between you and me because . . .

Helen turns around to face him with a pitying smile. Harry grabs her hand. He's excited. A few guys at the bar see this gesture and that raises some eyebrows.

Phil squeezes behind Helen on his way to the other end of the bar.

> HARRY
> (*raising Helen's hand*)
> Phil! Yo Phil! I'm in love with your wife!

Phil turns and gives Harry a scarey half-smile.

Harry rises from the bar, hands up. He's laughing nervously, winks in a "you know me" gesture.

25/26 INT: MUNICIPAL COURTROOM — DAY

City courtroom — full up with spectators.

JUDGE'S POV — Harry dressed more conservatively, sits with Emmet Gorgon, 18, huge. He's got a neck brace and a cane. He's fidgety, keeps twisting his neck as if the brace is giving him a skin rash. Seated across from them is Cuda Sanchez, super-flyweight contender, miniscule, wearing a rust three-piece suit, black shirt, open collar, Zapata moustache, rattlesnake stare; and Sanchez's lawyer, Bonney.

The courtroom is silent.

> JUDGE
> Will counsel please approach the bench?

Harry and Bonney approach.

>JUDGE
>Will the defendant and the plaintiff please rise?

Gorgon and Sanchez rise. Harry turns his head back to Gorgon.

>JUDGE
>No . . . Fabian, look at me.

Harry turns back to the judge.

>JUDGE
>(*almost whispering*)
>OK . . . Harry . . . now, turn around . . . see if you see
>what I see.

Harry turns, Gorgon is six-foot-six. Sanchez is five-foot-two.

HARRY'S POV — The judge is leaning his cheek in his palm, regarding Harry calmly.

>JUDGE
>(*tiredly*)
>Fabian . . . get the fuck out of my courtroom.

27 INT: HALLWAY OUTSIDE COURTROOM

Municipal glazed tile, semi-crowded.

Gorgon is standing with a bunch of friends — Long Island heavy metal rednecks — designer jeans, long, parted hair, gold peppers on chains, disco types out of Penn Station. Gorgon has his girl on his arm.

>GORGON
>(*touching Harry's sleeve*)
>Whad I do, Harry? I didn't do nothing. I did everything
>you said. Did I do something?

>HARRY
>You were great, Emmett, the judge's a fuck.

>GORGON
>Am I getting any money?

Harry nods no.

> GORGON'S GIRL
> (*grabbing Gorgon's arm and whispering*)
> The car . . .

> GORGON
> We bought a car.

> HARRY
> What do you mean you *bought* a car. You took ownership already or you just ordered?

> GORGON
> I ordered.

> HARRY
> When?

> GORGON
> Yesterday, cause you said . . .

> HARRY
> Yeah, I know. OK, what you put down, a thousand?

> GORGON
> Fifteen.

> HARRY
> Awright, call the bank . . . call in a stop payment. Fuck 'em. You want a car?

Harry scrawls in a name and number on the back of his card.

> HARRY
> Call this guy, tell him you're a client of mine . . . he'll throw you a almost new Caddy for half what you pay this other cocksucker.

> GORGON
> I wanted a new Trans Am.

> HARRY
> Yeah? I wanna live forever.

Harry extends the card. Gorgon hesitates, then smiles sheepishly, takes the card. Harry grins, pinches his cheek.

GORGON
Thanks, Harry.

HARRY
Listen, you get out of here. You get in a cab, don't take her on the subway, the animals'll go nuts on her down there. Get in the cab, wait a few blocks, take that fuckin' brace off.
(*he rubs the side of Gorgon's neck*)
You're getting a rash.

Gorgon, his friends, and his girl back off, hailing Harry. Harry wheels and walks right up to Sanchez, his lawyer, Bonney, his manager, a few reporters and fans.

HARRY
(*taking a gunslinger stance in front of Sanchez and Bonney*)
You're welcome.

They just stare at him. Sanchez gives him beady death ray stare.

HARRY
Thank you for saying thank you to me after what I just did for you.

They continue to stare.

HARRY
I just got this fucking kid,
(*pointing at Sanchez*)
more fucking publicity . . .
(*Harry wheels away and turns back*)
You know what the headlines are gonna be tonight?
(*counting on fingers*)
"*Jack* the Giant Killer." "David and Goliath." The picture of them standing up in court? Forget it! Up till today Superfly was a strictly chink and greaser division . . .
(*to Sanchez*)
no offense. What's gonna happen now? Everybody and

their fucking cousin is gonna wanna see Jack the Giant
Killer fight . . .
> (*counting on fingers*)

whites, blacks, P.R.s, *grand*parents, Eskimos . . . kid's a
fucking hero now. *I* did that . . . What . . . you didn't
think I knew what I was doing?

Harry cocks an eyebrow. He walks off, then wheels.

> HARRY
> Tell Grossman it's on the house!

28 EXT: FRONT OF COURTHOUSE

Harry trots down the steps. Gorgon and his girl are waiting for
him.

> GORGON
> (*walking after him*)
> Harry! Harry!

> HARRY
> Yo!

> GORGON
> What . . . are you gonna send me a bill?

> HARRY
> You paid me.

> GORGON
> No I didn't.

Harry winks dismissively.

> HARRY
> (*peering at him speculatively*)
> Gorgon . . . you ever box?

> GORGON
> What?

> HARRY
> Big white kid . . . change your name . . . Irish Billy . . . put
> shamrocks on your trunks . . . call me.

Harry walks off, face illuminated by the idea.

29 INT: WOLFE TONE — DAY

CLOSE-UP of a nun with a tin can hitting up everybody at the bar for a donation.

People start dropping in bar change.

CLOSE-UP of Phil — glaring.

> PHIL
> Fucking cunt!

Phil vaults over the bar top and shoves her in the chest towards the door.

> PHIL
> Out! Out!

The nun protests. Phil shoves her to the floor and drags her out, cursing.

The bar is stunned.

Phil throws her donation can after her, the change can be heard spilling over the sidewalk.

> PHIL
> (to the bar)
> Sleazy bitch!

> HARRY
> (laughing)
> Phil Nasseros! The meanest bartender in New York! Fucking guy just eighty-sixed a nun!

> PHIL
> Kiss my ass . . . she's no fucking nun. Last April she came in here dressed like the Easter Bunny.

> BOOM BOOM
> (standing with two heavies)
> Fabian! It's a case!

Smiling, Harry bolts for the door; a good sport.

30 EXT: BAR FRONT

Harry standing in the doorway. Everybody can hear him.

> HARRY
> (to nun picking up change on the sidewalk)
> Yo, sister! I'm a lawyer, I saw the whole thing. We'll sue
> his ass.

> NUN
> (looking up from the sidewalk)
> Go fuck yourself.

31 INT: BAR

Harry dashing down to the bar.

> HARRY
> She just told me to go fuck myself.

> BOOM BOOM
> I agree.

> HARRY
> (forced laugh)
> He agrees . . . this guy . . .

> BOOM BOOM
> Fabian'd see a bird digging up a worm, he'd get the worm
> to sue for assault.

> HARRY
> No . . . whiplash.

> BOOM BOOM
> Harry Fabian . . . defender of worms.

> HARRY
> (forcing a smile)
> Boom Boom, I lost the case, I'm a good sport about it.
> What are you drinking? You'll never believe this . . . I got
> a promoter's license. I'm inspired by you, man. I'm gonna

take a shot at promoting. Nothing on *your* level obviously.
What are you drinking? Phil, throw Boom Boom a Remy
on me.

The bar has gotten tense. Boom Boom is in a murderous rage under
the banter. This is obvious to everybody except Harry.

Phil looks at Boom Boom. Boom Boom nods OK. Phil pours a shot
and puts it in front of Boom Boom. Boom Boom rises, swirling his
Remy casually. Escorted by his heavies he saunters over to Harry.
Harry's surrounded, hemmed in.

> BOOM BOOM
> This Remy's on you?

Harry tightens, grimaces. He knows what's coming. But instead of
dumping the drink on Harry's head, Boom Boom places it on the
bar. Harry doesn't move. If he moves he might get beaten to death.
Boom Boom places a huge hand on the side of Harry's head, gently.
He touches a thick finger of the other hand against Harry's opposite
temple.

> BOOM BOOM
> I knew this guy once, he was a shitty fighter but what he
> could do . . . I saw this once. He could hold a guy's face
> like this . . . take a finger like this . . . and *push* it.
> (*he applies pressure to Harry's temple; Harry winces*)
> right through into the brain.

Boom Boom relaxes the finger and cups Harry's face between both
hands. Boom Boom gently pats Harry's cheeks and walks out.

The bar is deathly silent.

> PHIL
> (*smirking*)
> Harry, you want a refill?

Harry, shaking with humiliated rage and subsiding fear, stalks out
of the bar.

3 2 EXT: BAR FRONT

As Harry exits, Tommy Tessler is heading in. Harry grabs Tommy's
arm.

HARRY
Who'd Al Grossman fight!

TOMMY
Who?

HARRY
Al! Al! Al Grossman!

TOMMY
Al Grossman. Jeez, that's going back.

HARRY
(*barking*)
Who'd he *fight!* Gimme a name! Tami fucking Mauriello like every other fucking meat pie?

TOMMY
Maxie Rosenbloom, I think, once? . . . Ol' Slapsie Maxie.

HARRY
And where the hell is *West* Field, *West* Park? . . .

TOMMY
West Park? I dunno, it's one of those new artificial towns in the Poconos. Some retirement village. You know, shitty construction, everything's called "Haus." Grocery Haus, Casino Haus . . .

Harry leaves the bar without comment.

33   EXT: A RETIREMENT VILLAGE IN WEST PARK — TWO HOURS LATER

Leisure-y condo-y, duck-lake development — new, but something cheap, like what Red Skelton would advertise on late-night TV.

Harry stands with an old man who points to a gaggle of old men standing a distance away.

CLOSE ON HARRY'S POV

He zeroes in on one guy in this gaggle of men. A big, beefy, ham-fisted alta cocker in a white dagger-collared shirt laid on a lime-green leisure suit. He's also wearing white patent leather loafers. He pantomimes an upper cut in SLOW MOTION as he holds court with his pals. This is Al Grossman.

Harry thanks the old guy who pointed him out, and makes a beeline right for Grossman.

> GROSSMAN
> (*gravelly Lionel Stander voice*)
> Then Tony . . . you should've known Tony . . . he
> looks up,
> (*raises his eyes, huge hands up in submission*)
> Tony says, "Hey, Al . . ."

> HARRY
> I wish my father was alive just for today.

The old guys turn.

> HARRY
> (*sad and awed*)
> Al Grossman . . . Al Grossman . . . my father worshiped
> the ground you walked on . . . he said the time you fought
> Maxie Rosenbloom was the greatest fight he ever saw.

> AL
> (*jerking back*)
> Which time?

> HARRY
> What?

> AL
> Which fight? The first or the second?

> HARRY
> (*with a knowing smile*)
> Which do you think, Al?

34 INT: CAFETERIA — RETIREMENT VILLAGE

filled with old people, fairly sad and grim to behold, despite the bright colors and the Muzak.

Al and Harry are sitting alone at the end of a long, folding table covered with a paper tablecloth.

> AL
> So now . . . I dunno, I'm down here. They gave me a nice apartment. This development, you know what it's called? Hawaiian Pines.

Harry breaks out in high-pitched laughter.

> HARRY
> Hawaiian Pines!

> AL
> (*shrugs*)
> The developers? They got seniors' village in Honolulu . . . Same setup? It's called Florida Hills . . . the fuck do *I* care.

> HARRY
> Hawaiian Pines.

> AL
> Yeah . . . so anyways . . . six months ago my wife Ettie . . . you know . . . cancer . . . thank God,
> (*he snaps his fingers*)
> she went fast . . . but ah . . . now that I'm available, you know? Out of the *sea* they're coming . . . this lady? Look, they're lonely . . . this one lady she comes to me, I'm playing shuffleboard, she shows me a bank book . . . forty-five thousand dollars . . . she says we don't even have to marry, just shack up.
> (*Al shrugs, hands up*)
> This other lady . . . bank book . . . *eighty* thousand dollars plus she owns a condo in Israel, we'll move there . . . her son's a something or other at some university there . . . she says, "We'll live like Solomon and *Sheba!*" Gimme a break. What the fuck I wanna go to Israel for. I got Jews in my building.

Harry beams at him as he eats.

> AL
> My health . . . thank God.

(*knocks his big fist on the table*)
Well except for one thing.

> HARRY
> (*suddenly alarmed*)
> What!

> AL
> (*pausing*)
> How old are you?

> HARRY
> What . . . you got trouble gettin' it up?

Al shrugs and takes another bite.

> HARRY
> You know why?

Harry jumps up and imitates playing shuffleboard, a scornful look on his face.

> HARRY
> Know what I mean, Al? What the fuck you doing down there. Alta cocka city. You're a New York guy. I watched you in that gym . . . you're like a man of forty-seven in there. Whata you gonna do, go down there, hook up with some little old pigeon with a bank book, make you a nice gidempta fleish every night . . . watch a little TV . . . go to a doctor, get a surgical implant with a little crank? Play cards with a bunch of hearing aids?
> (*smacks Al's arm*)
> Gimme a break, Grossman . . . it's the Greyhound station for *death*.
> (*cagey pause*)
> Could you see *Boom Boom* living down there?

> AL
> I told you, don't fucking talk to me about that prick.

> HARRY
> (*squinting, testing*)
> I don't understand that, Al . . . in fact it makes me
> depressed.

> AL
> I don't fucking talk *to* him or *about* him. There's like at
> least two good kids each in three divisions who can't get a
> title crack cause they're not signed up with that
> sonofabitch.

> HARRY
> (*watching, watching*)
> Hey look . . . my brother's an orthodontist . . . but he's
> still my brother, no?

> AL
> Hey, I'm no angel. I was no angel. When I was a kid? I
> pulled some armed robbery . . . it was a different time but
> still . . . Do you know what I mean? I had a *gun,* I said
> stick 'em up or some shit. It was a *honest robbery,* not
> like . . .

Al's become red-faced with aggravation. He takes a pill out of a
vial.

> HARRY
> What's those?

> AL
> Nothing . . . don't fucking talk to me about Boom Boom.
> Boom Boom,
> (*snorts*)
> you know what his real name is?

> HARRY
> Ira.

> AL
> Who gives a fuck.

> HARRY
> So what do you think about what I'm saying? We'll get

you a nice apartment, you spot me my talent, we'll bring
back the good old days.

AL
(*studying Harry*)
There was never no good old days . . . boxing was always
a poor man's out.

HARRY
Whatever.

AL
I'll say yes on one condition . . . You answer me honest
. . . Were you bullshitting me about your father?

HARRY
(*clear-eyed*)
Absolutely not, Mister Grossman.
(*pause; Harry shrugs, smiles*)
Yes . . . I was lying out of my ass.
(*leaning forward*)
Yes.

35 INT: WOLFE TONE BAR — LATE AFTERNOON —
DEAD HOUR

Harry is hunched over the bar in Phil's face. Helen at the till.

HARRY
(*hands curled into his own chest*)
Phil . . . Phil . . . There's like a million guys out there I
could be offering this to. I come to you first out of respect
and friendship . . .
(*rearing back in disbelief*)
Take a *hike!* Take a *hike!* . . . In all due respect a man
comes to you, offers you twenty large back on a fifteen-
thousand-dollar loan . . . a man you've known for *years,*
Phil . . . Take a *hike!* How could you say that to me?
Bing Bang in a bag, a paper bag back to you right from
the ticket taker to you, I won't even *touch* it . . . two
thousand seats at fifteen a pop plus beer? I won't make
it *back,* Phil? Please, in all due respect.

PHIL
Get outa my face, Fabian.

HARRY
(*stepping back, almost obsequious but pushing it*)
OK, look . . . I don't want to use the wrong *word* here . . .
I don't want to say *scared* because that's not you, I know
. . . but are you con*cern*ed about Grossman? This I would
understand, normally I would be too but circumstances
have turned out such, that at present, I fucking *laugh* at
Grossman, all due respect to him . . . Grossman won't go
fucking *near* me. I can't tell you why right now because
it's a surprise but hear this . . . if Grossman's Superman,
which he's *not*, I'm Kryptonite, trust me on this.

PHIL
(*menacing calm*)
You saying I'm scared of Grossman?

HARRY
(*backing to the wall*)
I said that? I would put *hot flam*ing *bar*beque skewers in
my *eyes* before I would say that *to* you or *about* you . . .
hear this . . . *to* you or *about* you . . . drop all thoughts of
that *here* and *now* . . . but let me take another tack while
I'm standing here with you . . . you are the most successful
of all my peers . . . my friends . . . this establishment is
legendary in its reputation and excellence *but! but!* and
once again I have to be painstakingly careful in my choice
of words . . . didn't you *ever,* in the middle of the night,
maybe, say, 4:30 A.M., didn't you ever want to be *more*
than . . . not *"just"* a bartender because you are a
legendary bartender but . . .

HELEN
(*wheeling in fury*)
Who the fuck are you to talk to Phil like that, you
worthless piece of shit ambulance-chasing shyster
bastard . . .

Phil glares at Harry letting Helen do the saliva spraying for a
change.

HELEN

You worthless mutt, you don't even *know* what it's *like* to
earn fifteen thousand dollars . . . come in here running
down my *husband*? *You*? *You* don't even trust *you!*

HARRY
(*blown back*)
Hey, Helen, really, just say what you feel, don't hold back
. . . we're all friends here.

HELEN

Jesus Christ, you make me . . . you *pathetic* . . . Yeah . . .
OK . . . tell you what . . . you go out. You raise seventy-
five hundred. Phil'll lend you seventy-five to match.

Helen puts her arm around Phil's shoulder. There's a terrible silence
for a beat. Then Phil with burning crazed eyes laughs low.

PHIL
I'll give you three days.

HARRY
Three days?

Phil starts to laugh again. Harry backs to the door.

PHIL
(*looking at his watch, laughing*)
Go!

As Harry pushes out the door we hear Phil:

PHIL (OS)
(*laughing*)
Go! Go! Go!

HARRY
(*to himself*)
Fucking bitch . . .

36 EXT: FARUZ MEN'S SHOP — BROADWAY —
LATE AFTERNOON

It's a large clothing store, the windows displaying discount men's
wear on the loud side.

Harry emerges from his car, a five-year-old large American model.

37 INT: FARUZ MEN'S SHOP

It's long, cavernous. Harry fingers a rack of synthetic fur coats.

A young Indian guy, Gupta, wearing a shiny acetate shirt emblazoned with murals back and front and a pair of polyester cream colored pants, comes up to Harry.

> GUPTA
> Help you, sah? Harry!

> HARRY
> (*shaking hands*)
> Guppie, what's happening . . . is a . . . Faruz around?

Faruz, the owner, 40, Indian, gold tooth, acetate shirt, flat hair, skinny, sideburns, gold chains, comes down the aisle beaming, hand extended.

> FARUZ
> Perry Mason!

> HARRY
> Hey, Abdul Ben Fazool.

Harry bows and makes a casbah hand flourish. They hug and pat backs.

> HARRY
> I was just thinking about you.

> FARUZ
> Me too, you . . . I dream about you last night . . . you become wealthy man.

Faruz says something in his native tongue to Gupta, nodding at Harry's car, then with a palm on Harry's back, ushers him down the aisle to his office.

38 INT: FARUZ'S OFFICE

It's claustrophobic. Sport jackets hang in plastic along the walls. Playboy pinups, an old desk smothered under invoices. A Dax cube on the desk with four color shots of Faruz's family.

Faruz makes Harry tea with an immersion cord.

FARUZ
Harry . . . I'm not interested in boxing.

HARRY
You don't have to be, Faruz, you just gotta be interested
in getting back nine thousand on seventy-five guaranteed.

FARUZ
No, Harry. Harry, I have something better for me and
you.

HARRY
Faruz, I could go to a thousand guys . . . I'm coming to
you first.

Faruz bends down under a coat rack and lifts a heavy rectangular
box to the desk.

HARRY
What's this?

Faruz opens the box and lifts out a VCR.

FARUZ
You have one of these, Harry?

HARRY
(*wearily*)
Faruz . . .

FARUZ
It's fantastic . . . four heads, cable ready plays dirty
movies, cartoons for the children, everything . . . take it
. . . a gift.

HARRY
What is this, a game show?

Faruz sweeps back a rack of coats TO REVEAL a few dozen stacked
boxes of VCRs.

FARUZ
A friend gave them to me . . . I give some to you . . . sell
them for four hundred . . . keep two hundred.

> HARRY
> (*rising*)
> Hey, Faruz . . . gimme a break. What am I . . .

39 EXT: STREET IN FRONT OF STORE

Harry gawks at empty space where his car used to be.

> GUPTA
> (*from door*)
> Harry, come around back.

> HARRY
> Aw no . . . fuckin' Faruz.

40 EXT: ALLEY BEHIND STORE

Three Indian guys in muraled acetate shirts are busy loading Harry's trunk and back seat with VCRs. Harry's yelling at them, trying to unload while they load.

41 EXT: STREET FACING "BRUCE LEE EMPORIUM"

— a giant supermarket of martial arts equipment and Hong Kong imports.

Harry pulls up in front.

42 INT: EMPORIUM

Harry leaning over glass display counter of mugger equipment and Kung Fu weapons, talking to Duk Soo Kim, the proprietor, who is unloading a carton of Bo's, razor-sharp Ninja throwing stars.

> HARRY
> Kim . . . I'm talking about expanding your sports empire here.

Kim puts down a Bo, takes a boxing stance and thrusts a leg in a kickboxing move.

> KIM
> Bah-sing!

HARRY
(*pinching the skin between his eyes as if he has a migraine*)
Not fucking *kick*boxing, Kim.

KIM
(*making a face, waving dismissively*)
Then without dice.

HARRY
What?

KIM
Excuse . . . I mean, "*no* dice." *No* dice, right? How you say it?

HARRY
(*sighing*)
You like VCRs? I got some out in back, at Crazy Eddie's, they're like five hundred each. I'll throw you two for eight hundred. They got six heads . . . each.

43 INT: ELAINE'S RESTAURANT — EVENING

Harry at the bar, exhausted, eyeing Alan King at a table. Harry takes a deep breath. He's trying to screw up his courage. He rises to go over then sees another celebrity with his wife come over to King's table first. (Someone like a TV anchorman.)

Harry feels overwhelmed; loses heart, drops a tip at the bar and splits.

44 EXT: PHONE BOOTH — AN HOUR LATER

Harry on the horn, forehead against the glass partition. He's gently rocking and banging his head on the glass.

HARRY
About fifteen minutes? Thank you.

45 INT: BEDROOM

Harry sits in a chair at bedside. It's an expensively appointed room. In bed is Mr. Peck, sixties, bundled up. His wife puts a mustard plaster on his white-haired chest as he hacks and wheezes. His face is white and red.

There's half a dozen humidifiers steaming around the room.

> MR. PECK
> (*trying to pull off the mustard plaster*)
> Will you stop with this already? I'm on fire!

> MRS. PECK
> On fire is good!
> (*she swats away his hands and gives the plaster a final pat*)
> A real child, you are. Big shot.
> (*she stalks from the room*)

Mr. Peck shrugs at Harry. Waits for the door to slam and peels the plaster from his chest.

> MR. PECK
> (*sighing*)
> So . . . Harry, this is why I say no to you.

> HARRY
> (*sputtering*)
> Mister Peck . . .

> MR. PECK
> Ssh! I'm talking now . . . you talked already, now me. You say two thousand seats at fifteen a pop . . . thirty thousand plus beer and pretzels . . . whatever, another three to five . . . But, Harry . . . you ever hear Murphy's Law? Anything that *can* go wrong *will* go wrong? That law was dedicated to guys like you . . . you remember you came to me a few years ago . . . Mr. Peck! Mr. Peck! What was it? You were gonna buy two tons of ash from that volcano? What?

> HARRY
> Mount St. Helens . . . I would've cleaned up.

> MR. PECK
> No you wouldn't have . . . no one buys souvenir ash from a volcano.

HARRY
Bullshit, Mr. Peck . . . how about the guy with the Pet Rock?

MR. PECK
Harry, please . . . I like you . . . you're a nice kid . . . If you insist, I have to say yes . . . I have to lend you . . . it's my business. But then, what will happen, says my crystal ball, is *some*thing . . . something I don't know what, will happen, maybe Grossman, maybe the state commission, *some*thing . . . and then I'll be out my money . . . you'll be in less than the best physical shape you've ever been in, which I would hate to see . . . and we won't be on speaking terms anymore . . . Harry, please, I *like* you . . . I'm such a last resort . . . don't be so desperate.

46 EXT: VILLAGE STREET — 3:00 A.M.

Harry's building. Harry walking down a quiet street to a tacky modern glazed-brick apartment house.

47 INT: LONG HALLWAY

Cold fluorescents, same brick. Music and loud dopey voices from one of the apartment doors. At the end of the corridor, a figure is leaning against the wall.

Sound of elevator opening. Harry emerges and walks down the corridor. He's preoccupied with his keys — doesn't notice the figure until halfway to his door. He stops, startled, realizes it's Helen waiting for him, and continues to the door. Helen lurches upright off the wall.

48 INT: HARRY'S LIVING ROOM

Small, cheap modern. Door Store furniture (Haitian cotton sectional, common high tech lamps, dingy shag carpeting — furniture of someone with no patience to have taste).

Harry sprawled gloomily on the couch, Helen crouched down by a record cabinet. Harry ignores her.

> HELEN
> (*searching*)
> What did you do with that . . . ah!

She pulls out an album and sits facing Harry on a coffee table. They're knee to knee almost. Helen pulls out a vial of coke, offers it to Harry. Harry listlessly waves it away. Helen takes a hit and holds it in her fist as she talks.

> HELEN
> You should alphabetize your albums.

Helen takes another hit.

> HELEN
> (*mocking him*)
> I have to pick my words carefully here . . . but uh,
> Harry, with all due respect . . . are you in a bad mood?

Harry sulks.

> HELEN
> (*to an invisible third party*)
> See, he's confused . . . he's thinking "Should I break the
> bitch's face for humiliating me or should I thank her for
> knocking down the loan to a reasonable request that that
> little cocksucker is now obligated to if I come up with
> the rest."

Harry looks at her; curious now.

Helen smirks, digs into her pocket book and comes up with two fat envelopes which she holds, one in each hand, elbows on her knees in front of Harry.

> HARRY
> (*straightens up*)
> What's that?

> HELEN
> (*holding up one, then the other*)
> This is money . . . and *this* is money.

> HARRY
> How much and for what?

HELEN
This is seventy-five hundred for you, this is five thousand
for a friend of yours. You get me something for this
  (*the five*)
and you get this . . . you take this seventy-five to Phil, say,
"Here you go," and make him cough up his end.

HARRY
(*wary*)
Who's my friend for the five?

HELEN
You know the Blue Dolphin on Hudson Street?

HARRY
It's closed . . . somebody bought it or something. It's been
closed like six months.

HELEN
You give this five to your friend, get me my liquor license
so I can open.

HARRY
You bought it?

HELEN
(*winks*)
It's nitey-nite for that little creep . . . I'm *gone*. Only thing
is, I can't get a liquor license because I had a shitty lawyer
for that trial.

HARRY
Hey, Helen . . . I pulled out all the stops for you.

HELEN
(*handing him the five*)
Forget it, Harry . . . just get your friend to get me my
license like you did for Marty Fatass.

HARRY
Hey, Helen, Marty Fatass got a goddamn hack license.
What *you* want is a whole different friend. I mean this is
the SLA now.

HELEN
You don't have a friend at the SLA?

HARRY
(*sighing, he probably does*)
Why don't you just get it under somebody's else's name?
Take a partner.

HELEN
No more *part*ners . . . no more Phils . . . The place is
called "Helen's" and that's the way it's gotta be . . . you
get that license for me you get this envelope . . . then we're
both home free.

Harry gets up, pacing, his back to Helen. He stands still for a beat,
then suddenly leaps into the air, throwing a fist like he's cheering
some great football play in front of him. He quickly wheels to
Helen, dropping to one knee.

HARRY
I was asking around . . . they say the best is when they had
a Jew fighting an Italian . . . *then* they'd line up for miles.
Also I was thinking what if I had a amateur night? Get
a cop to fight a fireman, or a sanitation guy, drop off
some freebees at the precinct, the dump, the firehouse.
Oh fuckin' Helen man, this is *it*. No more bullshit, no
more. I can't *stand* it, man. I'm better than this. I'm no
jerk. I mean I *am* a jerk, but it's like playing possum so
far . . . the light under the bushel with me. I been eating
shit with a shovel but this is *it* . . . right? *Fuck* Alan King.

Harry leaps up, clears his throat, pretends he's on TV.

HARRY
Do you know me? People know me around the boxing
world but sometimes in a restaurant, or at an airport, I'm
just another Harry . . . that's why I carry this . . .

Harry pretends he's holding up an American Express card and
makes a noise as if a computer is embossing his name on the
bottom.

HARRY
American Express . . . don't leave home without it.

Helen applauds, slowly, wryly.

Harry's eyes brighten. He's got another idea. He grabs a bottle of Scotch, sits and strikes a pose.

> HARRY
> Dewars Profile . . . Name — Harry Fabian, Age —
> Thirty-seven, Occupation — Attorney, President and
> Chairman of the Board, Knockout Productions. Latest
> Accomplishment — In a series of boxing cards at the Felt
> Forum he unified six out of eight weight class boxing titles
> for the first time since whenever. Motto — Fuck Boom
> Boom Fuck Phil Fuck Alan King.
> (*to Helen*)
> And don't think I won't.

49 INT: OFFICE — DAY

The walls are now covered with blowups of fighters. Personality posters that can be bought in a sports shop in the Madison Square Garden arcade.

Harry is on the phone. The envelope with five thousand dollars on the desk blotter.

Al Grossman is sitting in a chair facing Harry. He smokes a cigar and cracks his knuckles.

> AL
> (*whispering*)
> Harry? I wanna fly up this lady friend from Miami.

> HARRY
> (*raising his hand for quiet*)
> Yes . . . John Dugan, please?
> (*covers the phone with his hand; to Al*)
> What lady friend? You turning sex beast on me?
> (*to phone*)
> Doogie! Fabian the Fox . . . Good . . . listen I need to buy
> you lunch . . . no can do! No can do! What's no can do, a
> Chinese appetizer? I just need to *talk* to you, man . . . I'm
> getting married . . . I want you to be my best man . . . I'm

serious . . . nothing else . . . yeah . . . yeah . . . why else
would I call? . . . Six o'clock? . . . you know Fanellis on
Prince? . . . Six o'clock.
    (*hangs up; to Al with burbly joyousness*)
Now . . . what's this, Al? Who's this woman? I have to
know. I can't have my personnel up on morals charges . . .

Al looks offended — no sense of humor

> HARRY
> (*chortling*)
> Look at him, look at him . . .

Harry rises, peels off a few hundreds from the five thousand and
slaps them in Al's palm.

> HARRY
> Rock 'n Roll, champ . . . use People's Express, OK?

50 INT: FANELLI'S BAR — 6:00 P.M.

Harry sits at a corner table under a wall plastered with old color
tinted framed photos of long-gone fighters. The place is a SoHo mix
of artists, New Jersey cruisers and a few working stiffs. Forced old-
time atmosphere.

John Dugan, S.L.A. agent, mid-fifties, accountant-type glasses,
squinty gravy-train-colored raincoat, sad-looking commuter snap
brim hat, *New York Post* and a briefcase.

> HARRY
> Doogie!

Dugan doesn't look happy to see Harry. He cops a seat, puts his
paper next to Harry.

> DUGAN
> (*permanent squinty wince*)
> You gettin' married, Harry?

> HARRY
> Not exactly.

DUGAN
I didn't think so . . . I couldn't imagine being your best
man, you know? We don't even like each other.

HARRY
I'm crazy about you, Doogie, you got a self-image
problem. Anyways a *friend* is getting married . . . this lady
and ah . . . I wanted to get her a unique wedding present
that I thought you could help me with.

DUGAN
I don't do that anymore, Harry . . . they're watching me I
think . . . I can't tell . . .

HARRY
I got five large to spend . . . more or less.

DUGAN
Seven five.

HARRY
Don't have it, Doogie.

DUGAN
(*rising*)
I gotta go, Harry.

Harry angered grabs his wrist and yanks him down.

HARRY
Don't you fuckin' walk on me.

DUGAN
It's *eight* five, now.

HARRY
(*sighing and hissing with remorse*)
How 'bout a blank? I'll print my own.

DUGAN
(*shrugging*)
Fifteen hundred.

Harry hisses, fingers his wad and looks around while sliding the
dough into Dugan's *Post*.

> HARRY
> It's in your paper.

> DUGAN
> (*laughing*)
> Nice going, slick . . . so's the blank.

51 INT: TINY PRIVATE OFFICE, BACK OF VULCAN
PRINTERS, AN OFFSET PRINT SHOP

An S.L.A. license, blank and unsealed, lays flat like a butterfly specimen in a cone of light on a draftsman's table. Harry and Herman (the master printer), barely visible in the perimeter of the light, stare solemnly at the document.

WE CAN ALSO SEE Herman's hands resting on the desk; blunt, stubby and blue-black with ink, but there's a surgical delicacy in the repose of the fingers.

> HERMAN
> (*breathing heavily through his nose*)
> Two thousand, Harry.

> HARRY
> Do it nice, Herman.

> HERMAN
> Uh-huh.

52 INT: HARRY'S LIVING ROOM — TWO NIGHTS LATER

CLOSE-UP of S.L.A. license in Helen's tremulous hands. The license is made out to "Helen's" — address and signature of S.L.A. Commissioner, embossed with seal.

CLOSE-UP of Helen's face. Tight trembly smile, eyes shining at Harry.

CLOSE-UP of Harry sprawled on his couch. He's smiling but there's a greenish cast to his face.

Helen folds up the license and puts it in her purse.

HELEN
(*voice quivery with quiet joy*)
You wanna celebrate, Harry?

HARRY
(*paranoid, depressed*)
Nah . . . I'm gonna crash.

Helen extracts a joint from her purse. Lights up, takes a drag and exhales for an endless moment. She's instantly high.

HELEN
Harry . . . do the American Express commercial again.

HARRY
Nah.

HELEN
C'mon . . . OK, I'll do it . . . *Hi!* I'm Harry Fabian, you don't know me . . . Harry, I can't do it. *You* do it.

HARRY
Not now, Helen.

HELEN
C'mon, *please?*

HARRY
Nah.

HELEN
(*joyous*)
Pleeeze!

Harry, freaked, guilty, tries to rally.

HARRY
(*flat*)
Hi, do you know me? In the boxing world I'm a household name, but sometimes, in an airport or a hotel, they treat me like everybody else . . . a piece of shit.

HELEN
(*clucking her tongue in annoyance*)
C'mon Harry, do it right.

53 INT: WOLFE TONE BAR — MID-AFTERNOON

CLOSE-UP of Harry's hands rippling through Helen's 7,500 dollars on the bar top.

Harry grinning. Phil, elbows on bar, peering deadpan at the dough. A cigarette between his lips. Phil slowly and deliberately stubs out the butt, smoke streaming from his nostrils.

> PHIL
> (*pissed*)
> What's this? Where'd you get this?

> HARRY
> From my friend at Chase Manhattan.

> PHIL
> You go to Peck?

> HARRY
> Peck! Do I look that desperate, Phil?

Phil glares at Harry, then slowly turns to Helen, who's signing a delivery receipt at the far end of the bar; the delivery man leaning on his empty delivery cart.

> PHIL
> Did you see this? Where'd he get this?

Helen shrugs — preoccupied with the delivery man.

> HARRY
> Hey Phil . . . you might have underestimated my resources
> . . . my resourcefulness . . .

> PHIL
> Fuck you.

> HARRY
> OK . . . fuck me . . . I won't argue . . . but ah, a deal's a
> deal, right? We're men of honor? Honorable men go with
> honorable men and all that?

> PHIL
> Where the fuck you raise seventy-five hundred?

Phil lights another cigarette. Harry fidgets.

> HARRY
> So, uh . . .
> (*Harry gestures for the dough*)

> PHIL
> (*grudgingly*)
> Just tell me when you need it. You'll have it . . .

> HARRY
> How about right now . . . I gotta rent a hall, lay down the
> bond, line up my meat . . .

> PHIL
> How much is the bond?

> HARRY
> Seven . . .

> PHIL
> OK, you got that without me . . . you don't have to lay
> out anything else till fight night, right? Give me some time.

> HARRY
> (*laughing through his tension, all teeth*)
> Hey, Phil . . . you're leaving me with five hundred here.

> PHIL
> (*starting to turn apoplectic*)
> You gonna break balls, Fabian? *I said* I'd give it to you
> when you need it . . . did I *not say that?*

> HARRY
> (*grinning, tense*)
> Yes you did . . . you *did* say that . . . and I believe you . . .
> *Ab*solutely.

54 INT: WOLFE TONE — THAT EVENING

The place is jammed, loud.

WE SEE Harry's white shoes come down the steps, through the
mob. As he comes into full view, WE SEE Al Grossman and an older
attractive woman, Frieda, on each of Harry's arms.

Al looks tentative. The woman is wincing at the noise. She's got her gray hair in one of those hairdos that looks like a wig. Her face and arms have that senior citizen-Florida-caramel-cancer tan.

Harry parades them through the bar area to the threshold of the dining room.

HARRY'S POV — Harry scans the diners. WE SEE Boom Boom Grossman eating with one of his tawny young things and two younger steel-jaw guys.

Boom Boom looks up. Tightens.

CLOSE-UP of Boom Boom as he follows Harry, Al, and the woman's progress to their table.

Boom Boom rises, says something to one of his steel jaws.

Harry, Al and Frieda at their table . . .

> FRIEDA
> I'm getting hocked in kopf with this hubbub, Harold.

> AL
> His name is *Harry . . . Harry . . .*

Harry laughs.

The steel jaw bends down to Harry's ear. Harry nods and rises.

> HARRY
> Excuse me for a minute . . . the soup's very good here . . . homemade.

> FRIEDA
> Homemade? In whose home?

55 INT: PHIL'S BACK OFFICE

Harry enters. Boom Boom grabs his jacket and slams him up against a wall.

> BOOM BOOM
> Whata you doin' with him!

HARRY
(*staring down at Boom Boom's hands*)
With who?

BOOM BOOM
What's he doin' with *you!* He's got a bad heart! What's he
doin' with *you!*

HARRY
(*calmly*)
Hey, Boom Boom, your hands are still registered weapons,
you know?
(*Harry shoves him away*)
So fuck off!

Al appears at the office door, ignoring Boom Boom.

AL
Harry . . .

BOOM BOOM
(*hand out*)
Al!

AL
Harry . . .

Al takes Harry's arm and guides Harry out of the office. Harry
allows himself to go, a gleeful fuck you on his face to Boom Boom.

56 INT: VESTIBULE OF DARK STAR DISCO — MANHATTAN
— NEXT NIGHT

Long rectangular movie-theater-like lobby filled with two lines of
kids, divided into boys and girls. Each line is being frisked before
entering a cavernous dark dance floor. The walls of the lobby are
smothered in Keith Haring–type fluorescent graphics. The kids are
a Latin-white-black urban mix — not a downtown crowd. The
friskers are a huge weight lifter (black) and a black leather Lisa
Lyons type (white).

On the slow-moving male line WE SEE both Al Grossman and
Harry. Al looks straight ahead, masking his embarrassment with an

aura of stiff upper lip preoccupation. Harry is trying to catch his eye, laughing.

We hear the black frisker bawling:

> FRISKER
> Yawll got something to shave with, take a walk *now!*
> These yere *ra*dar hands! You got it I'll find it! *R*adar hands!

Harry gets frisked and almost shoved inside.

Al raises his hands, face red.

> FRISKER
> (*standing back*)
> Eee-yo! Father *Time!*

Al glares at him, hands still up, forming war-club fists.

57 INT: DISCO DANCE FLOOR

The place is immense — huge floor — with spinning flying dance-action. In deep long shadows along the walls at least a few hundred kids drink, freak, shriek, etc.

Standing amidst the chaos is Al and Harry. Harry is ecstatic, absently moving to the beat. Al still looks firm-faced.

From Harry's POV, WE SEE the possibilities; the height, the depth. We see kids on elevated tiers looking down on the floor.

> AL
> (*shouting in Harry's ear over the din*)
> I'm goin' out there and break that nigger's face, Harry!

> HARRY
> (*shouting*)
> Forget it! What ya think? This place big enough or what!

58 INT: DISCO DANCE FLOOR — NEXT MORNING

Harry walking through the eerily still room — debris strewn — dull, sullen lighting — echoey.

A trim young straight-looking businessman picks his way through the muck to shake Harry's hand.

> OWNER
> (*as they walk*)
> Come to my office . . . boxing, huh?

> HARRY
> It takes balls, Mr. Resnick, but balls you have by the dozen . . . I can tell.

59 EXT: ALLEY BEHIND THE DISCO — 30 MINUTES LATER

Harry sits at the wheel, paradiddling as three bouncer-types unload all the VCRs from his trunk.

Harry sees his entrance onto the street from the alley is blocked by a car. Two steel jaws lounge on the side of the car, arms crossed, staring at him.

> HARRY
> Shit . . .

60 INT: CAR

driven by steel jaws. Harry slouched in back seat, resigned.

61 INT: ELEVATOR BANK

facing outer offices of Champion Enterprises, Boom Boom's organization. Plush, lush, hushed. Giant photo blowups of every fighter in Boom Boom's stable.

Elevator opens. Harry and the two steel jaws exit.

They all sit outside Boom Boom's office. One of the steel jaws takes a *New York Times* from the secretary's desk.

> HARRY
> Can I have the crossword?

Boom Boom's door opens and Cuda Sanchez and his manager exit. Boom Boom, in shirtsleeves, stands in the doorway.

Harry and the two others rise. They meet Sanchez and his manager halfway across the lobby.

> HARRY
> Hey! Cuda!

Sanchez stops, recognizes Harry. He slowly walks up to him, his nose at Harry's chest, his eyes drilled into Harry's. Harry starts laughing, nervous. Cuda slowly walks forward, making Harry walk backwards. It's a frightening, deliberate dance. Any second seeming likely to explode into violence. Harry backs into a wall, Cuda an inch away staring up at him. Everyone's quiet, watching — the secretary, Boom Boom, the steel jaws, the manager. Everyone's calm, curious, clinical. Harry's hands fidget, he absently covers his balls; his hands flutter around various vulnerable parts as Cuda stands tensed, snake-eyed. Harry looks ready to cry with humiliation.

Deathly silence for a long beat . . .

> AL GROSSMAN (OS)
> Make move *one* . . . I'll step on your fuckin' head.

Al Grossman stands a few feet away by the elevator bank, dressed in his leisure suit.

Cuda turns to Al, truly twice his size.

> BOOM BOOM
> No!

Boom Boom races across the lobby.

> BOOM BOOM
> Al . . .

Al hauls off and cracks his brother across the mouth.

> AL
> You wanna do strong-arm shit, Ira?

Harry watches all of this, a "wow" plastered across his face.

Boom Boom stares at the carpet. He wasn't hurt by Al. He could easily kill him with his bare hands.

BOOM BOOM
You're a foolish man, Al . . .

AL
That's OK.

BOOM
Do you *know* anything about this little prick, Al?
(*jerking his head towards Harry*)

AL
He's OK . . .

Al puts his arm around Harry's shoulder and roughly steers him towards the elevator.

BOOM BOOM
Al . . . can I talk to Harry for a few minutes?

AL
(*turning*)
G'head . . .

BOOM BOOM
Alone? Please?

HARRY
(*filled with immunity from harm*)
Al . . . g'head . . . it's cool . . .

62 INT: BOOM BOOM'S OFFICE

Chrome and lucite. Photos of Boom Boom as a fighter, Al as a fighter, Boom Boom shaking hands with boxing greats, Boom Boom and Ali on either side of Joe Louis in a wheelchair.

Boom Boom sits on the edge of his desk, playing with a letter opener. Harry standing, leaning against a wall, hands in pockets.

BOOM BOOM
(*sighing*)
Harry . . . Harry Harry Harry.

HARRY
That's my name.

BOOM BOOM
You're really gonna go through with this thing, huh?
What if I pay you, you know, to forget it. It's rough . . .
it's very . . . It's not for everybody. How much you want,
Harry?

Harry plays with the edge of a picture frame, not looking at Grossman. He speaks in a voice uncharacteristically sober:

HARRY
All my life I been angling to settle out of court one way or
the other . . .
    (*shrugs*)
You know, get somebody by the balls . . . make 'em pay
. . . like you . . . like now . . . I never . . . you know . . .
One time about ten years ago? I had these clients . . .
Puerto Rican family from Avenue C . . . the police were
looking for some guy . . . broke in, beat everybody up,
looking for this guy . . . they had the wrong house . . .
took the police department to court . . . me . . . Harry
Fabian, right? They gave *me* five thousand and my *clients*
five thousand to go away . . . I took it . . . you know,
I don't know how much we could've got . . . but ah . . .
I dunno. I could've . . . you know . . . I could've taken
the New York City police department to court . . . and I
could've won . . . I could've scored . . . not money . . . but
. . . *scored* . . . you know, so . . . anyways . . . no . . . I'm
tired of this shit, Boom Boom. Why can't *I* have a piece?
Why can't *I* be the man, for once? . . . I'm gonna be a
boxing promoter . . . if I go all this way just to get you
over a barrel . . . you know? I *do* that all the fucking
time . . . *all* the fucking time.

Silence.

HARRY
Just for the record though, how much were you gonna
offer me?

BOOM BOOM
(*calmly*)
Harry, you're not wearing a wire or anything, right?

Harry, still pensive, just makes a no with his face.

> BOOM BOOM
> No offense . . . I didn't think so . . . look, you wanna go
> through with this, I can't *make* you stop, but ah, Al, my
> brother? He's truly one of the world's great jerks . . . but
> what can I do . . . he's my big brother, I love him. I worry
> about him. I send him money. But he don't like me . . . I'm
> ruining boxing . . . whatever . . . Anyways my point is this
> . . . you sure you're not wearing a wire?

> HARRY
> I *said* no . . .

> BOOM BOOM
> Good . . . my point being . . . is that if *any*thing should
> happen to Al, in New York, which is where he is because
> of you . . . if *any*thing, flu, heart attack . . . he's had two
> . . . if he so much as gets a fucking headache around
> here . . . I will have you killed, Harry . . . fuck you and
> your registered weapons . . . you will *die*.

Harry and Boom Boom stare at each other soberly.

> BOOM BOOM
> You *will* die . . . so take care of my brother, Harry . . .
> don't let him get too excited.

63 INT: OFFICE BUILDING LOBBY — ELEVATOR BANK —
5 MINUTES LATER

Al standing, hands in pockets. Elevator opens. Harry strides out
grim-faced, all business.

> HARRY
> Let's roll . . .

64 INT: STEEP STAIRWAY LEADING TO THE GYM

Harry and Al climbing.

> HARRY
>
> The fuckers want five thousand for the night. I threw
> them the VCRs as collateral. I got four hundred dollars to
> my fucking name. I got to pay the printers, the doctors,
> the judges . . .

> AL
>
> You gotta pay Al . . .

> HARRY
>
> *You!* The fuck I gotta pay *you* for? I thought you loved
> boxing, you got any money I can borrow?

Silence as they trudge up the stairs.

> HARRY
>
> How 'bout that old tune . . . your girlfriend there . . .
> she win at cards a lot?

65 INT: GYM

Harry and Al stand in the mirror room scanning the action.

> AL
> (*pointing out a number of fighters*)
> You know who I like? That kid there . . . that one there
> . . . the lightweight there . . . the kid eating the Fritos . . .
> fast hands . . . he's got a brother I like too . . . also fast
> hands . . . that kid there . . .

> HARRY
>
> Wo . . . wo . . . wo . . . the brother thing I like . . . we'll
> get 'em to fight each other . . . Cain and Abel . . . I like
> that . . . the others . . . I dunno, everybody's from uptown
> . . . it's too same ol' same ol'.

Harry points to a white guy working out in a Williams College
sweatshirt.

> HARRY
>
> How about Adam Carrington there.

Harry points to a Chinese kid working out the heavy bag.

> HARRY
And this kid . . . Battling Chan.

Harry points to a kid shadowboxing wearing a yarmulka.

> HARRY
We gotta get Moshe Dayan.

> AL
> (*rears back, staring at Harry in dismay
> and distaste*)
Hey . . . are you gonna be serious here?

> HARRY
> (*walking towards Williams College*)
I'm serious as cancer, Jim.

66 INT: WOLFE TONE BAR — DINING ROOM — SAME TIME
AS ABOVE

Phil and Helen sit facing each other across a table in the deserted room.

They're silent, stony. Phil is wheezing with asthma. He suddenly lunges across the table and smacks Helen.

> HELEN
> (*licking her cut lip*)
Feel better?

Phil, hands trembling, pulls an asthma spray from his chest pocket and gives himself a hit.

> PHIL
How'd you get the license, Helen?

> HELEN
I earned it.

> PHIL
> (*popeyed, wheezing*)
You're goin' *down*, Helen.

Helen rises, smiling, bloody-lipped, and walks away. Phil watches her go, takes a few more hits of asthma spray and points to the floor with a violent motion.

67 INT: GYM — SHOWER STALLS

Harry leans against the doorway talking to Cotton (Williams College guy) who's under a shower.

> HARRY
> You know why you're here, Cotton?

> COTTON
> (*soaping up*)
> Why . . .

> HARRY
> It's cheaper than a shrink . . . you know . . . get out the aggression.

> COTTON
> Is that so?

> HARRY
> Yeah, that's so . . . also I bet you're one of these frustrated Hemingway heads . . . it's childish . . . you should be ashamed of yourself . . . these black kids, they're trying to claw their way into a decent life, stay off the streets, make a living here . . . you . . . you're whacking the heavy bag humming the theme from *Superman II* in your head. This place is about survival, Cotton. It's about man versus man. Why don't you join a fucking racquetball club? I'm giving you a chance to test yourself, 'cause frankly, after what I'm saying to you now, I don't see how you can come in here anymore you don't take me up on it . . . What . . . are you scared?

> COTTON
> (*face in the water stream*)
> Yup . . .

> HARRY
> That's *exactly* why you should do it . . . do you follow me?

COTTON
(*turning off shower and toweling his head*)
You left out the part about how I'm probably a repressed
fag . . .

HARRY
You know you're probably better than you think . . .
scared is OK . . . terror keeps you slender.

COTTON
Yeah, look at you.

HARRY
Exactly . . . you know a trainer or a manager or
something?

68 INT: GYM MIRROR ROOM

Harry walks around the bend from the shower room looking smug.

Facing him is Al with a cluster of older guys — managers. Al points
to Harry.

AL
Harry, this is Jap Epstein, Bobo Santiago, Tommy Carver,
Freddy . . . Freddy *what?*

FREDDY
Di Marco.

Harry shakes hands with everybody.

AL
They all got good boys.

HARRY
Who's the guy with the brothers?

SANTIAGO
Me.

HARRY
You think they'd fight each other?

SANTIAGO
Not without knives.

Everybody laughs. Harry laughs, raises an eyebrow.

69 INT: BACK ROOM AT THE PRINTING SHOP —
FEW DAYS LATER

Herman and Harry peering over a mockup of a fight poster, announcing the disco, the date, a six-fight card and the legend "THE RETURN OF PEOPLE'S BOXING TO N.Y.!!!"

>   HERMAN
> You should put their records under their names, Harry.

>   HARRY
> You do it . . . No, wait, *I'll* do it.

Harry takes a pencil and scrawls 11-0, 8 KOs, etc. under every fighter's name.

>   HERMAN
> Anything else?

>   HARRY
>   (*scanning the poster*)
> Yeah . . . yeah . . . put Irish in front of Steve Cotton . . .
> and ah . . . put Chocolate in front of Eddie Chase.

>   HERMAN
> You finished?

>   HARRY
> For now. Hey wait . . . Hy-Leow . . .

Harry scrawls "GET PUNCHY, N.Y.! FREE BOXING GLOVES TO THE FIRST 200 CUSTOMERS!" on the poster.

>   HARRY
> There's this sporting goods store; Hy-Leow's? One of the
> guys, Hy Feldman? He sued his partner — I got him the
> store, more or less . . . the guy still owes me . . . this is
> great . . . this is a truly great idea . . . there . . . wa-lah!
> Truly great idea . . . Finished.

> HERMAN
> OK . . . three hundred posters . . . the tickets . . . two
> thousand tickets.

> HARRY
> Two thousand and one — one for yourself.

> HERMAN
> And one . . . Fifteen hundred dollars.

> HARRY
> Sounds fair.

There's silence for a beat.

> HARRY
> I'll pay after the fight.

> HERMAN
> Bullshit.

> HARRY
> OK . . . before the fight.

> HERMAN
> Harry . . .

> HARRY
> Herman . . . you want a bad check? I'll write you one right
> now . . . My backer can't pay me until right before the
> fight . . . What are you worried about . . . worse comes
> to worse you take it out of the receipts . . . you'll be
> right there.

> HERMAN
> (*yelling into front room*)
> Levon!

A huge black kid in a printer's apron enters.

> HERMAN
> I'm gonna give Levon my ticket, Harry. You know
> what I mean?

HARRY
(*mildly uptight*)
I don't give a shit . . . give it to anybody you want.

70 INT: WOLFE TONE — DINING ROOM — DAY

Empty save for Phil sitting with Boom Boom at a small table. The same table where he'd sat with Helen.

Phil looks apoplectic, bug eyed. He's pumping asthma spray. Boom Boom looks aggrieved, burdened.

PHIL
Who the fuck are you to *talk* to me . . . to *tell* me something like that!

BOOM BOOM
(*deep sad sigh*)
Phil . . . I almost didn't . . . I said to myself . . . Boom Boom, keep your nose out where it don't belong. But then I says to myself . . . Phil's your *friend* . . . but even *then* I says to myself . . . don't do it, Boom Boom . . . but *then* I hear like the straw that broke the camel's back, that you *lent money* to the guy . . . I said enough's enough, Boom Boom . . . do your duty . . . weather the storm of outrage.

PHIL
Helen . . . and Fabian . . . Harry Fabian.

Boom Boom shrugs helplessly.

PHIL
Go fuck yourself.

BOOM BOOM
(*martyred sigh*)
OK . . . just ah . . . where do you think he got the money from? The Money Store? And, ah . . . how'd she get that liquor license with her record . . . She must know some funny phone numbers down there . . . or know somebody who *knows* some funny phone numbers. You do this for me, I do this for you. Please, Phil . . . I don't wanna go on

. . . this is like agony telling you . . . he's an utter *fuck* . . .
this is no revelation to you, is it?

Boom Boom rises as if he's finished paying his respects at a wake.

> BOOM BOOM
> I'm sorry . . . better from me . . . you know what I mean?

71 INT: LOBBY OF DARK STAR DISCO — NIGHT

There's the frisking lineup of kids again. Harry and Al enter from
the street. Harry with a bunch of posters under his arms.

They head for the huge black frisker.

> HARRY
> I'm supposed to see Mister Resnick.

The frisker semi-shoves Harry inside. Al tries to follow. The frisker
stops him with a hand on his chest.

> FRISKER
> Eee-yo! It's Father Time!

> HARRY
> He's with me.

> FRISKER
> Gotta check him for *hard*ware!

All the Dark Star people laugh.

Al looks like he's going to explode. He grips the wrists of the frisker
on either side of his thighs as the guy is patting him down.

There's a silent struggle as the frisker tries to break Al's grip. It's all
done without anyone noticing. Al is white-lipped and unblinking
with rage. Kids on the line start yelling "Let's go!" The two men are
nose to nose. Suddenly the frisker relaxes and grins. He can't break
Al's grip.

> FRISKER
> G'head in, Pops.

> AL
> (*letting go — still nose to nose*)
> Fuckin' piece of shit.

Al stalks in. The frisker looks wigged out, staring after him.

> NEXT KID IN LINE
> Let's go! Let's go!

The frisker wheels around, freezing the kid with his look.

> KID
> (*small voice*)
> No offense.

The kid gets the bum's rush as he's shoved, plowed through the crowd towards the street.

72 INT: RESNICK'S BACK OFFICE AT DARK STAR

Harshly lit — three desks — invoices everywhere. People screaming into phones — bartenders and bouncers running in and out. Rock posters on the walls.

Resnick is an island of cool composure and correct businessman's attire in this sea of angry franticness.

He sits at his desk looking up at Harry and Al. The boxing posters lay before him.

> RESNICK
> Very nice, very exciting.

> HARRY
> Good . . . good.

> RESNICK
> Listen . . . I'll handle the security . . . we'll use my people.

> HARRY
> I was gonna have some of my own people.

> RESNICK
> I'll do it . . . on the house.

HARRY
Really?

RESNICK
Yeah, no problem . . . and ah . . . I'll also handle the bar.

HARRY
What do you mean, handle the bar.

Suddenly the door flies open and a bouncer flings a kid into the desk.

BOUNCER
This scumbag was pushing blow in the john.

Resnick looks up calmly and nods. The bouncer kidney punches the kid, who drops to his knees by the desk.

RESNICK
(coolly)
OK . . . OK . . . look, we know your face so say goodnight and goodbye forever here.

Resnick nods to the bouncer and the kid is hustled out of the room.

HARRY
What's with the bar . . . you'll take care of the bar . . .

RESNICK
I'm equipped . . . I have the stock, the people, the set up . . . It's my problem, you concentrate on the gate, the fighters. I'll also get you the ring and chairs . . . we'll add it onto the rental.

HARRY
Screw you.

Resnick slides the poster on to the floor.

RESNICK
Then fuck off . . . go rent a VFW hall. I don't need this.

Al lunges for Resnick, grabs him by the throat. Three heavies materialize out of nowhere and have Al pinned to the wall. Resnick flicks at his shirt front. Harry's trying to pull the bouncers off Al.

> HARRY
> (*screaming, wheeling*)
> You know who this guy is! You know whose brother this is!

> RESNICK
> I figure your tab is now nine thousand . . . love it or leave it. Guys . . . guys . . . let him be . . . that's Al Grossman . . . let him go, guys, or we'll really be swimming in blood. So, yes or no, Fabian . . . there's a circus I'm talking to for the same night.

> HARRY
> OK, OK . . . but you gotta take it out of the gate.

> RESNICK
> No dice . . . up front . . . always up front . . . out of the gate the insurance'll run you another three . . . I say this as a friend . . . Where you getting the two hundred gloves? That's a nice touch . . .

73 INT: HARRY'S CAR — NIGHT

Harry and Al screaming at each other as they drive through Manhattan.

> HARRY
> Where the fuck else we gonna go! We got six days!

> AL
> I don't care! I'm gonna kill him *and* the big nigger!

> HARRY
> You're my goddamn matchmaker! Just make matches, hah? *I'm* promoting this! Christ! Nine grand! I owe *Her*man now, I gotta pay the . . .

Al starts seizing his chest. Harry freaks.

> HARRY
> What! What!

Al hisses in pain.

HARRY
Take a pill! Take a pill!

Al cools out. He's sweating. Harry drives bug-eyed.

HARRY
You OK? You shouldn't get excited. Take a pill . . .

AL
(*taking a pill*)
I shouldn't get excited? You kiss everybody's ass and *I*
shouldn't get excited . . .
(*working himself up*)

HARRY
(*excited*)
Whose ass did I kiss! Whose ass! I'm saving your *life*
jumping in saying Fine Fine to everybody. *You!* Always
with the *hands*, the *hands*. I gotta kiss ass to keep you
outa trouble!

AL
Me! I'm standing up for *you,* yah pissant! You let
everybody walk all over you!

HARRY
Who's walking all over *who!* Who!

AL
Everybody! Everybody! You couldn't promote a fuckin'
pillow fight!

Al seizes up again.

HARRY
Take another pill! Take another pill!

AL
(*subsiding*)
I'm OK . . . I'm OK.

HARRY
You get too excited, Al! . . . Nine thousand . . . cock . . .
sucker . . .

74 EXT: VILLAGE STREET — FRONT OF HELEN'S NEW
BAR — DAY

It's one of those fake Tiffany-fern bars. Woody, old-fashioned-style
ceiling fans, beveled mirrors.

Harry stands on the street looking through the plate glass window.
WE SEE Helen standing in front of an assembly of her waiters,
waitresses and kitchen staff who are seated at the dining room
tables. Harry watches the silent lecture. Harry is wincing. Helen
sees Harry on the street, waves him in. Harry hesitates, silently begs
off pointing to his wristwatch, gives Helen the thumbs up and starts
to back off.

Helen runs to the door.

> HELEN
> (*beaming with excitement*)
> Harry! Get in here!

75 INT: HELEN'S NEW BAR

Helen holds Harry up to the assembled staff.

> HELEN
> This is Harry Fabian. Know this face. Memorize it.
> You are *never* to accept money from this man. This man
> is *family.*

> HARRY
> (*staring at his shoes*)
> How ya doin'.

ANGLE as the staff works setting up around the joint. Helen is
sitting on the customer side of the bar with Harry.

> HARRY
> Helen, this is the bottom for me to come to you like this
> . . . I need a loan . . . five thousand. I'll pay you back six
> five the night of the fights, I swear on my mother's eyes
> . . . they're jerking me around again.

> HELEN
>
> Harry . . . if I had it I'd give it to you . . . if you came to
> me yesterday I'd've had it. You see that?

Helen nods to a cruvinet, an atmosphere-controlled wine cooler.

> HELEN
>
> Your loan's in there . . . that's a cruvinet . . . it keeps open
> wine fresh so I can serve glasses of good stuff without
> ditching the bottles . . . there's your loan money . . . it's
> something with a nitrogen balance in there . . . that's a
> sixteen-thousand-dollar wine cooler . . . there's like only
> ten of them in all Manhattan . . . I'm almost in tap city
> myself . . . Why don't you ask Phil? Who knows? It's a
> good deal . . . I just don't have it.

Harry sighs, rises.

> HELEN
>
> Harry, you want to see great art?

Harry pauses. Helen takes the framed bogus liquor license off the
wall and grins. Harry goes white.

> HELEN
>
> Harry . . . if Phil can't come through, come back to me,
> I'll make some calls.

76 INT: WOLFE TONE — DAY

Phil at the bar. Only a few customers. Dead hour. Harry comes
down the stairs. Phil pours him a drink.

> HARRY
>
> It's not good, Phil.

> PHIL
>
> What . . .

> HARRY
> (cagey)
>
> It's off . . . I appreciate the loan but ah . . . save your coin,
> there, Pops.

PHIL
What . . .

HARRY
I need twelve grand if I need a dime . . . the disco I was
gonna use? They wanna hold me up for *nine* now . . . it's
over . . . I tried to raise a few more dollars . . . it's very
tight out there . . . cheers.

PHIL
(*with uncharacteristic mildness*)
OK . . . so we'll make it twelve.

HARRY
(*stunned*)
You're shittin' me.

PHIL
Not at all . . . I want fourteen five back.

HARRY
(*light-voiced in disbelief*)
Phil . . . you're OK, you know that?

PHIL
You still gotta wait until the day before or so . . . it's a
lot of money.

HARRY
Phil . . . they broke the mold with you.

PHIL
You hear the news?

HARRY
What . . .

PHIL
(*studying him*)
Helen walked out on me.

HARRY
Aw Jesus! What a cunt!

PHIL
You know what else? She's opening the Blue Dolphin . . .
that place on Hudson Street?

HARRY
Fuck her! It's better, you know? It's better that . . . if she's
that kind of person to be*gin* with, you know? Aw Christ,
man I am really sorry . . . sorry for her *more* because
hey . . . a person is like that *you* can always leave *them*
but *they,* they have to live with themselves all their lives
. . . you know what I mean? You have to live with
yourself.

PHIL
(*studying him*)
You make your own bed, right, Harry?

HARRY
(*animated*)
Ex*actly* . . . now *lie* in it.

PHIL
(*casual, dry*)
Hey Harry . . . how did Helen get a liquor license?

HARRY
(*shrugging*)
They're so fucked up down there — God knows. She
lucked out I guess, you know? When you're hot you're
hot, when you're not, you can't give it away.

Phil stares at Harry for a beat. He smiles; a rictus of a grin.

PHIL
Harry . . . I'm gonna throw you a good luck party . . .
how many kids are fighting. Ten?

HARRY
Twelve.

PHIL
OK . . . twelve . . . I'm gonna blow you to a dinner party
here the night before . . . you know, prefight night . . . it'll
be nice publicity . . . you, Al, the kids.

> HARRY
> Yeah?

> PHIL
> Why not . . . protect my investment . . . get some publicity maybe . . . good for the place, too . . . no booze 'cause of the kids . . . so . . . well . . . look, come in with them Monday night early . . . so they get out early . . . they got the weigh-in Tuesday, right? Say six . . . I'll throw dinner for them, and I'll have the dough for you.

Harry is buggy with joy, snapping and clapping.

> HARRY
> Mister *Phil!*

> PHIL
> De nada.

Harry makes for the door and splits. Phil is alone smoking a cigarette. He picks up the phone.

> PHIL
> Yeah . . . State Liquor Authority, please.

77 EXT: STREET — DAY

Harry in phone booth.

> HARRY
> Yo! Irving! Is Hy there? . . . Harry Fabian.

Harry jerks back as phone slams down. Harry grabs a kid on the street.

> HARRY
> (*handing him a dollar*)
> Do me a favor . . .
> (*Harry redials*)
> ask for Mister Gabler, then give me the phone back.
> (*hands him the phone*)

> KID
> Is Mist' Gay-blow there?

> (*to Harry*)
> The man says who's calling?

> HARRY
> Athletic Department of ah . . . Tilden High School.

> KID
> Athletic Partmint of Tilden High . . . my name is Rollo
> . . . *yeah,* I'm a fuckin' teacher!
> (*hands phone to Harry*)

> HARRY
> Hy! Harry . . . what's Irving doing there, cleaning out his
> desk?
> (*laughing*)
> Yeah . . . an listen, Hy . . . how much you owe me . . .
> yeah, hey, I can wait. I can wait . . . or we can do
> something else. How you fixed for boxing gloves?

78 INT: WOLFE TONE — NIGHT

Harry, his mom on his arm, leading a party of twenty men, the fighters and their managers, into the bar. He's like the Pied Piper, gleeful, walking backwards to shout to his troops.

> HARRY
> (*yelling*)
> Go round the bend . . . there's the tables . . . Phil! They
> brought their managers . . . I couldn't say no . . . OK?
> (*shrugs and grins*)
> They can sit on each other's lap, OK? This is my mother,
> Mrs. Fabian.

> MOM
> (*to Phil*)
> You used to be a wrestler, right?

People at the bar gawk as Harry plays traffic cop, standing there ushering everybody into the dining room.

> HARRY
> (*sing song*)
> Go on . . . Go on . . . Go on . . .

79 INT: WOLFE TONE — DINING ROOM — LATER

ANGLE on Harry standing and clinking his glass in front of a few tables of fighters and their managers.

>   HARRY
>   (*raising drink*)
> To you all . . . to *me* all, the hell with *you* all.

Some laughter.

80 INT: WOLFE TONE — BATHROOM

ANGLE on the two brothers that are scheduled to fight each other, leaning against the wall, staring at each other, as David and his drug dealer exit the john. They continue to stare at each other for a beat and then dive into a packet of blow.

81 INT: WOLFE TONE — DINING ROOM

ANGLE on Harry, still speechifying, Al seated with Frieda at his side, Harry's Mom next to Al.

>   MOM
>   (*whispering to Al*)
> So what do you think, a boxer versus a wrestler . . . I think
> if he can get in there, tie up his arms, a wrestler will kick
> the hell out of a boxer nine times out of ten.

>   AL
>   (*whispering*)
> Wrestling's a joke.

>   MOM
>   (*smirking*)
> You're a fucking joke.

Al raises an eyebrow.

>   HARRY
> Now let me tell you about this man Al, here . . .

Cotton and his date, a Muffy type, stand tentatively at the threshold. Cotton is wearing a business suit. He looks nervous.

> HARRY
> Hey-y! The great white hope!
> (*Harry beckons him in*)

The coked-up brothers reenter. Two other fighters rise. They bump into the brothers, the blow passes hands and the other two disappear into the bathroom.

One of the coked brothers takes his seat, looks up at Harry, winks and makes a fist.

Harry's face goes white with premonition but then he shrugs it off.

82 INT: WOLFE TONE — BATHROOM

Al trying to take a leak. One of Boom Boom's steel jaws is washing his hands and talking to the mirror.

> STEEL JAW
> Look, Mr. Grossman, I'm not hassling you. Boom Boom sent me over just to ask . . . how long you plan to stay up in New York . . . he's concerned. He don't even know where you live . . . if you got money . . . he respects your privacy which is why he sent *me* instead of himself to ask this . . . he knows you don't want to talk to him. He just wants to make sure you're happy.

> AL
> Fuck off . . .

83 INT: WOLFE TONE BAR — LATER

ANGLE on Harry in the bar ushering everybody out of the dining room.

> HARRY
> Right to sleep! Right to sleep! Nine o'clock! Don't be late!
> Ma! Take that cab out front!

Harry turns to Phil.

> HARRY
>
> You got something for me?

> PHIL
>
> Oh, yeah, listen . . . there's a little delay. I'll give it you tomorrow morning.

> HARRY
>
> Tomorrow! Phil!
> (*laughing*)
> You're cuttin' it close on me here . . .

> PHIL
> (*calm*)
> Nah . . . There was a delay at the bank . . . look, just have your weigh in, pay your bond, I'll meet you here after.

> HARRY
> (*laughing*)
> Phil . . . c'mon, man . . . I gotta pay these guys or I'm fucked.

> PHIL
> (*angry*)
> Hey! I said I'd have it, OK?

> HARRY
> (*laughs*)
> OK . . . OK . . .

84 INT: HARRY'S BEDROOM — EARLY MORNING

Harry sprawled asleep, sleep mask on, mouth agape. Sound of key in the door.

> HELEN (OS)
> Harry?

Harry leaps up, flipping off the mask.

> HARRY
> (*scared*)
> Helen?

Helen enters the bedroom.

> HELEN
> Long time no see.

> HARRY
> What happened?

> HELEN
> (*confused*)
> What's the matter?

> HARRY
> I don't know . . . nothing happened? I just . . . you got me
> out of a deep sleep . . . everything's OK?

> HELEN
> Yeah! What should be wrong . . . everything's fine . . .
> I thought I'd come over and make you some breakfast.

> HARRY
> Yeah?

> HELEN
> Yeah, why not . . .

Helen picks up the phone and dials.

> HELEN
> Yeah, Oddysey? Delivery . . . two orange juices, two
> coffees.
> (*to Harry*)
> What kind of eggs?

Harry winces: no eggs.

> HELEN
> No eggs, two rolls with butter . . . Fabian . . . 31 Jones
> Street. 4B.

She hangs up. Harry lights a cigarette. He's sitting in his underwear
on the side of his bed. Helen alongside him.

> HELEN
> I'm opening tonight, Harry.

> HARRY
> Yeah? I'm having the fights tonight.

> HELEN
> Big night for the both of us, huh?

> HARRY
> Looks that way.

> HELEN
> I couldn't have done it without you, Harry.

> HARRY
> Yeah, well, I couldn't, you know, have done it without
> *you* I guess, right?

> HELEN
> Harry, I feel great.

> HARRY
> Good.

> HELEN
> Do you feel great?

> HARRY
> Yeah, I'm good, I'm good.

Helen stares at him with an amused smile.

> HELEN
> What a Harry . . . I got you something.

> HARRY
> What . . . you didn't . . .

Helen gives him a wrapped gift.

> HARRY
> Wait a minute, what's this . . .

It's a gold herringbone chain with two gold boxing gloves dangling
as a double pendant.

> HARRY
> (*awed*)
> Jesus Christ . . . this is beautiful . . . this is beautiful . . .
> what you do this for?

HELEN
I'm happy, Harry. I've never been happy like this . . .
you're my friend, Harry . . . you're my pal . . . that's all
. . . I don't have a lot of friends . . . you're my buddy . . .
so I got you this . . .

Harry stares at her, touched and seasick.

HELEN
I'm happy . . . I dunno . . .

85 INT: STATE ATHLETIC COMMISSION WEIGH-IN
ROOM — 9:15 A.M.

The room is bare bones. A folding dais table at one end. With
Harry, Al, a doctor and an SAC official. At the other end is four
rows of sky-blue plastic bowling-alley-type chairs in which are
seated various fighters and their managers. On one wall are a series
of crudely drawn and colored portraits of a half-dozen famous
fighters. In a corner near the dais is an old-fashioned heavy stand-
up scale. Connected to this room is a smaller medical examination
room.

Boxing personnel (women clerks in designer jeans, doctors in sloppy
suits) ferry back and forth from the hallway across the room to
the examination room. Cotton, the white college graduate, paces
the room looking aggrieved. He holds a plastic urine sample cup
(empty).

The kids are dressed in three-piece Vegas flash or Adidas sweat-
wear.

One fighter stripped down to a ratty colored pair of briefs is getting
weighed on the scale by a boxing official.

BOXING OFFICIAL
Santiago! One hunnert forty-two pounds!

The kid, all sinew and muscles, raises his hands in triumph. No one
gives a shit.

Another boxer exits from the medical room in his street pants,
no shirt and sits down with a bunch of papers. Santiago vanishes

into the examination room. Another kid strips down to his holey shorts and steps on the scale. Another fighter hands in papers to Harry & Co.

At the dais, ANGLE on a manager pointing out the portraits on the wall to his fighter.

> MANAGER
> You see that? That's Sugar Ray Robinson . . . it's hand-painted.
> (*he puts on glasses*)
> No that's Sugar Ray *Leonard* . . . hand-painted all the way.

> BOXING OFFICIAL
> Nunez! One thirty-*four!*

HARRY'S POV — WE SEE Cotton pacing, pacing, tapping the Dixie cup against his leg.

Harry rises

> HARRY
> (*whispers*)
> Cotton . . . drink some water . . . c'mon already . . .

> COTTON
> I can't pee!

> DOCTOR
> (*emerging from the examination room*)
> Fabian . . .

> HARRY
> (*to Cotton*)
> Run water on your fingertips.
> (*to doctor*)
> Yo!

> DOCTOR
> Morales flunked his CAT scan.

> HARRY
> What! What's *that* mean?

> MORALES'S MANAGER
> Give it to him again. I think he moved his head.

> HARRY
> What's that mean?

> DOCTOR
> I'm not letting him fight.

> OTHER MANAGER
> Fabian . . . those pictures, they're hand painted, right?

> HARRY
> What am I, an art critic?

Harry waves him away.

> DOCTOR
> I'm not letting this kid fight.

> HARRY
> Ah . . . Christ.

> MANAGER
> I got another kid . . . I'll give him a call.

> HARRY
> Get him down here.

Harry stalks back to Cotton.

> HARRY
> C'mon . . .

He grabs Cotton's hand and drags him out of the room.

86 INT: BATHROOM

Harry holds Cotton's hand under a water tap. Cotton has his dick in the cup.

> HARRY
> C'mon, Cotton . . .
>   (*pissing noise*)
> pss! pss! pss! pss!

> COTTON
> Cut it out.

> HARRY
> Cotton . . . this is the easy part, c'mon pss! pss! pss! . . .
> Shit . . . gimme that!

Harry grabs the cup, turns his back and pisses in it himself.

> HARRY
> (*charging out of the john*)
> . . . On the house.

87 INT: S.A.C. WEIGH-IN ROOM

Harry reenters, holding urine sample. Doctor is waiting for him.

> DOCTOR
> More good news . . . the brothers both flunked the piss-
> test . . . cocaine.

> HARRY
> Fuck! . . . Cotton! here take your pee pee here . . . give it
> in . . . fuck!

> DOCTOR
> Get your matchmaker to run down to the gym.

Harry looks at Al, bullshitting with the boxing official at the dais,
another old-timer. Al is at his ease, in his element.

> HARRY
> I'll do it myself . . . Stay right here.

Harry runs out of the room, screeches to a halt at the door. One of
the fighters is going over an information sheet with his manager.
They're both moving their lips.

> HARRY
> (*leaning over*)
> You see here? "Ring name?" Put down King Kong
> King.

They stare at him. Harry throws his eyes, grabs a pencil and writes it in himself.

> HARRY
> King . . . *Kong* . . . King . . . did you pee yet?

88 INT: TURNSTILE ENTRANCE OF TIMES SQUARE
GYM — 30 MINUTES LATER

Harry flying through, barging in like the guy that almost knocked him over on his first visit to this gym.

> HARRY
> I need two welterweights for a six rounder!
> A middleweight for *eight!*

Harry repeats the shout and races around the bend.

89 INT: WOLFE TONE — 1:00 P.M.

Harry enters. There's a young bartender. No Phil.

> HARRY
> Phil here?

> BARTENDER
> Phil?
> (*shrugs*)
> He's doing some business somewheres.

> HARRY
> *Some*wheres . . . where's *some*wheres? I'm a little late . . .
> I had to . . . you wouldn't believe what happened.

> BARTENDER
> (*shrugs*)
> He hasn't been in.

> HARRY
> He's *coming* in though, right?

> BARTENDER
> I guess.

> HARRY
> You guess . . .

Harry sits down, checks his watch. It's one o'clock.

90 EXT: STREET OUTSIDE WOLFE TONE — 1:30 P.M.

Harry pacing. Clock over Smiler's reads one-thirty.

91 INT: WOLFE TONE — 2:15 P.M.

Harry on the phone, dialing. Bar clock reads two-fifteen. Phil saunters in. Harry almost jumps on top of him.

> HARRY
> (*controlled, nervous laughter*)
> Where you been, Phil?

> PHIL
> (*casual, raised eyebrow*)
> Why?

> HARRY
> (*laughing*)
> Why?
> (*puts out his hand, wiggling fingers*)
> Let's go, let's go, you're fucking with me now.

> PHIL
> (*confused*)
> What . . .

> HARRY
> What? The money.

> PHIL
> What money . . .
> (*mock surprise*)
> What . . . oh . . . you were serious? I thought you were joking about that . . .

Harry turns white.

> PHIL

You thought I was gonna really lend you twelve thousand?

Harry laughs, wipes his mouth, laughs, looking at the ceiling, shakes his head then suddenly grabs Phil's throat.

Phil goes berserk finally. Kicks Harry in the balls, gets him down. Kicking, punching, biting. Mayhem and murder time.

> PHIL
> (*choking and sputtering*)
> Fuck with me! Fuck with Helen! With my money! You cocksucking mother*fuck*er!

Harry is curled in a ball as Phil kicks, beats, etc. Phil is pulled away by the bartender and the kitchen help. Harry on all fours crawls to the stairs leading up to the street.

> PHIL
> (*held back*)
> You're in *hell!* Ya fucking dead on *earth!*

Phil breaks free and stomps on Harry's back.

92 EXT: BAR FRONT

Harry stumbles into daylight. Phil at his heels, screaming, held back by his bartender, kicking the air.

93 INT: DARK STAR DISCO — 3:00 P.M.

The ring is being installed. Workers are setting up rows of chairs. Al sits sprawled in one of the rows, waiting.

The black frisker is swiftly unfolding a new row of chairs, moving closer and closer to Al with each chair.

> FRISKER
> Father *Time!* Bad ass from the *hey*-days.

> AL
> Stay out of my face, ya fucking orangutan.

> FRISKER
> (*building the row down the line*)
> The *hey*-days! The *ol'* days!

A delivery man carts in huge boxes from Hy-Leow Sporting Goods filled with the two hundred pairs of boxing gloves.

94 EXT: PHONE BOOTH — STREET — 3:00 P.M.

Harry on phone, head against the glass, his face fucked up.

> HARRY
> Mr. Peck, please . . . Harry Fabian. Mister Peck . . . Harry
> . . . Listen to me, just listen to me.

95 INT: MISTER PECK'S APARTMENT — 4:00 P.M.

Harry sitting on a couch in an overstuffed living room. Sitting next to him is a razor-faced guy his age dressed in a business suit. Their knees touch. The guy speaks softly, menacingly gentle. He's got a manila envelope filled with money on his lap.

> GUY
> As you know, Mister Peck feels very nervous about this.

> HARRY
> No problem . . . it's a twenty-four-hour loan.

> GUY
> Just so we understand each other. If there's a problem, it'll
> be all *yours.*
> (*he hands the money to Harry*)
> We'll have a few people there tonight, just to make sure.

> HARRY
> Loan officers, no problem.

96 INT: DARK STAR — 4:30 P.M.

The frisker opens one of the boxes of gloves and pulls out a pair.

> FRISKER
> Yeah . . .

He puts on a pair and starts shadowboxing for a moment, then works unfolding a new row of chairs with the gloves on. He's unfolding the row directly in front of Al's chair. He works his way down towards Al. WE SEE him coming from Al's POV.

> FRISKER
> (*working his way down*)
> Father Time be bad in *his* day but his day is *his*-to-*ree*.

The disco staff laughs.

> AL
> (*choking with rage*)
> Hey, go eat a fuckin' banana.

The disco staff whoops and whoos.

> FRISKER
> (*closer to Al*)
> Father *Time* should be eatin' a banana . . . keep him *reg*ular.

Disco staff laughs.

Al is quivering with anger.

Frisker moves closer, working swiftly — two seats away from Al.

> FRISKER
> (*almost directly in front of Al*)
> Father Time be dealin' with time marchin' *on*.

That's it. Al rises and in one swift motion clocks the frisker on the side of his head sending him into a pile of chairs. Al is up on his feet, squared off.

> AL
> Let's go, you piece of shit, get up.

The frisker rises, squares off, grinning. Al still has skill and he's taking the bigger man apart for a few exchanges, cutting up his face. The disco staff stands by, watching, amazed and amused.

Suddenly Harry comes flying out of nowhere, trying to break it up.

>   HARRY
>   (*screaming*)
>   Stop it! Stop it!

He gets swatted away and goes down. The frisker, frustrated, flings off his gloves and charges into Al, tackling him.

>   HARRY
>   (*screaming to the assorted people hanging
>   around watching*)
>   Stop 'em! Stop 'em!

The frisker, his face a bloody mess, is sitting on Al's chest. He rears back to finally slug Al. Al is bug-eyed, gasping wildly, his tongue thick in his mouth. The frisker freezes, his arm cocked back.

>   FRISKER
>   What's he *doin'!* What's he *doin'!*

He leaps off Al and steps back. Harry scrambles over to Al. Harry wildly improvises half-assed CPR. He doesn't know what he's doing.

>   FRISKER
>   I didn't do *nothing,* man. He beat *me!* He *beat* me. I didn't
>   do *no*thin'!

Al stops gasping. He's dead. Harry pounds on his chest, trying to get his pump going. He looks around wildly.

>   FRISKER
>   He *beat* me, man! I didn't do *noth*in'.

Harry, on his knees, watches everyone walk swiftly out of the disco.

Harry gets up, stunned, backs away, turns and quickly leaves by another exit.

>   FRISKER
>   (*alone in the disco; to no one*)
>   He beat my *ass,* man. I *lost!* I *lost!*

97 INT: HARRY'S APARTMENT — AN HOUR LATER

Harry sitting alone on his couch, the money in his lap, his knees fanning in nervous shock. He looks beat up and dazed.

NIGHT AND THE CITY • 357

> HARRY
> (*jabbering to an invisible third party*)
> This is a *tragedy* . . . terrible . . . terrible . . . to *see* what
> happened . . . Oh! What a fine *man* . . . a *lea*der . . . this is
> a tragedy . . . it's so terrible . . . a man so *loved* . . . a man
> so . . .

Harry sighs, his knees fanning, he's silent for a beat.

> HARRY
> But I wasn't even *there* . . . I *grieve* for him but . . .

Harry sighs again, falls into silence.

> HARRY
> (*singing a bank jingle*)
> the road to *rich*es starts at the *Dime* . . .

He pats the money on his lap.

> HARRY
> I wasn't even *there!*

Harry's face is twisted in fear and desperation as he plumbs his
brain for a saving angle. Then he gives up, suddenly slumping with
resignation.

He sighs, lights a cigarette, slides down on his couch a little and
becomes composed; sad but not panicky anymore. It's over. His
life, his dream.

98 INT: HELEN'S BAR — TWILIGHT — 6:00 P.M.

Harry enters the bar. It's deserted except for Helen smoking at the
bar.

She sees Harry standing at the door, the big envelope of money
under his arm. She doesn't react. She looks bushed.

Harry takes a stool next to her.

> HARRY
> (*grim*)
> Hey . . .

Helen doesn't say anything, just stares at him calmly dragging on her cigarette. Her face looks puffy.

Harry stares back, his hand over his lower face.

> HARRY
> Helen . . .
>   (*he exhales*)
> Helen . . . I fucked you over . . . that's a forged license.

> HELEN
>   (*softly*)
> Oh really?

Helen looks towards the frame in which the license was kept. It's empty. Also, the liquor is gone, and the sixteen-thousand-dollar cruvinet is empty.

> HELEN
> Yeah . . . I . . . I ah, found that out about three this
> afternoon . . . they showed up, some people . . . you
> know.

Harry doubles over trying to catch his breath, when he straightens his eyes are shiny.

> HARRY
> Helen, I couldn't help it . . .

Helen gazes at him, past him, shakes her head and ditches her butt.

> HARRY
>   (*near tears*)
> Here . . . there's like twelve thousand in here.
>   (*puts the envelope on the bar*)
> This is all I got . . . maybe I could make a call . . . we can
> pay someone down there . . . there's other guys besides
> Dugan . . .

Harry catches himself pulling his usual Harry shit. Harry smirks, amazed at himself.

Helen doesn't even look at the envelope. She just stares into his face.

> HARRY

Helen . . . you're my best friend . . .

Helen slides the envelope towards Harry.

> HELEN

Harry, keep the money . . . you're gonna need it.

> HARRY
> (sober)

What, are you kidding me? All's I need is pennies for my eyes.

> HELEN

Harry . . . you better get going.

Harry sighs and shakes his head in resignation.

Harry rises. He tries to smile a final apology, then walks slowly towards the door.

> HELEN

Hey, Harry?

Harry turns.

> HELEN

Gimme a kiss.

Harry embraces her gratefully. He's facing the bar. WE SEE Helen's face, chin on his shoulder.

From her POV, WE SEE through the street glass, a long Charon-like car pull up alongside the bar. It's Boom Boom's men — or maybe Mr. Peck's men. Helen's eyes register fear, then recede into fast-think.

> HELEN

Harry . . . come downstairs.

> HARRY
> (misinterpreting it as sexual)

Helen . . . c'mon . . .

Harry straightens up — looks in the bar mirror and sees what Helen sees.

Without a word and without panic, he follows Helen behind the bar.

The thugs come into the bar, which is now deserted.

They've vanished — apparently down a trapdoor below the duckboards into a supply cellar.

99 EXT: REAR OF BAR — DAY

Crappy alley. Helen and Harry run out, get into Helen's car, take off.

As they fly around the corner, heading away, one of the steel jaws, who's now standing behind the bar sipping bourbon, sees Harry in the shotgun seat.

He calmly gestures, drink in hand, through the picture window, for the other steel jaws to give chase.

Helen driving down Seventh Avenue. There's a car of two blue jaws tailgating at great speed.

> HARRY
> (*blurty, terrified, trying to be funny*)
> You drive like a friggin' man!

> HELEN
> Put your seat belt on.

> HARRY
> It's on! What are you, kidding me?

> HELEN
> Tighten it! Tighten it!

Helen slams on her brakes coming to a dead stop, causing the speeding car behind her to smash into their rear. The jolt is terrific, but Helen and Harry are unhurt save for a cut over Harry's eye. Harry turns around to see two smashed heads embedded in the shattered front window of the pursuing car, like red blooming poppies.

> HARRY
> (*almost in falsetto of shock*)
> They're fucking chewed up.

Helen, fighting hysteria, hands trembling, tries to smile in a "We did it!" sort of way.

As they sit there a beat, a second car of steel jaws regally cruises behind the first.

Helen sobs in despair.

ANGLE — HARRY AND HELEN

bolting from their car and running like hell as the other car leisurely follows through the narrow streets of the West Village.

Harry pulls them into a large abandoned structure, an old store, a gym, something institutional facing the Hudson River piers.

100 INT: ABANDONED STRUCTURE

Two steel jaws, guns drawn, walk calmly through the ghost structure — no one home.

They spy a big bathroom with a lane of stalls.

They look at each other. Cruise the lane with sadistic casualness, not even trying to open any of the doors.

They hear breathing behind a stall. Stop in front and fire into the door near the top and other places, obviously away from where the person is standing or crouching — it's sadistically poor marksmanship. The gunfire is deafening in the echoey hall.

Suddenly Harry appears in the doorway to the bathroom. (Helen was the one hiding in the stall.)

> HARRY
> Stop it! Stop it! I'm here! I'm here!

Harry runs in front of them, flings open the stall door — Helen sits there, unscratched, but in shock.

Harry puts his arms around her and carry-walks her out of the stall.

> HARRY
> (*covering her with his arms — pushing her
> towards the exit*)
> I'm here! I'm here! You shoot *ladies*, you fucks! She's a
> good person!

Harry turns to them, Helen standing behind him in the door-way.

> HARRY
> You want to shoot *me?* I don't give a shit. I loved Al so
> much, you know what I got for it?
> (*taps the bloody head scrape from the car smash*)
> This is from the guy who beat Al to death. The guy you
> cowards should *really* be after. *This* is *me* doing *your* job.
> Fucking *me* with my *bare* goddamn *hands,* standing in
> between some giant fucking animals hated Al from the
> *gitty*-up, beating him to *death.* I'm using *my* goddamn
> body to save his life. He's laying there, I'm holding his
> face in my hands.
> (*Fabian starts getting sobby*)
> . . . don't fucking die, Daddy. Don't you *die!* These big
> bastards *kicking* me, I'm holding Al's head, the bastards
> *kick*ing me, nobody's doing *noth*ing!

Fabian rips up the rear of his shirt, shows the bruises from Phil's beating in the bar.

> HARRY
> Don't you fucking *die,* Al. Please! I won't let them kill
> you, man.
> (*sobs; wipes his nose; with explosive outrage*)
> Where the hell were you sonofabitches when we *need*ed
> you! When *Al* needed you!

CLOSE ON HELEN

She's awed by Harry's balls. He's hustling death now.

The two steel jaws are momentarily thrown by Harry's ferocious outrage.

HARRY
(*pulling out the twelve grand envelope
from his pants*)
What do you think me and Al were in this for, the money?

Harry opens the envelope, hocks a gob of spit into the contents and disdainfully spills the cash on the floor, kicking it towards them.

HARRY
Hey, I got kicked, punched and smacked around six ways to Sunday. I held a dying man in my arms. So *fuck* you.

He turns his back on them, starts to walk out, winks at Helen. Helen is breathless.

HARRY
(*whisper-hissing to Helen*)
How'd I do?

Suddenly Cuda Sanchez steps out of the shadows. Stands in front of Harry. Shock-face as Cuda stabs him in the gut.

HOLD ON Helen's face. WE SEE Harry's death in her eyes.

THE END